PRAISE FOR

The Four Ms. Bradwells

A Ms. Magazine Summer Read Selection

"A great read for any woman . . . It invites the question: would you encourage your own daughter to follow in your footsteps—and why?"

—*Glen Ellyn Tribune*

"Gifted, entertaining, and mysterious—a gem of a novel! I love a good 'girlfriend' novel—and *The Four Ms. Bradwells,* like its predecessor, *The Wednesday Sisters,* did not disappoint. . . . I predict this will be a popular book club title—pick up a copy!"

—Book Club Cheerleader

"A thriller of a whodunit, a tender love story among friends . . . When the story ends at a not-too-distant point in the future, there is a clear line of sight between the Court of Bradwell and Bradley and that of Ledbetter and Sotomayor. Don't let that scare you, though. Did I mention the mystery and tenderness? They are tremendous. And the brains—oh, the brains!"

—AnnArbor.com

"[This] quartet of smart, witty women . . . meet in law school, but they get their real education many years later, when one of them is nominated to the U.S. Supreme Court and an old scandal flares up."

—*Chicago Tribune*

"Fans of Elizabeth Noble, Ann Hood, Elin Hilderbrand, and other luminaries of female friendship fiction will find much to captivate them."

—*Library Journal*

"Meg Waite Clayton writes with intelligence, wisdom, and humor about women's friendships. To steal from Holden Caulfield, after reading *The Four Ms. Bradwells*, you'll wish the characters were terrific friends of yours and you could call them up on the phone whenever you felt like it."

—TATJANA SOLI, *New York Times* bestselling
author of *The Lotus Eaters*

"Clayton has an exceptional ability to get to the heart of women's friendships and to truthfully depict the complexity therein. . . . An excellent book club pick."

—S. Krishna's Books

"As she did in *The Wednesday Sisters,* Meg Waite Clayton introduces us to a group of extraordinary women. . . . A fine, smart, compelling novel about the deep friendships that guide and nurture our most difficult choices."

—ELIZABETH BRUNDAGE, author of
A Stranger Like You and *The Doctor's Wife*

"*The Four Ms. Bradwells* are women we admire, amazing and strong, who are doing something special. [This novel] is well written and beautifully told."

—Romance Reviews Today

"The strength and love that stretches through three generations of women is endearing."

—*RT Book Reviews*

"A stirring and compelling novel about women's changing roles."

—*Booklist*

"A compelling contemporary novel that questions the power of love, loyalty and friendship."

—*Walnut Creek Magazine*

"A wonderfully written story . . . highly recommended . . . I truly felt as if I knew each of the characters, as though they were sitting in front of me, talking like old friends. At several points in the book, I quite literally had to put the book down and take a breather, the emotions so real and vivid that I experienced them myself."

—Jenn's Bookshelves

"A beautiful story about love, friendship and what people are willing to sacrifice in exchange for those things."

—Chick Lit Reviews

"A great read. The premise is fabulous and the plot well developed."

—Great Thoughts

"Meg Waite Clayton's gift for portraying the complex issues women face made her a bestseller with *The Wednesday Sisters*. She returns with *The Four Ms. Bradwells,* a multi-layered, character-driven novel about the enduring power of female friendship."

—World Talk Radio

"The four women in this book were beautifully written to be strong, smart, honest, flawed and loyal. . . . I love a novel that makes me feel or makes me think. Meg Waite Clayton has succeeded in doing both. Bravo!"

—Alison's Book Marks

"Great for book clubs. By the time I finished it I felt a sort of renewed and increased desire to achieve some of the goals I've laid out for myself and assert my independence as a woman. There was also a lot to think about in terms of friendships. . . . Definitely a read that made me feel Girl Power!"

—Take Me Away

"I'm loving this trend of books written about smart women (*The Weird Sisters,* I'm looking at you too) and I really hope it continues."

—Book Addiction

The Four
Ms. Bradwells

The Four
Ms. Bradwells

A NOVEL

~

Meg Waite Clayton

BALLANTINE BOOKS TRADE PAPERBACKS

NEW YORK

2011 Ballantine Books Trade Paperback Edition

Published in the United States by Ballantine Books, an imprint of
The Random House Publishing Group, a division of
Random House, Inc., New York.

BALLANTINE and colophon are registered trademarks of Random House, Inc.
RANDOM HOUSE READER'S CIRCLE & Design is a registered trademark of Random House, Inc.

Originally published in hardcover in the United States by Ballantine Books, an imprint of
The Random House Publishing Group, a division of Random House, Inc.

Grateful acknowledgment is made to the following for permission
to reprint previously published material:
AMY SUE NATHAN: Amy Sue Nathan's interview with Meg Waite Clayton
that was posted on the blog "Women's Fiction Writers" on May 11, 2011
(http://womensfictionwriters.wordpress.com). Used by permission.
GRAYWOLF PRESS: "Let Evening Come" from *Collected Poems* by Jane Kenyon,
copyright © 2005 by The Estate of Jane Kenyon. Reprinted by permission of
Graywolf Press, Minneapolis, Minnesota, www.graywolfpress.org.

This book contains an excerpt from the forthcoming book *The Wednesday Daughters*
by Meg Waite Clayton. This excerpt has been set for this edition only and may not
reflect the final content of the forthcoming edition.

Library of Congress Cataloging-in-Publication Data
Clayton, Meg Waite.
The four Ms. Bradwells: a novel / Meg Waite Clayton.
p.   cm.
ISBN 978-0-345-51709-8
eBook ISBN 978-0-345-52435-5
1. Female friendship—Fiction. 2. Middle-aged women—Fiction.
3. United States. Supreme Court.—Officials and employees—Selection and
appointment—Fiction. 4. Judges—Selection and appointment—United States—Fiction.
5. Secrets—Fiction. I. Title. II. Title: 4 Ms. Bradwells.
PS3603.L45F68 2011
813'.6—dc22   2010033479

Printed in the United States of America

www.randomhousereaderscircle.com

2 4 6 8 9 7 5 3 1

Book design by Victoria Wong

For the Hot Tub Gang, the Women of Division Street,
and all my Michigan Law School friends,
Section Four and otherwise

and, as always,
for Mac, Chris, Nick, Dad, and
(for this story about motherhood)
my amazing mom

You must be the change you wish to see in the world.

—Mahatma Gandhi

PART I

~

The natural and proper timidity and delicacy which belongs to the female sex evidently unfits it for many of the occupations of civil life. . . . The paramount destiny and mission of woman are to fulfill the noble and benign offices of wife and mother. This is the law of the Creator.

—U.S. Supreme Court Justice Joseph P. Bradley, from his 1873 opinion in *Bradwell v. Illinois*, denying Mrs. Myra Bradwell the right to practice law

Mia

∽

BETTS IS SITTING alone at a table with two untouched water cups, the pen I gave her the day we graduated from law school, a clean legal pad, and a microphone. On the dais, one of nineteen senators talks his way toward a question he hasn't arrived at quite yet. Cameras whir mercilessly as photographers on the floor between them vie for the better angle, capturing the small fatty deposit on Betts's freckled face, her perky mouth and shattered-crystal eyes. The chair she sits in is poorly chosen; her square diver's shoulders, in a suit the washed driftwood gray of her hair, fail to top its leather back. Still, she looks impressive as she leans toward the microphone, listening in the same intent way she has always listened to Ginger and Laney and me—the way we all need to be heard.

The senator's voice booms, "You were born in an Eastern Bloc country, Professor Zhukovski, a communist child of communist parents," as if this is something she might not have realized. The photographers edge closer on the journalistic racing pit of a floor, none pausing for fresh batteries or different lenses. Television cameras, too, peer down from booths in the side walls, relentlessly recording each intake of breath. "At least the TV cameras are shooting me from above," Betts had joked over the phone a few nights ago. "The still photographers are shooting right at my crepey old neck."

My own crepey old neck feels warm and moist as I stand at the back of the room, behind the computer-laden tables of reporters. Betts has already answered a week's worth of questions, though, sticking to the script. She praised *Brown v. Board* and deplored *Dred Scott* and *Korematsu*, uttered "right to privacy" and *"stare decisis"* while avoiding "abortion," "gay rights," and "guns." She's managed to appear to answer every question without actually stating a single view, all while demonstrating that she has great judgment without ever having been a judge. And the committee vote is scheduled for Tuesday, with the full Senate expected to confirm.

"How are we supposed to believe, Professor Zhukovski," the senator asks finally, "that a communist child of communist parents is the best person in this whole free country to be the arbiter of our laws?"

Betts smiles warmly. "My mother, a doctor in Poland, scrubbed floors here . . ." she responds, her voice rolling gently against the senator's snap. A softer sort of self-possession than she uses in her classroom is called for here, where the minds she is working to win over are still overwhelmingly older, and white, and male.

Scrubbed *toilets*, I'd suggested—words met with a long, expensive, overseas-line silence before Betts had responded, "You'll be surprised when your mom dies, Mia, how much her dignity means to you."

She's taken my advice, though, I realize with a small measure of triumph: she's gotten a friendly senator to ask about the Widow Zhukovski fleeing Poland with Baby Betts in a way that doesn't seem friendly. And the gang back here in the press gallery is taking copious notes.

"My *mother* actually would have made an amazing justice," Betts says. "A fact she would *not* have hesitated to tell you."

The senators laugh easily, as does the audience, the stenographer, and even the press.

I WAS ON assignment when Betts called to ask me to come for this weekend; we'd practically had to shout to be heard over the rickety line. "So let me get this straight, Betts," I'd teased her. "You want me to fly back from Madagascar? *Madagascar*, that's off the coast of Africa, you know that, right? To hold your hand while you worry over a Senate confirmation there isn't a shred of doubt you'll get."

"My crystal ball must be murkier than yours, Mia," she said, her laugh as cozy as the room we'd shared in N Section of the Law Quad our first year, as comfortable as the couch on the porch of the house we'd shared with Laney and Ginger our second and third. I'd slipped my camera strap over my neck and set the Holga aside, laughing with her. Betts, the Funny One. Ginger, the Rebel. Laney, the Good Girl. And me, the Savant.

"Or else . . . Hmmm," she said, "maybe *no one* is exactly a slam dunk for the Supreme Court?"

Laney had told her I'd be back home that week anyway. "They want to meet in D.C. for the hearings and then train up to New York for the weekend," she said. "I told them they could come for the last afternoon. The part where my supporters make me sound like Superjudge." And she laughed again. Betts is always the first to laugh at her little jokes.

"We're thinking *Les Miz* Friday night," she added.

"No doubt we'll be seeing something about a bad mother on Saturday if we let Ginger choose."

"Maybe not, now that Faith is gone." Then, with a crack in her voice, "God, Mi, I wish Matka had lived to see this."

"Matka," Betts always called her mom, the only Polish word she was allowed outside the songs she sang in church, and in church she usually played her zhaleika. Here in front of the Judiciary Committee, though, she calls her "my mother." I stick my hands in my pockets, feeling the cut of waistband, the little roll mushrooming over the top of my slacks as I head for three open seats in the back row. I settle into one of them, imagining Faith and Mrs. Z both cheering wildly together in whatever mom-heaven might exist.

BETTS IS FINISHING speaking in her short, straightforward sentences—her "rehearsed immigrant-widow speech," she would call this, although she's avoiding hyphenating here—when the click of high heels sounds. A young woman edges through the crowded room to whisper to a senator we in the press call "Milwaukee's Finest" for his professed love of his home state's Blatz Beer over the Russian vodka he really drinks. I'm reminded, oddly, of the Wizard of Oz as he turns toward her, his gaze as dull-eyed as my editor's—my *ex*-editor's, now that he "let me go," as if I'd just been waiting for his permission to lose my job.

My ex-editor. My ex-paper. My ex-husband and my ex-almost-fiancé. What a fool I am not to have made time to see Doug this weekend.

At the dais, Milwaukee covers the chairman's microphone and whispers, the creased lines around his narrow eyes leaving me wondering if my own eyes are as lined as his are, as lined as Betts's, too, above her pearls. Leaving me wishing my budget allowed for Ginger's expensive facials and creams—a smell trigger, I realize, as Ginger throws her arm around me, not a hug so much as a coach's arm drape. The soft fabric of her quilted winter white wool jacket tickles against my skin.

I turn back her collar to read the label: Kamila.

"I love the buttons," I say.

Her slight overbite disappears into a double-wide grin. "Found-ebony wood chips," she says. Fair trade. Eco-conscious. Fruit of the gods. "You can borrow it this weekend." Evoking memories of the four of us sharing medium-sized Fair Isle sweaters, raiding each other's closets before parties and dates.

Laney slides her long legs gracefully into the empty seat beside Ginger, whispering, "Mi," and reaching across her to grasp my hand.

I pull us all into a three-way hug. "If you two had been much later," I say, "you'd have missed the whole show."

The guy in front of us shoots me a look.

"God, it's so good to see you both!" I say more quietly, trying to tuck my rush of joy at being with them again into a smaller voice.

Ginger presses a folded scrap of paper into my hand—a faded old Juicy Fruit gum wrapper. I extract my reading glasses, a bamboo frame that cost next to nothing in China, and examine the tight loops of blue ink on the backside, Ginger's angular, almost illegible scrawl. Laney takes the gum wrapper and reads without the need of glasses as I remember the four of us studying together in the Law School Reading Room, the hush unbroken but for the occasional *thwick* of a page turned in frustration, the scrape of a chair, the hushed *swoosh* of the revolving doors, and, if you listened closely enough, the *tick* of a small folded gum-wrapper note hitting the table in front of Laney or Betts or Ginger or me, like a spitball hitting home. Gum-wrapper humor-fortunes like this one, which reads:

LAW QUADRANGLE NOTES, September 2018: Elsbieta ("Betts") Zhukovski (JD '82) has been appointed Chief Justice of the Supreme Court, the first woman and the first foreign-born justice to be appointed to the country's most important legal post. The line to kiss up to her forms outside N-32.

"She's already missed first woman justice," Ginger whispers. "By decades."

The chairman announces a five-minute recess, and the photographers reach for new batteries and memory chips while, behind us, reporters tweet quick recaps.

"You're forgetting the 'Chief' business, Ginge." Laney's Southern accent soft and warm and proud. "Betts could still be the first lady *Chief*. She's got years before that silly gum-wrapper 2018."

I swallow against a scratch in my own throat, envy too stingy to voice. I've always been as jealous of Betts as Ginger is. Not of her smarts so much as her discipline, her courage to imagine she might actually get what she wants.

"*Female* Chief," Ginger says. "Let's not be expecting proper, ladylike behavior from Betts when we don't require the male justices to be gentlemen."

"A real-life Justice Bradwell," I manage finally. "Not made of stone."

Laney's dark fingers smooth the folds in the wrapper. Fifty-some-year-old fingers, fifty-some-year-old hands, but her short nails unbitten now, there is that. Her teeth aren't as white as they once were and she has a few smile lines at her eyes and mouth, but the only place she shows her age in a real way is in her hands, bony and unevenly colored, lighter splotches against her African American skin where I have darker spots on my own Irish pale. I suppose she's imagining, as I am, what a real *Law Quadrangle* magazine alumni update might look like after the full Senate vote:

Elsbieta ("Betts") Zhukovski (JD '82) has been appointed to the United States Supreme Court, following in the steps of Ruth Bader Ginsburg, for whom Ms. Zhukovski clerked on the D.C. Circuit.

One of us would write the note for her. We've written every one of each other's alumni notes ever since Isabelle was born and Zack died in the same few short weeks and Betts, who'd somehow managed through it all, broke down over the writing of this irrelevant announcement. "How do I do this?" she wanted us to tell her. "How do I announce in fifty words or less that my daughter is born and my husband is dead?" The bones of her wrists as fragile as Zack's had been, as if she'd gone through chemotherapy with him: an aggressive form of non-Hodgkin's lymphoma, dead at twenty-nine. It had been, surprisingly, Ginger who had put her arm around Betts's shoulder and said so soothingly she might have been reading a favorite poem, "Let me, Betts. Let me do this for you, this one small thing." It's something we've done for each other ever since, too: set out the words to announce each other's joys and sorrows to the world.

Or joys, really. Only joys, not sorrows. Betts would never have thought to submit a class note about Zack's death if it hadn't so closely coincided with Izzy's birth. We don't ever announce bad news in the alumni magazine. Ginger didn't submit anything the fall she was passed over for partner, any more than I did when I divorced. And I sure don't plan to submit a class note announcing I've been fired. If I find a new job—*when* I find one—Laney or Betts or Ginger will compose a note that makes it appear I've moved up in the world, even if I haven't. That's the way of alumni notes.

"Betts is wearing your mama's black pearls," Laney realizes in a whisper—"your mama" being Ginger's mom and the pearls not really black so much as unmatched shades of gray tinted silver-green and blue and eggplant, with a looped white-gold clasp now resting at the base of Betts's throat. They're the good-luck pearls I wore to the Crease Ball our first year at Michigan, and Laney's "something borrowed" on her wedding day. "'Next to my own skin, her pearls,'" Ginger says in what Betts calls her "look-how-well-I-quote-poetry voice."

I don't remember ever seeing the pearls on Betts, but they look better on her than on any of us; it's the hair color, I think, the echo of gentle gray.

She's too thin again. She could stand to participate in one of those paczki-eating contests from her childhood—those celebrations of the Polish jelly doughnut Betts swears is not a doughnut. It's the stress, of course: the months of interviews and background checks, and the worry she'd lose the nomination to someone with judicial experience—not that she regrets having stayed in Ann Arbor for her daughter's sake. Then the weeks of holing up in a windowless room at the White House, crafting answers to every question the staffers could imagine, then practicing them again and again and again. And now the daily hearings, the cameras and questions, the news clips, a short few words taken out of context, replayed at 5:00 and 6:00 and 10:00, and then again on the morning shows. Betts's confirmation may very well be as secure as I think it is, but that doesn't make good press.

"We should make Betts color that hair this weekend," Ginger says as she smooths the cowlick at my right temple into submission. *Let me do this for you, this one small thing.* "That gorgeous auburn it was before Zack died."

"I'm liking the gray," Laney says, and I agree. Betts's refusal to color it is an odd form of penance, as if colorless hair could make up for not having loved Zack enough to keep him alive. Ginger needs to let her be.

"So you both like the gray on Betts, but not on yourselves?" Ginger says.

"Betts beats us all the way to heaven at being smarter," Laney says. "Surely she'd allow us prettier, Ginge."

I reach across Ginger to touch Laney's hair, which, after twenty-five years of being chemically straightened and shoulder-length, has been allowed to reclaim its natural spring. It frames the curves of her jaw in loose rings of dark curls her face has clearly wanted all along. "I love this," I say, meaning the hair, I think.

"Betts isn't smarter," Ginger says. "Just more disciplined."

Laney and I lean our heads on Ginger's quilted winter white shoulders.

"You're right. You're right," Ginger says. "Smarter, too. I can admit that now: Betts is smarter than me."

Laney and I each pat one soft, black-wooled knee of our dear, not always so humble friend as Milwaukee's Finest requests and receives permission to ask one last question.

"But not you two. I get to be second smartest," Ginger says, fingering an ebony button. "Damn, Betts is really going to do this, isn't she?"

"Mrs. Zhukovski," Milwaukee says.

Ginger, Laney, and I all whisper, *"Ms."* in unison and smile at each other as if the shared thought is a shiny penny found heads up.

"Professor," I whisper.

The cameras, as quiet as they are these days, snap off each moment as though any single shot might capture the whole of what's happening here, rather than distorting it. The TV cameras roll on, delivering every blemish in detail so the folks at home can wonder why Betts doesn't have that little fatty deposit removed. The thought crosses my mind that Justice Sotomayor might never have been confirmed if her "wise Latina woman" comment had been caught on film. Visuals are so powerful, even when they're untrue—or only a piece of the truth that, taken alone, is a lie.

I sit up straighter, leaning forward, wanting suddenly to warn Betts to be careful here: Milwaukee is sporting an expression like the one she'd dubbed "Professor Pooley's you're-about-to-be-called-on stare," but without the humorous underlay. My hands go icy, my neck and my feet, too, my spine. Like the shock of that first plunge into the Chesapeake all those years ago.

"Mrs. Zhukovski," Milwaukee repeats, "I'd like to ask you what you know about a death that occurred in the spring of 1982, at a home in Maryland where I believe you were a guest?"

"Oh, shit," Ginger says—mercifully not before the silent blink of the crowd absorbing the question gives way to a collective murmur, the photographers surging forward as even the senators exhale their surprise.

I take Ginger's hand and squeeze it. She looks startled, but if she was going to say more, she doesn't. She links hands with Laney, and we watch as Betts, oddly, unlatches the clasp at her throat and lets the pearl necklace slide into her hand. Every moment of the gesture is caught in a shutter snap: a single manicured nail flipping the catch; her competent fingers opening the necklace; the gray globes of pearls following the white-gold loop into her palm. She fingers the dark blue-gray end pearl, worrying it between thumb and forefinger as if saying a Hail Mary over rosary beads.

The adviser sitting behind her looks like he's praying for divine intervention, as does Senator Friendly up on the dais, but Betts looks unfazed. She doesn't even seem to realize she's removed the pearls. For a moment, I think she is going to stand to answer the senator's question, the way we were required to stand to answer in law school. I think removing the pearls must have something to do with this.

She doesn't stand, though. She remains in her chair. She leans forward from the seat back that is higher than her shoulders, moving closer to the microphone. She smiles the way she smiles when you stumble upon her doing yoga on her screen porch in the morning: a little embarrassed, but somehow more for you than for her. And in the same soft, self-possessed voice she and I rehearsed again and again over the telephone—a voice even I almost believe—she says, "Senator, I don't believe I have anything to add to the public record on that."

Betts

~

"I DON'T BELIEVE I have anything to add to the public record on that," I say, thinking, *You just close the damned door and walk on as if you haven't left anything behind.* Faith's advice had nothing to do with dead bodies floating to the surface of Senate hearings. Still it comes to me as I lean toward the microphone and spit out the answer Mia and I rehearsed. Always from private lines in private rooms. Always with an irrational our-phones-might-be-tapped unease.

The senators all stare back at me. Thin layers of I'm-in-control-here cover each what-the-hell? expression. The question is a dreadful one on which to end this. But the chairman announced it as the final one. And it'll be worse if I let this drag out. So I walk on. I launch into my prepared closing remarks without waiting for an invitation. I allow no possibility there might be anything more to ask or say. No doubt I'm violating every Senate protocol by wrapping things up here without being invited to first. One of the few benefits of being a woman: men are reluctant to call out your transgressions to your face.

I hope to hell the Ms. Bradwells have a plan to get us out of here without the press.

I slash whole paragraphs from my closing remarks as I say them. I need to stand and leave before a single senator interrupts. The chairman, a big supporter of my nomination, adjourns the hearing almost before I finish thanking him.

I stand and walk out. Jonathan follows. If every camera in the room has every moment of my leaving on film, well, then they have it on film.

I can't run, obviously. And the press can. Jonathan and I are not out the door before I'm eating microphones. "Maryland" and "death" bounce around me like echoes in a deep pit.

"Frankly, we're appalled at the senator's willingness to muckrake when there is no dirt whatsoever here," Jonathan answers. Pretty bold of him. He wouldn't have been ten years old when Faith hosted that party at Chawterley. 1982. He wouldn't have been watching the news even if this particular death had been news. Which it wasn't. Maybe an obituary ran in *The Washington Post* or maybe it didn't. I don't even know. It wasn't the unexplained death the senator is suggesting it was. The police didn't interview a single party guest about it. They talked to Doug because Doug found him. They talked to Faith and Mr. Conrad because they owned Chawterley. I don't think they even talked to Ginger. If anyone thought it was anything other than an accident, they thought suicide. "More often than you think, it's suicide rather than accident," I overheard one officer say as we were loading our suitcases the next morning. "But that only makes the family blame themselves, and Faith Cook has always been an awful nice lady, she and her sister Grace both." So the police just added our names to the hundred other names. They filed their accidental death report. They sent us on our way.

Mia's arm links in mine as we near the outside door. She whispers that Laney and Ginger ran for the car before the gavel banged.

A tap at my other elbow. Jonathan. It's my turn to speak.

"The only death I can imagine the senator might be referring to was ruled an accident," I say. Words I might have said to the Judiciary Committee if I hadn't just blurted out the line Mia and I had rehearsed. But without that response at the ready who knows what I might have said?

"As I told the senators," I say now, "I don't have anything to add."

Mia squeezes my arm again. The nondescript silver rental car Laney took me to breakfast in this morning pulls into the drive. Ginger holds a cellphone to her ear in the passenger seat.

Mia's hand at the small of my back pushes me forward. Ginger is opening the rear car door. The microphones chase us. Mia pushes me into the backseat. Climbs in beside me.

"Like the cliché of every criminal and his lawyer fleeing the court-house press," Mia mutters under her breath.

Isabelle is occupied taking a midterm this afternoon. At least there's that. And Matka is gone.

I hope the president isn't watching this. I don't know why it matters but it does.

"Good lord, you guys need to get a life," Mia calls out as she slams the door on the press. Laney is already driving off.

We burst into laughter. As if this is some law school prank.

"*Get a life?* Tell me I didn't really just say that." Mia's wry smile so familiar that for a moment we're Izzy's age again. Or even younger than my daughter. Mia and me sitting on our beds in our tiny room in N Section discussing the latest dirtbag of a guy Ginger had chosen to date.

"That's *my life* they're living!" she adds. "*They* need to get a life?!"

We laugh and laugh. It isn't even funny, but what else are we going to do? Gallows humor. The way we always survived finals weeks. Laney is laughing so hard it's a miracle she can still drive.

She hurries through a yellow light, the locks clicking down as we reach some critical momentum.

Mia wipes away laughter-tears.

"I'm guessing you need to turn your cellphone back on, Betts," she says. "I'm guessing you should call whoever you need to call before they call you."

Ginger says into her phone, "Max, I'm hoping the fact I have to leave a message means you're already on your way."

In the rearview mirror, I watch a press van pull into the Hart Building drive. Another follows just behind it. A third opts for the curb at the street. The reporters and cameramen load in no more efficiently than Mia and I did, despite being unhampered by microphones thrust in their faces.

I strap on my seat belt. "I guess the great break-the-bank orchestra seats for *Les Miz* are off the table," I say. "So where the hell do we go?"

Mia

~

THE FISHY STINK of the Chesapeake is as overwhelming now as it was the first time Ginger and Laney and Betts and I made the trip to Cook Island, spring break of our third year in law school. Ginger had wanted us to go to Mexico, but a week in Cancún wouldn't explain all that well to the financial aid office for Betts and me. Ginger's father's sixtieth birthday was that week, anyway, and Ginger's mom—"Faith," she'd asked us to call her—thought it would be "just grand" if Ginger brought us all along. So with "*Sub Judice* Bradwell at 4:05" as the plan, we'd muddled through Friday classes imagining the warm waters of the Caribbean—never mind Ginger's insistence that the bay wasn't exactly balmy in August, much less in the spring. After Ginger's Corporate Tax class, with the trees the dead gray of late winter and clouds spitting something between mist and rain on the windshield of Mrs. Z's rusty Ford, we'd set off at the mandated gas-saving fifty-five miles per hour (more or less) to conquer the five hundred miles from the Law Quad to this same yacht club.

A boat to take us across to Cook Island waited for us then just as one does now. I hope Ginger is right that my fellow members of the press will have a harder time following us to Cook Island than they would to New York. She's a poet; she has no idea how resourceful we journalists are.

Betts has been on her cellphone nonstop since we closed the car door on the thrust microphones and rolling cameras, as if to make up for having spoken so little in the Hart Building lobby. Her restraint there showed how good her prep was; Betts is not one to stand down when there are things to be said. Now she's assuring one White House aide after another that the death the senator was questioning was indeed ruled an accident. I pretend not to be listening, but of course I am.

"A *blog*?" she says.

Laney is intent on the road ahead and the press vans behind as Ginger directs her into the yacht club parking lot. "Max says to pull right up to the entrance," Ginger says. "He's got someone to take care of the car, and the press won't be allowed in the door." She and Laney either haven't heard Betts or it doesn't surprise them that this mess has broken in a blog.

Betts is being so Betts here. Calm and even. I hear the edge of alarm in her voice only because I've heard it before, that fall of our third year when she realized she'd forgotten to turn in a take-home midterm. Just forgotten, which was so unlike her. She was so unlike herself that whole term that I'd begun to imagine she was in trouble, unwed girl trouble. But she'd handled that midterm like she's handling this: she'd simply taken it to the professor and explained what happened, direct and honest and sure of herself. And he'd accepted it and given her an A.

"I can't imagine what the senator is thinking," she is saying over the phone now. And then, "Yes. Yes, of course I'll hold."

A few frantic minutes after we pull up to the door of the yacht club, we slip out the back of the building to a waiting boat, an elegantly simple one with a clean white deck and a hull some color between royal and navy, its masts bare, the boom wrapped in canvas the blue of the hull. It's the boat's name, though, written in the same blue on the white stern, that announces in no small way that this was Faith Cook Conrad's boat: the *Row v. Wade*.

As we board—Laney and Betts teetering in their pumps, leaving me glad of my practical flats—a faint whiff of Faith's menthol cigarettes mingles with the salt air. I remember the waxy up-close scent of Faith's "trademark red lipstick"—really more of a dark pumpkin, but some detail-challenged journalist called her lips red in the days of black and white newspaper photos, and his "trademark red" stuck. I imagine Faith still with us, in the cabin maybe, improbably hunched over a legal brief in a pleading clip, with pages rolled back over the top and the graphite of a chewed pencil spilled all over the page. Faith talking easily to the press we're running from, her wide smile so like Ginger's, or Ginger's so like hers. I can almost hear her voice, gravelly and certain, Faith advising us . . . but what would she advise us to do now, stuck as we are between the truth and our own unwillingness to accept it all those years ago?

And Faith has been dead for months now. The only person with us is Ginger's friend Max.

"All right. Thank you, Mr. President. Yes, I will. Thank you." Betts closes her cellphone and looks up, surprised to find herself already on the boat.

"Mr. *President*," Ginger repeats. "As in, of the United States?"

In Betts's perky, small-mouthed smile, I find the girl she was when I first met her, all that irreverent humor and kindness and drive. "He said if anyone catches us skinny-dipping this weekend, I should deny, deny, deny."

"Lordy! Betts is joking with the president of the United States!" Laney says.

I'm thinking it's us Betts is joking with. I didn't hear the term "skinny-dipping" cross her lips.

"I promised him we'd all do our best not to get photographed in the buff," Betts says.

I say, "Ginge, the press will have a boat in thirty seconds," trying to hurry her.

"Won't, actually," her friend Max says. "The club members are more loyal than the press is persistent, and there's no other boat for miles. Nor another way to get to Cook Island except by boat."

Ginger pushes the bracelet sleeves of her jacket up over her elbows and takes one of the two steering wheels at the back of the boat. Why two steering wheels? I remember my Holga and pull the camera out, framing Ginger's broad hand on the white wheel as the engine hums to life, low and easy in the reddening afternoon light. And we are out on the Chesapeake again, with only the briny stretch of water and the inadequate stretch of years between us and Chawterley and the lighthouse, and everything that happened that spring break of our third year at Michigan Law.

Laney

∿∿∿

Law Quadrangle Notes, Summer 2010: Ms. Helen ("Laney") Robeson-Weils (JD '82) has accepted the Democratic Party nomination for Georgia state senator from the forty-second district. For information on establishing residency in the area (which includes parts of suburban Atlanta) prior to November voting, please contact any of the Ms. Bradwells.

THE FIRST THING we Ms. Bradwells ever did have in common was our nickname, "the Ms. Bradwells," which came about in the very first hour of the very first day of law school, 8:00 a.m. Constitutional Law class. It was a Thursday in May of the year 1979. May rather than September, because we were Section Four "summer starters," a fine way to go about starting law school; the long days can get as hot as old-time revival meetings, too pasty-hot to work at anything too hard. So everyone just settles for doing their own best rather than trying to slaughter everyone else.

Have you ever seen the Michigan Law Quad? Think gothic stone cathedral but no altar, or a different kind of altar, something you can't quite see. Its centerpiece is the Reading Room, the scene of all our gum-wrapper tossings. It's an enormous room with a vaulted fifty-foot ceiling and tracery stained-glass windows, a place at its finest on the few evenings a year when a renegade brown bat careers back and forth up in that high expanse of wood beam and blue and gold tile, winging gracefully around the wrought-iron chandeliers. The unearthly quiet of the room explodes in a chorus of chatter that echoes from the hard stone walls, like the voices of monks lifted from their vows of silence by that unexpected creature of God. The good Lord knows there's nothing to do then but open the doors and hope the poor thing finds its way out.

It was Ginger's particular good fortune, Ginger's and mine both, to be nicknamed in that first hour of law school; we'd have walked out of that class with nicknames in any event. "Gunner G," Ginger likely would have been, for the seat she chose, front and center before the professor resat us alphabetically, and for the way her hand shot right on up into the air, too, while the rest of us were still blinking at the fella in khaki shorts and Birkenstocks writing his name on the chalkboard rather than settling in with the rest of us. Professor Charles E. Jarrett. "Sundance," *we* nicknamed *him* on account of his easy blond good looks.

"Ladies first, then," Professor Jarrett said in a Southern accent Betts would call "edible," although it sounded just like folks from home to me. "The facts of *Bradwell v. the State of Illinois,* Miss"—he peeked down at his seating chart—"Virginia Cook?"

"Conrad." Ginger stood, freeing hair the color of a shiny taffy apple threaded with gold from between her back and her chair—long, long hair pulled away from her clear forehead and secured with a red barrette at the nape of her neck, then looped down her back and up again so the end was caught in the barrette, too. "And it's *Ms.* The idea that a woman ought to be identified by her marital status is demeaning." Her full lips pressed together over teeth that were too big, but every fella in that classroom focused on her charming little overbite. There was not one hint of a question in her statement, which isn't so dramatic nowadays, mind you, but this was years before *The New York Times* allowed women the option of "Ms." in lieu of "Mrs." and "Miss."

"Is there . . ." Professor Jarrett glanced to his seating chart, then to the fellas beside Ginger. "I'm sorry, I don't think I have a . . . You're not Virginia Cook?"

"It's a mistake." Ginger fingered her barrette again, her knuckles spreading, her hand just about too wide and heavy for her narrow wrist. "Cook is my middle name."

"But it clearly says . . . Oh, you're the—"

"Ms. Virginia Conrad. The folks in admissions just got my name turned around."

"I see, of course." Professor Jarrett leaned back against the chalkboard. "Miss Conrad."

"*Ms.* Conrad."

"*Ms.* Conrad, yes," he said.

"Even the admissions office here addressed me as Ms."

"I see," he said, and he asked if she would accept his apologies, he was new to Michigan. "Clearly you're the perfect choice for the little discussion we're fixin' to have here, Ms. Conrad. So the facts of *Bradwell v. Illinois?*"

"Ms. Myra Bradwell applied for a license to practice law in Illinois but was turned down because she was a woman," Ginger answered, using "Ms." although the plaintiff was referred to as "Mrs." in the opinion. "She appealed the decision to the Supreme Court, alleging violation of her Fourteenth Amendment rights."

The two of them proceeded through the meaning of the privileges and immunities clause and whether someone born in Vermont but living in Illinois could claim the privileges of Vermont law, Ginger tripping over the ends of Professor Jarrett's questions in her hurry to answer: "The clause says, 'The Citizens of each State shall be entitled to all Privileges and Immunities of Citizens in the several States.'" Then, "The Court cites *Cummings v. Missouri* and *Ex parte Garland* to say the choice of a vocation is an inalienable right."

"'Inalienable.' Excellent," Professor Jarrett said. "Our first word for the day. Y'all will want to write it down."

Heads bent over the long, dark arcs of wooden lecture room desktops. Pens scratched. I spilled blue ink into my spiral binder while the fellas beside me wrote on yellow legal pads.

"So in your humble opinion, Miss *Conrad,* did the Court come to the right decision?"

"Ms."

"*Ms.* Conrad. With apologies. Old dogs and new tricks and all that."

"You don't seem such an old dog to me, Professor," Ginger said.

We all tittered, but he only smiled slightly. "And in your humble opinion, *Ms.* Conrad?"

"The Court uses this trumped-up excuse that since a married woman can't enter into contracts without her husband's consent, her clients wouldn't be able to count on her doing whatever she said she'd do for them. They point to the *Slaughter-House Cases* and say *stare decisis.*"

"*Stare decisis.* Now that's a big phrase we haven't covered yet," Professor Jarrett said, provoking another full-class titter.

Ginger again fingered her hair clip, but her pale-eyed gaze didn't leave the professor's face, and her straight brows didn't move one little bit.

"For those of you who haven't yet memorized the entire contents of your *Black's Law Dictionary*, that's Latin for . . . do you know, Ms. Conrad?"

Then, "Anyone else?"

No one answered for such a shameful long time that I finally said, "To stand by that which is decided."

Professor Jarrett leaned back against the chalkboard and studied me as if something about my white Oxford shirt or my gawky height or the fact that I was a black girl who understood Latin puzzled him and pleased him all at once. I stifled a nervous urge to giggle as the whole class craned their scrawny necks to have a look at me. *Orbis non sufficit*, I was thinking. The world is not enough: James Bond's family motto, from *On Her Majesty's Secret Service*. That's where I first got interested in Latin, seeing bad movies with my daddy when I was thirteen.

"Exactly: to stand by that which is decided," Professor Jarrett said. "In general, matters decided in earlier cases are to be followed by the courts. That's why what the Supreme Court does in any one case is so important: it becomes an interpretation of law that can't be ignored. But that's tomorrow's lesson." He wrote *stare decisis* on the board. "Y'all better get working if you plan to keep up with your colleague here."

Colleague, not classmate. An awful nice distinction.

Professor Jarrett consulted his seating chart again. "Thank you, Ms. Helen Weils, is it?" he said, pronouncing it "Wiles."

"Weils, like on a bicycle, actually," I confessed.

"Ms. Helen Weils." He frowned, a poor foil for the chuckle in his eyes: Hell on Wheels, the nickname that had followed me from Birmingham to Denver and on to Wellesley, finding me again at Michigan Law.

The whole class observed me again. Damage done, Professor Jarrett must have decided, because he said, "Your parents had a sense of humor?"

"I'm afraid they did, sir."

My "colleagues" had a nice little laugh, my treat.

"You've studied Latin, Ms. Weils?"

"*Omnia dicta fortiora si dicta Latina.*" Everything said is stronger if said in Latin.

"Ms. Cicero-Bradwell!" he said delightedly, and that was it for Hell on Wheels. Who knew having it out there would be easier than pretending it didn't exist?

Professor Jarrett returned to Ginger. "So you don't agree with what the Court did here, Ms. Decisis-Bradwell?" he asked, and forever thereafter Ginger had a nickname, too. Every time Professor Jarrett was looking for that particular answer he'd call on "Ms. Decisis-Bradwell" and Ginger would pop up and answer *"stare decisis,"* even on mornings she wore her glasses rather than her contacts and nearly drowned in her Styrofoam cup of Dominick's coffee, Professor Jarrett having a good bit of fun with Ginger like he did with all us Ms. Bradwells.

"I certainly do not agree with what the Court did here," Ginger said that first morning, her eyes shining like new money even as Professor Jarrett again eyed the seating chart.

"*Ms.* Porter?" he said, looking to a pale gal in a middle row. "You look like a sympathetic sort to me. What do you think of these poor clients not being able to make their lady lawyer do the job she told them she'd do?"

Mia tucked weedy-blond hair behind the tiniest little ears I ever have seen on a grown-up, before or since. "It does seem—"

Professor Jarrett spread his arms palms up, Jesus Christ the Lord allowing this poor sinner to rise up and be healed. "If you complete this class having learned nothing else, you will have learned that you *can* speak while standing," he said. "It'll serve you well."

Mia stood, her knees so shaky that the fella sitting next to her, a big fella in a Dartmouth T-shirt, whose open casebook did not have a mark on the page, whispered something to her.

"It does seem it could be a problem if a client can't make Mrs. Bradwell do the job they paid her to do," Mia conceded.

"You might end up in prison for want of a lawyer when you've already emptied your pocketbook to pay the big retainer," Professor Jarrett said, and the class again laughed. "So you'd agree with the Court here?"

Mia looked like she wanted to say *Heavens no* but couldn't come up with a single reason why not.

He turned to Ginger. "Ms. Decisis-Bradwell?"

"But the Court says the ruling applies to unmarried women, too," Ginger said.

"What about that, Ms. Porter?" Jarrett asked Mia. "What if our friend here is Ms. *Miss* Bradwell? Then shall we let her sit for the bar exam?"

Dartmouth rested a hand lightly against Mia's blue jeans, behind her knee. I felt a calm roll through me, too.

"You can't say what the Court would do from this, I guess," Mia said. "The stuff about— The language about the destiny of woman to be wife and mother, that isn't the whole Court speaking, it's just one justice."

"*Just* one justice?" Jarrett's face lit in mock astonishment. "Do you know how qualified a man has to be to be appointed to the Court?"

"Person," Ginger said.

"Pardon?" Professor Jarrett said.

"Person," Ginger repeated. "You said 'man,' but a woman can be a justice, too."

"All evidence to the contrary notwithstanding," Jarrett said.

"All evidence to the contrary notwithstanding," Ginger agreed, "and despite the holding in *Bradwell v. Illinois*."

"Do you know how qualified a *person* has to be to be appointed to the Supreme Court, Ms. Porter?" Professor Jarrett asked.

"But one justice can't make law by himself, can he?" Mia said. "He'd need to have a majority of the Court speaking with him. Or she, I mean. With her."

The set of Professor Jarrett's mouth didn't alter one little bit, but there was a new smile in his eyes that we would come to call his bravo gaze.

"Well, that's a pretty good guess. I'd bet on that one if I were you, Ms. Porter, if you're a betting kind of gal."

As the professor eyed the room again, Dartmouth scrawled *Good Job!* in elephant letters on Mia's notepad.

"So tell me this, Ms. Cicero-Bradwell: Why isn't the right to practice law an inalienable right?" Professor Jarrett asked, giving me the same Jesus Christ the Lord bit.

I rose slowly, trying to cobble together an answer; it would have been easy if I wasn't having to stand. "I don't believe the Court . . . The Court as a whole only says . . . They're just saying the right to practice law isn't protected by the privileges and immunities clause. The *Slaughter-House Cases* are *stare decisis* on the issue."

I too was graced with the bravo gaze.

"I hope you gentlemen are taking careful notes," Professor Jarrett said to the class. "These ladies'll be a tough act to follow."

He turned to Ginger. "So, Ms. Decisis-Bradwell, what if our Ms. Cicero-Bradwell here promises never to marry? Okay or no?"

"Indubitably okay," Ginger said in a tone that left everyone chuckling and me green as the spring grass on the Quad in envy at her ease in front of the class. "Okay with me, anyway. Although not with this Court."

"And what if Ms. Porter wants to be a soldier rather than a lawyer? Sergeant Porter-Bradwell."

"There's no more excuse to prevent her becoming a soldier than a lawyer," Ginger insisted. "Although the Bradwell Court would disagree. And the current Court, too."

Jarrett mock-frowned. "Those guns can be mighty heavy."

Ginger's topcoat of cool gave way to something more like an eight-year-old with a bright new bicycle, the sexy mouth disappearing into an overwide grin. "Any gun you choose, and you can have five shots to my one. There's a shooting range out West 94."

Professor Jarrett's professorial mock-stern softened ever so briefly; he'd just warmed to Ginger as surely as I had. Funny how lovable we become at the first crack in our perfection-seeking façades.

"Let's say Sergeant Porter-Bradwell's choice of weapon leans more toward hand grenades. She looks awfully innocent, I see that." He nodded to Mia. "But she just has an irresistible urge to hear those little things explode. So she turns to terrorism. She comes to Room 100 here for a secret rendezvous with"—another glance at his chart—"the Drug Lord of Section Four, Ms. Els-bee-et-a Zoo . . . Zoo-cow-sky? Am I pronouncing that one right?"

Betts, who is the most improbable of drug lords—she's no bigger than a minute, with chipmunk cheeks and eight million freckles—popped up from her seat as if spring-released. "Elsbieta *Zhu-kov*-ski," she said.

"Ms. Zoo-*kof*-ski."

"Close enough. I'll respond to that," she said, and we all laughed.

He returned to Mia. "So Ms. Terrorist-Bradwell, here you are buying your cocaine—that's the drug of choice in the law school these days, right?—from Ms. Zoo . . . from Ms. Drug-Lord-Bradwell, we'll call her. You're planning to resell it to raise funds for more terrorist grenades, but you're caught red-handed. Would the Bradwell Court here allow the state to treat you differently than a man?"

Mia cleared her throat. "I guess . . . Yes! The Bradwell Court, yes. They would say it was okay to treat me differently because I'm a woman."

Professor Jarrett tsk-tsked for a minute, the way he would do repeatedly all year. "They'd probably spare you the Iron Maiden and even the rack, I suppose."

The bell rang then, and he called out, "Let's all thank the four Ms. Bradwells for illustrating 'the natural and proper timidity and delicacy which belongs to the female sex' the Court talks about here!" Causing the class to laugh yet again, and then to clap.

He called out over the rumble of gathering books that there would be a handout at the distribution center after noon, and we should read pages eight through thirty-three from the casebook, too. And we all shuffled out of that first class: Ms. Ginger Decisis-Bradwell with her unchanging opinions; Sergeant Mia Terrorist-Bradwell, whom Professor Jarrett brought in whenever he introduced violence to a hypothetical; Ms. Betts Drug-Lord-Bradwell, the improbable Drug Lord of Section Four; and me, Ms. Laney Cicero-Bradwell, tapped for every Latin translation the rest of the class whiffed on all year. The names would stick, too. They'd be the way Ginger worked us into her first law school poems at the end of that summer, silly little things that made all of Section Four laugh. It was the way we appeared on "Aristocracy Bingo" at the end of the year. That first morning, though, as Dartmouth took off before Mia could say how do you do, Ginger parked herself at the door and collected us like a kindergarten teacher herding hopscotchers off the blacktop. I see now she was setting out to make us her friends as surely as she'd meant to make her South African playwright love her. That's the way Ginger is. And if it seems a bit manipulative, well, it's hard to hold it against her once you realize how enormous her heart truly is, and how often she fails to get what she thinks she wants, or even to recognize that what she thinks she wants is a different thing entirely from what will bring her happiness.

"Well, that's over for us, isn't it?" she said as she gathered us. "We've all survived our first 'up.' You guys want to study together in the Arb after Torts class? I'll bring champagne."

So that afternoon we met in one of the Law Quad archways, under a gargoyle with dislocated shoulders and legs twisted in awful angles, who nonetheless smiled underneath his silly stocking cap. "Justice Bradwell," we nicknamed that contortionist gargoyle, which would become our gathering place for ex-Quad activities: Saturday night dinners and movies; that first shopping expedition for navy blue interview suits; even the Cook Island vacation our third year, after we'd moved to the Division

Street house. "Justice Bradwell at three o'clock" we'd say, or later, "*Sub Judice* Bradwell at three," and although there was another gargoyle meant to represent the law, we weren't ever confused. That first afternoon of law school, though, we simply headed side by side up South U toward Geddes, the Ms. Bradwells of Section Four.

Mia

ON THE *ROW V. WADE*
FRIDAY, OCTOBER 8

WHEN THE REPORTERS are specks in the distance, I turn back with my Holga to photograph the roiling lace of wake opening out to the disappearing shore. As I frame the shot, I recall the shiny teak battened-down world of that earlier sailboat, the teenage boy who helped us at this same yacht club saying, "Ought to be smooth sailing to yer island." To which Laney had said, "*Your* island, Ginge?" Cook Island: Ginger's middle name that was her mom's maiden name—Faith Cook Conrad—and also the name on the sitting room in N Section of the Law Quad, the name of the women's dorm across the street.

Max, a slightly goofy-looking fifty-something guy in jeans that bag at the knees, studies Ginger from behind fashionably nerdy glasses that, on him, are all nerd and not the least bit fashion. He's my type, I realize with surprise; I've always considered my type more like Professor Jarrett—*handsomely* boyish and charming rather than nerdily so—but this guy looks like so many of the men I've slept with over the years that it must be true. He looks like the one man I married, not unlike the one I nearly did. He looks, I realize, something like my father—a disturbing thought.

Ginger declines his offer of help and he retreats below deck, leaving me to wonder if he's the kind of guy Ginger loves or the kind who loves Ginger. Ginger's taste in men tends toward total dicks, with the single and fortunate exception of her husband, Ted.

I peel back the electrical tape from the red shot counter to manually advance the film, then pan upward to catch a flock of white birds passing overhead. They'll blur a little but the motion might be interesting. Maybe the light leak that is characteristic of this particular Holga—a leak that creates a lightning bolt from God himself at the top left of the frame—will appear in the shot. You never quite know what you'll get with a Holga, which is, I suppose, why I'm drawn to it.

"Ducks?" Laney asks. Ginger always kept a photo by her bedside in law school: she and her dad and brothers in hunting gear after a day of duck hunting, their guns in hand. And "Ducks?" seems a better question than "What the hell do we do now?"

When Ginger doesn't answer, Laney says her name and repeats, "Ducks?" more loudly, to be heard over the motor and the lapping water, the thump of the boat against the waves.

"The rare Long-Necked Honking Ms. Cicero-Bradwell Duck?" Ginger smiles—a little smugly maybe, but maybe not; maybe that's just me remembering how Ginger used to be. "Tundra swans," she says. "Coming from Alaska for the winter, like Mia's mom."

I blink up at the birds: their long, graceful necks, their widespread wings. This is the way all the Ms. Bradwells imagine my mom even still. Maybe I've told them about the summer the car overheated in Death Valley, the many flat tires on the many roads to nowhere, the dusty pavement through the grimy car window always slipping over the horizon, always leading home again at the end of August, just in time for school. Or maybe I haven't ever told the Ms. Bradwells any of that; I don't even know anymore. But I know they hold this unreasonably glamorous image of my mother: in a convertible with the top down, a scarf blowing behind her like Beryl Markham in her airplane as we set out from Chicago to Alaska, me in the passenger seat, my brother, Bobby, in the back, Dad calling, "Drive carefully, Ellen!" as we leave him behind with three months of frozen dinners and a lonely trek back and forth to the office every day. Except the Ms. Bradwells don't see Dad, they only see Mom. She has Alzheimer's now, Mom does. She refers to Dad as "that nice man who takes care of me." Ginger and Laney and Betts would be appalled at how unswanlike her thin neck looks, how frail.

Betts frowns at her cellphone, then asks to see mine. I flip it open but have no reception either. We're too far out on the water.

"Remind me to call Isabelle when we get to the island," she says.

I'm godmother to all the Baby Girl Bradwells: Izzy, who is in law school herself now, and Ginger's Annie and Laney's Gem, freshmen at

Princeton and Stanford. Half the reason I came back from Madagascar was to see Iz and Annie in New York this weekend. But an express train from Princeton or New Haven to Manhattan for a dinner is one thing; a train to a car to a boat to Cook Island would be nearly as ridiculous a trip as Gem flying to New York from Palo Alto for the evening. Ginger left Annie a message while she and Laney got the car, telling her daughter not to come.

"What's with that camera, Mi?" Laney asks. "It looks like the kind of thing only you could love."

"Like Dartmouth!" Betts suggests.

"But we all loved Andy," Laney protests. "Maybe he wasn't such a good husband choice for Mia, but . . ."

The *Law Quadrangle* note Andy and I submitted the spring we married:

Mary Ellen ("Mia") Porter (JD '82) and Andrew ("Dartmouth") Cooper IV (JD '82) were married in Chicago, and will be making their home together in San Francisco. The former Ms. Porter has taken the name Mary Porter Cooper in defiance of the wishes of her friend Ms. Ginger Conrad (JD '82), who has vowed hereinafter to refer to all future issue of the couple as "the Babies Terrorist-Bradwell."

It had seemed so funny at the time, that whole name business, Ginger insisting Andy should become a Porter rather than me taking his name. ("Porter-Cooper?" Betts had suggested. "Cooper-Porter? I know! Coopporter! You can start a business transporting chicken coops!") But I'd gladly tucked Porter aside and abandoned Ellen altogether, shrugging off my mom's name and all her expectations for me with it, *claiming* the person I was rather than abandoning any part of me. After six months of wedded unbliss, though, Andy started coming home far too late at night—which might have been work or might have been another woman but wasn't either. We split after less than a year, and I took the apartment and I took my name back, and he quietly moved into his new lover's house in Pacific Heights.

"So," I say, hoping the film isn't scratching as I turn the plastic knob to advance it, seeing that even Laney's neck is starting to go. I position the wrinkling skin under her jaw in the center of the plastic lens, where the focus is sharpest. She's too close, though, and the Holga is just a cheap toy camera: the focal length doesn't adjust. "So, I'm thinking this return to Cook Island might be as bad a move as Andy's and my marriage was."

Laney, running unbitten fingers through her spring of loose curls, says, "I expect a roll of film costs nearly as much as that camera, does it, Mi?"

"She says the camera creates a mood," Betts says quickly, with a warning glance in my direction: where else is there to go?

"Foreign?" Laney says.

"Remote," Ginger says.

I turn the camera first to one, then to the other, wondering how we are ever going to face this if we can't even talk. "Nostalgic," I say. "The camera creates a nostalgic mood."

"Nostalgic!" Betts snorts. "We'd best be careful or Ms. Terrorist-Bradwell here will have us wanting those awful navy blue suits back from the Goodwill. And those goofy silk scarves we used to bow at our throats, too—like we belonged under a Christmas tree!"

"Remember all those conversations on the couch on the Division Street porch?" I ask.

"That place surely was a dump," Laney says.

"It wasn't," I say.

"That place made the Hamtramck apartment I grew up in look spiffy," Betts says.

"Definitely a dump," Ginger says.

"Ugly is in the eye of the beholder," I say.

Ginger puts me at the helm for a minute while she removes the blue casing over the sail. She's completely at home on the water, even in her fancy suit, which, as perfect as it is for our planned New York theater evening, is exactly the wrong thing to wear sailing. One splash of bay water and that gorgeous jacket is trashed.

"Pooley's cocktail party first year," Laney says. "Manhattans or Martinis, and not a drop of water."

"Plenty of water in that hot tub," Betts says, and we all laugh at that memory.

"That was the first time we got naked together," Laney says.

BETTS AND I had been rooming together only a few weeks the night of the hot tub party. We were all taking a Thursday night wine tasting class held, improbably, in one of the law school lecture rooms, and a class-mate had invited eight Section Four women to a private tasting at her va-cationing parents' house. I can still see Laney and Ginger standing to strip off their suits in that hot tub, their nipples hard against the unsea-sonably cold September night before they sank back into the water. Laney's nipples almost black to Ginger's pink, her breasts dark to Gin-ger's milk-water white. Salt and pepper, such different spices, but always passed together. They'd stretched their long legs out, side by side, allow-ing their feet to float up to the surface, Laney's long and narrow without being fragile while Ginger's were sturdy and calloused, inelegant. Their toenails were painted an identical red, where Betts's and mine were bare. Just the four of us in the hot tub, our other friends already gone back in-side the house.

They seemed so comfortable in their nakedness, Laney lanky and easy, Ginger more aggressive, wielding her body as if it were one of her much-loved guns. I imagined a girl had to be tall and thin like they were to be comfortable naked, even just with friends, with no guys around. I imagined every girl who was tall and thin was comfortable with herself.

"You know what I hate?" Ginger asked as she played footsie with Betts, kicking up the smell of chlorine. "I hate waking up in the morning and having no idea what the name of the guy in bed next to me is."

She fixed her gaze on Betts as if she somehow knew Betts was still a virgin, the only one of the Ms. Bradwells who was. As if she already knew Betts would beat her out for law review. I'd slept only with the college boyfriend I broke up with just before starting law school, and Laney only with her medical student, Carl. I don't suppose Betts or Laney ever imag-ined climbing in bed with a boy they didn't love, any more than I had, much less one whose name they didn't know.

Betts, though, simply met Ginger's look in that very frank Betts way and said, "But think of the possibilities for the morning. Twenty ques-tions: Does your name start with a letter in the first half of the alphabet?" She laughed then, and we all laughed with her.

Ginger sank completely underwater, her long hair drifting toward me before she reemerged with it slicked back from her pale forehead.

"So what's your future, everyone?" she asked.

And when that evening was over, I still had no idea that Betts was a virgin, that Ginger had indeed once woken next to a guy whose name she didn't know, that she'd dropped out of college a week later to move to

South Africa with him. But I did know more about the Ms. Bradwells than I would have imagined learning in just those few hours.

Laney meant to return to Atlanta after law school, maybe after a few years in D.C. with a politically connected firm, she said, to which Ginger said she ought to run for the Senate someday.

"Not president?" Betts offered, palming a spray of water in Ginger's direction. "If Margaret bloody Thatcher can do it, can't we?"

I admitted no real idea what I was doing in law school. My childhood dreams had included becoming a guitarist, movie star, news reporter, and Catholic priest. My mom had convinced me to take the LSAT, though, and I'd done well—a perfect 800, I found myself admitting in response to their inquisition.

"Mia, the Savant," Ginger said, reaching for the wine bottle at the edge of the hot tub and refilling my glass.

She, unlike me, had her whole future laid out and *she* wasn't afraid to admit it. She meant to join a Wall Street firm, make partner on an accelerated basis, have a weekend place in the Hamptons where she would race sailboats, and marry someone with a fortune to match the one she meant to make herself.

"The Prince of Wales is still available," Betts suggested. "The Crown Princess Ginger? Ginger of Wales? Haven't you always wanted to be 'of' somewhere, really? And you wouldn't have to worry about recognizing him when you woke up. Then you could be beheaded or burned at the stake when you got caught waking up next to one of those guys whose name you didn't know!"

"A *handsome* millionaire," Ginger insisted. "I don't care if he's royalty, although I'm not opposed. And a flat in Paris—I forgot the flat in Paris."

"I, on the other hand, just want my head on a coin," Betts declared.

We talked for a minute about the Susan B. Anthony coin just out, the first U.S. tender ever to sport a woman's face. Progress, I said, to which Ginger scoffed, "A dead woman's head on a coin is progress?"

"It *is* a dollar," Laney said.

A dollar that would be forever mistaken for a quarter—what does that say?

"*Progressio advenit sensim,*" Laney said. "Progress comes slowly."

Ginger thrust her hands toward Laney, index fingers crossed at right angles as she juggled her wineglass. "*In manus tuas, Domine!*"

"Into your hands, Lord?" Laney said.

"From *Dracula*," Ginger said. "You know—when they're about to finish off poor Vlad? *In manus tuas, Domine!* It's the phrase the professor uses to ward off evil spirits, evil like Latin spoken outside the classroom. We'll have none of that in this hot tub."

Betts made a finger cross too, then, her Speedo swimsuit puckering over her flat chest, and I followed, both of us mangling the Latin verbal shield, saying something that sounded, between us, like "In manners, too, dominate."

"In manus tuas, Domine," Ginger repeated more slowly, as if she knew at least as much Latin as Laney did.

"In manners, too, dominate!" Betts and I insisted, laughing as much from the abundance of wine as anything.

"So your turn, Betts," Ginger said. "What's your dream?"

"My head on a coin isn't ambition enough?" Betts floated onto her back in the water, looking up into the fuzzy dark sky. "I have humble ambitions, really," she said. "I'd just like to be called 'Judge Zoo'!"

The truth was that Betts dreamed of being on the Supreme Court even back then. Thirty years, that's what she figured it would take to get there. No woman had ever been admitted to the Court at the time, and part of her hoped to God it wouldn't be another thirty years until one was appointed, but another part of her—maybe the bigger part—hoped the opportunity to be the first would wait for her. That much truth, though, would roll out gradually, the way most of the truths about the Ms. Bradwells have.

"You should get a D.C. Circuit Court clerkship if you can, it's the most influential appellate court," Ginger said—a clerkship being a one- or two-year position working for a judge, not for the shabby paycheck but for the experience and prestige. "My mother has connections, that might help."

"And then a Supreme Court clerkship," Laney suggested, and Ginger said, "Right."

No one said anything like, "Gosh, you need to graduate at the top of your class and be some kind of freaky genius to get a Supreme Court clerkship." No one pointed out that Nixon and Ford together had appointed exactly two women to the federal courts in their combined twelve years in office, two out of almost three hundred appointments. No one said that Caruthers, Smythe & Morgan, the law firm Ginger meant to join, had no women partners—much less that it would still have none the year our class would come up for partnership. And none of us uttered a word suggesting that Laney should plan on being a widow or facing a short term in office if she wanted to be a senator, even though half the fourteen women who'd sat in the U.S. Senate by then had filled their late husbands' seats and none of the others had served longer than nine months.

That was one of the things we Ms. Bradwells had in common pretty much from the start: we might laugh at ourselves or at our own chances, but even when we didn't know each other very well yet—when we might have mistaken light tones for lack of seriousness—we never did laugh at each other's dreams.

Mia

~

GINGER HOISTS THE sail on her mom's boat, calling out to me, "Hold that helm tight and straight for a minute, Mi!"

"Lordy, how *did* we get back to the Law Quad, as drunk as we were?" Laney asks, and I can almost hear her voice saying "Lordy, Lordy" in that hot tub all those years ago, after confessing to claiming an A at the grade wall when she'd actually missed it by two points that would cost her law review. I'd confessed to the opposite: pretending the grade beside my student number wasn't an A when it was so that Andy wouldn't think I'd done better than he had. And Ginger, much later that night, after the drugs had come out, had confessed that the man in the portrait in the Cook Room, the man who donated all that money to build the Law Quad, was her great-great-uncle—in response to which Betts had demanded, "Why in the world is that any kind of confession?" Ginger had said she didn't know, but it was.

Ginger takes the helm back from me, the sail billowing gracefully in the afternoon breeze, the boom swinging out to accommodate the power of a wind we can't otherwise see as I remember Betts waking to the coffee I'd made her the morning after the hot tub party, the two cups I'd carried across the Quad and up the stairs to Ginger and Laney's room. Despite my efforts, we were all late for class.

"Makes you worry about what our daughters might be doing right this minute," Betts says.

"I can't imagine Annie is anything like I was," Ginger replies with a hint of melancholy that suggests sadness, or relief, or both.

"Gemmy doesn't *want* to be like me," Laney says. "She'd like to be not-me. She'd like to be reborn a Baby Terrorist-Bradwell."

I shoot a frame of her dark eyes looking directly at me as I imagine that: me taking Laney's place in her annual holiday photo-cards—Laney and her picture-perfect family with their picture-perfect needlepointed Christmas stockings hanging from the mantel behind them. William, Laney, Willy J, Manny, Gem, and Little Joe. I send holiday photo-cards too these days: Mia with birds swarming overhead outside the Wazir Khan Mosque in Lahore, Pakistan, where I was researching a piece on honor killings; Mia at a school in Angola, with too-thin children and something that passes for a chalkboard; Mia in Kenya, helping plant indigenous trees. But I don't have a Christmas stocking or a fireplace, much less a family.

"I loved the expression on that *Washington Post* fella's face at the yacht club when your friend Max said he was calling the police, Ginge," Laney says. "It was even funnier than when he told them there wasn't a boat within fifty miles that would take them anywhere."

I shoot another frame, Betts's face in the upper right corner so her gray hair will bleed off into the vignetting.

"We're not exactly in for a quiet weekend on the island," I say. "The press is going to catch up with us."

"You say that like you're not one of them, Mia!"

Betts means it in good fun, but I'm left wondering if she really thinks I'm like the journalists who had conniptions when Max in his pale-kneed jeans informed them the yacht club was members-only, and pulled his phone from his pocket lest they think he'd hesitate to call the police. The headlines tomorrow will be wicked, but the papers will be reduced to running a photo of our backs entering the club, or perhaps a long-lens shot of the boat disappearing into the bay. And I suppose Ginger is right that it will take them some time to find us, since Cook Island is only a small dot of unnamed land on navigational maps, and nonexistent on your average visitor map of the Chesapeake.

"How does this mess surface in a *blog*?" Betts says.

She looks at me, I'm sure she does. My roommate, and then my housemate, who knows me better than anyone in the world.

"Half of D.C. was there for Mr. Conrad's party, Betts," I say. "A hundred guests. Someone shows up with . . ." With their guts blown out.

"Someone turns up dead like that, anyone at that party might have doubts."

Or anyone on the whole island. Any of the "slutty island girls."

I turn the camera to Ginger, remembering her words: *Tessie McKee? She was just a slutty little island girl everyone seems to think popped Beau's cherry.* Remembering how fiercely loyal Ginger was to her brother Beau, and he to her. How fiercely loyal they still are, I'm sure. I focus on the soft white of Ginger's jacket, her ebony buttons. The contrast unsettles me. I raise the camera higher, to her pale gray-blue eyes, her wide mouth, which is not smiling, not even trying to hide the bare sorrow as she looks ahead, guiding her dead mother's boat toward her dead mother's home.

As I press the shutter release, I imagine the Cook Island house as empty today as it was thirty years ago. That emptiness had been rich with possibility, though, a whole week of fun stretching out before us. Now, even in the warm afternoon light, the emptiness looms dark and murky, as bottomless as the Chesapeake.

Ginger presses a knee against the wheel to hold the boat straight, then pulls a barrette from her trouser pocket—found-ebony to match the suit buttons—and battens down her hair. The long loop from law school is gone, her hair now barely long enough to catch in the clip. She cut it all off after Betts's husband, Zack, died, and she donated it to an outfit that made wigs for children going through chemo, although she never told me that. She only said she needed a change. Laney was the one who told me Ginger gave up all that beautiful hair for some kid who was as bald as Betts's Zack was when he died. I don't think Betts knows that to this day.

"You okay, Ginge?" I ask.

A few strands escape around her face, whipping against her cheeks as she realizes I'm addressing her. "I was just imagining who you Ms. Bradwells would be if you were poets," she says brightly, with the smile that isn't a smile, that is only the same screen she has always thrown up to mask sorrow or disappointment or wounded pride. "You, Mia, would be Elizabeth Bishop: the way she never settles, she's always going somewhere. And something about her reaction to the moose: 'Why, why do we feel / (we all feel) this sweet / sensation of joy?'" She doesn't look at me as she speaks, as she repeats the phrase "this sweet sensation of joy." Nor does she turn to Betts when she says, "Betts, you'd be William Carlos Williams's red wheelbarrow, simple and pure and fun." When she does look at Laney, her pale eyes are as tired as they ever were in law school. "I was thinking of you, Lane, as Marianne Moore. 'The deepest feeling always shows itself in silence; / not in silence, but restraint.' "

Laney considers this in silence or restraint or both. "What about you, Ginge?" she asks.

Ginger's eyes do actually brighten—although not enough to match her voice—as she decides that she would be Emily Dickinson. "'Tell all the Truth but tell it slant—' "

"Slanted beyond recognition sometimes, as I recall, and maybe not quite *all* the truth!" Betts laughs then and we all laugh with her, a gentle sound that barely registers over the motor, the waves, the wind in our ears.

"And your mom, Ginge?" Laney asks gently. "Which poet would she have been?"

It's hard to imagine any poet capturing the spirit of Faith Cook Conrad. It's hard to imagine her as anyone but herself. When I think of Ginger's mom, I think of that poster from the mid-1980s, the women who showed up at art museums naked but for gorilla masks, to draw attention to the dearth of work by women artists included in museum collections. I think of the newspaper photos of Faith arriving at the steps of the U.S. District Court for Idaho dressed as Susan B. Anthony on life support during the appeal for *Idaho v. Freeman*, where despite her efforts the Court upheld state rescissions of earlier Equal Rights Amendment ratifications, killing any chance the ERA would become law before the deadline for ratification passed. I think of her arriving at a men's steam room with a tape measure, singing "Is That All There Is?"—which in reality was Gloria Allred trying to end the Friars Club's all-men policy, but it's the kind of thing Ginger's mom crowed about even if she didn't do it herself. Humor, she always said, was a much more effective way to get press coverage for something you cared about than was rage.

I think, too, of the many ways Faith urged *us* to care, the monthly letters she made us write to *The New York Times*, calling their resistance to addressing women as Ms. rather than Mrs. or Miss "a total crock." She always called on Saturdays rather than weekdays or Sundays; a Saturday call undercut any excuse we might have to avoid rolling stationery into the typewriter—this in the days before you could simply email a petition link. "If change is needed and it doesn't start with us, then where the hell does it start?" she liked to say. "Timing and persistence are everything, and if you're persistent, your time will come."

Did she have the nerve to say that to her daughter after Ginger was passed over for partner? *If you're persistent, your time will come.* I used to believe it myself, before my marriage failed, long before the current state of newspaper sales and advertising left me without a job.

Ginger slides a carefully manicured hand down the boat's white steering wheel, then back up again. "Maybe you guys can help me clear out Mother's things," she says. She stares ahead the way she does when anyone touches anything raw in her, the way she did that time she'd insisted that if *our* mothers were the ones forcing women members on a club that didn't want them, *we'd* be the ten-year-olds alone on our towels at the pool, the debutantes no one asked to dance. If we got pregnant, maybe the guys would marry us or maybe we'd get abortions or give up our babies, but no one would read about it in the *Times.*

I raise the camera, framing the circle of the wheel, the straight line of the horizon, the textured triangles of her jacket and the triangular bow of the boat. In her admission—that even though the house and all its contents have been left to her, Ginger has not, in the months since her mom died, returned to Cook Island to sort through her things—I feel the ebbing away of a small anger I've been nursing since Faith died. Faith was important to the rest of us, too, but maybe Ginger's refusal to have us at her mom's funeral *wasn't* the same kind of selfish thing Ginger has always done, the way she tries to hoard everyone close to her lest they abandon her for someone else.

"You have clothes on the island, Ginge?" I ask. Betts's suitcase was in Laney's trunk—they'd all had breakfast together—and Laney and Ginger took mine when they ran for the car. But Ginger took the Acela Express from New York this morning, meaning to train back with us in tow tonight.

"Not so much as a swimsuit," she says, her gaze fixed on the uncluttered horizon.

"None of us brought swimsuits this time," Laney says gently, and although it's obvious why—we brought clothes to wear to the theater, heels, the light evening jackets in which Laney and Betts and I now huddle, little protection against the wind of the bay and the speed of the boat—still, it seems a bad omen, as does the silence that settles over us.

I squint against the coloring sunlight, wondering if the shadow darkness I think I see at the horizon now is anything at all, torn between wanting this journey to end and not wanting to arrive at Cook Island again.

Cook Island. I remember Ginger telling us that even though it looks like two islands, the two ends are attached by a strip of earth barely wider than the one-lane no-name road that crosses it, connecting her family's half of the island to the public end: the little white village with Haddy's Market and Brophy's Bar; the fishing docks; the Pointway Inn where the four of us had dinner with Ginger's brothers and Trey Humphrey and Doug Pemberley before we went stargazing all those years ago, where Doug and I stayed the week he asked me to marry him.

We all watch silently as the horizon shadow grows closer, taking shape, but just barely, a raggedy outline that is the tops of the trees— hackberries that Ginger once told us "drop shit everywhere but are the only tall things that grow in this salt pit, unless you count my brothers and me." The high slate roof of Chawterley asserts itself as a flatness in the treetops then, and because I see the roof now, the house, too, emerges: three stories of green shingle bleeding into trees that are not the new-leaf-spattered tangle of limbs they were that spring break but rather a tired camouflage tinged with yellow and dying brown. I can make out the white trim of all those windows now, the stone chimneys rising over the blue-green of the roof, the pale foundation stones washing into the sand or the fall-dying marsh grasses—what *does* front Chawterley?

I finger the electric tape holding the back of my Holga in place, resisting the urge to turn the lens on Ginger or Laney or Betts, to look without being seen. The words are on the tip of my tongue: *I came here once without you guys, with Doug Pemberley, remember him? I don't know why I never told you.* But I would have to shout the words to be heard over the wind, and I can't imagine shouting them. Because Ginger's friend Max is on the boat? Because it feels a bit like a betrayal, not to have told them? Because even now I don't understand why I returned here with Doug Pemberley, why I ever thought I could marry him, why I still need the lifetime guarantee I know doesn't exist.

Ginger turns the wheel a degree or two, setting our final course, headed directly toward the pier taking shape now: a long stretch of wood reaching out into the bay, with what looks to be a great blue heron perched on one round wooden post. The little boat tied up there, or one like it, was the way we got to town that spring break, up through the winding marsh streams that riddled the island—"guts," Ginger called them, or "channels," or "cricks." The mail is brought here by boat from the mainland, and the garbage truck is a trash boat, the school bus also a boat. It's the way you arrive and the way you leave, the way even Trey Humphrey left. The way Faith, too, must have left, her body taken to the mainland to be cremated. It doesn't make sense to bury anyone on Cook Island; the rising ocean levels caused by global warming are slowly absorbing it into the Chesapeake.

A second little boat is upside down on the shore—which is disconcerting, finding something unexpected already. Why two skiffs? As if ready for the eight of us again to race through the marsh channels, shouting and laughing into the darkness. I remember the longing I felt as we first arrived at Cook Island, impatient for the end of law school and the beginning of whatever life would have in store for me: marriage and jobs, apartments and houses and children. I remember imagining owning a summer home like Chawterley with Andy, something grander than his parents' cabin, somewhere more exotic than a small Midwestern lake. I remember wondering if Mom would have wandered so—frighteningly? Is that what she was, frightened?—all those summers if she and Dad had had a place like this to get away to, if she'd had a family and a future she was willing to embrace.

The details of that first night on Cook Island flood me, then: the bright stars and the splintered roughness of the pier, the drip of bay water down my back after that initial cold plunge, the wet tug of my swimsuit as I'd pulled it from my unlined body, leaving me wearing only the small diamond engagement ring on my left hand, my promise to Andy and his to me. I remember the slick push of the cold, dark water as I dove back in again, the startling shock of something wrapping itself around me, refusing to let me go. I was twenty-four and unmarried, undivorced, unaged—and as quick to laugh as Ginger and Laney and Betts were when the water daemon I screamed in terror of turned out, in the sweeping beam of the lighthouse, to be only a tangle of seaweed and marsh grasses clinging to my skin.

As I settle in to the reality of the second skiff now—Max's, of course; he would have run from the village down to the Chawterley pier to bring over the *Row v. Wade*—it occurs to me that it was Max's boat we stole that night we went gut-running with Frank and Beau and Trey and Doug. "Borrowed," Ginger and Trey had insisted. Does Max know we took his boat? Would he want to know? Would he even care? I think of the things I know that I never wanted to, and I imagine how I might start to tell the Ms. Bradwells what I've done, knowing I should.

It's Ginger's voice, though, that breaks the silence as we approach the pier. "Anne Sexton. My mother would be Anne Sexton," she says softly, uncertainly. "'I'm no more a woman / than Christ was a man.' Except Mother would never have killed herself."

She begins issuing directions before any of us can respond. She puts me at the helm again—just for a second, she says, just hold it straight—and she lowers the sail, then directs Laney and Betts to take their heels off and hurries them to the front of the boat. She sticks a coiled length of rope in Betts's hands, then turns to Laney and says, "When we're close enough, you're going to jump across to the pier." Then to Betts, "You just toss her the line when she's ashore."

She's setting them to their tasks when Max pokes his head up from below, the lenses in his fashionably nerdy glasses catching the light as he peeks around at her. He must know Ginger pretty well, because he doesn't emerge. He allows her the entire stage.

"How do I stop this thing?" I mouth to him. Despite the fact that the sail is down, there is a reason the heron's cackle is sounding alarm, its black flight feathers springing to action, opening into a wide blue-gray of gracefully pumping wings.

Ginger, with her back to me at the front of the boat, can't see Max grin in response, a smile that matches the nerdy glasses, that makes me like him all the more. His neck is going just as surely as ours are—his neck *and* his hair; how does he pull off boyish and charming even with his wrinkled neck? He looks a little like that heron, but in a good way.

"Hold on tight," he says, his words blowing toward me, "so you won't fall overboard when we smash into the pier."

He disappears below just as Ginger turns and heads back toward me, her jacket still improbably spotless, its shawl collar still perfect at her neck. I point to the heron, and Ginger turns and looks. "Wish on it!" I call out as we watch the bird skim low over the water, then rise up on the wind.

"WISH ON IT!" Ginger had called out all those years ago, that first night on Cook Island—not pointing to a bird or to a shooting star but rather to our champagne cork rising up over the mast. The cork from a bottle we'd brought all the way from Ann Arbor, stored first in the trunk and then in the galley fridge. In the gunshot echo of that cork pop, we'd sent our wishes up into the night sky, into the hoot of an owl and the gurgle of briny-grassy water sucking around in the marshes, the thrum of insects pressing in under the bottomless stars.

"Who's up for skinny-dipping under the moon?" Ginger had called out, already pouring champagne as the cork plopped into the bay. We'd accepted plastic cups spilling foamy white, and skinned off our shoes, dropped our jeans, pulled off our sweaters, all as lighthearted and full of laughter as Ginger was.

She was pale pale pale as she stood naked in the moonlight, no swimsuit under her clothes like the rest of us. Her face, still baby-fat round then, seemed a reflection of the moon itself as she raised her cup.

"All the planets will be aligned this week," she said. "There's going to be a syzygy Wednesday night. All the planets banded together on the same side of the sun."

"Like us," Laney said. "Like we'll always be, banded together on the same side, even when we aren't sharing rooms or houses anymore."

Betts had said, "To the Syzygy Bradwells!" then, and we'd all raised our cups together, our unspotted hands clicking plastic on plastic as we shouted, "To the Syzygy Bradwells!"

As GINGER TAKES the wheel back from me this time, skinning off her pumps, I imagine she might wrap a whole poem around that funny word: "syzygy." I imagine her stirring the word into the awkward call of the great blue heron, mixing these two things that don't go together at all and capturing in iambic pentameter the joy of being who we were the last time we arrived together at Cook Island, four happy young women just weeks away from graduating into lives we were sure would be more real than the days and months and years we'd shared. It's the kind of poem Ginger would do well—not that I know the difference between good poetry and bad. The kind of poem I want her to find inside herself. A poem about a time when we could strip down to swim naked in the cold water of the bay, focused on the wide stretch of our wings, on the few bright planets in an endless darkness that would, in just moments, break into beautiful dawn.

GINGER

~~~~~~

Skinny-dipping: you have to wonder how different that shitass week at Cook Island might have been if we hadn't shed our suits that first night, when we were still road dead after driving all the way from Michigan in that tin can of Mrs. Zhukovski's. That's what I'm thinking as my feet touch the rough wood of the Chawterley pier now. *A night: mysterious, tender, quiet, deep; / Heavy with flowers; full of life asleep; / Thrilling with insect voices; thick with stars; / No cloud between the dewdrops and red Mars.*

My biggest worry then was about the miniature *Sonnets from the Portuguese* I'd stolen, protected in a sandwich baggie all the way from Ann Arbor to keep it dry on the boat. Mother could have told you all about that goddamned "volume," which was what she called it: that it was published in London in 1900, by Leopold B. Hill; that the cover was hand-colored (cream-yellow leather embossed with a rose-vine border of Christmas-morning red and green and gold, with a paste-down panel of a golden-winged peacock); that its value was so low that my theft of it was only a misdemeanor. She could recite every one of its flaws from memory, too: the fading *o* and first *n* of *Sonnets;* the slight bend where the covers overlap the smaller pages they bind; the missing corner fragment of page twenty-three. But it was the peacock on the cover I was drawn to when I was thirteen, when I slipped it from its proper place among Mother's miniatures. The lovely peacock sitting on the shelf in Mother's library, his unreadable face turned toward a puff of angel-white clouds, his elaborate back turned to me.

I have this idea that my relationship with Mother must have been easy at some point, when I was three or seven or nine. Every child imagines her mother loves her, doesn't she? Every mother imagines she loves her child. So how is it that we cross over from love to something more . . . complex? Is anything more complex than love?

The first poem I wrote, when I started writing again, was about that night after Mia and Laney and Betts came with me to Cook Island, the moonlit bay water slipping over our skin. The second poem, oddly, was about the music Betts made on her zhaleika. Or that's what I thought it was about. My teacher, when I went back to taking classes, decided it was about motherhood. So maybe it is. Maybe the bagpipe-y, oboe-y sound of that weird reed instrument, the giggle of it, is the sound of Betts and her mother, the sound I wanted to make with my own mother but never thought I could. The sound I want to make now with Anne.

Annie with her long, long neck. Too long. I used to wonder which possibility I should dread more for my daughter: that she would grow into that neck, or that she wouldn't.

Annie would trade me in for Mia in half a heartbeat, but Betts assures me her Isabelle went through a phase of this excessive Mia-love, too. "Mia gets to parachute in from whatever exotic place she's on her way to or from," she says. "Bearing godmother gifts that our daughters mistake for pumpkin-disguised carriages. Ones that will take them off to exciting lives like hers. You can't compete with that. You just have to let it blow over and be glad it's Mia and not some nutcase your daughter has fallen for. Like that jerk you dated that first summer in law school. What was his name? Or his scrawny brother who thought he could take over when—Steve! That was his name. When Steve left for New York."

I guess the truth is I'd trade me in for Mia, too. She hasn't ever been the prettiest of us, or even the smartest, probably, but there is a casual joy in her that creeps up on you, that makes you reluctant to walk away from the way she makes you feel about yourself. So I try not to worry that my own daughter prefers her to me, that my son does, too. And I think I'm succeeding, but then every bullshit rejection I get back, from *The New Yorker* or *The Atlantic* or *Poetry*, comes with a scrawl of ink on the form saying they aren't wild about motherhood poems, do I have anything else? Poems that aren't even about motherhood. Poems about red giants, pulsars, neutron stars, supernovae, black holes, the Rosette Nebula.

Am I anything but a mother anymore? I'm not even a daughter now.

I'm a spouse, true, at least for the moment. I'm a sister who almost never sees her brothers. And I am a friend; there is that. I guess that's the oldest decent relationship I have left, this friendship with Laney and Mia and Betts.

Who are, it appears, no better sailors than they were thirty years ago.

"The cleat, Laney! Wrap it around the cleat!" I call out, jumping to the pier before the boat swings farther and Laney either lets go of the docking line or follows it into the bay. Thank God for Mia at the helm.

Mia will sleep with Max this weekend. The thought catches me by surprise as he emerges from below deck, where I've forgotten all about him. The way he helps Mia while I secure the boat makes me a little . . . not jealous, exactly. I certainly would never sleep with Max. He's a schlumpy dresser, for one thing, which I know doesn't seem like it would matter once we were in bed, but it would. He dresses like Steven used to, but not: the same blue jeans, the same outdoor-guy jacket over a T-shirt, or sometimes a button-down. But he fills it all differently. Or fails to fill it. Clothes droop on Max where on Steven they wrapped up sex appeal. Max is losing his hair, which my husband, Ted, is too, of course, but Ted wears his baldness with confidence while Max clings to what's left as if longer hair on the sides can make up for a shortage on top. Probably even Steven is balding, though; I haven't seen him since I visited him in New York the fall of our first year, when Mia always kept her knickers on and I was the promiscuous one. I was so proud of myself back then. Or I thought I was. Imagined I was? Pretended I was? It's hard to understand, even now, how I felt back then, why I claimed to be the girl I did.

Mia looks like she needs a baggie even more than that miniature *Sonnets* did the last time we arrived here: her hair is blown every which way, in short, thinnish wisps that pivot around her cowlick. Her nose is red from the cold, and she's got that tacky little camera at her neck. Yet she looks happy. It's there not just in her face but also in the way she moves, in her unconscious comfort with her body. Maybe it's the way Max sets his hand on her hip as she steps from the boat now. To steady her, of course, but the way she smiles back at him suggests there's electricity in that touch.

I'm the one who startles as if shocked, though. Shit! Have we said anything we ought not to have said with Max aboard? We haven't, I don't think. We haven't.

"Don't drop that swanky camera in the bay, Mia. That'd be quite a loss now, wouldn't it?" Max says with a tease in his voice that makes it clear to me, at least, that the current runs both ways. I wonder if Max's daughter would love Mia, too, or if that's just a Baby Bradwell thing.

As I offer a hand to steady her from boat to pier, I wonder what it would be like to be free of the expectations of a husband and children, not forever on the brink of letting everyone down. To flirt with some journalist in Madagascar, or some guide in someplace so foreign it would seem another world. A man my age or older or younger, who maybe speaks my language or maybe, more intriguingly, does not.

I wonder if Mia ever flirts with women, or even goes home with them. I don't know why, but the idea seems less improbable than I would have imagined. The thought, I see, reflects a deeply imbedded prejudice even I can't shake, despite all Mother's efforts to change the way we think: the eligible bachelor vs. the old maid, or the lesbian.

Mia's flat, sensible shoes take easily to the wood pier, her ankles where they show between slacks and shoes unstockinged, nearly as red as her nose. My own stockings are shredded to hell. Funny, the way I dressed so damned carefully for a day in Washington, an evening in New York, only to end up on the water. Who was I dressing for, anyway? For the press cameras I imagined might capture Betts and Laney and Mia and me? For my friends?

Max helps Betts step ashore, then joins us as Mia says, "The house looks exactly the same."

Victorian shingle-style architecture, built in 1893, Mother used to tell everyone. If the house has any flaws, she never mentioned them. It looks abandoned now, though. Haunted. Not in a ramshackle way, but in the way an old dog, left behind on his master's death, lies prone, his face on his paws, patiently awaiting a return that will never be.

"Exactly the same," Mia repeats with a quick glance at Max (who is looking his Max-goofiest, his hair trying to escape his head in little wisps like Mia's).

Max, surely you'll meet me at the Ritz at five. / Hurry up somebody's dead, we're still alive. The line from Anne Sexton's "February 20th" comes to mind along with a vision of Sexton in her mother's fur coat as she wrote the lines, the coat she wore three years later when she locked herself in her garage with the car running.

I ask Max if we couldn't impose on him to help us get our things up to the house. He looks away just as I see echoed in his eyes my own reluctance to enter this place I've come to think of as Mother's tomb.

He focuses on Mia, which she must feel because she raises her camera, hiding behind it as she takes a shot of Max. She *will* sleep with him, I decide. The only question is where, and perhaps whether it will mean anything. A thought which, oddly, leaves me imagining Max and Mia and Ted and me out here on the island together, boating to the Pointway Inn for dinner or playing cards in the Tea Parlor, lying out on the pier late at night identifying stars.

Mia is wrong about Chawterley, of course. It *isn't* exactly the same. Max starts explaining this, in Mother's defense or to keep Mia's attention or in embarrassment at being photographed, I'm not sure which. He trots out the details of the library Mother added five years ago. I find myself saying, "Max designed it all," the first time he pauses for a breath, before Mia can disparage it as not green enough. He added a whole new library wing hidden in the trees to the right, with special lighting and humidity and temperature controls. He replaced the upstairs windows with triple-pane low-emissivity ones made to match the first-floor windows he left in place because Mother wouldn't give up the original wavy leaded glass despite how energy inefficient it is. He repaired the slate roof with new slates brought from the same quarry as the original roof, carefully cut to match the size gradations and color variations of the existing ones. He designed it all to be better while looking the same as it always has to anyone who hasn't seen the cycle of neglect and rebirth. That's the beauty of what Max does. His restoration work is a bit like well-done plastic surgery: things looks fresher in a way that leaves everyone marveling at how nothing has changed.

Nothing important *has* changed. The redwood floors inside still creak invitingly. The whole place still smells of dusty chintz, polished wood, Mother's Chanel No. 5, and cigarettes. The chimney in the Captain's Library still whistles on a windy night the way my great-grandfather wrote of in his journals, a low whistle that generations following him have come to call the Captain's Ghost.

At least it did the last time I was here, before Mother died.

"It's funny to think of this as your house now, Ginger," Betts says, two small lines creasing between her brows. "It must feel so odd."

I wonder, then, if Chawterley does still smell of Mother: her tobacco, her perfume, her shelves and shelves of unread books. I don't know whether I want it to or not. It's the way I feel whenever I go backwards: back home to Virginia before Mother sold the house; back to Ann Arbor; back to New York.

Max says, "I'm glad you're here, even if just for the weekend, Ginge. It's been bleak, looking out every night to see Chawterley gone dark."

Gone dark. It's an expression I've heard so often from Cook Islanders, but never about our house. We were always summer people until Mother moved here. Chawterley was always dark all winter. That never bothered islanders the way a house in town sitting vacant did. No one could see its lights anyway. We shared this end of the island with no one.

Now Max has a house here, too, on a one-acre lot Mother sold him not far from the no-name road. Mother never would have sold to anyone else; she didn't sell for the money. My brother Beau approached Max, then suggested the idea to Mother, who'd been fond of Max even when he was just one of the many island kids we ran around with. It made Beau nervous to have Mother out here alone.

"Mother goes to all this trouble to make sure Max builds a house that she won't even have to admit is there," I tell Laney and Mia and Betts, "then asks him to leave a light on at night."

"Just an eight-watt LED," he says. "It's not like she was asking me to drill in the Arctic Refuge to keep it lit."

"What about the lighthouse?" Laney asks quietly, addressing Max as if she can bear to talk to him about this even if she can't talk to us. "The lighthouse puts out a lot of light."

"Built a new one down to town, where the ferry stops in," Max says, the funny preposition choices identifying him as an island boy despite the many years he spent in New York. He alone looks north, to where the old lighthouse sits as silent and empty as Chawterley, its white shingle tower rising up to the red of the lantern deck and cupola, the lightless beacon. "The darkness out here'd make anybody lonely," he says.

I turn my back to the lighthouse, looking down the marshy shoreline to Max's house. I've never imagined Mother lonely out here. It's hard to imagine Chawterley without a dozen Cooks and Conrads and Humphreys setting off to hunt in Goose Marsh or sail to Lightning Knot or stir up whatever trouble we could find in town. And Mother wasn't a woman to be lonely. She didn't indulge much in emotions that couldn't be channeled into bettering the world.

Mia follows up on Max's LED comment, the two of them launching into an enthusiastic discussion splattered with terms like "autoclaved aerated concrete," Kirei Wheatboard, "passive solar gain." Who knew post-industrial denim batt insulation (recycled blue jeans in the ceilings and walls) could be as sexy as unrecycled blue jeans falling away from bare hips? *That's* where they'll slip out of their blue jeans together, I think: at Max's house, with the low-e glass sliders wide open to the water. Maybe on the sustainable bamboo floor. What would it be like to have sex on a bamboo floor? Or perhaps in the spa, in the glow of the LED landscape lighting, although fucking in water (even solar-heated water) isn't as great as it sounds. So maybe on the spa's wide stone edge, with their feet in the water to help keep them solar-heated, too.

I try to imagine Ted and me slipping out of our blue jeans on the stone coping of Max's spa, with the waterfall splashing away from us, pouring toward the bay. Ted used to love to slip my blue jeans down my hips anywhere outdoors. Or slide his hands up under my skirt to find I wasn't wearing underwear. He liked public places, with the risk of being caught, and so did I: the woods in Central Park in broad daylight; a conference table at the office late at night; a little alleyway in the East Village where, to be honest, a couple seen in the act probably wouldn't have fazed anyone.

We have a spa in the backyard in Cleveland. No waterfall, but it is solar-heated, with a gas heater, too, because you can't get to a hundred degrees on solar alone. We sometimes share a bottle of wine and a soak out there, but we always come inside to make love, if we make love at all. It's one thing to have an adventurous lover in an anonymous city like New York, another entirely to have reckless public sex in a place where your fellow executives or churchgoers or co-presidents of the PTA might recognize you. Although Ted wouldn't mind being caught in flagrante delicto himself. It's the possibility of me being seen that gives him pause. Me, the mother of his children. So I guess the truth, or Ted's truth, anyway, is that it's one thing to have an adventurous lover, another entirely to have the woman who breastfed your son brought up on an indecency charge.

We've never even made love outside here on Cook Island, now that I think of it. I have: at Rogues' Point, in the skiff in Hunters' Gut and Little Thoroughfare and Kizzie's Ditch, and the first time, at Fog's Ghost Cove in bright moonlight, with no fog in which to hide. But whenever Ted and I have made love here on what he calls "Faith's Island," it's always been in the old four-poster in Nana's Room. Quietly, so no one would hear.

"Did you know that in Christian art, the peacock is a symbol of immortality?" I ask, half expecting Mia and Laney and Betts to roll their eyes. They just look at me like they understand exactly what I'm thinking. Only Max looks perplexed.

"Immortality and the incorruptible soul," I say. "Flannery O'Connor raised them. Peacocks. She used to send feathers in her letters to friends. She once sent a five-foot-long one to Robert Lowell, after a particularly bad one of his 'spells.'"

"That's what this weekend is missing!" Betts says. "Imagine the trouble we could stir up with a supersized peacock feather or two."

I smile even though I don't feel like smiling, because I know she wants to make me smile. *Heartbroken / But wearing / Fresh / Smiles,* like Alice Walker's friend arrives to visit her. It strikes me then that Laney and Betts and Mia haven't been back here since that spring break, that this can't be easy for them either. Laney looks a little green, and she doesn't get seasick.

"Clearly *you* ought to be the poet here, Betts," I say. "That was Lowell's response, too: 'That's all I need, a peacock feather.'"

I look up at Mother's empty house looming over us. "Well, I'm sorry to report there will be not one drop of tequila in the liquor cabinet, decent or rotgut," I say. "Believe me, I've looked before."

Laney

I'M FINE ENOUGH till I'm breathing in the stench of sea air and the grumble of bay water I see now I never have quite washed away. *Ad undas.* "To the waves," literally, but what it really means is "to hell."

I stand on the bird-dropping-splattered pier, trying to attend to what Ginger is saying about her mama's peacock book. This is hard for her, too. But I can't find my way beyond the smells and the looming red of the lighthouse, the birds squawking and trilling and something that sounds like a cross between laughter and barking. The joy of them seems worse than anything nasty could be, laughter at the edge of a newly dug grave. Although this particular grave isn't new. This grave is peeking out from under decades of weedy underbrush.

It's only three days, and Betts needs me. Surely I can tolerate three sunny autumn days with my dearest friends.

I try to focus on how much I did love this place those first days: the white houses at the public end of the island perched like lilies on a soft summer pond; the boats arriving with their catch, all the men here crabbers; the children luring baitfish into mason jars with bits of bread and lines of string. I recall one mama crying out, "Run nor'east, honey!" to a girl with a kite who changed direction as if she were a compass. I almost wish Willie J and Manny and Gem and Joey were still little like that, still needing me to help them decide which way to run to catch the wind.

As the splattered purple-red berries on the path smush into the thin soles of my pumps, I try to find comfort in thoughts of my life now: William and the children and our home in Decatur, the many friends pitching in to help with my campaign. My own mama deserves the credit for my running for political office, or perhaps the word is blame, and Faith, too, played a role. But I'd be nowhere at all without friends. Even my first job in government came through a friend of Daddy's from his Morehouse College days: Maynard Jackson, who was by then the first black mayor of Atlanta. After I'd graduated from Wellesley, not long after my parents moved to Atlanta, I found myself interviewing to work for a spell on Maynard's reelection campaign.

I hadn't been working but about a week when someone collected me to take me to Maynard's office, and before I knew it I was following him to speeches and press conferences, in charge of his outreach to young vot-ers. He took me under his wing the way a man does when he's known your daddy since the two of them were eighteen. He urged me to apply to law school, and took me back into his fold three years later, when I just couldn't go back to Tyler & McCoy.

Maynard was the one who talked William and me into buying the house in Decatur, and after we'd already made an offer on a place in Fulton County, too. "*Any* black is going to have a tough time getting elected in Fulton County unless the white folks in north Fulton manage to se-cede and re-form Milton County, in which case what's left of Fulton is going to be poor as the red Georgia clay," he advised me over fried chicken at Paschal's, his favorite place for soul food. "A black *gal*—even one as pretty as you, Laney—she won't stand a chance. You and William just go on now and have a look at this little house."

He wiped his hands on a paper napkin, then handed me a note card with an address, a house that was close enough to Agnes Scott College, where William teaches, for him to walk. Maynard had this all thought out.

"Mrs. Davidson doesn't think she's quite ready to sell yet," he said, setting at the chicken again. "But you and William give her a fair price and the only one to suffer will be the real estate agents." And when I in-sisted I would never run for office, he replied, "You just go on and make a deal with Mrs. Davidson. Your time will be coming, whether you want it to or not."

That was the way Maynard did things. He wasn't a gradualist; he be-lieved the time for change was now. If he offended a few folks or even a lot of folks on his way to getting black Atlanta a fair shake, well, then he offended some folks. That was how he got to be the first nonwhite mayor of a major Southern city, and Maynard was a big believer in dancing with the girl you brought to the party, except maybe when the girl was Bunnie, his first wife.

I ought to have run for office back then if only to give Maynard the pleasure of seeing me run, but it wasn't until I saw Faith at his funeral that I gave it a sturdy thought. June 28 of 2003, a Friday, with Coretta Scott King and John Lewis there, and President Clinton remembering Maynard's "gift of gab that could talk an owl out of a tree."

"Maynard believed politics should be practical, not radical," President Clinton said that day, and I had to stop to think whether that was true or not. "That we should all strive to be righteous, not self-righteous . . . and that it was wrong to claim to have the truth and then use it like a stick to beat other people with."

Half of Atlanta was at that funeral, and Faith must have been eighty by then, but she plowed through the crowd to find me. She pulled out the same key Ginger is jiggling in the lock now and pressed it into my hand at Maynard's graveside, when she urged me to run for office, when she said she and Maynard had talked about it, that she'd promised Maynard she would see me along. I remember the buttery feel of the silver keychain engraved with the Oxford University seal, from the year Faith studied there. I remember reading the inscription, *Dominus illuminatio mea*, "The Lord is my light," and wondering at the irony of that, and then at the irony of her very name, since Faith never did believe in God.

"Come visit me," she said. "Come next week." And I promised her I would. I didn't take the key, though, I said she needed it and she would be there to answer the door. The truth, though, is that even as we stood watching friends scoop earth over Maynard's coffin, I'd thought I never would return to Chawterley. I never meant to come back.

It took me another seven years to work up my nerve to run for office. Seven years of visiting the simple stone marker on Maynard's grave as if he might advise me from the other side. Seven years of Faith's introductions to people at the National Women's Political Caucus and the Women's Campaign Forum and Emily's List, her constantly evolving advice about what office, exactly, I should run for. At Maynard's funeral, it was the Georgia state congress, but she upped the ante to the U.S. House of Representatives when Denise Majette tossed aside her representation of the Georgia fourth to run for Zell Miller's Senate seat.

Seven years of Faith's advice and my excuses: I was better behind the scenes; I'd never be able to raise the money for a campaign; the children were too young to have their lives disrupted; William didn't have the stomach for being a candidate's spouse. And underlying the excuses this worry: that questions would be raised about Cook Island, about things I'd not told even William. I'd always meant to, but then as time passed the telling became complicated by the years of things left unsaid.

I told you so, Maynard, I'm thinking as I stand on the berry-splattered steps at Chawterley. But I didn't, actually. I never did tell Maynard the truth about why I didn't want to run.

The fact is I felt the guilt of sitting out all the hard stuff my whole life while most folks like me weren't left with that option. I may as well be white for all the suffering I haven't been put through. When the civil rights demonstrations tore apart Birmingham, we picked up and moved a thousand miles west, to Denver, to a university where Daddy was welcomed as an important young professor, the heir to the head of his department. I grew up in a world that was all safe neighborhoods and tidy lawns, and if anyone didn't like me because of my skin color they knew better than to say so because my daddy was an important man. My parents moved back to the South, to Atlanta, only long after the violence had ebbed, when I was safely off at Wellesley anyway.

The only moment that doesn't fit in my whole happy almost-white childhood is one memory from just before we left Birmingham. I was in the first grade, but I hadn't been allowed to go out for days, not even to school, like I was sick except I wasn't, I was baking things with Mama, I was reading books Daddy brought home. He and Mama were always talking, always shushing me and sending me away. And then I was helping Mama pack things in boxes for moving to a new house where I could have my room whatever color I wanted. I wanted purple.

That particular day, the boxing-up day, Mama told me to put on my best dress, we were going out but I mustn't tell Daddy. This would be our secret and it would be fun to have a secret and Daddy wouldn't mind if he didn't know. Mama looked pretty in her church dress, with her hat and gloves, too, and when I asked where we were going, she said we were going to church.

"To church?" I asked. "Will I have to go to Sunday school? I don't want to go to Sunday school, I want to stay with you and Daddy in the big church."

Mama stooped down and looked at me, then hugged me and told me Daddy wouldn't be there. "Remember, we're not telling Daddy; this is our secret," she said. And she promised I could stay in the big church with her.

When we got to the church, though, it wasn't our regular church, and it was already full, with a big crowd of folks outside, too. I couldn't see anything, so Mama lifted me up and put me on her shoulders. There wasn't much to see from up there either, though, just the tops of a lot of heads and everyone shushing to hear the preacher.

"You pay attention now, Laney," Mama said. "You won't much understand, but you pay attention. You try to remember." And she patted my leg.

I think Mama was already crying when she said that. She didn't want me to see she was crying but there were so many people crying that I only could wonder why she wanted to take me to someplace so sad. I thought it was going to be a fun time, a secret.

And then the preacher was talking about some little girls like they were heroes. He was saying, "They have something to say to every Negro who has passively accepted the evil system of segregation and who has stood on the sidelines in a mighty struggle for justice. They say to each of us, black and white alike, that we must substitute courage for caution." And I couldn't tell from the way Mama just kept crying, the tears on her cheeks and her shoulders shaking, what she wanted me to think. Did she mean for me to be like the girls Dr. King was talking about, or *not* like them? My daddy must have wanted me to be *not* like them, I decided. That that was why I was meant to keep secret that we were there.

Do we want our children to be heroes, or to be safe? As a mother now, I see Mama's answer would have been "Both A and B above" if that answer had been available. But I don't expect it ever is.

Even after Mama had her stroke, when she looked up at me from that hospital bed and wept like she had at that funeral for those little girls who died in the church bombing, I wasn't sure what she wanted from me. It wasn't until she died the next night, until I was on the telephone telling Ginger she was gone, that I heard what Mama had been trying to tell me my whole long life, what Maynard had been trying to tell me and Faith still was. It's a different thing, though, when your own mama is trying to do the talking with a final breath she doesn't have.

So what am I doing now? I should be standing up and shouting out the truth, saying This is what I did and the consequence belongs to me or to folks long dead or perhaps to us all, to every one of us *except* Betts. But

I'm standing idle, saying nothing. Even in my campaign, I've been cling-ing to caution. I'm running for office, but I'm running a safe race. I take pains to offend no one. I'm as white as a black woman can be.

AT THE CHAWTERLEY door, Ginger rattles the key in the knob furi-ously, but still the thing won't open.

"Shit shit *shit,*" she says.

"Let me," Max insists. *Let me do this for you, this one small thing.*

Ginger surprises me by stepping aside to allow Max her place at the door. He works the lock without any fuss at all, and opens the door just a crack before handing Ginger back the key.

The door creaks wide at Ginger's touch: to the dim interior, to a back foyer wider than William's and my bedroom in Decatur, with twin stair-cases rising high to the second floor. What strikes me first is the musty, slightly moldy odor of an old house closed against the damp for months but unable to keep it out. I taste it deep in my throat, and I turn back to the bay as if it's one more glance at the view I'm after, and not the pier and the boat and the possibility of escape. This is the best alternative we have, I understand that, I do. And I suppose Ginger never did say the lighthouse was gone, she only said a new lighthouse had been built closer to town and that if we didn't get here before sunset the approach to the house would be awfully dark. I've only imagined that they tore the light-house down, that no one could ever again turn off the lantern and lean out over that rail.

White sheets cover the upholstered chairs in the back foyer, the rat-tan furniture in the Sun Room to the left, the grand piano in the Music Room to the right. The thin white fabric floats above the floors like ghosts moving in, taking over, claiming this as their home.

Ginger is trying to look sturdy, but she's more spooked by the ghostly furniture than I am. Poor Ginge. She's forever bluffing without so much as a pair of twos in her hand. We need Betts to say something to make us laugh, but she just stares into the Music Room as if the ghost of Mrs. Z is settled in the chair by the fireplace, her zhaleika to her lips.

It's colder in the house than outside: cold stretch of marble floor, cold expanse of high white ceiling, cold empty stone hearths in every room.

Max settles our bags and places a gentle hand on the small of Ginger's back. "Wish I'd known you were coming," he says. "I could at least have uncovered the sofas."

Betts thunks down her swanky little black leather briefcase like she might mean to crack right through the cold marble, which maybe she doesn't intend to do or maybe she does. A disturbance is just what we do need, though. When we all startle at the noise, she makes a face that is Betts at her silliest, and everyone smiles.

"Well, I'll leave you to yourselves then," Max says. "I'm just down the road if you need anything." He gives Ginger a friendly peck on the cheek and then, on a second thought, wraps his arms around her and holds her for a long moment. She closes her eyes, her lashes moist, unblinking.

"Neighbor," he says, the single word loaded heavy with fondness, with the kind of love that comes with being friends as children and ever since. "Really, if you need anything at all." It might be his attention lingers on Mia just before he closes the door quietly, or it might be it doesn't. It might be I just want to think it does.

Ginger gathers up what she hopes looks like courage. I half expect her to say something like "The thing I hate most is waking up next to a fella whose name I don't know." Except that here her bluff would be something more like "The thing I hate most is returning to the home of a dead mama I understood so very well." My face flushes with the guilty memory of Faith's gravelly rough voice over the telephone, conversations Faith would have liked to have with Ginger rather than with Betts or Mia or me, but Ginger and Faith never could talk. Which was true of Mama and me, too, I suppose. It's the weight of the dreams, the feeling you're meant to do what your mama and daddy couldn't do, that the path you choose will complete their lives, or not.

Mia

CHAWTERLEY HOUSE, COOK ISLAND
FRIDAY, OCTOBER 8

"FIRST, WE CHANGE into something more comfortable," Ginger says, and you can see the thought register through the continuing bluff: she doesn't have a stitch of clothing to change into. It's there in the careful stillness of her eyes, the tightening in the tendons of her lotion-smoothed neck, the stiff shoulders under the soft white jacket. She pushes on, though, cranking up the thermostat, grabbing my bag, and heading up the right side of the double staircase, the tromp of our feet as we follow her intruding on the house's silence.

The second-floor rooms here at Chawterley bear the names of people who are long dead: Old Aunt Betsy's, Betsy being the first wife of the father of Ginger's great-great-uncle William Cook, who built the Michigan Law Quad (although one wonders how old she could have been if after she died Uncle Willy remarried and had a dozen more kids); Chauncey's Room and Governor Waller's; Hamlet's Retreat, named for a dog who slept at the foot of the bed of a child whose place in history has been ceded to his beloved mutt. The third-floor rooms above us, referred to in the aggregate as the no-name rooms, do in fact have names, too: the cook's room, the upstairs maid's, the waitstaff's bunkroom where we slept that spring break.

Ginger throws open the first door we come to, saying, "The Captain's Office," the Captain being the ancestor who built Chawterley; there is a Captain's Bedchamber that was Faith's bedroom, too, and a Captain's Library downstairs. Perhaps the Captain used this room as the office its name suggests, but it's a bedroom now, with twin four-poster beds, more maritime paintings than reasonable, and a fireplace—which every room here has, Chawterley having been built before the island had electricity.

"Of course, the Captain only ever captained his business, unless you count a dinky sailboat he took out with no crew," Ginger says. "I don't even know why he's called the Captain."

As she tells me I can take this room, she realizes what I, too, am just realizing. "And you too, Laney?" she says. "You guys want to share?" She takes charge, pulling a sheet away to reveal a love seat upholstered in dark green pencil-striped chintz. She opens a heavy wooden armoire, and says, "You can hang your things in here." She sets my bag beside it, leaving neither Laney nor me an opening to say we'd prefer to bunk alone.

The chair at the business Captain's rolltop desk swivels to a fine view of the Chesapeake: seawater all the way to the mainland shore, where, on a clear night, you can glimpse the faraway lights of a village. A bird lands on the broad windowsill, cocks his head and peers into the glass as if puzzled by his own reflection there, or by us.

"*Rāra avis,*" Laney says. "Rare bird."

"'Words for birds and their Latin names, too,'" Ginger recites.

Outside, the light is deepening to red, the sky a swirl of deep magenta and pink tingeing what's left of the blue, all of it reflected again in the water of the bay. From the rooms on the front of the house, the sunset must be gorgeous; this northern end of the island is narrow enough that Chawterley has a view of the sunrise out its backside and the sunset out the front.

Ginger settles Betts in Emma's Peek, a room with a bed that belongs in a Merchant Ivory film, although it's missing its bed curtains. "Guess who Emma was," she says as she starts pulling sheets off a sitting area by the fireplace: Queen Anne chairs and a tapestry couch clustered around a white marble-topped coffee table.

Betts, standing tall and breathing deeply as if about to touch her palms over her head, foot folded up against thigh in that yoga pose I call Flamingo, says, "The sister to the queen of England! Third in line for the throne."

As we laugh, I wonder why we never heard the stories behind these rooms when we were here in law school. How full of ourselves we were back then. How uninterested in stories that didn't revolve around us.

"Mrs. Everett Whitman, a society 'lady' who was the Captain's wife's best friend and the Captain's mistress." Ginger grins her wide grin. "Emma spent whole summers here doing the Captain behind her best friend's back while her poor sod of a husband worked in New York. Or so the story goes. The family would never admit to any scandal, of course, but check this out." She opens an armoire, squashes aside the bed curtains hanging there, and points to a section missing from its back panel. "See?" She kneels and opens a small square door cut into the wall there, just large enough to crawl through. "Where do you think this goes?"

Betts grins. "It's a passageway to the venting system so the thieves can steal the crown jewels!"

It hits me where it must go—"The space under the big rolltop desk in the Captain's Office?"—although I can't imagine why.

"Gives new meaning to the pleasures of working at one's desk, doesn't it?" Ginger says.

No wonder Faith became a feminist, I think as I realize she's talking about Emma and the Captain and oral sex, perhaps with the office door open and Mrs. Captain passing by in the hall.

Ginger closes the door and stands again. "We'll have to make the beds ourselves, I'm afraid, but let's change and eat something first."

We hadn't made beds here that spring break; Faith had arranged for our every comfort. With her gone now, I'm the only one of us whose mother is left, I realize. And what's left of my mother isn't much.

THE LAST TIME I saw Faith was over dinner in D.C., the night I met Doug Pemberley again. We were in the bar, waiting for a table, and Faith was advising me on a point my editor was quite opposed to seeing in print. Her suggestion: start a blog to say the things that really needed to be said.

"Blogs don't often pay the bills, Faith," I said.

"Just do it anonymously, dear, and never admit a thing," she insisted with such delight in her voice that I was quite sure, suddenly, that she'd had a hand in that whole naked women in gorilla masks thing, and almost certainly additional body parts as well.

I imagined taking her advice. Starting a blog. Going naked where I've always been edited, an anonymous moniker as my gorilla mask. No more fighting to hold on to the things I felt were important to say. No more defending my words against the onslaught of largely male editors and their frustrating certainty that they know best what readers of both genders want to read. No money in a blog, true, but the other rewards might be worth it. That's what I was thinking as a tall, well-dressed man with graying, wavy dark hair leaned down to kiss Faith's cheek.

"Mia, you remember Doug Pemberley?" Faith said.

"Of course she doesn't remember me, Faith. It's been thirty years since we met, and I was tall and geeky and soft to her smart and beautiful," he protested, and at the sound of his voice I instantly did remember, and wondered if he could still sing. "But I do remember you, Mia," he said. "From Cook Island, when you were in law school and I was still suffering the delusion I could support myself by writing. Like you do so well now. I watch for your byline. And will plead guilty to insisting Faith include me in this dinner when she told me about it this afternoon."

"You've come a long way since safari jackets and blue jeans," I said. "I don't suppose you carry a flask of scotch in the pocket of that fancy suit, do you?"

"Not half as far as you've come, Miss Just-Won-the-Women's-Media-Courage-Award," he said, his grin accentuating the slight imbalance in his face.

"The International Women's Media Foundation Courage in Journalism Award," Faith said.

"Faith does love bragging on you girls," he said. "She tells me your friend Betsy is on the short list for the Supreme Court, should the need to replace one of the current nine arise."

Chief Justice Zoo, I thought, remembering Professor Jarrett getting Betts's name wrong that first day in law school, Betts saying he was close enough that she'd answer to that.

The maître d' took us to our table, where we settled into fine steaks and fine conversation about the state of things in Washington. Doug, it came out, had been a lobbyist for most of the years between Cook Island and that dinner. He'd just retired, and he wanted to go back to writing now that he didn't need to make a living. That was why he was so interested in meeting me again, he admitted with refreshing honesty.

When dinner was over, Doug offered to walk me back to my hotel, and we had another drink together in the hotel lobby—scotch straight up, for old times' sake. He didn't wear a wedding ring, and I suppose I assumed Faith wouldn't have invited him to dinner if he was married, though why I assumed Faith was putting us together as anything more than friends I can't now imagine. So maybe I simply didn't want to know whether he was married or not.

He was going to be in London at the same time I was, a week later. And when I left London he went with me. I knew he was married by then. I knew he and his wife were still together. I knew how disappointed Faith would have been in us both. But his children were off at college, and I wasn't thinking he would mean to leave his family for me. That didn't occur to me until months later, when he and I returned to Cook Island. Until I awoke that first morning at the Pointway Inn to the sound of Doug singing outside the sliding glass doors to the beach, "Morning Has Broken," like that morning at the lighthouse, watching the dawn.

I walked out onto the balcony to see him writing huge letters in the sand: MARRY ME, MIA! inside a big heart. I believe I laughed, actually. I believe I said something about him having spent too much time in Arab countries, that harems weren't legal here.

He didn't laugh back, though. He stood there, holding tight to his lopsided grin.

"I've told Sharon she can have everything," he said. "The house. The money. I don't care. I want the kids to know she's taken care of. I don't want them to think their dad is a schmuck.

"They're going to love you, Mia. My daughter Jane especially. She's going to love you. She already loves the things you write."

How could I decline the engagement ring in the velvet box he'd dropped right after the exclamation mark drawn in the sand, then? What choice did I have but to be the happiest woman in the world? Faith had died just a few weeks before; I didn't even have the disappointment she would feel in us as an excuse. Her death was the reason I'd wanted to return to Cook Island, to say my goodbyes to her.

"I . . . God, I just . . ." I walked down the steps and onto the beach, the sand creeping warm around my toes. "I'm fifty-four years old, Doug. I'm . . . I don't know if I'm fit to marry anyone at this point."

He smiled the way I remember all four of the guys smiling in the Captain's Library that first night they arrived on Cook Island: like the world would always bend their way. He put his arms around me and lifted my chin, and kissed me, his talent for kissing nearly as amazing as his voice. He picked up the ring and he put it in my hand, closed my fingers around it. "Think about it," he said. "If I can't convince you to marry me before this week is up, I don't deserve you anyway."

And so I spent most of the rest of that week settling into the idea of hearing Doug Pemberley's lovely voice singing in the shower every morning of the rest of my life. I would take the ring out from the box on the dresser as he bathed and sang, and I'd slide it onto my finger for just a moment, one he couldn't see. How many other men would likely be willing to follow me to the places I needed to go: to Brighton, England, to write about 200 naked cyclists with "Burn Fat, Not Oil" written on their skin; to Copenhagen in December; to a remote reserve in Madagascar just to hear a lemur mating call? A man who proposed in the sand, who serenaded me with Cat Stevens songs sung as well as Stevens himself.

To be honest, I felt a flip of hope every time Doug started singing that week. So much hope that, late one night while Doug was fast asleep, I climbed from bed and slipped on the ring, went downstairs and outside to call Laney from the public phone by Haddy's Market, to ask her if she could bear it if I married Doug.

Betts

◇◆◇

CHAWTERLEY HOUSE, COOK ISLAND
FRIDAY, OCTOBER 8

AFTER WE'VE CHANGED our clothes Mia and Laney and I wait forever just outside the Sissies' Square. Mercifully, neither of them mentions the Supreme Court or the press. We stare through the small room's door to windowless walls and built-in-side-rail beds meant to keep toddlers from falls small and large. The bed rails remind me of the ones Matka helped me install in Isabelle's room in Ann Arbor after I'd taken a job teaching back at Michigan Law. I still remember how fraudulent I'd felt standing to lecture in the same room I'd taken exams in just a few years before. But teaching seemed the job best suited to my daughter's needs. We try so hard to make our children safe. But we never know where the dangers lie.

Yet you have to wonder who tried to take care of whom at Chawterley. Sissies' Square and Baby's Room and the Nursery are all here on the guest side of the house. Far from the family wing from which Ginger emerges, finally.

She's dressed in khakis and a white oxford shirt like her mother wore everywhere. Her feet are bare. The wide expanse of her manicured toes presses against the dark wood floor.

"Well," she says. "Food? And then maybe a game of Scrabble?" Scrabble: a game Ginger used to play to the death.

The front doorbell rings. The same can-the-press-have-found-us-already surprise registers on each of our faces. Ginger slinks barefooted toward the back stairs. Mia, Laney, and I slip off our shoes and skulk along behind her. We cross the sheathed-furniture Sun Room. The kitchen. The serving pantry. The outside end of the Dining Hall.

The damask drapes of the Front Parlor are drawn. Ginger peeks through the center gap. "Shit!" she says in a tone that renders obvious the absence of reporter-wolves at our door.

She hurries to the front foyer. Throws open the door. Calls loudly, "Max!"

An electric car slips soundlessly onto the one-lane road. A red fireball of setting sun takes its place at the end of the drive.

Three tan reusable grocery sacks with a tree-and-mountain logo sit outside the door. A substantial pile of firewood is topped with a note that there is more outside Faith's Library. I choke up as I realize this is the way the new library will be forever known. Faith's Library.

I wonder if any of us ever imagined that Hamlet actually slept at some little boy's feet. That he was a puppy. A young dog. An old and faithful companion. An emptiness at the end of a bed.

I think of Matka as we watch the sun set. I still sometimes pick up the phone to call her about some song I've worked out on the zhaleika. I imagine Izzy hunched over a casebook at Yale. As sure of herself as Faith ever was.

The last blink of sunlight sinks into the water. A rainbow swirl of color graces the horizon.

"*Diem perdidi*," Laney says. "I have lost the day."

"'And have we room for one more folded sunset, still quite warm?'" Ginger's wide mouth registers a hint of self-satisfaction as she picks up a grocery sack. Does she think she's just one-upped Laney? Like that night in the hot tub when she'd answered Laney's Latin with the *Dracula* quote. Latin that was literary, too. I see this so often with my students: the need to be the smartest. But I've always imagined Laney and Ginger are closer than that. I thought after they both failed to make law review they'd settled into a more intimate friendship. Left the competition to Mia and me. For years I've envied a closeness that perhaps never was.

Laney and I lift the two other sacks as Mia stares out the door with her hopeful-toddler look. Eyes the brown of a paper bag but not so plain. Surely Max reminds Mia of Andy. He seems so like Mia's ex to me. Like the kind of guy who might understand her weird mix of confidence and insecurity. Her fear that anyone she loves will leave the way her mother left her father again and again. Without ever letting him go.

Mia wants to follow Max. But she just stands there. She watches in the rearview mirror as everything she wants slips away.

There is no room for romance this weekend anyway. We're in a tight spot. And Mia is the one who more often than not leads us out of tight spots.

Back in the kitchen, Ginger flips on the lights. Opens the refrigerator. Stares, pale-eyed and taken aback. The refrigerator is spotless inside. Completely empty. If Ginger didn't do this then who came in to wash the bourbon glass Faith drank from the night she died? Who threw away the half carton of milk and the tin of coffee? The brie. The last few eggs. Whatever else Faith might have eaten if she'd wakened that morning three months ago. All those things Isabelle helped me do after Matka died.

Ginger fingers the clip that holds back her still-windblown-from-sailing hair before she starts unpacking the Sierra Club bags. She pulls out a half loaf of bread. Hummus and bananas. Goat cheese. Green onions. Butter. Whole wheat fettuccine. There are nine brown eggs in a cardboard carton. Three slots empty. Locally farmed.

"Have you ever met anyone sweeter than Max?" she says. "Too bad he's vegetarian. I sure could use a hamburger." She means this to temper Mia's attraction to Max. Mia likes her meat pretty much just short of a moo.

Ginger disappears into the Sun Room. Flips on a light. Van Morrison sounds at high volume. Her hips swing as she returns. But the courage she's marshaled is leaking out from under her mom's khaki slacks and white shirt. She thinks she's fooling us.

She's all wide mouth and straight bleached teeth as she resumes unpacking groceries. "Ah, here we go! Sipping tequila. Thank you, Max!" She looks at Mia. "You can see why even his own kids adore him. The man doesn't miss a thing."

Mia is unwilling to risk making a fool of herself by voicing the question: Max is married?

Ginger hands the bottle to Mia, saying, "Pour."

Mia finds four small jelly glasses. Spills a generous shot into each. We lift them. There's an awkward pause. What the hell is there to toast?

"Ad fundum!" Laney says.

Mia and Ginger and I smack our glasses down on the counter. Thrust finger crucifixes at Laney. Shout, "In manners, too, dominate!"

In manners, too, dominate. A phrase no one but a Ms. Bradwell would laugh at. But ever since that night in the hot tub it's been the way we laugh together at ourselves: at Laney for relying on Latin to make her seem smart; at Ginger for forever needing to one-up us; at Mia and me both for steadfastly rejecting the possibility that someone else might know something worth knowing that we still need to learn.

It feels so good to laugh.

The first sip hits sharp on my tongue. I let it sit in my mouth. Savor it for a moment. It burns its way down my throat as "Crazy Love" gives way to "Caravan."

How different that spring break would have been if we'd scraped together the money and gone to Cancún. If we'd settled on the white sand of a Mexican beach where there was no one to share any tequila we might have bought. So much depends on which turn you take. And you never know which one is best until the reasonable, responsible path leads you to places you spent your whole life avoiding. Without even realizing you had.

Van encourages us to turn up the radio. Ginger turns the knob on the stove and sets a cast-iron skillet on the burner. Tosses Laney the green onions. "Chop."

Laney takes a sip of tequila. Pulls knives from the block on the counter. Finds just the right one.

Ginger tosses the half loaf of bread to me. "You're toast."

"Any senator in that room today could tell you that," I say. They all stare at me for a second. Then burst out laughing. What else are we going to do?

"Who wants to be a judge, anyway?" I say. I launch into a riff on *Who Wants to Be a Millionaire?* "I'd like to phone a friend, Meredith," I say. I do my best phone ring, the old-fashioned kind that was all we had in the days before cellphones and ring tones. *Bbbrrrring. Bbbrrrring.* "Mia! Thank God you're . . . where *are* you? How did they find you? Well, never mind. There's no time for that. So here's the situation. This woman, Lilly Ledbetter, discovers as she's retiring that the Goodyear Tire Company has been paying her less than the men she's worked beside for nineteen years. She sues. Her victory is appealed to my Supreme Court. Will we (1) Decline to reconsider the case, leaving a very sensible decision to grant Ms. Ledbetter actual and punitive damages intact? (2) Uphold the decision, giving it authority as Supreme Court precedent? (3) Throw out the punitive damages but leave Ms. Ledbetter with nineteen years of back pay? or (4)—"

"Or (4)"—Mia grins—"Make the improbable and ill-considered decision that Congress—which can't agree to delete a comma without a month of deliberation and a compromise that makes no sense—meant to give Ms. Ledbetter the right to sue for discrimination but intended to limit her damages to six measly months of back pay so the good people at Goodyear will know discrimination is fine for as long as you can get away with it?!"

I do miss Mia. Most of the time.

In my best Mia rhythm and Chicago *O* I say, "So let me get this straight, Betts." I add the *ccccckkkkkcccc* of an overseas line. "You're calling me in Madagascar? *Madagascar,* Betts. That's off the coast of Africa, you know that, right? To hold your hand while you answer a question there isn't a shred of doubt you know the answer to?"

And we all laugh. Humor is a much more effective way to get your point across than rage. One of the many things Faith taught us all.

Mia lifts her glass of tequila. "You know what I was doing that day you called me in Madagascar, Betts? I traveled halfway around the world to drive forever in a bumpy jeep to hear the song of an endangered Indri lemur, a furry little animal that sings for maybe three minutes. This is my *life?*"

Laney puts an arm around her. I'm not sure exactly why.

"Spill, Mia," she says.

"It's actually two Indri calling together, they sing together. They sing more during mating season, too. And they mate for life. I know all this because I'm a good journalist," Mia says with a tiny crack in her voice. "Because I do my research before I go."

I'm thinking I see where this is going. This is about the fact that Mia can't seem to find anyone to take Andy's place. To be honest this particular record has gotten a little old. Could she stop to think of Ginger for a moment? Could she stop to think about the direct hit I just took? Or the glancing blow Laney will take in her campaign?

"You could write such an amazing poem about the Indri, Ginge," she says. "The name of the reserve—the Analamazoatra—is a poem all by itself."

Leaving me embarrassed at my quiet indignation. She *is* thinking of Ginger.

"Spill, Mia," Ginger says. "Spill."

Mia protests: there isn't anything *to* spill. She starts telling us some myth about two Indri brothers who live together in the forest until one of them decides to leave and cultivate the land. He becomes the first human, while the other sends out this mourning cry for his brother who went astray.

"Don't read my piece this weekend," she says. "It's too heavy-handed. As if the reader can't figure out himself that the human brother from the myth is now destroying the rain forests the lemur brother lives in, destroying his kin. God, my writing sucks."

We all just look at her.

She shrugs. "Who wants to be a journalist, anyway? I'd like to ask the audience, Meredith. Is the only way to keep your job: (1) to sleep with an editor who has the worst beer gut in the city; (2) to cover Hollywood gossip instead of women's rights or the envir—"

"You didn't tell us you were cut, Mi!" Even I can hear the irritation in my voice. As if her unwillingness to trust us is worse than losing her job. But isn't it?

"Canned," Mia says. "I preferred 'canned' to 'cut.' It sounds so much more . . . in the tin!"

"In the soup?" Ginger says.

"It sounds less bloody," Mia says.

"Hic est enim calix sanguinis mei," Laney says. "For this is the chalice of my blood."

"It's not a big deal," Mia says. "Just budget cuts."

"You could start a blog," Ginger suggests. "You can make a fortune blogging these days."

"You can start with, say, a scandal involving your ex-roommate Supreme Court nominee!" I suggest. Recalling Jonathan's words over the phone: *How does the senator have the nerve to try to derail a Supreme Court nomination on the basis of an anonymous post?*

"Mia didn't want to spoil your moment," Laney says to me. Her tone says, *hush*. Her tone says, *why are you being so nasty to Mia?*

I bury my uneasiness in a chirpy voice. "And such a moment it's turned out to be! You and me, Mia. We can be mates for life. Who else would want us with our luck?"

"I would," Ginger says.

Laney says, "I would, too." She raises her glass and says, "To friendship."

"To friendship," we all say.

We clink our glasses and we throw back whatever is left. Mia opens the bottle again. Refills us all. I think I shouldn't. I should keep my wits about me. But I've just been through a week of Senate hearings ending in disaster. I have no wits left to keep.

"Shoot, I need to call Izzy," I say. "Can I use the phone, Ginge? I get no cell reception here."

Ginger folds one empty Sierra Club bag before she answers, "I left a message for Annie not to come to New York. I asked her to call Iz and let her know."

"But I'd still like to—"

"I had the phone disconnected." Ginger reaches into another Sierra Club grocery bag, ignoring the now hot cast-iron pan. "Frank and Beau gave me endless shit for it: the family would still come here, we still needed to have a phone. But . . ." She sets aside a can of black bean chili. "But I couldn't bear dialing this number and having someone who wasn't Mother answer, any more than I could bear the phone ringing and ringing without answer in the silence of this goddamned house." She blinks back tears. Pulls a head of lettuce from the bag. "Shit," she says, "who'd've guessed I'd be as able to wallow in my own feelings at fifty-one as I was at twenty?"

"Fifty-two, Ginge," I say. I don't know why I know this will make her laugh, but it does.

Ginger pitches the head of lettuce good-naturedly at Mia, saying, "Still, I'll always be younger than all of *you!*"

Mia groans as she catches the lettuce. She has always hated making the salad. And we all laugh. This is such familiar territory, making a meal together. You can almost see the tension begin to seep away.

In a few minutes we have a green onion and goat cheese omelet. Toast with blueberry jam Ginger found in the cupboard. We grab the Scrabble board and tiles from the Captain's Library. Set the game and the food up in the Sun Room. Pull sheets off the furniture before Ginger says, "Let's do the library instead." Without explanation, she turns the music and the lights off. A small nod to Max's efforts for a greener world. She leads us through the Music Room, the Tea Parlor, the Ballroom Salon. We're headed the back way to that funky hidden door from the Ballroom into the Captain's Library. A door hidden behind a bookshelf on the library side and behind a large painting on the Ballroom side.

But she goes instead to a door I'm pretty sure used to be a window.

Stares at the brass knob. The wood floor. The door into Faith's Library. A room hidden in the trees outside. It will be considerably harder for anyone approaching Chawterley to see us in the new library than in the brightly lit Sun Room.

Laney touches her elbow. "Those lines you were saying at the front door, Ginge, about the folded sunset, did you write them?"

Ginger grasps the handle finally. Stares at the door as if meaning to bring it down with her look and nothing else. "Elizabeth Bishop," she says. "From 'Questions of Travel.' 'Should we have stayed at home and thought of here? / Where should we be today?'"

GINGER

FAITH'S LIBRARY, CHAWTERLEY HOUSE
FRIDAY, OCTOBER 8

THE DOOR TO Mother's library sucks open, the seal ceding its job of protecting the room's contents to the positive pressure. The subtle blow of air from inside brings traces of Chanel, menthol cigarettes, the mustiness of old books. You can almost see Mother sitting in a chair by the fire, reviewing a legal brief or an opinion, looking up, saying, "Ginger, do close that door before the mold spores follow you in." Never mind how bad her cigarette smoke was for her goddamned books. For her goddamned self.

Someone is dead. / Even the trees know it.

Max's note about the firewood comes to mind as clearly as if it were in my hands, his careless scrawl: "Faith's Library." I fight the sudden longing to pull every book one by one from the shelves. Touch them. Open them. The *Sonnets,* too? Maybe. Maybe I'll read the poems one last time before boxing them up, sending them insured mail to . . . to whom? Mother's will included a specific bequest of the *Sonnets* and a volume of Sexton poems to her friend Margaret Traurig from law school, but Margaret died the day before Mother did. Aunt Margaret, who'd been the only other woman in Mother's class at Michigan Law. "We weren't allowed to eat in the Lawyers Club and we couldn't room there either, and our classmates weren't always welcoming," Margaret once told me, "so your mother's and my choice was to learn to like each other's company, or learn to love being alone."

There's a part of me that wants to steal the book again, to send some other more valuable volume in place of the *Sonnets* to whatever heir of Margaret's is entitled to them, with a note that the long-ago missing *Sonnets* have again disappeared but I'm sure Mother would want . . . But what would Mother want? Mother wanted Aunt Margaret to have the *Sonnets* just so that I wouldn't.

I put Mia and Betts to setting up the Scrabble board while Laney and I bring in firewood. The particles wood fires emit make a mockery of the air controls, but Mother wouldn't have gas logs. "You think these books have never been exposed to wood fires, Max?" she'd insisted. "If Ginger values the preservation of my books over her enjoyment of them after I'm gone, she can put in those awful fake things, or never light the damned fire." It was the first I'd realized she meant to leave her books to me. If I hadn't been so overwhelmed, I might have realized she meant to leave me this library, too, and Chawterley itself. I might have realized that, being Mother, she would leave me all the books except one worthless Sexton volume and the *Sonnets,* just to make sure I realized she'd always known I'd stolen it, that she'd never forgiven me the theft.

Betts and Laney and Mia all rejected this interpretation. "When I die, I expect I'll leave something for each of you," Mia had reply-emailed. "I can't imagine *not* leaving something for each of you." Which sent Laney and Betts into a silly frenzy about the special things of Mia's they wanted her to leave them. "Can I have the hat from that photo of you by the dead tree in that cemetery? The one that looks like you stole it off a refugee?" Betts wrote, and Laney claimed a pair of plastic teeth she'd once seen on Mia's desk in Andy's and her San Francisco apartment, in the days when Mia had a desk, or an apartment for that matter. They were doing what we always do for each other, making me laugh when I would otherwise fucking cry.

The wind picks up as Laney and I go out for more wood, whipping my hair into my eyes. *Up above the sea grass / flew like a woman's hair in labor.* The moon is setting already, following the sun into the bay to the west. It seems a bad omen, somehow, to have the only thing lighting the darkness disappear just as the long night begins.

Back inside, Mia and Betts look a little pale. You'd think they'd had some bad omen, too. When the wind howls through the chimney in the Captain's Library, Betts demands, "What *is* that?"

"It's just the Captain's Ghost," I say. "Don't worry. He's . . ." *He's partial to virgins,* a long line of Cook men have claimed, my grandfathers, my uncles, my brother Frank among them. *He's partial to virgins, so he's no threat to anyone here,* Trey used to joke.

"He's just the wind in the chimney," I say.

but the rain / Is full of ghosts tonight, that tap and sigh / Upon the glass and listen for reply

The islanders will tell you the Captain's Ghost never leaves Chawterley, that it's Mr. Humphrey's Ghost who ventures out to the marshes during duck hunting season, felling birds no one else claims to have shot. It's his reflection they see in the mirror over the bar at Brophy's, bellying up for a shot of the single malt scotch they keep on hand, superstitiously, for Trey. His chin is still square in these sightings, his smile *GQ* white. His eyes, dark espresso against blue-white china, always laugh behind the long lashes. His hair falls to his shoulders as he'd let it grow after he made partner at Tyler & McCoy. And when ghost hunters claim to hear him running the guts, the laughter they describe is that of the young man they see at the bar. Trey manages to stay young and tragic in everyone's memory while those of us left behind fight sagging asses and wobbly arms, age spots and jowls.

His favorite haunt, of course, is the lighthouse. The lantern goes on and off when no one is there, the islanders insist, and no amount of assurance that it hasn't been operational for years does a bit of good. I guess if you believe in ghosts who drink high-priced scotch and shoot ducks, a broken lamp isn't much of an impediment to providing light.

"Mr. Humphrey's Ghost, he's restless, restless," they say, even the islanders who played kick the can with us according Trey the honorific "Mr."—a courtesy always extended to the occupants of Chawterley except when we were playing games as kids. Even Max, who wouldn't hesitate to call me "Ginger, you fucking moron" when I dropped a pass in a game of touch football out on Sheep Neck North, called me "Miss Conrad" when he delivered groceries to the door. Or "Miss Cook." More often than not, islanders called me "Miss Cook." I guess the strangest thing about that was that it never seemed strange to me. It's a rare person who sees things that have always been as even the least bit odd.

"Mr. Humphrey's Ghost," they call Trey—as if he deserved anyone's respect, as if any god that might exist wouldn't send him straight on to hell.

Damn. How am I ever going to sleep here without my pills?

Betts asks about the flat screen television hanging over the mantel just as Laney says, "Look, Mia. Faith has that first news piece you wrote." She's picked up a small black frame from a shelf by the miniature books: Mia's damned "The Curse of the Naked Women." After she and Andy split, Mia took off in her car for South America and who knows where else before somehow snagging a visa to visit her brother, a geologist working for an American oil company in Nigeria. There, she saw a group of African protesters, and called Mother, and the next thing we knew Mia had a byline and a job as a foreign correspondent, and Mother had herself a brand fucking new pseudo-child. Six paragraphs that didn't even run in a major paper, but Mother has kept a framed copy ever since.

Mia takes the frame, smiling slightly, doubling her chin.

Betts reads over her shoulder, mock-dramatically:

"Early dawn, the entire womenfolk of Ogharefe, Nigeria, have laid siege to the offices of the United States multinational oil company Pan Ocean. Their mission: payment for lands seized and for damage to health and property caused by pollution. These women want only a very few basic things—reliable drinking water, and perhaps electricity—from a foreign corporation selling millions of dollars worth of crude oil extracted cost-free from oilfields here."

Betts says, "You do a great job of describing it, Mi: the dawn light and the shine of the women's breasts, the dancelike quality of their protest. It's just . . . thousands of women stripping naked to make a point?"

"Their well water was laced with heavy metal, and the ash from the natural gas flares dissolved their corrugated iron roofs," Mia says. "Their kids were getting sick. Wouldn't you do anything to stop something from making Izzy sick?"

"Turns out all they had to do was take off their clothes," I say dismissively.

"Exactly!" Mia says, undismissed. "And honestly, it was one of the most moving sights I've ever seen, all those . . ."

Christ, she's tearing up.

". . . all those women standing naked together, saying this is who we are at our very cores, and we are powerful, too."

"And we are powerful, too," Betts repeats, rolling the phrase around in her own voice, admiring it.

"Why do you think the piece didn't get more exposure?" I ask.

Laney shoots me a look; she thinks that's my way of digging at Mia, saying the article was not very widely read. Which, okay, it is. I turn my back to them all, setting about finding the Sexton *Transformations* that

Mother left for Aunt Margaret. The book, when I find it, falls open to an envelope and a photograph stuck in the pages, Trey and me in hunting gear.

"It doesn't take an Einstein to figure out that thousands of naked women protesting you is a public relations fiasco," Betts says. "The oil company wasn't stupid. They caved immediately to keep it from becoming a story."

In the awkward silence, I suppose we're all thinking the same thing: we should have caved immediately at the Hart Building this afternoon. Is it too late to cave?

Betts takes the frame from Mia and continues theatrically:

"A woman's exposure of her body in this society is believed to cast a lifetime curse on those to whom the nakedness is directed, a curse related to productivity and fertility. This curse, used by women in South Africa, Kenya, and elsewhere, is one no local man would dare provoke. Any foreigner upon whom the curse is believed to be cast—and any corporation with which he is affiliated—would find his ability to transact business in the Nigerian oilfields severely compromised. So the sight of thousands of naked women did the trick: the local officials and police all fled to avoid the curse, leaving the company with little option but to—"

"A little sensationalist, I know," Mia interrupts. She takes the frame from Betts and sets it back on the shelf. "We could turn on the news, Betts," she says.

"Or not." Betts's tone evoking Katie Couric's voice as she might begin this story: *In what was expected to be a quiet final day of Senate confirmation hearings for Supreme Court nominee Elsbieta Zhukovski . . .* "Unless you want to, Laney?"

"Or not," Laney agrees.

"Music," I suggest. I set the Sexton volume on Mother's desk, find the iPod I gave her last Christmas plugged into the Bose cube speakers I also gave her. It's surprising how much it touches me to know that she used them, that she hasn't, as she so often does, regifted them to some women's shelter. When I hit the play button, an almost unbelievably gentle piano piece begins, a few notes that call to mind the bay at sunrise, the Law Quad in moonlight after a new snow, Mother reading by the fire just before she realizes I'm there. When Mia asks what the music is, I realize I don't know. Ted is the one who puts together the playlists. This music I like to think I chose for Mother is in truth music Ted chose for me, that I copied for her.

"That's a long way from the Bee Gees, Ginge," Betts says. "Gymnopédie Number One by Erik Satie. It was inspired by a poem: 'Les Antiques.'"

"'The Ancients,'" Laney says.

"I don't remember the poem exactly, but there was something about a fire in it," Betts says.

Fire longs to meet itself / flaring, longing wants a multiplicity of faces. Not the lines that inspired the music, but from Mark Doty's "Fire to Fire." The book it's from, *School of the Arts,* is the kind of book Mother ought to have collected, but Mother never had much use for new books, or for the kind of desire Doty explores. Most of what she read was the news, actually, with a preference for the kind of things Mia writes, pieces about crazy people doing crazy things to try to change the world in whatever crazy way they think it needs to be changed.

Mia and Betts and Laney and I sit on the floor around the Scrabble board, the way we used to in Laney's and my suite in the Law Quad and in the living room of the Division Street house.

"Why did you call my mother, Mia?" I ask.

Taking her time / she looks the bus over, / grandly, otherworldly, like Bishop's moose.

"With the naked women thing," I say.

"The women made me think of her," she says, as if it's just that simple.

"Those women didn't bare their asses to draw attention."

Mia shrugs. "Didn't they? Anyway, it seemed so like something your mom would do."

The way she glances at Betts leaves me sure they've talked about this in a way that has something to do with me. Leaves me imagining Mother's hands wrapped around the telephone as she talked not to me but to Mia or Laney or Betts.

My mother's hands are cool and fair, / They can do anything.

"I didn't expect everything that came after, Ginge," Mia says gently. "You can't possibly think that when I called her I meant for her to write it down and send it to her newspaper contacts."

"Have her *secretary* write it down."

Mia flips a Scrabble tile from inside the cardboard lid: a one-point *E*. She won't be going first.

"She liked the part about the curse," she says. "She said she was going to use the idea of the curse sometime and get naked for a cause."

"The curse of the naked feminist!" Betts says as she flips over a *J* (eight points), winning the right to play first.

We flip the tiles back over and mix them around, then pull our seven. When Betts plays her first word, "jargon," I eye the *J* with suspicion, sure she kept an eye on it after she flipped it back over. But I don't challenge her because even as I think it I know it isn't true. Betts would never cheat at anything, much less at something that doesn't matter. I'm the one of us who would cheat at a Scrabble game.

"'Jargon' with the *J* on the double letter score. And the whole word doubled!" she says. "That, friends, is forty-four points."

If she can set aside that awful senator and his awful questions, surely I can ignore the looming presence of the shelves and shelves of Mother's books.

"I think Ted wants to retire and move here," I say.

Laney looks around the library as if I might intend to move our king-sized bed into this very room. "He's only, what? Fifty-five?"

"Work isn't fun for him anymore, if it ever was."

"Could you live out here, do you think?" Laney asks.

Mia plays "raw" on the *R*, the four-point *W* on a triple letter square giving her fourteen points for what really is a pathetic effort, but I don't complain because I play next. I've got "ember" with the *E* next to her *W* so I get "we" as well. A pretty nice play even if does only get me one point more than Mia's "raw." And the placement will make it hard for anyone to use the triple word box that falls below and to the right of my *R* for more than a two-letter word.

"Shit," I say when Laney lays out "choose" with the *S* falling at the end of "ember," the *E* on the triple word score. I look around at the books as if they might be as appalled at my language as Mother forever was. Never mind that I learned to swear from her.

"Shit," I repeat. The word feels as good as it ever has in my mouth, here in her library.

"Ten for 'embers' plus fifteen tripled to forty-five for 'choose.'" Laney grins at Betts. "Fifty-five makes your forty-four look awful shabby, doesn't it?"

Betts settles for "teeth" and Mia plays "anger," leaving me gleefully close to the bottom left triple word score space. I sink into the warmth of the fire as I work like hell for something that uses my ten-point Z on the double letter space above the *A* in Mia's "anger." "Zap" is a word, but I need four letters to get to the triple word space. I have another *P,* but "zapp" with two *P*s isn't a word, much as I want it to be. Zape? Zaep? Zare? If I had an *F,* I could play "faze," but I don't. I consider playing "zap," taking the twenty-four points, but then if Betts has an *S* she can play "zaps," which would be forty-five points for a single tile, a play she would gloat about for the rest of her life.

The sand is falling fast as I give up on the *Z* and look for another way to use the triple word score. I focus on the *P* which, at three points, is the next-highest-point tile I have.

"Tick, tick, tick," Mia says.

I see it then: a word I can't possibly play.

I pull the tiles, set them on the board in a different order: "pear." Six points. Which is fine. I'm fine with six points.

Laney counts the points, adding the six to my fifteen for twenty-one, but Mia is watching me, her little mind spinning, wondering how I missed snagging the damned triple word score, if only as a defensive move. She sees the better play too, then. She hesitates, looking from me to Betts, then to Laney. She has never been a good bluffer, at least not with us.

"Your go, Laney," I say.

Mia's expression makes Laney and Betts study my play again, too. Maybe they see it or maybe they don't; I'm distracted because I see now what I ought to have played: "Pare!" Like with a knife. With the three-point P on the double letter space and the *E* on the triple word.

Mia begins rearranging the tiles, though, forming the word I simply could not play. "We've managed to stick our heads in the sand for almost thirty years, but the nasty little grains are filling our lungs now," she says. "We need to talk about this."

"We weren't ever going to talk about it," I say quietly.

"We didn't start the conversation," Mia says as we all sit staring at the tiles, which now read R-A-P-E.

PART II

~

The sexual assault exam began at 6:30 a.m. . . .
Two clean sheets were spread on the floor. . . . Patty
stood over these and removed her clothes . . .
provided a urine sample . . . was asked to lie naked
on a table for a head to toe examination. Her
knees were up high, her legs spread apart, her
feet in stirrups. . . . Patty's pubic hair was
combed, and pubic hair samples collected.

Poarch examined Patty's vagina with a
Wood's lamp, which casts ultraviolet light to de-
tect body fluids like semen. She did a "wet mount
exam," which involved taking a swab from Patty's
vagina . . . inserted a medium speculum into
Patty's vagina to search for evidence of internal
injury. Lastly, she used a colposcope—a kind of
sophisticated magnifying glass attached to a
video camera—to probe Patty's vagina and rectal
areas.

—from *Cry Rape: The True Story of One Woman's
Harrowing Quest for Justice,* by Bill Lueders

GINGER

LAW QUADRANGLE NOTES, Winter 1993: Virginia ("Ginger") Cook Conrad (JD '82) and Edward Hudson are delighted to announce the birth of Annie Hudson-Conrad. Little Ms. Hudson-Conrad's brother, B.J., is working hard to get his nose back in joint, as is grandmother Faith Cook Conrad (JD '53), who calls the baby "little Faith." Annie's Aunt Betts (Elsbieta Zhukovski, JD '82) has nicknamed the child "Ye-Of," which her Aunt Laney (Helen Weils, JD '82) insists is Latin for "Princess Annie of Manhattan Island." Ms. Conrad, a senior associate at the New York firm of Caruthers, Smythe & Morgan, was back in her office billing time within just a few six-minute increments of her daughter's birth. Mr. Hudson, a partner at Caruthers, is on leave for two months, a sabbatical he would describe as "paternity leave" if his firm offered such a thing.

IN RETROSPECT, I wish I'd never told the Ms. Bradwells about Daddy's damned sixtieth birthday party. I wish I'd rented a villa on a tropical beach and claimed it was a friend's place so it wouldn't have cost Betts or Mia anything. I can't imagine hearing even our conversation at the Lightkeeper's Cottage about crab fishing described to the Senate Judiciary Committee, although I fear that's what we have to look forward to. It's only hindsight that's twenty-twenty, though, and we were young and single and on the last spring break we would ever share.

You had "such fun," you said, that classic summer.

That week started out with the best two days we Ms. Bradwells ever spent together. The afternoon we set off for Cook Island, we were as excited as schoolgirls (which, okay, we *were*, but we thought of ourselves as school *women*, so you take my point). Betts was more than a little embarrassed about the state of her mother's car we were borrowing for the week, but as she pulled up to the curb and peered through the windshield wipers at us, Laney and Mia and I literally jumped up and down under Justice Bradwell folded in his contortionist pose. It was 4:05, because I'd refused to cut Ross's Corporate Tax class, a class the rest of those pathetic little clucker Bradwells refused to take, afraid for their grade point averages although the excuse they gave was that it met at three on Friday afternoons.

The dark settled on us well before we hit the Ohio-Pennsylvania border, but we amused each other with extravagant stories of where our classmates might end up (as television game show hosts, truly incompetent parents, inmates at a maximum security prison in upstate New York). We sang along with every song on the only eight-track we had, Carole King's *Tapestry*. (Even Betts, who, as Laney would say, "can't carry a tune in a bucket with a lid on it," doesn't sound dreadful singing along with Carole King.) And we had a long discussion about Andy, to whom Mia was engaged by then.

"He's great, he's great, I know he is," she said. "I know I'm the luckiest person in the world, but . . ."

She hesitated for such a long time that Betts finally joked that Andy was into kinky sex.

"Conservative Episcopalian Dartmouth-sweatshirted son of a prominent banker Andrew Cooper IV," she said (Andy, who sported a conservative haircut even before all the guys cut their hair for interview season), "prefers handcuffs and whips?"

"No, of course not!" Mia protested while the rest of us were all still laughing. "But when we lived together last summer, *phwutt*. New York City. Greenwich Village. It should have been fun, but when he wasn't working late, which he always was, or playing softball with his firm or doing some other summer clerk thing, he was tired. And even in Paris at the end of the summer . . ."

"Blame that on jet lag, there's always too much pressure on those romantic getaways, they always disappoint," I said.

I sometimes wonder how different Mia's life might have been if we'd taken her seriously as we drove eastward from Ann Arbor. But it never occurred even to me that Andy might have been seeing a man in New York that summer, or perhaps several men, that when he proposed to Mia in Paris that August it had more to do with not wanting to disappoint his father than with wanting to spend his life with her. That whole thing with Andy was probably the real reason the rest of us kept our names when we married. I like to take credit for it, but the fact is when Andy, who is basically the nicest guy in the world, the kind of guy who would never leave you, did leave Mia, it made us all nervous. How do you give up your identity for something you can't be sure will last?

We had champagne on the pier that first night on Cook Island. I shot the cork and we wished on it, and Betts remembered the bottle I'd brought to the Arb the first day of law school, which I'd neglected to tell the newly minted Ms. Bradwells was my birthday champagne. That first day of law school had been my twenty-first fucking birthday, but Mother had an important meeting back in Washington, something about the Equal Rights Amendment, which, okay, *was* on life support at the time, but it was my twenty-first birthday and she'd just dumped me the night before in that skanky little basement apartment I'd sublet for the summer term. Left me alone to wonder whether to change my mind and enroll in Georgetown, where she taught, knowing she'd hate having her failure of a daughter splashing in her pool as much as I'd hate drowning under her watchful gaze. Then she showed up at my door the next morning, saying she'd be late for her meeting but they wouldn't get to anything important before lunch. And she took me for birthday fragels, deep-fried bagels dipped in cinnamon, an Ann Arbor delicacy. It was hard enough to say goodbye once, but she made me do it twice on the excuse of bringing me a bottle of birthday champagne. "A new day, a new year, a new life," she said. "An opportunity to leave the sordid past behind."

The sordid past: my turbulent teenaged years, which included a slew of cut classes; a suspension from school; a drunk driving arrest Daddy arranged to have stricken; my sketchy performance at the University of Virginia; and of course my year in South Africa. Now that I'm a parent, I have to admit that would have alarmed me as much as it alarmed Mother and Daddy, me taking off to a place as far away from them as I could get with a playwright who called himself "Scratch." Love at first sight. That's the way I always presented that relationship, the way the Ms. Bradwells and everyone else heard it because that was what I wanted them to hear.

That night skinny-dipping in the bay though, I admitted, "I had no idea Scratch was writing a character that was me into his play." *And my heart, old hunger motor, with its sins / revved up like an engine that would not stop.*

I'd been living in South Africa with Scratch for almost a year by then, waiting tables and playing housewife, all in support of the cause of great art. His art, not mine. Mother would have been appalled. I went to the market and made fancy dinners, washed clothes, waited tables at night, flirting with customers for the bigger tips. All while Scratch scribbled away day and night on a play I wasn't allowed to see, not even after a local playhouse offered to do a staged reading.

I told everyone I knew about that, of course. Extra flirting at my tables, a subtle line dropped about this staged reading perhaps they'd enjoy. I twisted arms to get friends to come, afraid Scratch, who was moody to start with, would be devastated if he failed to draw an audience. "Not even a real play? Just some actors *reading* a play?" they asked. To which I promised champagne. Champagne is always good for drawing a crowd.

The first shock came when the curtain opened. A single actress stood with her back to the audience, her long hair looping down her back and upward again, caught in a clip at her neck. The dark hair of a woman named Abigail, whom Scratch had slept with. He slept with lots of other women, I knew that. He was an artist, he needed a variety of experiences from which to create. I was free to sleep with others, too. But Abigail was the only one we'd ever argued over, the only one with whom he spent the night.

"I won't see Abby if you don't want me to. If you need that limit on my life," he'd pleaded to my threat to return to the States. "What would I do without you as my muse?"

He hadn't told me he'd cast her in his play. That he'd spent late nights rehearsing with her. Abigail, who wore her hair long and loose. I was the one who wore my hair looped into a clip.

The character Abigail played, which Scratch had the nerve to name Ginny, was a child in a young woman's body, a spoiled rich girl, a promiscuous slut who, despite the fact she had everything anyone could possibly want, remained hungry for approval and desperate for love. All of that was apparent in the words, in the non-movement of the non-actors, the readers who were only Abigail and Scratch.

I sat there in the darkness, growing smaller, shrinking into a tiny atom, a black hole of anger sucking in whole constellations of hurt. Watching the pathetic Abigail-Ginny with her long loop of hair beg and cry for the loss of Scratch. Scratch, who was reading a character named Beau, my brother's name.

When I did stand, finally, I didn't say a word to defend myself. I slipped quietly from my seat before the lights went back up, walked out of the theater, hailed a cab.

"I couldn't bear to go back to the apartment even to collect my things," I told the Ms. Bradwells that first night on Cook Island, as we drank champagne on the pier. "I called Beau from the airport. Beau called Mother, Mother arranged a ticket, and I flew home."

I dumped my jeans and top onto the rough wood of the pier and dove off, regretting, suddenly, having told the Ms. Bradwells about Scratch. They stripped, too, though, down to the swimsuits under their clothes and then, without thinking much longer, down to bare skin. We all swam naked in the bone-cold water, Mia screaming bloody damned murder that some sea monster was devouring her when it was only seaweed twisted on her leg. Shit, how we laughed at that. Teeth-chattering laughter. That water was cold as hell.

Laney

~~~⧓~~~

LAW QUADRANGLE NOTES, Fall 1994: Ms. Helen ("Laney") Weils (JD '82) has been appointed Special Assistant to Atlanta Mayor Andrew Young, in charge of interface with the Olympic Committee in preparation for the 1996 Summer Olympics. She will hereinafter be known as Special Assistant Cicero-Bradwell. The line for tickets forms behind the other Ms. Bradwells, and you'll have to be nice to her for two full years. Is it really worth it?

THE BAY WATER off the wood pier that first night on Cook Island was as cold as Aunt Frieda's freezer, but not half so cold as when we found we had no towels. We left every little thing on the pier except the champagne, and we ran bare naked up the path, laughing so hard it nearly kept us warm. Inside, Mia and Betts and I collected the bay in little puddles on the marble floor while Ginger fetched us towels, her hair still unloading bucketsful when she returned to the landing above us. She slipped at the top step, and we all started or gasped or held our breaths, whatever expression you like for "were scared to death she'd tumble headfirst over the rail and splat on the marble floor." The only thing that flew over that banister, though, was a pile of pure white towels.

Ginger laughed as she regained her balance, while huge, baby-soft bath blankets smelling of cedar and bleach landed with a *flooop* right in front of me. As we wrapped ourselves up in them, I thought if Chawterley were mine, never mind just one of my several homes, I wouldn't have a friend in the world who didn't know all about it. Bigmouthed as Ginger was about so many things, though, she never did like to talk about her family wealth.

The thing I best recall about that first night at Chawterley, the thing I best *like* to recall, is taking the Scrabble board and the rest of the champagne into the Sun Room, still wrapped in fluffy-soft towels. Ginger set a match to the fire, forgetting the flue at first, and the four of us curled up on the couch and chairs to choose seven letter tiles each. We weren't sleepy. We were on that second-wind kind of day-after energy that would carry Mia and Ginger and me through all-nighters at work. Betts never did pull an all-nighter even clerking for the Supreme Court, which says something, that deals to buy grocery stores require Herculean efforts of sleep deprivation while the highest law of the land does not.

Maybe it was the fact that we'd brought no casebooks, that we had a whole long week ahead of us with nothing we much needed to do. Maybe it was that we were about to go separate ways in just a short while, that this would be the last time we ever would have to say *this is who I really am* to friends who wouldn't be elbowing us in the ribs for the best assignments and bonuses, and partnership. Or maybe it was Chawterley itself.

The house had been shut up all winter, but it was as welcoming as if Faith had just run out for some something, never you mind that she was still deep into the *Idaho v. Freeman* appeal to the Supreme Court back in Washington. Ginger liked to call Faith's efforts to save the Equal Rights Amendment back then "hours and hours of time wasted on a case that is going to be moot before it's decided." But Faith always did believe the ends aren't the only things that matter, that process is important, too. "Losing a fight is better than never coming into the ring," she liked to say.

We weren't more than two words into that Scrabble game before I spilled out, "So I had this thing happen to me last summer." An inarticulate way to set into a conversation about sexual harassment, a label you didn't hear back then, but I'd worried how to begin that conversation so many times over the intervening months—or whether I ought to begin it at all given the fella involved—that it was a mercy to have it out. I never am as articulate as I imagine, anyway, in Latin or otherwise.

"This fella I was working with at Tyler & McCoy," I said, "he just pulled me to him and kissed me in the elevator one night as we were leaving." Like a bad cliché.

"Shit," Ginger said. "Not Frankie."

"No! No, of course not. I swear on my grandmama's grave." I pulled my towel close around me, shivering again. "I didn't even meet your brother, Ginge. He was working in Abu Dhabi or someplace like that."

"Shit, Laney," Ginger said. "A partner?"

I'd been one of only two women and the only black lawyer—or almost lawyer—summer-clerking at Tyler & McCoy. I was invited to all the outings: the boat trips and the shows and the weekend gatherings at swanky country clubs, but I was the only one ever mistaken for staff at those clubs, and if I wasn't the only summer clerk never invited to grab a sandwich at lunchtime, it surely felt like I was. Then I was assigned to work on a project supervised by a senior associate who'd been written about in *Esquire* and in an early issue of *The American Lawyer*, the latter with a full-page photograph of him on his boat and a caption claiming he never did go out on the water without a client aboard. He expected to be accelerated to partnership that fall, he told me, never mind that no Tyler associate had ever been made partner early. And if he was arrogant about his prospects, he had the good grace to be right: he'd been an associate when he kissed me, but had made partner that fall.

He was also undaunted by my gender, my race, my accent. He liked my work, too, or liked working with me, or both. He gave me a whole lot of rein, and credit for every clever thing we did together. He told everyone who would listen that when I returned to the firm after taking the bar exam they would have to stand in line behind him to get my time. Comforting words in a firm that didn't always invite its summer clerks back for permanent jobs. And I wanted that job. Tyler & McCoy was one of the most politically connected firms in the country. Its ranks included an ex-attorney general and three partners who'd been in various cabinets over the years. Working there would provide me all the how-do-you-dos I needed to enter politics at the national level, not by running for office but by appointment or invitation to work on a senator's staff.

A loud backfire popped from the fireplace, startling us as Ginger laid the word "drift" on the Scrabble board. "Well, what the hell can you do in a situation like that?" she said.

Mia and Ginger nodded while Betts sat silently watching the flames pop red and yellow and a blue that was neon compared to the blue-green of the bay lapping against the pier outside.

"Thank goodness the elevator stopped at the next floor," I said. "He introduced me to the receptionist who joined us, and then chatted with her." Flirted with her, as if he hadn't just had his lips pressed to mine.

"A receptionist saw you kissing?" Ginger asked.

"Lord, no, Ginge. The elevator dinged and . . ." And he'd stepped away from me as if he kissed women on the elevator about every time he pressed the button for the ground floor. "No, of course not," I insisted, wondering which ruffled me more: that he'd kissed me like he was entitled to, or that he didn't seem to much care that he had.

"The fastest conduit for any rumor is a law firm receptionist," Ginger said.

Betts asked, "Was he married?"

"*Lord* no! At least I don't think . . ." *Was* he married? But I recalled a conversation earlier that night he'd kissed me, about folks he took out sailing: not *only* clients.

Maybe he'd thought I was flirting with him, that I was angling to go sailing. Was that why he thought he could kiss me on the elevator, in the middle of a conversation about where I should start my research the next day? I'd lain awake the whole long night worrying over what I would say to him the next morning, but in the end I'd said nothing and neither had he.

"I bet he's sleeping with the receptionist," Ginger said. "Half the guys at Tyler have slept with that receptionist, including Frankie. Do you think it was . . . I don't know how to say this so I'm just going to say it. Maybe he wanted to try a different flavor?"

"*Ginger!*" Betts said.

"I know, I know," Ginger said. "It's just . . . even my brother, who isn't a bad guy—"

"Laney is beautiful!" Betts said. "What guy wouldn't want to kiss her? This doesn't have to be about race."

"But I think maybe it was," I said, the words coming out more hushed than I meant. I shrugged, recalling his thin lips pressed against mine, his pale hand, his probing tongue. "I don't know why. I just think maybe it was."

I laid three tiles on the board, spelling the word "hour," not many points. "Your turn, Mi."

"It's inexcusable whether it was about race or not," Ginger insisted. "He kissed her on the *elevator*. At the *office*."

"Men and women who work together are going to fall in love sometimes," Betts said.

"So you recommend this as a dating strategy?" Ginger shot back. "We should all corner attractive subordinates on elevators and kiss them before they can object?"

This was long before Anita Hill, and even when she came forward to challenge Clarence Thomas's appointment to the Supreme Court nine years later, we watched the way one watches a wreck occurring close enough to touch when there is not a single thing you can do but step back. "That woman is committing career suicide," I recollect Betts saying. We played by the old rules; if you didn't, you'd sure enough be shown the door. No one would ever admit you were let go because you'd ruffled feathers, but the truth was if a prominent partner liked to kiss young associates in the elevator, your job as the young associate was to avoid any elevator he might be on.

"He never did bother me after that," I said.

"See," Betts said. "He was a perfect gentleman after that. He was great to work for. He made a pass at her. She rebuffed it. He respected that. I don't know how you can fault either of them."

We talked late into the night about problems we'd encountered at work the prior summer. Ginger was asked if she could take dictation. Betts was asked to fetch coffee despite the suit she was always careful to wear, and one partner liked to take her to lunch at his men's club, where they had to ride the back "pink" elevator up to the "pink" dining room in which "ladies" were allowed. But Mia suffered the worst indignities. She was asked if she'd been a cheerleader, if she wore pantyhose or garters, if women liked to sleep in the nude. She and Andy shared an apartment that summer, and although she'd been careful to be discreet about it, not even admitting her living arrangements to her parents, word had gotten around. She wasn't offered a permanent job at the end of the summer, although Andy was: the difference between being a stud and being a slut. This was 1981, when the firms we were joining had no women partners and few women associates. The class that graduated before us marked the first year large firms hired women in substantial numbers, and the medium and small firms had yet to follow suit.

The judiciary, where Betts herself was headed, was perhaps the worst of the old-boy networks. Carter let a few women climb up onto the federal bench, but Reagan went right back to the tradition of senators recommending their golf buddies for judge. The "old boy" Betts would be clerking for on the D.C. Circuit after graduation was one of those Carter girls, though: Ruth Bader Ginsburg. They'd spent Betts's interview discussing Judge Ginsburg's notion that laws banning abortion are gender discrimination rather than violations of privacy.

To this day, I don't know why I didn't go on and tell Ginger it was her cousin Trey who kissed me on that elevator. Trey, whom I'd met thanks to Faith.

I'd had dinner with Faith at the Conrad home outside Washington regularly that summer; it was my home away from home. One night, she was showing me a miniature science text with beautiful flowers decorating the diagrams and text—"As if the scientific truth isn't beautiful enough," she said. The book, by Johannes Kepler, had put us into a discussion about the path astronomers wove to avoid the wrath of religion: Galileo forced by the Roman Catholic Church to recant his belief that the earth orbited the sun, Giordano Bruno, another believer in Copernican theory, burned at the stake. "The work of putting powerful men in the position of being seen to be mistaken is often dangerous work," Faith said.

Profane, I recall thinking. *From the Latin* profānus, *outside of the temple.* And I found myself confessing I'd blundered into telling a partner he was mistaken earlier that week. With no audience, I'd been able to back off and suggest *I* was the one who was mistaken, only to hear him touting my idea as his own in a meeting the next day.

Faith lit a menthol cigarette and exhaled, then asked if I'd met her sister Grace's son, Trey Humphrey. "You should introduce yourself. Tell him you're Ginger's roommate. Trey has always been fond of Ginger, like siblings without the competition, or without much of it. He's spent summers on Cook Island with us ever since his father wrapped his car around a tree when Trey was ten. Just tragic, as you can imagine. Grace could barely take care of herself, much less Trey.

"I should warn you that Trey doesn't suffer fools lightly," she said, "but you're a smart girl, you'll love working with him."

I was like a calf staring at a new gate when I walked into my office the next morning to see a fella sitting in my desk chair, reading a brief I'd been working on. "You're Helen," he said, his gaze so intent that I wanted to deny I was. "My Aunt Faith tells me I ought to meet you. She says you took my cousin Ginger's spot on the *Law Review.*" He stood and shook my hand, grinning suddenly, his face opening into boyishly oversized front teeth. I didn't have the nerve to tell him I hadn't made law review, that I was only ALR, "almost law review."

"You can't be nervous about meeting me," he said, wiggling his fingers as if to warm them; my own hands were cold cold cold. "We're practically family, and really, despite all the rumors you've no doubt heard, I don't often bite.

"Sit," he said, moving to the visitor chair. "Sit. I've been raised a gentleman, so until you sit I have to stand here waiting for you to do so."

A New York City gentleman. Where does a father wrap a car around a tree in New York City?

I sat, pushing away the rumors I had indeed heard, about secretaries who didn't type fast enough and copy machine operators who wouldn't stay until three in the morning now looking for new jobs. He settled his lean legs into the guest chair and extracted a pack of Marlboros from his pocket.

"Smoke?" he asked, extending the pack. When I declined, he asked if I minded if he did, and although I didn't much look forward to working all day in an office that smelled like an ashtray, I didn't have the nerve to say so.

He grilled me on what I was working on, which wasn't much. "Shit," he said, his expression so like Ginger's that I might have laughed if I hadn't had fresh in my mind that conversation with Faith about offending powerful men.

"Okay, so I can't get you unstaffed from that. It would ruffle feathers, and I'm up for partner this fall, or that's the speculation anyway. But I've got this project . . ."

And not much later, the work coordinator poked his head in my office to say Trey Humphrey had heard that I was a superstar and wanted to work with me. "I'll tell you honestly we don't often let Trey close to summer clerks," he said. "He has a reputation for being . . . demanding."

From the Latin meaning *responsible for more than one summer clerk not getting invited back to the firm.*

I DON'T KNOW what time we finally did fall asleep that first night on Cook Island, but we woke with a start to Ginger exclaiming, "Oh, shit! I left the book on the boat!" She bounded from the couch, her towel dropping away and her fanny jiggling as she bolted out into the bright daylight and sprinted down the path. At the pier's end, she leapt onto the boat like it might take off without her, and disappeared below deck. A chill set in to the Sun Room, but none of us rose to close the door before she burst back into the house with what looked to be a sandwich-sized baggie in her hand, the kind Betts had used for her Ms. Drug-Lord-Bradwell Halloween costume herb-drugs. It contained something the size of a pack of cigarettes or a deck of cards.

"A prayer book?" I guessed. "Except that thing is even smaller than any prayer book I've ever seen. And considerably more colorful."

"The Holy Church of the Blessed Virgin Flamingo?" Betts suggested.

"It's a *peacock* on the cover," Mia said.

"Oh! That's much more likely: the Holy Church of the Blessed Virgin Peacock!"

"A *male* peacock," Ginger said, still catching her breath. "Female peacocks are an undistinguished brown."

"Female pea*hens*," Mia said.

"A male can't be a blessed virgin?" Betts asked Ginger. "That sounds sexist to me, *Ms.* Decisis-Bradwell."

Ginger pulled off the tape sealing the baggie and extracted what we could all see now was a beautiful miniature book.

"*Sonnets from the Portuguese?*" Mia took the book from Ginger and opened it. "'The face of all the world is changed, I think.'"

"It certainly is!" Betts said. "Or at least it will be when we're through with it. Us in our navy blue skirt suits and high-cut blouses. But really, Ginger, even *you* don't jump up from a warm fire to run naked in the cold without a reason."

"You're forgetting the hot tub party, Betts," I said.

"Let me rephrase, your honor: even you, Ginger, don't jump up from a warm fire to run naked in the cold without a reason unless you're drunk."

I lifted one of the empty champagne bottles, pointed it at the cold ashes and the sad remains of a half-burnt log.

As Betts reloaded the fireplace, I said, "It's your mama's book, Ginge?"

"Why would you think *that?*" Ginger shot back, the astonished expression in her gray-blue eyes confirming the book's ownership.

I pulled my soft white towel more securely, huddling lower, wishing we all had on clothes.

"I stole it," Ginger said, plucking the book back. "Laney's right, it's Mother's. I lifted it from her library and no one missed it for so long that it was impossible to track when it had disappeared or who might have taken it, and I've had it ever since." Her smile not real but rather what Betts calls her the-thing-I-hate-most-is-waking-up-next-to-a-man-whose-name-I-don't-know smile.

"And you just"—Betts waved a hand toward the book or the growing fire or both, inexplicably annoyed—"carry it around with you wherever you go? That's why you happen to have it with you? Why you sprinted in a panic to the boat when you realized—"

"What exactly is a sonnet?" Mia interrupted. Betts never could begin to understand back then that the stolen *Sonnets* volume was about more than a silly book. That the fact of Ginger's family owning this big old house and another in Virginia while Betts grew up in a tiny apartment in Hamtramck didn't mean Ginger grew up with the kind of ubiquitous happiness Betts thought she did.

Ginger touched a hand to her still-damp hair, flipping it over the back of the couch. "Fourteen lines in iambic pentameter. 'How do I love thee? Let me count the ways.' A pentameter is five feet."

Betts glanced at her toes, the nails bare like Mia's where Ginger and I had painted ours red before we left Ann Arbor.

"Five two-syllable pairs. Iambs, so the second syllable is stressed," Ginger said.

"Now is the spring break of our wildness spent," Mia chimed in, and we all smiled.

"Except that has a trochee at the beginning," Ginger said. "An inverted foot." She stretched out her own leg and twisted it so her toes were nearly pointing to the floor.

"Is *now* the spring break of our young wildness spent?" Betts amended.

"Is now the spring of our dreams yet unmet?" Ginger proposed. "And that's eleven syllables, Betts."

"Did y'all know the word 'verse' comes from Latin that means something like a plow at the end of a furrow turning around to begin again?"

They threw couch pillows at me, calling me "Ms. Cicero-Showoff-Bradwell."

Ginger ran a hand over the cover, the lovely peacock, as the fire crackled, the room warming again. "I didn't even read poetry when I was thirteen," she said. "I had no idea what a sonnet was, much less anything about Elizabeth Barrett Browning." Then after another moment, "She grew up on an estate in England. Hope End."

"There'll be a million people here for your dad's party, Ginge," Mia said. "You could just leave it here somewhere after everyone has arrived and no one will ever know who took it. You could leave it in the library here, or maybe not, maybe leave it where it will be *sure* to be noticed after the party, so it's clear any of the party guests who'd ever been to your house in Virginia could be the thief."

"*I* might could leave it somewhere here," I offered. "If I was to be caught carrying that little book, I'd just say I found it somewhere. No one would expect *I* was the thief since it disappeared years before you and I met."

And we left it at that, no one saying another word about that book, but it was clear we'd made a plan.

Mia

〜

LAW QUADRANGLE NOTES, Winter 1985: Mary Ellen ("Mia") Porter (JD '82) is now on staff as a foreign correspondent at the *St. Louis Post-Dispatch.* She has no intention of accounting for the eight months after she left Belt & Bayliss, so please don't ask.

OUR SECOND NIGHT at Chawterley that spring break—Sunday night—we were skinny-dipping off the pier again, giggling and splashing in the bright moonlight when a spotlight fixed on us. It came out of nowhere, from out on the water where nobody ought to have been.

"Shit, we have company," Ginger said with laughter in her voice. "No one else was supposed to be here before Tuesday!"

The spotlight flashed twice before fixing on us again.

"Shit, it's Frankie and Beau."

"Your brothers?" Laney said. "How do you know?"

"Sorry guys," she said, "but we can climb naked from the water now, while they're close enough to see but far enough away for plausible deniability, or we can wait until they pull up to the pier, at which point we're screwed." She was laughing: this was a joke she'd had played on her before, or that she'd played on her brothers; the difference wasn't quite clear.

She climbed from the water into the spotlight and grabbed the top towel from the stack we'd been smart enough to have handy this time. Suits, no, but towels, yes.

Wolf whistles sounded from the boat.

"Shit, it's freezing," she said, pulling the towel around her and directing us to swim over behind the *Row v. Wade,* where we'd be at least partially hidden as we climbed from the water, and where she would cover us each in a towel as we emerged.

"Shit," she laughed. "Those bastards." She called out as loudly as she could, "You bastards!"

The sound of male laughter arose from beyond the light—more than two voices—and the light went off and on again, as if winking at us, or trying to catch us dropping our towels to dress in the momentary dark. She grabbed my hand, saying, "Come on!" and pulled me along behind her up the path, all of us laughing now.

We bolted into the house and through the Sun Room to the kitchen, then up the narrow servants' stairs to our third-floor, no-name room. We dressed quickly, Ginger hurrying us as we pulled on jeans and the sweaters we'd worn in the car, the only sweaters Laney and Betts and I had brought. Despite Ginger's warnings, we'd imagined a tropical island right up until the moment we jumped into the cold Chesapeake.

We shared the single comb Ginger handed us—she was the fastest to dress—and followed her as she bolted back down the servants' stairs, through the Dining Hall and the Front Parlor and across the front foyer to the Captain's Library. There, she flipped Betts a deck of cards, saying, "Sit! Deal!" When we didn't sit, she pointed to a round table in the center of the room. "Sit, you dipshits!" She grabbed a canister of long matches from the fireplace mantel.

"What are we playing?" Betts asked.

"Just deal something!" Ginger struck a match and set it to the paper and kindling and logs already on the grate. She plopped down in the last chair, her back to the door, and took the cards from Betts. She gave a few to each of us, not dealing so much as handing out random numbers of cards. "Mia, do you have any threes?" she asked before she'd even looked at her cards.

"Go fish?" I said.

She hopped up and ran out into the foyer, where she peeked around the corner and down the hall to the back door and the pier beyond it. "Shit, they came in Trey's boat." She hurried back to her seat and picked up her cards again. "We can't imagine who might have been skinny-dipping off the pier but it certainly wasn't us. That's the party line."

"Even though our hair is still dripping?" Betts asked.

"With this gang, it's all about the bluff," Ginger insisted. "Your turn, Mi."

Four voices singing in harmony—lovely music, actually—sounded from somewhere between us and the bay. Again, Ginger hopped up and peeked down the hallway.

"Dougie is with them." She plopped down in her chair again. "Dougie is a holy asshole, but he's been Trey's best friend since before my uncle died. He keeps Trey from getting morbid. And he sure has a beautiful voice. Don't let him sing to you. I swear to God, you'll want to screw him just because of his voice."

The door in the back foyer opened a moment later, a song I couldn't quite place sounding in four-part harmony: "She's so cold cold cold like an ice cream cone!" A barbershop quartet version of the Rolling Stones? We sat listening as the music made its way into the Music Room, then across the back foyer again and through the Sun Room. In the kitchen, the banging of cabinet doors joined their voices.

"*Voilà!*" one of them said as the others continued singing. A moment later the singers made their way through the Dining Hall and the Front Parlor, into the foyer where we could be spotted through the open library door.

"You got any threes, Betts?" Ginger asked.

Betts pulled a three of hearts out and tossed it to Ginger, who tucked it into her hand, ignoring the foursome now singing in the doorway. The smell of sea air and aftershave and scotch and cigarettes came with them: four men in blue jeans and hunter-cum-sailing duds, the least cocky in a down vest while the others wore unbelted tan safari jackets, all those empty pockets. With the bottle of scotch in Down Vest's hand and the highball glasses each carried, they might have sailed in on the wind without need of a sail. Even the down-vested one had that air of confidence that comes from always having been one of the cool guys.

I recognized the tallest of the four from a photo Ginger kept in her bedroom: her older brother Frank. A clean-shaven face and hair the color of whiskey—shortish for the time, meaning not much below his ears. He had Ginger's wide mouth and her overbite which, on his profile, accentuated a too-sharp nose. He had thin lips and thin brows, but there was no lack of confidence in his blue, blue eyes. He didn't look to me like the kind of guy who would be "tasting flavors" just to be tasting, but what did I know about what men did and didn't like when it came to sex? He was the kind of guy who would have plenty of flavor choices if he wanted them.

The cute one in the down vest looked familiar, too. His long, thick hair reminded me of Professor Jarrett, although Jarrett was always clean shaven, while this guy had a mountain-man beard and mustache, and eyes the polished green of sea glass, with straight-across brows and long lashes and such a nice-guy expression focused on Ginger that I liked him at once. I looked down at my cards—I *did* have a three among the disorganized mess of hearts and spades and . . . I ran the fingers of my right hand over my left behind the cards, over my diamond engagement ring. Down Vest grinned as the foursome finished their song, a smile as wide as Ginger's and Frank's emerging from all the thick mess of facial hair. *Beau!* Ginger's brother. The face buried under the beard was an older version of the one in Ginger's other photo: Beau sitting on the bench in a basketball uniform, his chin bare and baby-soft.

One of the others, a taller, softish guy with wavy dark hair, a slightly crooked face, and an amazing singing voice, said, "You're forgetting your manners, Ginge?"

Only then did Ginger look to them. "What kind of shit do you morons have for brains, sailing in at night?"

"Thank you!" Beau said. "That was my point, too, but Trey—fine, it's his boat, but—"

"Let it go, Beau," the taller guy suggested in an unthreatening voice that was melodic even when he wasn't singing. "We're here. Let it go."

Ginger stood then and, tugging affectionately on Beau's down vest, said, "This is my brother Beau, who likes always to be prepared for a snowstorm."

"I *did* come from Chicago," he protested.

"I don't know about this, Beau," she said, touching his beard.

"And this is Dougie," she said of the guy with the voice. Was it the angle, or was his face really crooked? Not just his nose, but his whole face just a little off symmetrical?

"We pretend Dougie is family because he's been running around with Frankie for as long as I've been able to say 'Dougie,' and we all feel sorry for him having to put up with such a sad excuse for a friend."

"I believe Trey was Doug's sad excuse for a friend long before I was," Frank said.

Ginger amended, "We feel sorry for him having to put up with *two* such sad excuses for friends: Frankie and *Trey,*" indicating the shorter, slighter guy, whose intense eyes drew you to him even as you tried to look away. "Trey who doesn't have the sense to wait until dawn to set sail."

"Bright moon," Trey said. "And I *did* bring the spotlight."

He extended his hand to Laney, saying, "Helen," his voice as deep and strong as his eyes.

Laney shook his hand.

"I was hoping Ginger would bring you along," Trey said, sounding like so many of the jerks I'd worked for the prior summer. But that was just the edge of New York in it, I decided as he said, "Very nice to see you again."

"Mr. Humphrey," Laney said.

"Trey."

Laney looked down to where the red Oriental rug fringed into the wood floor. "Trey."

"And she's Laney," Ginger insisted, bristling at Trey's overruling her introduction by calling Laney Helen even though that *is* her name.

"Helen did some work for me this summer," Trey explained to the rest of his quartet. "We're lucky to have her returning to Tyler and McCoy after she takes the bar, Frankie." Then to Betts and me, "I'm Ginger's cousin."

He pulled out a pack of Marlboros, shook one forward, and offered the pack toward Laney. She waved her hand slightly, declining, and he offered it to Betts, then to me. I had half a mind to take the offered cigarette even though I hated merely the smell of cigarette smoke. He seemed to expect it.

Ginger, to my amazement, did take one. Trey pulled out a monogrammed silver Zippo and flicked the wheel. She took a half step back as if needing more space, but leaned forward to dip the end of her cigarette into the yellow-white flame.

"So there were some ladies skinny-dipping off the pier as we approached," Trey said. He snapped the lighter shut and returned it to his blue jeans pocket, the look in his eyes easier now without, somehow, being any less intense. He took a drag on his cigarette while reaching with his free hand to touch a strand of Ginger's damp hair, just where the pattern around the neck of her Fair Isle sweater brushed her breast.

"'Ladies?' Were there really?" Ginger's words emerged in soft puffs of smoke as her hair fell from Trey's fingers. She turned to Doug. "Maybe you called Tessie McKee to let her know you were coming, Dougie?"

Frankie and Trey laughed the way guy friends laugh at each other. Betts and Laney and I shared an uncomfortable glance; none of us had grown up as the lone girl in a pack of brothers and boy cousins, as Ginger had.

"Tessie?" Doug said. "I seem to remember Tessie being *Beau's* particular favorite, Ginge. And I sure don't remember her ever having such attractive friends."

"You saw so much, obviously," Ginger said.

"It takes a certain amount of persuasion to get an island girl skinny-dipping this early in the year," Doug said. "Doesn't it, Beau?"

"Not that any of us would know anything about that," Beau said, trying, I thought, to spare us all embarrassment, but I was left with no doubt that they all did, in fact, know exactly how much persuasion an island girl might need to shed her suit.

Trey was a bastion of manners after that, though, directing Frank to be a good host and fetch four more glasses, pouring scotch for each of us, straight up, all the while asking solicitous questions about what we were doing after graduation, applauding how well we must be doing in law school to land the positions we had.

"Belt and Bayliss? That's a great San Francisco firm," he said to me. "Were you law review?" Then to Ginger, "All three of your friends here on law review, Skunky, but not you?"

Ginger looked to Laney, who said, "Just Mia and Betts."

"Oh?" Trey was quick to mask his surprise. "Well, you and my cousin here are the smart ones, then, aren't you, Helen? Law review is an unreasonable amount of work for anyone who doesn't get their jollies out of telling prominent professors their commas are in the wrong places. Isn't it, Betts?"

Betts, startled, looked to Trey, then stole a hopeful glance back at Beau, whom she'd been staring at as fantasy-romance moonily as she and I both used to stare at Professor Jarrett. "Sure. Right. Commas."

"So we're going gut-running, Ginger," Doug said. "You and your friends in?"

Ginger pulled the curtain back from one of the windows: darkness. The clock on the mantel showed almost one a.m. "All of us in one skiff?"

"Just as far as the McKees' dock," Doug said. "We can borrow Max's skiff."

"I thought Max was at Columbia," Ginger said. "In architecture school."

"So he won't be needing his boat, now, will he?" Frank said.

Ginger considered this for a moment. "It's high tide?" she asked.

The guys all laughed, and Doug said, "What? Are you afraid of getting a little mud on the bottom of your boat?" and they all laughed again.

Frank's idea was that all eight of us would pile into the skiff and go together to "borrow" a second one, which we could return before anyone knew it was gone.

"I personally don't mean to be found at the bottom of Fog's Ghost Gut in a boat that sank in the middle of the night because eight foolish souls overloaded it," Trey said. "Dougie, you and the brothers amuse Ginger's friends here. Play Go Fish. Ginger and I will nab Maxie's boat. That way if we're caught we can claim to be out spooning, right Ginge?"

"I gave up spooning for Lent," Ginger said.

We laughed at that, at the idea of Ginger letting go of the armor of her sexuality for a day, much less a full six weeks. Everyone but her brother Beau laughed. Beau stuck his hands in the pockets of his down vest and studied his Top-Siders, toeing his right shoe against the oriental carpet.

"I'll go with you, Trey," he volunteered. "Ginger will want to stay here with her pals."

I imagined him kicking a friend's face in if he took advantage of his little sister. I imagined how many faces he might actually have kicked in over the years. But Trey had already thrown an easy arm around Ginger's shoulder. He was laughing and saying, "No spooning then. If we're caught, we're reclaiming the boat in the name of Jesus Christ our Lenten Lord." And then Ginger was calling back over her shoulder, directing Beau to gag Doug if he started to sing again before she returned, and she and Trey disappeared down the hallway and out the door, two fresh cigarettes glowing red toward the pier.

Betts

LAW QUADRANGLE NOTES, Summer 2005: Elsbieta ("Betts") Zhukovski (JD '82) has just returned to the law school after a six-month sabbatical carrying state secrets to the governments of Russia and the Eastern Bloc countries, including Poland, where she was born.

"BEAU, YOU AND I better take the two law review ladies," Trey suggested after he and Ginger finally returned with the second skiff. "They'll have had too much boredom already this year to be made to put up with Frank and Dougie on their spring break." We were out on the pier by then. All eight of us. Ginger not even protesting being called a "lady." And Trey's hand on the center of my back. A gentleman dancer escorting his partner onto the starlit-bay-water floor.

"Hey, Skunky!" he called out to Ginger. She was already climbing into the other boat. "You protect Laney there, you hear me? Don't you let Dougie start singing to her."

My spirits lifted as our laughter rang out into the insect thrum of the starry night. Trey was guiding me into his boat. He'd chosen me over Ginger and Laney. Who were, let's be honest, the passengers I would have chosen if I were a guy.

Before that summer in New York and the trip to London maybe I would have thought these guys were too old for us. Too old to bring home to Matka. They were grown-ups with jobs and responsibilities. Or all of them but Beau were. Beau was twenty-six. Laney's age. Three years older than Ginger. And there were no closer friends than Laney and Ginger.

Trey had just made partner in the same D.C. firm Laney planned to join that summer, but even he wasn't yet thirty. He'd already managed to work into the conversation that he'd graduated from Harvard at nineteen and from Harvard Law at twenty-two. He'd been accelerated to become the youngest partner ever at Tyler & McCoy.

But we Ms. Bradwells were only weeks away from jobs and responsibilities ourselves. And one thing I'd learned that summer I'd worked in New York was that no one ever really feels like a grown-up.

It was such an odd time for me, law school was. I no longer fit in back home in Hamtramck, if I ever had. I knew how to pray over the paczki and I could stand in the line stretching from the New Palace Bakery before sunrise as long as anyone. But I didn't dare tell my unemployed friends that my summer job at Caruthers, Smythe & Morgan paid more each week than my mother's monthly take-home at the industrial cleaning job she worked. They already imagined me enjoying some cushy student life that didn't exist. No one saw the long hours I spent bleary-eyed over casebooks. The pressure I felt to validate Matka's leaving my missing father behind in Poland for my sake, if my father was even still alive. And no one in law school was anything like me, either. They'd never had to decide between going to the doctor and paying the electric bill. Even the Ms. Bradwells were nothing like me, although I did feel I belonged with them. That long late-night drive east from Ann Arbor to the Chesapeake. Stopping only for gas and potato chips and cans of Tab. As I listened to Mia babble on about Andy being unenthusiastic in bed, I thought I might even tell them about Ben. The only person I'd ever tried to tell about Ben, though, was Matka. And she'd refused to hear.

November first. I remember the day exactly because we'd all dressed as the appropriate Ms. Bradwells for a Halloween party the night before. Laney Cicero-Bradwell in a toga. Ginger in judicial robes. Mia in military garb. Me in a very attractive hooded sweatshirt, the pockets stuffed with "nickel bags" of herbs. I'd washed off the makeup I'd used to make myself drug-addict-looking, but there were still dark circles under my eyes when I arrived in Hamtramck.

"I'm just here for the day, Matka," I insisted. "For Mass and supper afterward." I hadn't told her I was coming. Afraid I'd lose my nerve.

Matka and I walked to Holy Cross and sat through a Mass said in Polish. We made potato and cheese pierogi in the tiny kitchen of the tiny apartment that had been home my whole remembered life. We talked about how not-well the neighbors were doing with ten percent of Michigan unemployed. We talked about my classes. The articles we'd chosen for the *Review.* Interview season. Applications for clerkships. And Laney and Mia and Ginge.

"Ginger, she is going home to Washington, Betsy?" Matka asked. She was always surprisingly fond of Ginger.

"New York," I said. "Caruthers, Smythe and Morgan. The firm we worked at this summer. She's going back there."

"New York." Matka shook her head, her thinning hair sprayed into utter stillness.

"Matka . . ." I said. I didn't know how to start, so I said "Matka" again.

She set her fork down on her plate. I remember how sad it looked. The cheap stainless. The chipped stoneware. Things I'd never noticed until that summer I'd dined at every Long Island country club to which any partner at Caruthers, Smythe & Morgan belonged. Always on spotless tablecloths with silver and carved crystal and food presented as art.

"I have a friend," I said. "I was wondering . . . She thinks she . . . You were a doctor in Poland, right?"

She touched worn fingers to worn cheeks. She picked up her cheap fork. Set it back on her plate. "This is Ginger," she said.

It would have broken her heart if I'd come to her saying I was pregnant. That the father was a partner I'd worked with that summer. That late one night when Ben and I were working on a case together he'd kissed me. That I'd kissed him back. That we'd gone to Los Angeles together on business. That he'd introduced me to Paul Newman at a party after a long day defending the deposition of a studio head client of his. That I'd had my own hotel room but after the party I went back to Ben's Jacuzzi suite. We slept together the next week, too. In Houston. Again on business. And at the end of the summer he flew me to London for a long weekend of theater and expensive dinners. Strolls along the Thames. This time with only a carefully orchestrated *story* of the business we might claim should we be seen together by someone who knew one of us.

I didn't know anyone in London, of course. Ben was the one who knew people everywhere. Who knew the little boutiques on Bond Street in Mayfair. Who spent thousands of dollars on clothes and jewelry for me. He liked to dress me and I was surprised to find I liked to be dressed. Not lingerie so much as suits, dresses, bags, and shoes. One silky-soft tweed cost over a thousand pounds. A month's wages for Matka. I told her I bought it on sale at Macy's. I didn't tell her Ben had insisted I have it because its mix of pale blue and gray and green matched my eyes.

"No, not Ginger," I told her.

She wet her lips. Studied me over the cracked wood of our kitchen table for such a long time that I knew she must know. She must understand. I took a bite of potato pancake. Made myself swallow it so as to have an excuse to avoid her. Wondered in the silence if maybe Ginger knew about Ben and me. She'd worked in the same firm all summer. We'd lived together. Did she never suspect? But she was wrapped up in her own life. Busy stringing Ted along. She was almost never home to find out that I wasn't either. And I had my history of innocence working for me, too. Ginger probably couldn't imagine me having a flirtation, much less whatever it was Ben and I had. And Ben and I were discreet.

"Elsbieta," Matka said finally, "this I cannot do, you must know that. In my country, yes, this I can do, but here I am not doctor. Here, to practice my medicine is not allowed."

I wondered for a moment if she would have said something different if I'd said "yes, Ginger." If I gave her a real face of a real girl in trouble, on whom she was turning her back.

"Your friend, she will have somewhere else to go?" she asked.

I made myself meet her lidded eyes. I made myself say, "It's expensive, is the thing."

She frowned, her face weary and dark. "In my country, yes, this I can do," she said, "but it is wrong for me here, it is against law for me here. I am American now, and I must be as America is, I cannot choose what is good here and leave what is not good. It is what is better in this country, Elsbieta: the rules apply to all the peoples. This I cannot throw away."

I nodded numbly, wanting to say, *But you're a good doctor. You would do this better than anyone. You know you ought to be a doctor here.* Wanting to say, *It's me, Matka, it's me.* But I couldn't make the words come out. Maybe over the phone I could have told her. But I couldn't bear to witness the disappointment. Everything she gave up for me only to have me return her this.

"Your friend, she will have somewhere else to go, Elsbieta?" she repeated.

I traced a crack in the pottery. A thin line of raw stoneware splitting a yellow rose. "Yes, yes, I'm sure she will," I said. "I'll help her. We'll find somewhere else." Because I could see then that she didn't know. She couldn't imagine I could be the kind of daughter who would sleep with a man who didn't love me the way my father had loved her.

"To be leader, Elsbieta," she said, "you must do what is right, even when it hurts you to do." She searched my face then. I could feel her wanting to look to my waist and I thought maybe she could imagine. I wanted to scream at her. To say this wasn't Poland and I didn't have the money for an abortion. That if I went to the father for the money or if anyone but her did it there would always be the possibility that it would be discovered. That I would never be able to reach for anything for fear it would come out. I wanted to explain to her that even in America, *especially* in America, no woman who'd had an abortion would ever be appointed dogcatcher. Much less judge. But I didn't say any of that. I only repeated that I'd help my friend think of something else. And I sat with her while we both pretended to finish our suppers without eating anything more.

She insisted on driving me back to Ann Arbor. A long, silent drive. In front of the Division Street house she took my hand in hers. "This you must remember, Elsbieta," she said. "To be leader you must lead, even when it will harm you. To be leader, you must always do what is right." Then after a moment, "When you are baby, Betsy, before you are born, I play the zhaleika for you, even then. After your father disappears and I am pregnant with you, I play for you every night. You are learning this music even before you are baby. You begin to play, and at first I play with you. Then it is time for you to play and you go up on this stage alone. Do you remember this? Only eight years old, but you are on this stage at your school and I want to go with you, to play with you, but it is time for you to play on your own." She reached over and touched my thick hair, my unlined cheek. "I am knowing it is time for you to play on your own, and still, I want to be playing with you. One person plays alone, it is one thing, but two plays together is so much more.

"I am so proud of you, Elsbieta, when you are playing only with yourself." The touch of her raw-skinned hand on mine. Her proud-Polish-mama smile. "Even though you miss half the notes," she said with a gentle laugh, "I am so very proud. I am always be proud.

"A child, she is blessing, Elsbieta. Everything is wrong sometimes and still a child she is blessing. Your friend, she must understand this before she is making decision." She sighed, and she pulled me to her and kissed the top of my head. "Your friend, you tell her I give her money if this she must do. I give her money, I get money somewhere. But you tell her, you make her understand: It is hard thing to raise child alone, this I know. But this is nothing to how hard it is to let child go."

I ANGLED FOR the seat next to Beau in the skiff that Sunday night. Monday morning, technically. I admit now to wanting to sit next to him, although I wouldn't have back then; I'd have claimed to be taking the front seat to avoid getting motion sick. But Mia seemed happy enough in the seat next to Trey.

He hurried us to sit. Fired up the pull-cord engine. The other boat was pulling away from the pier.

Already, we were behind in something I hadn't realized was a race.

"Whoa, Nellie!" Beau's large hands steadied my shoulders. I'd be in the bay if Trey hadn't waited for me to sit before he opened up the throttle. I gripped the narrow plank seat lest I fall onto the skanky bottom of the boat as my hair whipped into my eyes.

"Try straddling the seat unless you want to go for another swim," Beau suggested. He glanced back at Mia already straddling the seat she shared with Trey. "A swim, not *another* swim." A smile as wide as Ginger's exploded from his beard. "Since that wasn't you skinny-dipping off the pier, right?" He tapped my right knee and flipped his hand: I should throw my leg back so I'd face inward. Face him. I was glad I'd run a quick toothbrush over my teeth while Ginger and Trey were so long borrowing the second skiff. Glad of the soft night. The gentle starlight off the water made it dark enough that my acne wouldn't look so bad. Doris-Day-moonlight gauze.

Ginger stood in dark outline at the engine of the other boat. Her long hair slipped its barrette and whipped back in a surreal streak. She laughed and called out a taunt I couldn't make out over the wind.

Trey bellowed out from behind me, "Go right, sure, Skunky! You need a head start!" at a volume that hurt my ears at such close range.

Ginger pushed the hair from her face and laughed again. Slowed her engine. Took a swallow from a flask as she let us round the pier and approach her boat. "Ready, set, go!" she called out. But she didn't gun her engine. She slowed even more. Trey had to turn sharply to avoid her.

She sped off. Gained several yards before we could correct course again.

"Damn," Trey swore. But something in his voice or his dark eyes or the way his body seemed sprung tight with energy left me sure he thrilled at Ginger's getting the better of him.

He gunned the engine again. The little boat dug into the water.

Ginger's boat swung straight at the darkened shore. The winter-dead land. All those dry reeds that would catch fire from the motor.

She didn't crash. She disappeared. Buzzing forward somewhere in the reeds.

"Damn, you really want to take Boat Scrape Gut, Ginge?" Trey said to himself as he slowed the engine and eased us into the shoreline just where Ginger's boat had disappeared.

The narrow stream we entered wound through cattails standing higher than my head. Creatures rustled from their nests by Ginger's boat stirred in the air.

"Boat Scrape is one of the shallowest of the tide channels that riddle the island," Beau explained. "Ginger is fearless. She's grounded boats a dozen times—she broke her arm once—but it doesn't slow her down."

Behind us the lights from Chawterley disappeared behind the dead reeds. The darkness seemed total. Even the moon was lost behind the clouds rolling in. It was scary dark. Foolish and exhilarating dark. Out in the middle of nowhere in a boat. I could barely see the shadow that was Beau sitting across from me now. How could Trey possibly see to steer?

I reached out toward Beau to steady myself. Touched the damp wool of his sweater. He'd shed the slick polyester vest before we left Chawterley.

"She raced a boat with a broken arm?" I said.

He laughed. A lovely laugh full of the night and the winding slither of the boat in the shallow water. Laughter that left me understanding why Ginger was so fond of him. Why any of us Ms. Bradwells could tell when he telephoned at school from the lift in Ginger's voice.

"Dark enough for you?" he asked.

I leaned forward. Maybe I would just kiss him. That was the champagne and the scotch talking. Of course it was. And the anonymous darkness. It all felt so good. The cool air. The sway of the boat in the moist night. The abandonment.

We might drown out here, unfindable in the dark. A thought that ought to be terrifying but made me feel alive and sexy and wild.

We passed through a tangle of spiderweb. It was all I could do not to spit away the bit of it I was sure was on my lips. I hadn't been with a guy since that London trip with Ben. I hadn't been with a guy before that summer, either. I'd had only the one forbidden entanglement. And that hadn't ended well.

The moon reemerged spotlight-in-the-darkness bright. Only to be blotted out by a flood of flashing light. Beau wiped spiderweb from his sweatered shoulder in the pulse of the lighthouse beacon. It stuck to his fingers. He dipped them into the water outside the boat.

I'd have sworn the lighthouse was in the other direction. I looked right, trying to use the lights of Chawterley to get my bearings. But the only lights were to the left. The direction of town? But we had to be miles from town.

"They went up Johan's Creek," Beau said to Trey.

Trey took a swig from a flask and passed it to Mia. Said he was taking Bald Eagle Cut.

"It was her left arm, the arm Ginger broke, so she could still steer," Beau said to me. "And I swear to God she helped me push the boat out of the mud, and she didn't say a word about the arm hurting. I had no clue until I woke the next morning to my father's voice bellowing about whatever the hell Ginger had done to her arm." He laughed again. "She swore she hadn't been out because of course we weren't supposed to be out running boats in the middle of the night. She claimed she must have fallen out of bed." He shook his head. "Ginger makes anyone but Trey look like a lightweight gut-runner, and even Trey can't keep up at night."

Trey tossed something from his pocket at Beau. It hit off his cheek and fell into the water.

"But it's true and you know it," Beau said to Trey. "The only one who can beat Ginger is Max."

"And we all know Maxie McKee isn't human," Trey said. "His heart doesn't pump any faster in Long Creek than it does when he's sleeping in his sad and lonely little bed."

"Clever angling on your part, to get the three lightest of us, by the way," Beau said. "I bet Ginger is carrying a hundred pounds more than we are. But you still can't beat her. Certainly not at this speed."

I edged backward on the seat. Watched the dark stir of disrupted wildlife. Where was the lighthouse beacon now? Feeling the little confidence I'd taken from the law review billing and the fact that Trey had chosen me over Ginger and Laney shrink into my lack of sex appeal. I didn't weigh much. That was why he'd chosen me. I wouldn't be much of an inconvenience if I straddled the bench and didn't fall overboard.

"You need us to drop weight? I can empty my pockets," I offered with my best you're-supposed-to-laugh-at-this face. Not that anyone could see. "Except . . . Dang! I don't have any pockets!"

Beau laughed. "I could shave my beard, that would save us a few ounces."

"You could jump ship," Trey suggested. "That's, what, a hundred and sixty pounds?"

"And the only PhD in the boat!" I said. "Now *that's* a lot of weight."

Beau stood and made as if to leap from the boat just as we turned sharply left. He fell back on me. Caught his balance by hugging me. His beard soft on my cheek.

"God, I'm sorry," he said. "Are you okay? I'm sorry."

I was fine. Really, I was fine. Hoping he hadn't noticed my heart trying to make a break for it through my chest wall.

I pulled out my best sultry Mae West: "'Too much of a good thing can be wonderful.'"

He paused in his effort to untangle his limbs from mine to say, "I'm not that heavy, actually; I'm not a PhD yet." He sat back, holding the side of the boat. "Ginger tells me you're a pretty heavy type yourself. She says you'll be on the Supreme Court someday."

I gripped the water-soaked wood more tightly as we swayed through the winding channel. "You can't believe everything that girl says."

"Can't you? I find she's pretty perceptive about everyone but herself."

"Herself *and* your mother," Mia said from behind us.

Beau's smile grew wider as he looked at her. A little bit of gum line showed above his top teeth. "About everyone but herself *and Mother*," he agreed. "But Mother isn't any better about Ginger than Ginge is about her."

"And you?" Mia asked.

"I'd say I'm pretty perceptive about them both," Beau said.

Mia pushed his shoulder gently. "I meant about *yourself*."

His gaze lingered on her for a moment. "I can usually recognize what I want," he said.

I looked away to a twinkle of lights ahead of us through a gap in the reeds. The house or the town or something else altogether? A ship out on the bay or even the faraway lights of the mainland shore?

What the hell was it that Mia had that I didn't? Why did the guys I liked always seem to go for her? She wasn't cuter than me. She didn't have a better figure. She wasn't any smarter or any less smart.

Beau, I thought, liked smart women. Like Ben did.

"Look: a bald eagle!" Beau said.

We all turned to see a shadow creature in the air above the reeds. A dark expanse of wings and a lighter head.

"The only sea eagle native to the United States," Beau said. "We get them nesting at this end of the island sometimes, because nobody lives here. They don't much like to live near humans."

"We've woken him," Mia said as the boat picked up speed.

"Probably." Beau's eyes lingering on her again.

Maybe she did things sexually that I didn't? Maybe guys knew this somehow? Maybe the way she held herself or the way she moved or some expression in her eyes let them know she would give them whatever they wanted. She hadn't had sex with anyone but that one guy she'd dated in college and Andy. But here she was engaged to Andy and still flirting with Beau. Or not so much flirting as capturing his attention without seeming to try.

We emerged from the winding marsh stream to see Ginger's boat disappearing into another channel at the other end of a more open marsh. Trey cranked the engine higher and we shot across the reedy water. I wondered how deep it was. How likely we were to run aground. How forcefully I would pitch forward. How much it would hurt when my arm broke against the prow.

"Ginger tells me you're headed to D.C., to clerk for a year," Beau said. To me, of course, because Mia was heading to San Francisco with Andy.

"I'm in Chicago for a few more months," he said, almost shouting now to be heard over the engine. "But I present my dissertation at the end of the summer, and then I'm in D.C., too."

"Doing?" I shouted back too loudly, the adrenaline rush of this faster speed finding release in the single word.

"Working on international development policy with the IMF."

"A lightweight job, I guess," Mia said.

Trey's hand was covering hers on the engine doohickey. Guiding her. Her expression positively gleeful. Like a three-year-old sitting on her father's lap thinking that because her hands are the ones touching the steering wheel she controls the car.

"Beau worked for our uncle there when he was getting his master's," Trey said exactly loud enough to be heard and no louder.

"From the Georgetown Public Policy Institute," Beau said.

"And you're at University of Chicago now?" Mia said. "I thought everyone in Chicago's economics program washed out."

Beau's round shoulders rose toward his shaggy-adorable face.

"You know," Trey said, "this is a really weird conversation to be having while racing around like lunatic adolescents in little boats in the middle of the night."

"You know, we're pretty weird girls," I said.

"Speak for yourself," Mia said.

She was just being flip. Still I was left wanting to point out that the hand Trey was touching was the one with her engagement ring.

"This is racing?" Beau said.

Trey's hand remained over Mia's as he opened up the throttle. We sped into a relatively straight channel through the reeds, spray dampening my face in the darkness, the conversation giving way to engine noise. The lighthouse was behind us now. I could see what I was pretty sure were the lights of Chawterley in front of it to the left. We could see Ginger's boat again, too. Not far ahead.

When we slowed to take another winding passage, Beau said, "I get that, too, that I'm a weird guy. Mostly from girls who don't understand that I can't take them to dinner and a movie when I have to work."

"Like Tessie McKee?" Mia said.

Trey laughed. "Don't you girls go believing anything Ginger tells you about Tessie McKee. That girl is a lunatic."

"And your version is . . . ?" Mia prodded. Pretty gutsy since we'd never heard Ginger's version of the story despite what they thought.

His hand nudged hers just a touch to the left to follow a tighter bend in the water. "We're only here for summers; what do we know? But the rumor was she slept with half the—"

"Tess was a nice girl," Beau insisted.

Trey tapped Mia's hand away and took over the steering. Ginger's boat had appeared up ahead. "Okay, here we go," he said.

"She had a scholarship to Vassar," Beau said.

"She was smart enough," Trey conceded, "but she was just a slutty little island girl. I bet half the boys on the island had her right here in her brother's boat."

He gunned the engine to bring us around the next bend. Right up behind Ginger. Everyone trash-talked each other across the water as we tried again and again to pass. The two boats nearly plowed into each other more than once. But Trey always gave way when Ginger stood her ground. In the excitement of that, the shock of Trey's answer, "she was just a slutty little island girl," was left behind. But it was the same answer Ginger gave us the next day. "Tessie McKee?" she said. "Who brought her up again? Trey? Shit. He needs to leave Beau alone about Tessie McKee. She's just a slutty little island girl everyone seems to think popped Beau's cherry. So maybe she did. I mean, she screwed just about every guy on the island that summer. And she was too shitbrained to use birth control. Or that was the rumor, anyway, that she got preggers. I heard she screwed two guys at once, like at the same time in the same bed. So if she really was preggers—and how should we know? we were never here except for the summers—the father could have been anyone."

Laney

≈≈≈

IT'S PLENTY EARLY, the thick red of sunrise glowing out the window, and I'm too old to be staying up with the hoot owls like we did last night. I feel it in my creaking joints. But Mia's bed is already empty, the spread neatly in place, the pillow fluffed. So I dig a pair of trousers and a sweater from my suitcase. I don't bother with panties or a brassiere or stockings. If I find myself dead in a car crash between here and the kitchen coffeepot, Mama will toss in her grave.

In the mirror over the dresser, the easy curls that looked back at me as I climbed into my pjs last night are flapjack flat in places, wild in others. I'm ugly as a mud fence this morning, no doubt about that. But it's only the Ms. Bradwells here, and they all saw me that night Carl telephoned to tell me he'd proposed to that medical student of his I thought was just a fling. I was ugly as a whole village of mud fences back then, for weeks and weeks.

I get as far as the landing overlooking the back foyer before I see Mia outside, sitting where the path steps down toward the pier. With a fella? The two of them are looking awfully comfortable together on that step, and most everyone Mia is cozy with these days is a reporter. I'm not offering up bed hair for some tree frog to write about in the morning papers. No thank you, ma'am.

I map out a plan: a one-minute shower and a little hair gel—I've come a long way from the hours I used to spend wielding a straightening iron—and thirty seconds with the toothbrush. I stand there staring down at Mia and the fella, thinking *screw it*. But my campaign manager will kill me if I let a journalist catch me with bed hair.

Through the open door I can just make out Mia saying something about Madagascar. The fella seems more interested than I would be, or considerably more polite. He sets something that was under his arm on the walkway beside him: a newspaper.

My smeller registers coffee, which I need even more sorely than I need to see what that newspaper says. But I just stand there unmoving, like the absolute fool I am.

"We stole your skiff," I hear Mia say, and I look to the pier, where a little boat is tied up next to the *Row v. Wade*. Now that's an idea. I'm playing it forward: we steal the boats the reporters arrive in so they're stuck here with no cellphone reception. But it isn't like there aren't landlines in town.

"Last night?" the fella says.

"*Thirty years ago*, Max," Mia says. "We went . . . gut-running, that's what it's called, right? A group of us. Too many for one boat."

Max. Ginger's friend who'd dropped whatever he was doing to bring the *Row v. Wade* across the bay. The reason we're not already chin-deep in press-wielded microphones, or starving half to death.

"You couldn't invite me along?" he asks with a playfulness in his voice only Mia could miss.

"You were away at school, I think."

"Ah. Well, I didn't need my skiff then, did I?"

I finger my unruly curls, run a tongue over my teeth, wait for Mia to spill all our collective guts to this fella she doesn't even know, like I surely want to do. I just want to get it out and be done with it.

"Did you have fun without me?" Max asks, still with the flirt in his voice. The fella is pretty shameless for a vegetarian man with children.

"We did, actually," Mia says.

I ponder this. Did we? Mia was in the other boat that night, but she's right: we had a fine time chasing each other through all those winding streams.

"I'd be happy to take you myself sometime," Max is offering when I hear feet shifting or someone breathing below me, or both.

Ginger peers up from the first floor, a steaming mug of coffee in hand. She's wearing eyeglasses like she used to on the hardest mornings in law school; it's too early for contact lenses. "Love blossoms," she whispers with a finger to her wide mouth.

I creep down the stairs to join her, and she thrusts her coffee into my hands. "Drink this, will you? I gulped down a whole second cup to have an excuse to leave them alone. If I have a third cup I'll be on such a high buzz you'll have to peel me from the balcony rails."

"I thought he was married."

"Divorced."

"You told Mia that?"

This isn't the first time Ginger has done something like this: introduced Mia to a divorced fella and then talked about his kids, leaving us all the impression he's still married. She always says afterwards, when Mia is halfway around the world again, that she doesn't know why Mia never likes the men she introduces her to. But there is no shortage of men in Mia's life, so I do what I so often do with Ginger: I let it go. If I call her on it, she'll only claim to have no notion whatsoever what I could be talking about. And it's possible that she really doesn't. Ginger never has been any better at understanding herself than she is at sharing her friends.

The coffee is black, and I'm milk and sugar, but I take a sip anyway, and we stand observing them. The conversation has faltered; neither seems to know what to say next. I hesitate, thinking I should shower and dress properly for when the press *do* show, which they will, likely this morning. But what does it matter?

"To the rescue?" I whisper.

Ginger pushes out the door as if it's her idea to help keep them talking. I can't but wonder what she would do if I weren't here. Would she sit and watch Mia and Max run out of conversation? Would she watch them part ways and then say, a month from now, that she doesn't understand why Mia didn't like her friend Max? But I am here, and she's fixin' to join them, calling out, "No sign of the press yet?"

"NO SIGN OF Andy yet?" Ginger had whispered as I'd slipped into her bedroom in our Law Quad suite to tell her to hurry, her date to the Crease Ball was knocking on our door. It was our first year, the year Ginger and I enjoyed a lucky stumble into rooming together in a two-bedroom suite with a fireplace and bay windows overlooking the Quad. Ginger had finagled a change in room assignments, giving up the single room with fireplace she may well have been given because her great-great-granddaddy or granduncle or whoever it was built the Law Quad. *Fidus Achates.*

Betts and I were attending that dance with classmates who had girls back home. Betts wasn't even particularly attracted to her date, but the fella I was going with, André, was an All-American football player who was both the nicest fella in the whole law school and also the studliest. Serious about his girl back home, though. And I was still in love with Carl in those days, or I thought we were in love.

Mia, though, was going on a first date with Andy, an evening engineered by Ginger that was to start with wine by the fire in our suite, the four of us and our dates. Ginger had left a Crease Ball invitation in Andy's mailbox, a silly thing made to look like a legal summons, "The Crease Court in and for the County of Nocturnal Enjoyment, State of Rapture" at its top in fancy script. She'd penned "Mia Porter" on the "in re" line and, for good measure, written N-32, Mia's and Betts's room, on the "docket number" blank, in the event there might be some other Mia Porter Andy might know. She left the "complainant" line blank, though, so he'd think Mia was inviting him to ask her, rather than being so bold as to ask him. The only hint Ginger gave of her own involvement in this little deception was the name she'd filled in on the "clerk" line: Justice Joseph P. Bradley, the justice in *Bradwell v. Illinois* who wrote the bit about the mission of woman being to fulfill the noble and benign offices of wife and mother rather than arguing the law. Mia would never in a month of Sundays have asked Andy out herself. Despite all our conversations about wanting our relationships to be something different from what our parents had, we were pretty well stuck waiting for the phone to ring the same way our mamas had.

Ginger mushed her lips together to spread her lipstick, checked for color on her teeth, pulled her dress from the hanger, and slid it over her head. "Am I rubbed?" she asked. She slipped her bare feet into strappy sandals and stuck dangly rhinestone earrings into her ears, having lent her pretty black pearls to Mia that night. I'm not sure Ginger ever wore those pearls herself, she was always so busy loaning them out.

I smudged the line at the side of her face where her blush wasn't quite blended. "You look way better than this toad deserves," I said, "and you've already kissed him, so you know he won't turn prince." I'd suggested she go for Andy herself, but bad as Ginger was at sharing friends, she was loyal to the ones she wouldn't share. If one of us Ms. Bradwells expressed interest in a fella, he was moved to the "just friends" column for her.

Ginger's date to the Crease Ball was another in a long string of Ginger's bad choices: a string that had started with a fella who'd graduated from Michigan just before we'd started, who'd stayed in Ann Arbor to study for the New York bar with friends. Ginger had gone to see him in New York twice that fall, both times on fly-backs for interviews with firms, and it looked like the romance was lasting through the separation. But he never did respond to the messages she left before she flew out the third time, and when she showed up at his door, he was entertaining—at 8:30 on a Saturday morning, in boxers and a T-shirt, so it wasn't like Ginger could pretend that was anything other than what it was. She'd fallen back on pretending she didn't care, and she went through a whole mess of overnight gentlemen guests that winter before Steven's brother, a second-year, asked her to the Crease Ball. When it comes to men, Ginger doesn't have the sense God gave a goose.

Did Ginger's good luck pearls work well for Mia and Andy? Let's just say Betts returned to her room to find them hung over the doorknob more discreetly than Andy's tie would have been. André and I were ready to call it a night by then anyway, so Betts and I shared the last of the wine back in Ginger's and my sitting room, where the embers had long since gone cold, and she settled in on our sofa. And if it was a little awkward when Ginger's date woke Betts with that awful fluorescent overhead as he left at four in the morning, well, he didn't seem to much mind. That toad would have laughed for days about finding Betts on that couch—so he could advertise that he'd taken his big brother's place in Ginger's bed without saying so—except that Ginger, to her credit, dumped him before noon that same day, saving herself the humiliation of his dumping her now that she'd slept with him.

FAITH, IN ANN ARBOR on business the next night, fetched us all for dinner at the nicest place in town. She showed up precisely when she told Ginger she would, talking about how nice it was that spring had finally arrived, polite conversation that seemed to irritate Ginger, never mind that Faith seemed more interested in making us feel welcome than in talking about herself. Even the things she said about herself at that dinner were in the context of Betts's admitting her hope to clerk for the Supreme Court. No women were Supreme Court clerks back in Faith's day, she told us. Yes, Lucile Lomen had clerked for Justice Douglas in 1944, but there wasn't a second female Supreme Court clerk until 1966.

"Connections and timing," she said. "Lucile Lomen's story is a lesson in the importance of connections and timing. Ms. Lomen graduated from Whitman College, so I suppose you can guess who else was a Whitman alum? And how many qualified gentlemen law students do you suppose were applying for Supreme Court clerkships when there was a war to be won?

"Connections and timing," she said. "You girls are going to have both."

I felt so approved of during that dinner, basking in Faith's certainty that we would all have lives even more interesting than hers. But the moment we'd climbed from the car and she'd driven off to her hotel, Ginger said, "'You can sure tell it's spring, can't you?'" in a voice mocking Faith. "She's such a bitch, criticizing how white my legs are like that."

Her legs? Mia mouthed to me behind Ginger's back.

"She's always criticizing me," Ginger said.

We all looked down at our legs in the glow of the streetlight: Betts's and Mia's intemperate shades of hosiery tan, mine dark, and Ginger's, it was true, nearly albino white.

"Your mama doesn't *expect* us all to be appointed to the Supreme Court, Ginger," I said finally. "She was just saying some gals of our generation have a real possibility of important court appointments and partnerships in firms that have been historically male."

"Yes, well, you're not her daughter," Ginger said.

AT THE SOUND of Ginger's voice calling out "No sign of the press yet?" and the Chawterley back door banging shut behind us, Mia and Max crane around to have a look at us. Max picks up the newspaper, and Ginger plops down on the hard, hackberry-splattered stone next to him without a thought of the stains she'll get on her khaki slacks. Her mama's khaki slacks.

I eye the gooey step, my back to Chawterley, the water of the Chesapeake stretched out before me as far as I can see.

Ginger bumps her shoulder against Max's, a suggestion that he should move on over a little to give us more room. He closes the gap between Mia and him which is, I expect, what Ginger has in mind. It strikes me that Ginger *did* get Mia and Andy together, that maybe the failure of their marriage has something to do with the way Ginger introduces Mia to fellas now.

The stone is cold on my feet. I, too, am barefooted this morning. My feet look veiny and callused. My nails would benefit from a pedicure, but where would I find time to sit still long enough for that? I campaign in conservative, closed-toed pumps that will offend no one. How my feet look is not a priority.

Max is the freshest of us this morning. He's still in baggy-kneed jeans but his shirt has been visited by an iron, and a small nick at one of his smile lines suggests scraps of toilet paper staunching bleeding, like William taught Willie J and Manny to do, and will teach Joey soon enough. It might be Max has even exercised already this morning, although he doesn't much look like the exercising sort. On the whole he looks surprisingly dapper, even in eyeglasses that are goofier than Ginger's without seeming very different.

Cleans up nicely, I decide, although the ironed shirt makes me think *married.*

Ginger said divorced, though. *A fella who irons.*

"Go ahead and show it to her," Ginger says to Max, and she nods her head sideways at me. She curls her red-nailed toes. "If we had one bar of cellphone reception out here, her campaign manager would already be screaming at her."

"Wasn't sure whether I should bring it," he says, "but nothing much is ever achieved by sticking your head in the sand. Or in the marsh grasses here, I s'pose it'd be." He hands the folded newspaper across Ginger to me.

The secretary of state smiles above the fold as she shakes hands with the Australian prime minister, a familiar face I can't put a name to for my life. The good voters of the Georgia 42nd don't much care about U.S. relations with Australia; they care about jobs and health care, poverty, and drugs on our streets.

"Everybody on this island knows this is nonsense," Max says.

I open the newspaper to the full front page and there it is: QUESTIONS RAISED ABOUT SUPREME COURT NOMINEE'S PAST. In the photograph, a bare-necked Betts stands between that Jonathan adviser fella and Mia at the Hart Building door.

No photo of me, I see, feeling the flush of shame at being so self-absorbed, but also relief. I wonder where the pearls are, Ginger's black pearls that Betts took off.

WASHINGTON, D.C.—Questions were raised about a death that occurred at an isolated summer home on the Chesapeake Bay when Supreme Court nominee Elsbieta Zhukovski was visiting thirty years ago, drawing uncertainty into a Court appointment that, until late in yesterday's confirmation hearing, was expected to be uneventful and swift . . .

I skim the text: no mention of me. Again, a selfish thought, but there it is. The article details only the indisputable truth (this *is* the *Post*):

David Charles Humphrey III died in 1982 of a gunshot wound in an incident believed at the time to have been the result of an accidental discharge of his own hunting gun. His family confirmed the day after the death that Mr. Humphrey had been hunting, and shotgun cleaning rods and solvent were found on a table beside the body. The deceased, a highly regarded new partner at the prestigious law firm of Tyler & McCoy at the time, was said to have been in good spirits, giving no reason to suspect suicide.

In good spirits, that much was surely true: spirits as in Trey's preferred brand of scotch. No one had said a thing about Trey's drinking after his death, though; Faith never did mind drawing attention to herself in the name of a good cause, but she wasn't one to air dirty family laundry in public.

It was a 12-gauge shotgun. Faith had pointed that fact out: her nephew Trey shot himself with the same sort of gun Ernest Hemingway had used. He'd fancied himself a Hemingway type even if he was a lawyer, even if he was only hunting ducks rather than big game.

Humphrey was experienced with guns, but no suggestion that the death might have been other than accidental was raised at the time.

A representative for the senator released a statement confirming that the question had been raised to him as the result of a post on WOWD: Washing Out Washington's Dirt.

I skim through a short list of people who have denied authorship of the anonymous blog: the chief of staff for a New York congressman, a prominent Washington hostess, the White House press secretary, of all people. I flip to the continuation of the article on page eight, and there it is: a second photograph, the four of us escaping on the boat. Our backs are to the camera, but the caption below the photo identifies me as Helen Robeson-Weils and, just in case there might be another Helen Robeson-Weils around somewhere, describes me as the Democratic state senate nominee for the Georgia 42nd. It leaves no room for doubt that I am the second woman from the right, standing over the "Wade" in the fancy blue *Row v. Wade,* which is easily readable in the photograph. My conservative Republican opponent will have a field day with that.

This will cost me the election, just when my children are old enough that I'll finally have time to do things properly rather than forever sticking my skinny fingers in leaky dikes. It won't take the Georgia papers any time to find that I, too, was at Chawterley when Trey died, that if his death was suspicious they ought to suspect me even before they suspect Betts.

I still have William, though; I still have Joey at home and Willie J and Manny and Gem not so far away, and I'm not even entirely sure how much I *want* to win this election, how much it's something I'm doing for Mama, something I've found the courage to reach for not on my own but because of Maynard's and Faith's confidence in me. What this mess means to me is nothing compared to what it means for Betts. Her Isabelle graduates from Yale Law School this spring, and hasn't lived at home in years. And a Supreme Court appointment is something Betts has been working for since about the beginning of time.

"Betts hasn't seen this yet?" I ask.

"The blog doesn't even mention Cook Island," Mia says. "It just talks about him being shot at the Conrad summer home."

I take a look back at the article. Did I miss that part?

"It doesn't?" Ginger says, and Mia, too, looks surprisingly surprised given that she's the one who said it.

"'The Conrad summer home in Maryland,'" Max confirms.

Mia says, "If we all hadn't lived together in law school, I doubt anyone would have connected it with Betts. Ms. Drug-Lord-Bradwell is still sleeping. I vote we let her sleep."

"All the long day," I agree.

"All weekend," Mia says.

"All year," Ginger says. "Shit."

I sit beside Ginger, staring out at the endless waters of the Chesapeake, wanting to say the words aloud: This is my fault. Y'all need to quit trying to protect me. It's time for me to step up and own the truth. We were all in the wrong place at the wrong time, it's true. But we did the wrong thing. *I* did the wrong thing. And here it is now. *Ira dei.* God visiting his wrath down on us all because of my sin.

GINGER

~~~~~~~~

THE TOP OF Max's arm is warm against mine as I lean into him. How many times did the two of us sit on these hard stone steps together, trying to make sense of all the things kids have to sort out on their way to growing up? *Doing all the little tricky things it takes to grow up, step by step, into an anxious and unsettling world.* I ask him how his kids are doing, and as he answers Laney glares. She wants me to tell Mia that Max is divorced, but what I say is, "Your son must get the science thing from his mom."

You hoard your friends, Laney is forever telling me. *You stick friendship in your pocket like a lone dollar bill that, if lost or given away or even spent on something precious, will leave you without.* She thinks friendships multiply when shared, and maybe they do for her. It doesn't occur to her that the wreck that will result if Mia gets involved with Max will take out my friendship with him, too.

The four of us stare out across the water, clear sailing and a clear view of the house for any damned reporter in a boat. Is that something on the horizon? I squint into the early sun. Wipe my glasses on Max's shirt (which provokes a halfhearted protest from him) and then squint again. It's not the ferry; that only runs in summer. I push back the sudden hope it's the girls. But Annie and Iz aren't coming; we told them not to. Any minute now the phone is going to ring, Annie saying she got my message.

But they can't call. Shit. They can't call.

Well, they don't likely even know what's happened yet. Betts's Isabelle is so absorbed in her studies and in the work she does at the legal aid clinic that she probably has no clue, and surely Annie wouldn't have watched the news on a Friday night.

I really *don't* want Annie to come all this way, even though I would give anything to see her. It's her first term at Princeton, and she has enough of a challenge to start with at college since she can't write any better than I can. Dysgraphia, they call it now, which I guess is a good thing, that they have something to call it, although God knows we worried about labeling her anything other than perfect. Annie tests as well anyone when it comes to filling in circles with a number two pencil, but the process of having to write out answers hits a glitch in her brain. She's smart enough to make up for it, and if her teachers think (as mine always did) that she is just being lazy rather than efficient when she writes the shortest complete answer possible, we can point to the report in her file which they *ought* to have read: thousands of dollars of doctor and occupational therapist time to conclude that Annie has "a processing difficulty." Which means she can't write worth shit.

I check my watch, worried she'll see the news on the Internet before she listens to her phone messages. But when has she ever cared more about the news than about friends? She'll have gotten my message and called me, and when she couldn't get me she'll have phoned Ted, who no doubt explained this to her the same way I explained it to him when we talked from the car: "Was it awful? Yes, absolutely. But there was no question: it was an accident."

Annie has been at Princeton since early September. Ted and I came home from getting her settled and, for the first time in twenty years, sat at the dinner table without a child. We took our usual seats, Ted at the deep gouge where B.J.'s robotics team powered up their robot only to have it topple over rather than roll, me at the sprinkle of pits where Annie's catapult for AP Physics took out the light fixture, scattering tiny lightbulb shards we picked from the table and chairs and floor for weeks. We sat kitty-corner from each other, facing empty chairs.

I'd been sitting next to B.J.'s empty seat for two years by then, but it's one thing to sit next to emptiness, and another to stare straight into it. I wanted to slide over into our son's seat, but I couldn't bear to do it. Then Ted slid over into Annie's seat and reached across the table and took my hand. And the next night, just before dinner was ready, he turned on *PBS NewsHour* and professed an interest in a story about the Taliban throwing acid on girls walking to school (a story Mia covered but that Ted never in a million years would have found interesting). We took our plates into the family room and settled into our club chairs, facing the TV.

It's not always an easy dinner, watching the *NewsHour*. Even the best homemade pasta doesn't go down that well with, say, children being pulled from earthquake rubble, or African mothers brushing flies from their children's faces, willing to do anything for food. It's always the mothers, too. These children must have fathers, but it's always the mothers shown on the news.

That's what I'd seen, mothers on the news, the night before Annie's eighteenth birthday, which is maybe why after Ted and I went to bed that night I lay awake wondering if she was as lonely as I had been the night before I started law school, the eve of my twenty-first birthday. Sometime before midnight, I got out of bed and pulled on the first clothes I came to. I popped in my contacts in the downstairs bathroom so as not to wake Ted, filled a thermos with coffee, left a note that I'd woken early and gone to the gym, and drove east from Cleveland across the endless stretch of Pennsylvania Turnpike and up U.S. 1 to Washington Road.

It was nearly dawn by the time I got to Henry Hall, a gothic stone building that had looked lovely the sunny afternoon Ted and I moved Annie into her dorm room—a single that was stark and cold even with its view of other pretty gothic buildings through leaded windows, even with her bedding and books and the WELL-BEHAVED WOMEN RARELY MAKE HISTORY poster from her bedroom at home. Rain was threatening as I pulled to a stop across the street and sat looking up at windows I knew weren't Annie's (her window doesn't face the street), remembering the way Mother had shown up at my door in Ann Arbor the morning of my birthday, after we'd said goodbye. I sat watching Annie's dorm in the darkness until I must have drifted off to sleep, because the next thing I knew the sky was a paler shade of gray and a rusty bicycle came so close to nearly clipping a girl right in front of me that I shouted, *Look up, for heaven's sake, Annie!* although the girl wasn't even blond.

Annie emerged from the dorm, finally, wearing her favorite leather jacket. No umbrella in evidence and, God, she looked unbearably thin. How could she have grown so thin in only two weeks? She walked with her too-long neck bent forward as if to shorten her gawky six feet. *Most near, most dear, most loved and most far.*

I rolled down my car window, wanting to shout *It's her birthday!* to the nearby students: a couple kissing far too passionately for this early in the morning, a group of girls giggling together, four boys singing in harmony as they walked in synchronized step down the puddled path. But I said nothing. After she disappeared into a nearby building, I sat watching through the open window, willing her to emerge laughing with a classmate about the red bow tie the professor wore or the way the nerdy guy from Arizona wouldn't stop hitting on her.

When she did emerge, she was alone again. She looked in my direction, as if sensing she was being watched. I thought to wave, but she turned and looked in another direction, then another, before ducking her head toward the pavement and following the path toward the heavy dormitory again. An old gray Chevy passed between us, its wipers pushing aside the drizzle as Annie mounted the old stone steps, heaved the door open, stepped inside. And then I sat watching the empty space she left behind.

I thought to go around to where I could see her window, but somehow I could no more move that morning than I could that first kidless dinner. I sat and watched the dorm for another hour as the rain came harder on my windshield, not a thunderstorm but just a long, steady rain, the kind that would likely fall all day.

It's her birthday, I kept thinking. *Her eighteenth birthday.*

I pulled my cellphone out, finally, and I dialed her number and sang "Happy Birthday" when she answered. I wanted to ask if she was eating well, if she was taking her vitamins, if she was making friends and who she ate dinner with when the dorm cafeteria was closed, who she ate lunch with every day for that matter, or if she ate lunch at all, if she wasn't too shy to sit at a table with strangers, if it had gotten harder rather than easier as the days passed. But I only asked if she'd gotten the package we'd sent.

She was waiting till after dinner to open it, she told me. She didn't yet know that it was an apple-shaped pendant encrusted with diamond chips, with a card saying she was the apple of our eyes and we hoped she'd always know how much we love her.

"We can't wait to see you at parents' weekend," I said.

"Me, too."

"I can come sooner. Do you want me to come sooner?" Not wanting to say the word "lonely," a word I realized only in that moment had hung over me long into that first year of law school, even after I'd met Laney and Betts and Mia, after we'd become the Ms. Bradwells I wanted us to be.

When Annie didn't answer, I thought of how hard it had been to say goodbye to Mother that second time, that morning after I thought I'd already said goodbye. How close I'd come to asking to go home with her.

Annie and I talked for a long, long time that morning, with me just outside her window and Annie imagining me pouring a third cup of coffee in the kitchen back in Cleveland five hundred miles away. We talked about her classes and the cafeteria food and the girls on her hall, the friends she had not yet made although she pretended she had. Then we said goodbye, and I listened to the click of her phone closing, her letting go of me. I turned the key in the ignition, and I turned the wipers on and I watched them push the raindrops from the windshield until the rain began to let up a little, and I headed back home.

I LEAN AWAY from the touch of Max's arm against mine, toward Laney, toward the comforting feel of her sweatered shoulder, remembering Mother's words that first morning I woke in Ann Arbor: A new day, a new year, a new life. An opportunity to leave the past behind. The *sordid* past? Had Mother actually used that word, or had I heard it in her don't-fuck-up-again tone? I wonder for perhaps the first time if it was hard for Mother to leave me at law school, if she worried about how I'd manage, whether I'd be lonely, whether I'd make friends.

Lonely. The word hangs over me now more than ever, with my children gone and nothing else in my life, really, with my days reduced to rattling around the empty house every morning after Ted goes to work. I have no office to go off to, which maybe *is* my "choice," maybe Ted is right about that. Maybe I could have gotten another job in the law when I didn't make partner at Caruthers. But if I couldn't be at the top of the legal world—or what I thought was the top—I didn't want to be in it at all. It's the same way with my poems: when *The New Yorker* and *The Atlantic* and *Poetry* reject them, I should submit to less prestigious magazines, but I never do. It's the way I am, I do see that. If I can't be the best, I don't want to be anything. I keep my failure to myself.

I have friends, of course: Trish from my spin class, my book club, our Saturday night dinner gang. But they aren't the Ms. Bradwells. They have no more idea than Ted does how I've longed for this weekend, and yet how I've dreaded, too, being with these friends who have within their reach the dreams I'll never achieve.

Lonely. I feel it worse here at Mother's empty house, even with Laney's arm warm against mine, with Max beside me and Mia on the other side of him. Was Mother ever lonely like this? Behind the frantic activism she lived and breathed for all the world to see, did she ever feel anyone knew her? Did she ever wonder if the person she'd grown up to be was the person she meant to become?

Betts

～～

I EMERGE FROM a dream under unfamiliar covers. It's about the eight thousandth time I've woken since turning in last night. Each time to a forlorn silence. No low bass note of a garbage truck dumper. No *ding-ding-ding*-striking-triangle bell as the truck moves backward. No car wheels on wet pavement. No airplanes. No voices passing on the walk outside. Just the devastation that I will soon be an ex–Supreme Court nominee.

Can Laney and Mia and Ginge really want me to stick with the story after all this time? Can they really want me to be appointed to the Court with this untruth swamping us? But the one truth that I'm sure of, the truth of the rape, isn't mine to tell. And my other "truth," the one about Trey's death, isn't really truth at all.

Why should I imagine I know more than anyone else? Something I pieced together from nothing, really. Just from something Ginger said that might not even *be* fact, it might be Ginger claiming things for reasons she alone could understand. And from that conversation with Faith, something that looked like one thing at the time coming into better focus in retrospect.

I turn to see the time. The small clock on the marble-topped nightstand is a windup that has wound down in the months Chawterley has sat waiting for whatever future it will have in the wake of Faith's death.

Were mornings here this quiet that spring break? Was it as hushed as this in the Captain's Library when I went to Faith the morning after the rape? Papers scattered all over the huge expanse of green leather inset that was the desktop. Faith looking up over her tortoiseshell reading glasses. Her eyes flashing annoyance at the interruption before she raised one index finger. The eternal wait as she scratched with an eraserless yellow Ticonderoga. The empty metal eraser-holder bitten flat. Not once as I stood there did the pencil go to her mouth.

I had this idea of Faith back then that was formed from things I'd read. That article in *The New York Times* that Laney (the only dedicated newspaper reader among us) had pointed out: Faith quoted in connection with congressional hearings praising the White House Office of Personnel's directive prohibiting sexual harassment. I'd have traded my own toilet-scrubbing-ex-doctor mom for Ginger's quote-giving one in an instant before that Saturday in the Captain's Library. And even after. Yes, after, too, I still might have traded Matka in for Faith.

The two stories of floor-to-ceiling books loomed darkly around me. The nonstop shelving was relieved only by a few windows, a large fireplace, and two narrow, railed walkways circling above me to allow the books to be reached. As I waited I started to see why Ginger balked at going to her mother with this thing. I stared down at the swirl of Oriental carpet. Glanced up occasionally to see Faith still writing. Had what I'd taken as a *just-one-second* gesture really meant *Don't you dare interrupt*?

Standing there deciding I couldn't possibly tell this cold fish anything. Trying to decide whether to apologize for bothering her and excuse myself or just slip out without another word. Then Faith set her pencil down and took off her reading glasses. One arm as chewed as the pencil.

"What is it, Betts?" she asked. Not unkindly or impatiently. Then with concerned alarm in her voice, "What's wrong?"

Her eyes pooled as I told her. As I stood on the thin layer of stiff carpet and dumped the burden at her feet. She listened intently. Spoke only when I'd finished. "Good Lord." But without shock or judgment or even that much surprise.

"Was it you, Betts?" Spoken even more gently. "Is that what you're trying to say, that he did this to you?"

I didn't trust my voice.

Faith sighed. Rubbed at her forehead. "You're sure it was Trey?"

I nodded, trying to make sense of her reaction. No suggestion that Trey would never do this. Just the question whether I was sure.

"Trey and who?" she asked. "You have to tell me, Betts. I can't help if I don't know the facts."

I managed to say, "She doesn't want anyone to know."

Faith dipped her head. Ran both hands through her hair and then left them there. "One of you? Not an island girl? One of you." She traced the join where the leather inset met the wood of the desktop. "She's okay?"

She looked up, then. The intensity in her green eyes startled me. Evoked Trey's darker eyes.

"Physically, I mean?" she asked.

"Bruises, but . . ."

"She needs to see a doctor. This is when we need a doctor in the family."

"She doesn't want to see a doctor." Thinking Matka was a doctor and that hadn't helped anything.

"Does she want to go home?"

"I don't think she wants her parents to know. I don't think she can bear for her parents to know."

Faith studied me for a long moment. "And there's no question that it was . . . Did she say no? Did she say no and *mean* it?"

I wanted to turn away from her. To run for the locker room the way I always had when I dove poorly. Head to a stall in the john where no one would see the tears of frustration I never could hold back. I couldn't let myself, though. I couldn't risk the possibility that Faith would take averted eyes as a sign that I wasn't sure.

"It wasn't *voluntary*." The word bitter. The tears spilling. If Faith could think Laney had wanted to have sex with Trey, it would be assumed by everyone else.

"I don't like it any more than you do, Betts, but it's a question that has to be asked, that will be asked by the police and by the press and by a jury, if it comes to that. Which it won't, probably. It's a total crock, I know, but even rapes that *are* reported—only one in ten to start with—rarely *get* to a jury. And so few of the ones that do ever result in convictions." She shook her head. "Christ, it doesn't even matter if she said no, no one was there to hear it. And the defense would just trot out that damned Schul-hofer survey that forty percent of girls admit to saying no when they mean yes. They don't want to seem promiscuous, for God's sake. They don't want to seem *promiscuous*? God knows men never worry about that.

"The defense will just say sure they had sex but it was consensual. Every two minutes a girl is raped and eighty-five percent of them know the rapist, and it never gets to court."

I don't know what I'd expected her to suggest that we Ms. Bradwells hadn't already decided together: that rape victims couldn't win, that if we wanted to be taken seriously as a lawyers we had to just bury this.

"What *aren't* you telling me, Betts?" Again in the gentle voice. "You've come to me. You were right to come to me. But now that you have, you may as well tell me everything."

When I hesitated, she said, "Ginger?"

Matka, too, had assumed Ginger was the bad girl among us. She'd thought Ginger needed an abortion when it was me. But *my* mother had assumed it *wasn't* me. Matka had assumed it was someone else.

"But it has to do with Ginger?" Faith said. "It has something to do with Ginger?"

My bare feet on the carpet looked pale and insubstantial. I wished I'd worn shoes.

"Ginger and Trey?" she said with a caution in her voice that made me nervous. That made it clear she didn't know. I realized then that I'd hoped she would know. That I'd come to her hoping she would know enough already. That I wouldn't have to explain. But how could she have known her daughter was sleeping with her too-old-for-her cousin and just let it be?

"Lord." She fingered the pencil. Distractedly picked it up. Worried it until she snapped it in two. The crack startled her even more than me.

"For God's sake, sit *down*, Betts."

I glanced to the door.

"We're talking about your clerkship with Ruth," she said more gently. "If anyone comes in, you're telling me about that."

She set the two halves of the broken Ticonderoga on the desktop. I sat in the leather chair across the desk from her.

"For how long?" she asked. She stood and turned to the bookshelf the same way Ginger had in Faith's Library last night when she hadn't wanted us to see her face. She ran a hand along the small vertical seam where the bookshelf hid the door into the ballroom. Then in a measured voice, saying it so I couldn't deny it, or maybe so I would: "How long has Ginger been sleeping with Trey?"

She came and sat in the chair next to mine. "You can tell me this in confidence, Betts," she said. "Ginger won't ever know that I know, much less that you're the one who told me."

My hands in my lap dry and useless.

"You must know by now how terribly Ginger blunders with men," she said.

I licked my lips. Continued to stare at my hands. *Ginger blunders with men.* Matka would have called them "boys." How bizarre it must be to have a mother who isn't appalled that her daughter has sex.

She took my chin in her hands and turned my face to hers. "A year?" she asked.

The press of her fingers on my chin.

"Less?" she said.

I blinked. Blinked again.

"Longer." She sank back into the chair. "How much longer, Betts? Since she was . . ." She cleared her throat, said weakly, "Seventeen?"

I looked down, shocked at her quick leap from an affair that might have lasted only a few weeks to one that had lasted years. She took it as a gesture with meaning.

"Sixteen?" she said with more doubt. She stared at me without seeming to see me. As if she might be trying to remember this thing she hadn't known. As if she would see in retrospect something she'd missed at the time.

"That summer that…" She blinked, her dark green eyes uncharacteristically uncertain. "Jesus, she was *thirteen* that summer."

She stood. Went to the bookshelves. Pulled the hidden door open, whispering to herself, "She was thirteen years old, she was a *child*," as she disappeared into the ballroom.

Thirteen. Ginger hadn't said that the night before. But Mia and I had done the math. Ginger was thirteen the summer she lost her virginity to Trey Humphrey. And Trey was twenty. Ginger hadn't seemed at all troubled by that, though. She continued to have sex with him again and again over the years. She had sex with him the night the guys arrived, when she and Trey went off to "borrow" a second skiff so we could all go gutrunning.

Faith reappeared a few minutes later with a full glass of bourbon in her hand. No ice. She took the seat next to me again. Studied me. Took a sip of the drink. She stared into the glass for a moment before starting the inquisition: Where had the rape occurred? At what time? That late? ("Shit," she said, the way Ginger would have, but it startled me to hear her use the word.) Had she gone with Trey voluntarily? Had she and Trey had sexual contact before? What about flirting? And did the girl have a sexual history?

Girl. Even with Faith, males were men and females were girls. Or was she still thinking of her daughter, who had been only thirteen?

"She had a boyfriend in college," I said. "But I don't think she's . . . you know . . . with anyone else."

"Not something less than sexual intercourse. Oral sex?"

I said I didn't know, although I did.

"Trey has a history, too, of course," Faith said. "But his dozens of one-night stands wouldn't be held against him even if they were admissible, while even that single serious lover she no doubt thought she would marry will bring charges of rape into question."

She took another sip of the drink, then drained it. Studied the empty bottom as if the glass might magnify the way out of this mess. I could almost see her measuring how damning it would be for Trey if it came out in court that he had seduced his thirteen-year-old cousin. But even a past rape conviction wasn't admissible if Trey didn't take the stand.

"Okay, you don't tell anyone, Betts," she said finally. "None of you do. Do you understand that? You have to understand that and you have to make Ginger understand that, too. Ginger and Laney and Mia. You know that, right? Having this made public . . . It will tarnish everyone."

I nodded dumbly, understanding in the same way I understood I could never have gone to Ben about the baby, that I'd have ended up splattered with a mess he would deny. Men can deny truths women are saddled with. And do. I like to think I wouldn't be like that if I were a man. But I suppose I might be. I suppose some would say I am. And maybe I would have to agree.

"You don't even let the girls know I know," Faith said. "You just explain to them that allegations of rape, true or not, provable or not, will hurt every one of you. You don't make her feel bad. You make it clear you know it's not her fault. But still there isn't anything to be done."

I blinked back tears.

"I know it's not right," she said. "It's not fair, but it's the way it is. The press can make a nice girl into a slut without even trying."

At the slap of the word "slut" my tears spilled in earnest.

Faith went behind the desk and pulled a small plastic packet of tissues from a drawer. She handed them to me. I wiped my eyes and blew my nose.

"A good lawyer would have a jury wondering from the opening argument if she isn't a call girl. You have to take my word on this. You have to promise me you won't say a word to anyone, Betts."

I nodded.

"You get them to promise, too, okay? You get Ginger to promise. You make her understand."

I nodded.

"Ginger will listen to you, Betts," she said. "She'll rush out to do the opposite of anything I tell her, but she'll listen to you."

Ginger *wasn't* listening to me, though. I thought we should tell someone and so did Mia. But Ginger insisted we couldn't say a word. We had to let this go. That's why I'd come to Faith. Looking for a way to hold Trey accountable for what he'd done.

I STARE UP through the bare frame of the Merchant Ivory bed in Emma's Peek. Remember now the quiet of Cook Island that morning Trey was found dead. I woke long before dawn to the moonlight across my face on the bottom bunk. The bunk across from me empty. When I got up to lower the window shade I half expected to see Ginger swimming off the pier. But the bay was as still as if it knew Trey was dead even if the rest of the world didn't yet. And when I'd turned back to the beds I'd seen Ginger. Her long body was wrapped around Laney's in the upper bunk.

A moment of this morning's dream comes back to me. Me wrapped around someone in bed. Was it Zack in my dream-bed? I was definitely in London in the dream. In that funky floor-that-slanted-so-much-it-left-me-motion-sick hotel room just off Soho Square. Where people in publishing liked to stay but high-priced New York lawyers did not. But Zack and I never went to London together. We never went much of anywhere. We clerked together and we got married and he got sick, leaving Izzy as fatherless as the never-child I'd carried those few months in law school would have been.

Betts

~~~

LAW QUADRANGLE NOTES, Winter 1993: Elsbieta ("Betts") Zhukovski (JD '82) and Virginia ("Ginger") Cook Conrad (JD '82) completed the Cleveland Marathon together this fall, raising $40,000 for the Leukemia Society through Team in Training and making them the first Marathon Bradwells. Friends Helen ("Laney") Weils (JD '82) and Mary Ellen ("Mia") Porter (JD '82) cheered from the sidelines, having chosen the quick pain of opening their pocketbooks over the extended pain of running ridiculous numbers of miles. Thanks to all the many law school alums, students, and staff who supported the run!

I PICKED UP the receiver to call Ben a hundred times that fall of our third year at Michigan Law. I knew Ben would give me money. But I didn't know if he would give me more than that. If he would give my child the father I never had. I thought I didn't even want him to. Rejecting something I knew I couldn't have. I'm more like Ginger than I like to think I am.

Ben would have had every reason to keep it quiet. But people do inexplicably tell secrets you never imagine they will. That was the thing I couldn't get past. That he might tell someone.

What I did instead: I stopped eating more than a few pieces of dry toast a day. I started swimming and diving again. Hours of laps followed by dives that landed me on my back and my belly. Dives that left me breathless and hurting. I told myself I was getting back in shape. I was just trying to get back in shape.

I told Matka I couldn't come home for Thanksgiving. There was so much to do with the *Law Review*. With finals just weeks away. No, not even for Thanksgiving dinner. Not even if she came to Ann Arbor to fix dinner at the dump of a house on Division Street.

Then a bright red spot appeared in my underwear the Wednesday afternoon before Thanksgiving. After Mia and Ginger and Laney were already headed home. My insides began bleeding out. My stomach cramped. A frightening gush of painful red poured into the toilet.

I would have driven to health services and given myself up if I'd had a car. The other Ms. Bradwells would have made me go if they'd been there. But I didn't and they weren't. And if I was dying that seemed a better solution than having Matka know. Not that any young person actually believes they can die.

I kept telling myself I could call an ambulance. If it got worse I would call an ambulance. And it did get worse. And still I didn't call. I just kept telling myself I could call if it got worse.

Then the cramping ended and the bleeding lessened. By mid-morning on Thanksgiving Day the worst was over. I was let free. That was the way I felt then. So thankful for everything that Thanksgiving. So relieved.

I called Matka just after noon. Told her I'd changed my mind. I couldn't bear to miss Thanksgiving dinner with her. "Just for the rest of the day, though. I need to come home tonight."

She drove down to Ann Arbor and took me back to Hamtramck. We had a small turkey breast together. Just the two of us. We played music for hours: Polish folk songs; church music; and three songs I'd improbably adapted for our zhaleikas, "Every Little Thing She Does Is Magic" because my singing along to that record had caused more groans in our house than anything else, and "Your Song" and "Hey Jude."

Midway through "Hey Jude" I couldn't blow another note. I coughed. Coughed again. A dry hack that wasn't a cough at all, that was only cover for the sudden realization that I wasn't waiting for anyone to perform with anymore. That the baby might have been a daughter. That I'd never play music with her.

"You are okay, Elsbieta?" Matka asked.

I nodded and picked up my zhaleika again. "Just something caught in my throat," I said. I coughed again.

And it was true in a way. Something *was* caught in my throat. The thought of another family having dinner around a table on Long Island. Ben and his wife. His son. His two daughters, one of whom was almost my age.

I told myself I'd done the right thing for everyone if I'd done anything at all. Which probably I had not. Ben had a family. He couldn't be a father to my child without leaving three children behind.

It wasn't until Matka was dropping me back at the Division Street house that she asked again about my friend. "She make decision?"

I gathered my things. Focused on the door handle. The breath-fogged window. The empty house just a few steps up the hard cement path. "It was a false alarm," I said. "She's fine. She wasn't pregnant after all." I pulled the handle and pushed the car door out into the chilled night. Climbed from the rusty old Ford. Looked up at the empty house. The dark windows. The ratty couch on the front porch, where the bulb we always left on had burned out.

I made myself turn and lean in through the open car door. Meet Matka's eyes. "She went home for Thanksgiving," I said. "She's fine."

I wonder sometimes what my life would be like if I'd had that baby. If I would still have met Zack. If he would have taken on a child as well as a spouse. If Izzy would have been a happier child if she'd had a big sister. If three of us would have felt more like a family than like Matka and me all over again.

I don't know how I'd have borne Zack's death without Isabelle sucking at my breast. The little coos she made and the milky smell of her all those lonely nights. I didn't want Matka there. I couldn't share the middle of the night with anyone but Iz. Which was selfish. I see that now. If Izzy was a widowed young mother I couldn't bear for her grief to hold me away.

Izzy had kept me company all those long nights after Zack died. That whole first year. And when I'd moved her into her own room in Ann Arbor, I'd moved myself into a twin bed, too. No empty space in a twin bed. No unused pillow. No space for anyone else; I see that now. But there it is. I'd been so focused on Isabelle. I would wake up to the garbage-truck quiet and bolt into her room to find her sleeping. Or, later, reading in bed.

I remember talking to Laney once about what a quiet child my daughter was. Laney saying she *wished* it were ever quiet at her house. Laney pausing. Perhaps sensing I was imagining a whole house full of family laughter two lonely voices can't duplicate. "Battery-operated chaos, that's the Robeson household," Laney had said then. The *Robeson* household. She'd kept her name just as I had. But neither of us passed our names on to our children.

I suppose that first child if I'd had her would have been a Zhukovski.

Named after a grandfather she never knew. A man I never knew myself. A man who for all I know might have abandoned my pregnant mother. Or never known about me. For all the time I spent on my "sabbatical," traipsing all over Poland in search of him, I never did find my father. I suppose at this point I'll only ever know him through the memories my mother shared. The same way Isabelle will ever know Zack.

Laney

~~~

BETTS HAS JOINED us; we're sitting beneath the six-candle chandelier in the Tea Parlor, finishing the last bit of griddle cakes made with flour from the canister in the kitchen, with syrup from the same cabinet in which we found the jam last night. Dead woman's syrup, but I don't say that. We've poured dead woman's syrup over dead woman's flour pancakes, in a dead woman's breakfast room where I'm relieved my campaign manager can't reach me to pronounce the death of my political career. *Cogi qui potest nescit mori.* She who can be forced does not know how to die. Whatever that means.

I expect every house that's been around for any time at all has belonged to someone who has passed. I suppose I *live* in a dead woman's house, since old Mrs. Davidson, who sold it to William and me, died last year. That's the silly kind of thing I'm thinking while I'm pretending to listen to Ginger and Betts.

Ginger has her contacts in now, having borrowed lens solution from Betts, so she doesn't have the excuse of something on her glasses that she used for the three boats she was sure she saw while we were out on the back steps. She does have a limited view now, though, since there are no windows in the Tea Parlor. She's peering through the doorway to the Music Room windows. And it does look like what she thinks she sees might actually be a boat this time.

As it takes shape, Max indicates an industrial smokestack-y thing toward the back. "Looks like a trawler," he says.

The tension ebbs from Ginger's shoulders: not the press. "Watermen setting crab pots," she says.

The sound of the word "crab" makes me puny even after all these years, but I try to look like I'm just fine. I do feel better than Betts looks. She hasn't said but about three words since she finished reading the article in the newspaper, which still sits beside her nearly untouched plate. We're all wanting to believe the front page piece is all the press coverage we'll get, that there are not journalists and photographers working their way across the bay this very minute. But it won't have taken all that much time for them to identify Cook Island as the location of the Conrads' Maryland summer home.

"I'm thinking I'll go for a walk after breakfast." Working hard to keep my voice even: just a stroll to listen to the birds, watch the waves, get my feet muddy along the edge of the marsh.

"You'll need the key," Ginger says.

When I try to look like I have no idea in this world what she's talking about, she says, "The lighthouse is kept locked. Too many teenagers and tourists looking for ghosts. You want company?"

Betts says she needs some exercise, too, she's been sitting at conference room tables for weeks getting ready for the hearings. But Mia hesitates, leaving me wondering how different her life might have been if she hadn't already been engaged to Andy that spring break.

"I hope Annie got your message, Ginge," Betts says. "I hope she called Iz."

Ginger says she's sure Annie has called Isabelle. She's sure Isabelle is settling in with her law books, Annie with her non-law ones. They would have called to say so, but they can't call, she reminds Betts. "But if you're nervous, maybe Mia could go see Max's place, and call the girls while she's there. If you and I tell them not to come, they'll find a helicopter to get here within the hour, just to defy us."

She glances in my direction. She can't help herself; she wants to make sure I see how hard she's trying here to share her friend Max with Mia. Part of me wants to scold her for needing applause *and* for letting Mia off the hook, but I don't quite trust Mia to come with us anyway. So a few minutes later, Mia climbs into Max's skiff, while Ginger and Betts and I head up the well-worn path toward the lighthouse. *Ad Pharum. Parate pessimo,* I hope. Although Ginger's bare toes on the dirt path leave me sure we aren't, in fact, prepared for a single thing.

As we step through the tunnel-like doorway into the lighthouse a few minutes later, I brace myself against the damp cement smell I remember from that spring break trip. What I register, though, is something more like the house smell, musty and closed up but not dank. The same black and white marble floor tiles are still lined with the same cracks (from lightkeepers' tools inadvertently dropping from above, I remember Beau explaining). The counterweights suspended from the top like the works of a giant grandfather clock are as immobile. The spiral of stairs as geometrically exact. But everything seems cleaner, and more still. The iron railings around the counterweight well and along the stairs are pure black where I remember more a tint of rusted-metal orange. The ocean outside more completely silenced by the thick cement walls. Is that the layering of emotion onto memory? I'm so sure I remember the cold scratch of metal on my palm as I climbed these stairs.

"The Lightkeeper's Cottage is gone?" I ask, just realizing I don't remember seeing it as we walked. The Lightkeeper's Cottage, where the fellas stayed that week, where I ought to have stayed myself that night. *Et hic sunt dracones.* And here are the dragons.

WE'D ALL GONE to the Lightkeeper's Cottage after we had our fill of gut-running that first night the fellas had arrived on Cook Island. Doug had carried on forever in the skiff about seeing the sunrise from the lighthouse, leaving me about split half in two between wanting to rush right up to the top so as not to miss it and wanting to fetch canvas and paints from Chawterley first. But Beau suggested we warm up in the Lightkeeper's Cottage. "It'll be cold up on the lantern deck, and Mia is already shivering," he said.

"You get that Mia is engaged, right, Beau?" Ginger responded.

"Jesus, Ginge," Beau said.

And poor Betts. As Trey began rubbing Ginger's shoulders from behind like a boxing coach readying his fighter to return to the ring, you could see Betts thinking Mia already had a fiancé, what did she want with Beau?

"How do we see any little thing at all with that beacon light on?" I asked, jumping in before Betts could poke at Mia. Those two sure have at each other sometimes, even still, and Ginger never can resist joining in on a brawl. "Won't the light wash out the sunrise?" I asked.

Frank said he had the secret code to turn it off, and Trey said if the Coast Guard caught us I'd have to be the one to take the rap.

"Shit, look at the moon," he said. And there it was, hanging soft with haze and nearly full. *"Ex luna scientia,"* he said, words that surely ought to have provoked a finger cross from the Ms. Bradwells, but didn't. "'From the moon, knowledge,'" he continued. "That was the motto of *Apollo 13*. Can you imagine being up there, looking back at Earth, thinking you might never return?"

"Getting morbid, Trey," Doug said, cuffing him on the shoulder. He echoed Beau about getting warm, and we headed to the Lightkeeper's Cottage, a ramshackle little house where, in the days when someone had to make sure the beacon flame didn't go out, the keeper lived.

As we walked, Doug suggested Trey tell us all about the syzygy that was supposed to occur Wednesday night.

Frank, in mock horror, said, "No, not that again!" but Trey, ignoring Frank, launched right on into the kind of interminable Trey Humphrey monologue the young associates at Tyler knew all too well. This one was about how all the planets would be aligned on our side of the Sun for the last time in our lifetimes. The next syzygy, which wouldn't include Pluto, would not occur until May 19, 2161. "But beware," he said. "This syzygy may exert a collective gravitational tug that will cause huge tides on the Sun's surface. The resulting sunspots could change Earth's rotation."

"No kidding?" Mia said.

Trey laughed. "Actually, it's all nonsense. It comes from *The Jupiter Effect*, but even the two astrophysicists who wrote the novel admit there's nothing to it. Still, people will believe what they want to believe."

"Trey isn't the only earthling who likes to imagine doom," Frank said as he unlocked the door to the cottage. He flipped a switch, lighting a dead bug burial ground in the frosted-glass ceiling lamp.

Spiders had set up house in just about every corner of the small sitting room. The lace curtains and the Oriental rug, the settee and the upholstered rocking chair were all faded to match the dust.

"I suppose Mother already had the wood laid in the fireplaces for *you*, Ginge," Beau said. Then to the other fellas, "And to think, I begged Mother for years to let me stay out here with you 'big boys' on party weekends, before she finally decided I was old enough."

He headed off to the single bedroom for blankets while Trey and Doug set to lighting the cast-iron woodstove. Frank announced that these accommodations called for a drink and quickly accepted my offer of help, leaving me following him into a dreary kitchen with an icebox that fell off the ugly tree and a pump-handle faucet that ran surprisingly clear from the start.

"So you're the famous Hell on Wheels," he said, but in a fond way.

"Thank you, Ginger, for sharing my beloved nickname with every soul you meet."

"It came from Trey, actually. But he means it with great respect. Trey likes a woman with spunk."

Back in the sitting room, our glasses filled with scotch from flasks in the fellas' pockets, Frank said to Doug, "So this is home for the week, I'm afraid. Not exactly watertight." They proceeded to discuss whether the roof would last the week, and the merits of dragging mattresses up to the lighthouse watch room.

"One hundred thirty-six steps," Beau pointed out. "And those mattresses aren't light."

Doug said, "The keepers used to carry fifty-pound drums of lamp oil up those steps."

"I think I'll take my chances here," Beau said.

"Only two mattresses," Doug observed, at which point the fellas all looked at each other and burst into laughter. "I guess your mother doesn't mean for us to sleep much this week, unless it's in someone else's bed."

"Don't even be thinking about singing to my friends, Dougie," Ginger said. "We've already got four in the waitstaff's bunkroom. We don't need your company."

Ginger and the fellas started sharing stories of past visits to the island, then: earlier parties where Chawterley beds were in high demand. There was the time ten-year-old Ginger, not meaning to be excluded, had snuck out here to spend the night with the boys, causing a flood of panic in the big house when she was missed. There was the time an even younger Beau, sleeping on the pier under the stars with the other fellas, rolled over and landed in the water, sleeping bag and all.

"That bag is still sleeping with the fishes," Frank said with a Godfather accent, brushing the back of his hand against his cheek. "It'll come up in a crab net some day."

And then they were talking about crabbing season, and whether there would be crabs for the party. It was early for crabs, but with the warm weather you never knew.

"You know how crab fishing works?" Trey asked Mia and Betts and me.

The others groaned.

"No one but you thinks this is interesting, Trey," Frank warned. "You and maybe Ginger, but that's only because she was young and impressionable the first time she heard it, and you were the older, much-adored cousin who could still beat up Beau and me."

Trey plunged ahead anyway, explaining how the shallow waters around the island were ideal for crabbing, how by mid-May millions of blue crabs would be digging their way up from their muddy-bottom winter homes and shedding their skins so they could grow.

Doug, in a heavy New York accent meant to imitate Trey's more subtle one, said, "A crab sheds its shell some twenty times in its short life."

"That's how it grows," Frank added in a similarly bad imitation of Trey. "It can't grow without shedding first, leaving its little claws naked and exposed."

"Its *crimson* claws," Doug corrected him. "Crimson and *cerulean*."

"'Cerulean': a word you've never heard before and will never hear again, but trust us, Trey means blue," Ginger said. "He thinks he means a particular shade of blue, but really he just means to impress you with the range of his vocabulary."

From the Latin word *caeruleus*, meaning dark blue or blue-green, which in turn derives from *caelulum*, diminutive of *caelum*, meaning . . . "Heaven," I said, "or sky."

Everyone looked at me. I shrugged. "*Caelum non animum mutant qui trans mare currunt.* Those who cross the sea change the sky, not their spirits."

"In manners, too, dominate!" Mia and Ginger and Betts all said, flashing finger crosses without missing a beat.

"And she's *not* law review?" Frank said to Trey. "Good thing we got into the firm when the competition wasn't so stiff."

"I think I'm the only one of us actually *in* the firm," Trey said. "I believe I'll be voting on whether or not you'll be made partner, m' boy, so you'd best be awfully nice to me."

"Meaning don't interrupt his story," Ginger advised her brother.

Frank grinned, and said (again in the fake Trey accent), "So it's the final shed . . ."

". . . that makes a she-crab a sook," Doug said.

"What good learners you gentlemen are," Trey said. Then to us, "And a sook's abdominal apron, her vaginal covering—"

"—takes on a triangular shape," Doug interrupted, "which resembles nothing so much as . . . all together, boys."

"The U.S. Capitol!" Frank and Doug and Beau shouted, although Beau seemed less enthusiastic about it than the others, and less drunk, too.

"The jimmy crab—that's the male crab," Doug continued. "His genital covering looks like . . ."

"The Washington Monument!" The words again delivered in synchrony, at which point Frank and Doug applauded themselves.

Trey, looking mightily peeved and trying not to, said, "*Slender and phallic-shaped*, like the Washington Monument. If you're going to steal my story, at least get it right. You're making it sound so unromantic." He caught me in the harsh beacon of his gaze. "It's really one of the most touching mating rituals you'll ever see," he insisted. "The jimmy cradles his girlfriend for as much as a week, and then he stands guard over her, literally makes a protective cage for her with his walking legs while she molts. He's a patient sort. Her striptease can take two or three hours, but he just stands over her, protecting her. When she's done, when she's all vulnerable and shiny, he gently helps her onto her back before he takes her. She extends her abdomen so that it folds around him, and they couple like that for as long as twelve hours. Afterward, he hangs around to protect her until her shell regenerates. He carries her around until she can protect herself again."

The whole conversation was creeping me out, though it didn't seem much to bother anyone else. Ginger was laughing with the fellas, and if Betts heard anything more than simple biology in Trey's voice, she was masking it well enough. Maybe she was too focused on Beau to tend much to what Trey was saying; Mia clearly was. Beau was sitting by Mia's feet, next to the wood-burning stove he'd settled her beside. So maybe I was the one whose mind was in the wrong place. Trey was a successful young partner in a conservative firm where every lawyer was an upstanding member of the community and no one was a creep. They were talking about something natural, something beautiful and loving if Trey was to be believed, and no one was disagreeing with him. They were laughing. They were having fun.

"You're leaving off the part about how crabbers take advantage of all this romance?" Doug said. "That's so unlike you, Trey."

But it was almost dawn, and there were 136 steps to climb for the view of the sunrise we meant to have.

Betts

❧

THE SUN HAS long ago risen this time. But here we are back in the lighthouse. The Lightkeeper's Cottage is gone just as Laney said. Ginger and I stare back through the tunnel-doorway to the blank space where it stood in 1982. Land now filled with tall grasses blending with the rest of the island. Filled-in emptiness.

"We tried to talk Mother into tearing this lighthouse itself down when they bulldozed the cottage and the oil house," Ginger says, "but she spent a small fortune restoring it instead."

The details fall into place then: The walls painted where they had been bare concrete. The sills of the windows along the winding stairs no longer flaking. The cracked panes replaced.

"So when it was a useful lighthouse it was a dump," I say. "And now that it's useless it's *Architectural Digest* material. Maybe that's our future, too! When we're useless we'll have time to polish our nails."

Ginger examines her hands. "I have a photo shoot with *Hand Digest* this afternoon," she says, her slight overbite disappearing into her grin.

Our feet clank and our breaths deepen as we wind up the webbed-iron stairs to the watch room, where the lighthouse keepers once monitored the light. As we catch our breath, I try to remember whether the whole floor was just one open room like this. Did the windows go all the way around for this amazing view? What I remember was a filthy service room. Its beaded ceiling flaking strips of dirty white paint. The room itself full of rusty old tools. Wire. A single chair and table. And not much else. Not even the telescope that first night. It was still in Trey's boat. If there was a view back then it was through windows that hadn't been washed in years.

But the walls and ceiling are now tongue and groove, painted a glossy white. The few tools left have been cleaned and polished as if for a museum. There isn't a loose nail in sight.

"*Spira mirabilis,*" Laney says. "Miraculous spiral." She's looking down steps as logarithmically perfect as the swirl of a nautilus shell.

Several books sit on a polished table next to a plain wooden chair. The original chair and table where Trey Humphrey shot himself? Or was shot. Trey Humphrey who we all want to believe brought his gun up 136 steps to clean it. To this space that has nothing to do with guns.

I pick the top book from the pile and open what looks to be a handwritten diary. "'Arrived at Cook Island at 9:10,'" I read aloud. "'Commenced making inquiries for an additional man. Could not find anyone who is competent.'" I flip forward a few pages. "'Snowed last night. Ice thick on the bay.'" And later: "'Took inventory of all the groceries here belonging to keeper at invoice prices to be returned or sold to incoming keeper.'"

I pick up the next book on the stack. Read silently for a moment. "Is this . . . ?"

Ginger stares at me. Or at the chair in which Trey died. Or both. She doesn't seem to register that I'm talking. Her eyes have faded to the color of dirty bathwater.

"Ginger?"

"They're the logbooks," she says. "From when the lighthouse was manned."

"Did your mother . . . ?"

Ginger offers no answer to whatever question it is I can't manage to put into words.

We haven't any of us asked the one question that needs to be asked. For thirty years. We've just pretended nothing to be questioned ever happened on this island. Someone must have talked, though. One of us must have talked.

My answer to the senator's question was too quick. My look too unfazed. Mia and I had never discussed how I should *look* when I answered. But that's what I was going for. Unfazed. A mistake. I was too well prepared for a question I didn't want to appear to expect.

I don't believe I have anything to add to the public record on that.

Ginger goes to the windows and stares out. She reaches up and touches the back of her hair. Like the day we met. Ginger standing in class insisting that her name wasn't Cook. Insisting that identifying a woman by her marital status was demeaning. Ms. Decisis-Bradwell. Stand by that which is decided.

I don't believe I have anything to add to the public record on that. It's the kind of nonanswer Mia might arm me with if she had in mind that I might need a weapon. If she worried that I might not stand by what we'd decided without the right words. Why did I let her talk me into this? Why did she want to? Mia, the one who thought we should go to the police. Who never has given up thinking she was right.

Except she didn't talk me into anything. I'd already talked myself into it. She just fed me the words. Mia has always been good at words.

Although not good enough to persuade Ginger and Laney to tell someone what had happened when it did. Mia and I were the only ones who thought we should say something. And it isn't me talking now.

"You don't think Mia was the blogger, do you?" I say. The treachery coming out in a whisper. Is this why Ginger suggested Mia go with Max? *Did* she suggest it? Or was that Laney?

I arm myself with arguments against the protest I expect from Laney: Mia was being vague in the blog so it would look like the information could have come from anywhere. She didn't need to name me specifically to implicate me. She only needed to mention the Conrad summer home. Practically every article about my nomination mentioned how sad the timing was. How Faith Cook Conrad had been a mentor to me. How she'd died only weeks before the nomination was announced.

Arguments I haven't realized I've been having inside my own head until I blurt out the charge.

Lordy, you've been blaming Mia since the first moment in the kitchen. That's what Laney must be thinking. Or simply *Lordy, how can you think Mia would do that to us, Betts?* Laney is so naïve about what we Ms. Bradwells will do, even still.

But Laney says nothing. Ginger says nothing. In the silence of the waves against the shore below, I wonder if this is what Ginger suspects after all or only what I suspect. Mia has just lost her job. And that's what journalists do these days when they're unemployed. They start a blog with a big splash so they can live on the ad revenues. They start with a messy, life-drenching post—like the one suggesting Trey Humphrey's death may not have been an accident—even when they *aren't* so jealous of what their best friend is accomplishing that they have to be begged to come help her celebrate.

Madagascar. That's off the coast of Africa. You know that, right?

But would Mia really do that to me? How can I even think that? What does it say about how poor a friend *I* am that I can even imagine she might?

Mia

THE HOUSE MAX pulls the skiff up to is the most gorgeous I've seen maybe ever. Until this moment, I would have told you I'm a traditionalist when it comes to architecture: Victorian or Craftsman or even Colonial or Tudor, anything but modern—not that I've ever owned a house. But this slender expanse of glass and wood is hardly noticeable even as I stand in front of it, which is part of what I love. It somehow smoothes the intersection of land and sea rather than interrupting the two, the house evoking trees, and the landscaping—not just plants but also streams hurrying down rocky paths and over baby waterfalls, pausing in shallow pools—evoking marsh grasses and seawater, as if a wave has washed up and will just as surely wash back to join the bay.

"Wow," I say.

He smiles. Man, the guy does look goofy when he smiles.

"How does it just . . . disappear? Blend? I don't even know the word."

Max shrugs, as if it's a small bit of luck, and perhaps it is. When I write, I'm not always quite sure a piece is going to work until it does. But it's one thing to approach without certainty a two-thousand-word article that I'm spending four weeks on, another thing entirely to risk a year and a million dollars on something you're not quite sure about. Like writing a book—risky business. What if, after all that time, it simply doesn't work? Which is why, I suppose, I cling to journalism even though a part of me longs to immerse myself in something larger.

It's partly the line of the house, I think. Everything is soft. It has corners, but they don't seem like corners because of the landscaping.

Max starts talking about the technical attributes of the house as if anyone looking at its beauty might be interested in its guts, but I listen because I know how this is, to be proud of something and yet reluctant to admit to the pride. I nod and look as he points and explains: the auto-claved aerated concrete, the rainwater recapture.

"Solar panels?" I say.

"Hidden behind the top edge of roof."

"But the glass goes up to the roof."

Again, he shrugs. "Solar panels are pretty thin."

He puts a hand on my back to urge me up the path and into the house. The shock of his touch shoots through me, like the first time Ginger's brother Beau touched me, when we were gut-running all those years ago. Ginger had warned us against Doug's voice, but it was nothing compared to Beau's touch. I'd been engaged to Andy already, which I see in retrospect was part of it: I was engaged, so any other man was forbidden fruit, and although the Midwestern girl in me—the side of me that is my father's daughter—didn't want anything to do with forbidden fruit, some other piece of me wanted a big, juicy bite.

Forbidden fruit never fails to stain everything, though. And Max, as a married man, is the worst kind of forbidden fruit, the kind that would leave me feeling as awful as I did that spring break when I was engaged to Andy and slept with Beau. How do you tell the truth about something like that? At the time, I'd decided you didn't. I didn't tell Andy about Beau until Andy left me for Michael, and when I did tell him, finally, it was under the guise of a kindness to him, to let him off the hook for leaving me. Although Laney insists that wasn't really why I told Andy; she says I told him because I wanted to have rejected him before he rejected me. She thinks I've never been any better at losing than Ginger is, that I'm only better at convincing everyone I haven't really lost.

Max's house, inside, is all smooth, curved walls, one room leading to another without barrier. The outside walls are made of large expanses of glass so that the outside is brought in, and yet the house feels private. That's the landscaping obscuring the inside without, somehow, disturbing the view.

"No doors? Or are they hidden somewhere, like the solar panels?"

Max raises his eyebrows in a way that makes me want to laugh, which I do. If we weren't here in a house he shares with his wife, I would think he was flirting. I wonder where the wife is. I half expect her to emerge and introduce herself.

The lack of doors leaves me wondering how quiet he and his wife must be when they make love, unless they don't care if their children hear them. But the photos of his children scattered about remind me that they're older, away in college—which they have been since before he built this house.

His wife is not in the living room, a room with cozy white couches and bamboo floors, with a bronze sculpture that could be a Rodin but isn't, and a small print he confirms *is* a Miró although he's quick to point to the seam in the middle, to say it's unsigned and not particularly valuable.

He pushes a button and a long wall of glass slides away, leaving no barrier at all between this room and the bay.

"The sunset from here must be delicious," I say.

"The sunrise," he says. "You're looking east. Only Chawterley is far enough up island to see both ways. Chawterley and the lighthouse."

"So you're a sunrise kind of guy?" Flirting even though I shouldn't.

"I like the freshness of early morning," he says, which maybe means he likes to have sex in the morning, but probably doesn't, probably that's just my attraction to him.

"How 'bout you?" he asks.

I raise both my eyebrows in the same way he did, wanting to make him laugh, which he does.

"I like both," I say, which sounds better than the truth, which is that I rarely see either sunset or sunrise with anyone, that I meet fellow journalists in bars—usually well after sunset—and I'm careful to go to their places rather than to mine so I can slip out before dawn, alone.

He shows me the kitchen, clearly a cook's kitchen: the eight-burner stove is the giveaway. When I ask who the chef is, he admits to learning to fend for himself when he went vegetarian. I'm about to go for the opening, to ask, "Your wife isn't vegetarian?" But I pause, wondering what the hell I'm doing here, why I'm so damned curious about his damned wife.

I think of Dad still cooking for Mom although she long ago ceased to recognize "that nice man who takes care of me" as her husband of sixty years.

As Max leads me around another curve to his study—where there is a welcome relief of untidily stacked magazines—I'm wondering if my mom can be blamed for the way she was on those summer adventures any more than she can be blamed for who she is now. Would I have done things differently if I were her, in those days when women had so few options to begin with?

"My dad always wanted a study," I say.

"How much of our lives do you s'pose we live trying to reach our parents' dreams?" he says. "My dad was a waterman. Spent far too many cold nights on a boat on the bay. His dream was for me to go out with him, but he died out on the water before I was old enough, and my mom's dream became for me to be anything *but* a waterman."

"I think my mom's dream was to have some time to spend with her lovers without my dad finding out," I say, inexplicably spilling my guts to this near-stranger, wondering if Mom didn't anticipate that someday she'd need Dad to take care of her the way he does now. "Not that I even know that about my mom. She's never hinted that the friends we visited on our summer jaunts were her lovers, and maybe they weren't, probably they weren't, probably they were just the best of friends, like Betts and Ginger and Laney and me." No men in my friend list, I realize too late, but maybe he won't notice. I didn't, or didn't think I did. The idea that those friends might have been my mother's lovers never occurred to me until Andy moved in with Michael. I never worked up the nerve to ask her about it, either, and the Mom who's left to ask now doesn't have any idea she ever set off each June for a three-month adventure with anyone.

"My father liked the whole island to know of his conquests," Max says. "Ma looked the other way, because what choice did she have?" In his voice is a certainty that he will never be like his father in anything he does. Whatever I'm seeing as flirtatiousness is something else. "I don't s'pose I can really blame him for everything bad in life, but my sister, Tessie, she's made a mess of her life, forever going out with the wrong kind of man. She has no idea what a decent man is."

"Tessie," I exhale, not meaning to say it aloud but remembering all that talk about the "slutty island girl," Tessie McKee. "Beau's particular favorite," someone had called her, but Beau had told me that night on the boat that he'd never slept with Tessie.

"I guess my mom did love my dad in her own way," I say, thinking I *do* know Andy loved me, that he still loves me in his own way. The two things don't always line up, though: love and need.

From Max's study, we wander down a hallway to the children's bedrooms.

"Bathroom doors?" I ask, and he does the raising eyebrows thing again.

"No bathroom doors," I say. I peek around a bend to find a doorless bathroom next to a closet that also has no door.

Max lifts a little metal tab in the archway between the bedroom's bamboo floor and the bathroom's stone, and pulls out a pocket door. "My daughter threatened never to visit if I didn't have bathroom doors," he says. "The things we do for our kids."

He asks if I have children.

"Calling the kids! That's what I'm supposed to be doing here!" I say, although the only kids I have belong to Laney and Ginger and Betts.

He shows me to a phone and I call, but I get no answer from either Annie or Iz. No answer at Ted and Ginger's; it's Saturday, so Ted is likely playing golf and I don't have a cellphone number for him. I finally reach Annie's brother, B.J.—Beauregard James, after Ginger's brother and Ted's father—who is pretty sure Annie was going to spend the weekend with us.

I call William, to let him know about the phone situation and tell him everyone is fine. He asks me to tell Laney to call her campaign manager, that the guy is about to bust a gut over the press coverage this morning. His voice is light, but that's the way William handles things: he keeps the problems low-key and hopes they go away—which, surprisingly, they usually do. He doesn't even ask why Laney isn't calling herself, or what she's doing. He only asks if she's okay, and when I say I think so, he says, "I'm glad she's there with y'all for this. You take care of her, Mia. And tell her I love her. Tell her I haven't heard a word from Willie J or Manny or Gemmy, so presumably they haven't flunked out of school yet. And Joey is fine: his debate team placed third and he's spending the weekend on an English project with that cute little Emily he's sweet on, so he barely realizes Laney is gone."

We chat for another minute and we're just saying goodbye when he asks, "Mia, is there anything to this?"

I hesitate, unsure how much if anything Laney has told him. In the silence, I hear music from his end of the line, something gospel-bluesy. "I don't think Laney had anything to do with Trey Humphrey's death," I say finally, "but that doesn't mean this isn't going to be messy." I almost blurt out what happened then, because I know William, I know he loves Laney and nothing will change that. But what if she hasn't told him anything?

The fact of Laney's not allowing him to help her—not trusting him—might just break his heart, and it isn't my place to break his heart like that.

"You know you're the best thing that ever happened to Laney, don't you?" I say.

"No, that would be you Ms. Bradwells," he says. "You gave her a sense of belonging. I just reap the benefits of that."

AFTER I HANG up, it occurs to me that Max must have Internet access. "You don't have a computer in the study?" I ask, saying the words as I realize I didn't see a computer there—or anywhere else.

"You want to take a look at that WOWD blog," he says. "Thought you might but didn't want to raise it if you didn't. I'll grab my laptop from the bedroom for you."

"Wireless? I can use my BlackBerry."

"The screen will be too small," he says.

It wasn't too small at Dulles Airport yesterday. But as I put my hand to my pocket, I realize my BlackBerry is back at Chawterley anyway.

While Max fetches his computer, I sit on one of the cozy white couches, imaging a crazy wife kept hidden in the bedroom on this remote island where she can't hurt anyone, like Rochester's mad Bertha from *Jane Eyre*. Never mind that in one of the photos I'd noticed—the whole family together at his son's wedding last summer—Max's wife didn't look crazy at all. She looked like she could be a Ms. Bradwell. She looked like someone whose husband I ought not to flirt with, much less do anything more than flirt.

Max returns with his laptop, boots it up for me, and leaves me for a minute on the excuse of checking something in some other room. As the computer chimes to life, I remain facing the bronze sculpture that isn't a Rodin and beyond it, through the empty space where the wall has been moved away, the Chesapeake. I listen to the lap of the waves, or the movement of water through the landscaping streams, or both, for a long time before typing into the browser a blog address I know all too well. The page loads then, WOWD appearing at the top of the page in a Tempus Sans font that is the exact blue of the sail on the *Row v. Wade*.

GINGER

THE THING I'M most ashamed of as I stand in Mother's remodeled lighthouse monument to Trey (with all its focus on this watch room: not a damned speck of dust, not a thing out of place) is that I didn't believe Laney. When Betts and Mia and I found her curled up in the top bunk in the waitstaff's bedroom, pretending sleep, what I remember feeling was relief that she wasn't still with Trey. And then disbelief.

The eight of us had been playing Risk in the Lightkeeper's Cottage. Beau was the first to be eliminated, followed shortly by Mia, and then Trey and Laney. They'd all gone off to look at the stars through the telescope while the rest of us finished the game. But when Mia and Beau came back without Trey and Laney, I'd imagined the two of them out in a skiff together, on Hunters' Gut or Little Thoroughfare or Fog's Ghost Cove.

I was the one who first said the word "rape," so I must have known it was true. When she broke down and told us the awful details, though— the lighthouse and the telescope and Trey—I shut down as quickly as she had. I couldn't believe it, so I simply chose not to. Chose instead to feel anger at Laney, fury at her for doing what I was afraid to do. I knew Trey. I knew he liked it rough sometimes, that he turned to the island girls when he wanted it rough.

I try to attend to what Betts is saying about Mia and the blogger, but the memory of Trey in this watch room is overwhelming. Trey, the first man I ever slept with, the only one I slept with for years. I had this idea that the fact of that meant we were supposed to be together, that if I was patient he would come around, too, and his doing so would prove I wasn't a slut as surely as it would prove the island girls he slept with were. Prove to whom, I can't say, because no one ever knew Trey and I slept together until I told the Ms. Bradwells. And the saddest thing about that confession is that I was offering it as proof that Trey couldn't have raped Laney. "Trey and *I* are lovers. Trey *loves* me," I'd insisted. "Why would he want Laney when he has me?"

Have you listened for the things I have left out?

I thought I was so grown up because a grown-up loved me; I thought having sex was the same thing as love, or would be. Trey, who was admitted to Harvard at sixteen, who was editor in chief of the *Law Review* at twenty-one. The one Mother set up as the example for us all, and Daddy loved him, too. Trey, who was the best shot on the island, the only one of the boys who could knock down a bird with more certainty than I could. Whose final view as he bled to death was these windows and the sea and the syzygy.

Syzygy. In poetry, two metrical feet combined into a single unit. I thought that's what Trey and I were.

"Statutory rape," Mia had said the night I told them about Trey and me, but I was so sure Trey hadn't raped anyone, not Laney and certainly not me. It wasn't until I was a mother myself—until Annie was thirteen or nearly so and I saw how very young a thirteen-year-old girl is—that I understood that a twenty-year-old man had no business seducing his thirteen-year-old cousin. *What voyage this, little girl?* Trey's attention had made me feel special. I thought that Laney was jealous of that, I thought she'd been jealous since the moment Trey stepped into the Captain's Library. I thought if she'd had sex with him (which maybe she had but I thought it just as likely that she was making it all up), she had wanted him.

Laney, who was the closest friend I ever had or ever will. It's a sign of how close we all were that she even told us; most rape victims never tell a soul, even today.

That following night when I'd curled up in bed next to her, Mia and Betts thought I was comforting Laney, and I let them think that. I let everyone think I was a good friend when I was no friend at all, when I was scared shitless and seeking comfort from Laney, not giving her anything.

I have always been such an ignorant fool when it comes to men. First Trey, and then L. Gordon Hayes, who I fell for in my junior year at Virginia. He was like Trey, but younger and better looking, and he pursued me until, finally, I slept with him after the Kappa formal. He took my roommate out the next night and slept with her, which would have been humiliating enough if he weren't a fraternity brother of Beau's, and Beau in D.C., too far away to reach L. Gordon Hayes's handsome but imminently breakable jaw. I escaped with my humiliation to New York, where I met Scratch, and I got drunk with him, and woke the next morning in his bed, suddenly counting three lovers where just days before there had been only Trey. When Scratch headed to South Africa for a playwriting fellowship in Cape Town the next week, I went with him. And when that ended badly, I came home and finished at Georgetown, graduated early, went off to law school bound and determined to make an even bigger fool of myself. I thought I'd be like Trey and Frankie, taking lovers and casting them off at my own whim. But it didn't make me feel quite the way I'd thought it would.

The truth is I wasn't even that wild about my husband, Ted, at first. I worked with him, and I'd determined not to sleep with anyone at work that summer, not meaning to blow my chance for an offer at Caruthers by tumbling into bed with the wrong guy. But we'd drunk too much together on a summer clerk sailing outing, one of the ones Betts worked through, already gunning for the Supreme Court when even the firm wanted her to be having fun. And somehow Ted and I ended up necking in a dark corner of a dark club afterward. He suggested screwing right there, but I was not so drunk as to have sex within a few (albeit dark) paces of our fellow office mates. Not smart enough to say no later that night, though; I let him come up for a drink after he walked me home. I'd slept with so many guys by then, anyway.

But Ted married me. He's stayed with me all these years. Maybe he's taken other lovers along the way and maybe he hasn't, I don't know and I'm not sure I want to. I haven't, that's the thing. I still want men to want me even when I don't want them. Even Max. But in all the years I've been married, I've never slept with anyone else. And the truth? It's a relief.

"Ginger?" Betts is saying, calling me back to the refinished table and chair, the clean windows, the bay. I try to think what she wants of me, but I can't shake the memory of Trey with his guts blown out. His eyes closed, but behind the lids the unblinking stare I'd gotten when I'd asked him in the Triangle Blind that morning if he'd fucked Laney.

"Did you fuck Laney in the lighthouse last night?" I'd demanded, feeling even more humiliated than I had sitting in that theater in South Africa, wanting him to deny it even if he had.

For years, I used to wake from the nightmare memory of Trey's blood pooled on the floor here. *Blood blooms, spreads / its wide foliage in my chest.* All that blood meant he'd died slowly, that the shot hadn't killed him immediately; he'd bled to death, and the dead don't bleed. I know it should bother me that Trey died slowly. The way it used to bother me when I had to break the neck of a bird I'd shot to put it out of its misery. But even after all these years, it doesn't. If there's a hell, I'll probably burn in it for the satisfaction I've taken from believing Trey knew he was dying before he was dead.

Laney

~~~

AND HERE I am, out on the lantern deck, not touching the railing, I can't tolerate that, but with my back again to the lantern room and the bay stretching away in every direction, like Noah looking out at the flood. It's the last place I'd have said I would come, yet when Ginger said I'd be wanting the key, I saw this was the graveyard I needed to visit. I expect what she says is true: she does know me better than I know my own self.

The light is well past dawn this time. We've missed the awakening that was such a beautiful thing that morning after we went gut-running, when we were exhausted and wet from boating all night, and not much drier for the time we spent warming in the Lightkeeper's Cottage. I'm comforted by the murmur of Betts's voice from below me, and then Ginger's. My friends, with me without being all over me, as I remember Mia (that coward) standing just here where I'm standing: a younger, thinner Mia leaning out over the rusted railing in a way that would panic me now, after twenty years of trying to keep my children from talking to strangers, and riding with friends who've been drinking, and leaning against high railings that just might not hold.

It's daylight and I can see so many things I couldn't see back then.

It was still dark when we circled the heavy black teardrop of counterweight again and again, heading up to the watch room on legs less weary than mine are now despite the scotch we were drinking even as we climbed. We were trying to hold on to the boat-racing buzz we'd already lost, I expect.

"Let me get the beacon," Trey said at the top of the stairs. "I'm not taking responsibility for you girls going blind."

We paused on the final steps while Trey disappeared into the lantern room, the bright light flashing onto the stairway giving way to a darkness that left me dizzy, imagining my skull crashed onto the ornate inlaid marble of the counterweight well 136 steps below. It seemed forever before I could begin to make out the dark form of Ginger on the stair above me, before we continued on past the glass darkness of the lantern and out to this higher view of the night.

The air was cold and damp, the taste of salt mingling with the aftertaste of scotch. An almost-full moon was setting to the west. Mia, though, went to the rail facing the eastern horizon, the lightening sky.

"Look, the sea is violet," she said in a hushed tone, as if she'd just seen Jesus rise.

Purple water? But she was right: a hint of violet shone from the black water.

I took a sip of scotch and held the sharpness on my tongue, thinking *I* was the painter, *I* was the one who was supposed to be noticing color. Mia the Savant and Betts the Funny One, even Ginger the strong-willed Rebel. But I was just the Good Girl, the one without courage even to break a rule.

"Sunlight scatters differently at sunrise and sunset because it comes at a tangent to the earth, through a bigger slug of atmosphere," Trey told Mia. "More of the shorter blue and green light waves are knocked off before they get to us, so more of what we see—what our brains perceive—is the longer-wave-length red."

In lumine tuo videbimus lumen.

"Hence the red sky," he said. "And as any kid who ever dyed an Easter egg can tell you, when you mix red and blue—"

"But why isn't the ocean red then, like the sky?" Mia asked. "Isn't its color just reflected light?"

As Trey explained that clean water absorbs red light—that's why water usually looks blue, but in coastal zones with high concentrations of matter like this it's more complicated—I considered this side of Trey: a man who cared about the different ways the sun's rays appear at dawn and noon and four, who imagined children dyeing eggs the colors of the changing sky. It was a side of him I'd never seen at Tyler & McCoy.

Mia nodded eagerly as Trey spoke, having no worldly idea that thirty years later she would write a six-page piece for the Sunday magazine about how satellite images of ocean color indicate increasing levels of pollution at our shores.

"Think about it," Trey had said. "If it weren't for Rayleigh scattering—light's interaction with air molecules—when we looked up at the sky we'd see the black of space." Then he started on about the optical illusion that made the moon appear big as all outdoors at the horizon, talking about upside-down Ponzo illusions and our brains seeing the sky as a flattened dome. I braced myself for another Trey Humphrey monologue. But he grew silent, then, watching with the rest of us as the moon sank into the earth.

It was the end of a long and wonderful night running through the island streams under a vast, dark sky. The beginning of a third day of a whole week enjoying life with my best friends before we set off our separate ways. It was going to be the first in a string of long and wonderful nights with Ginger's brothers and friends, smart fellas who could teach me something about the sun and the moon and the sea, the creatures on the island, the stir of life I hadn't much noticed in law school, or perhaps ever. How often in my whole life had I just relaxed and enjoyed a moment without any thought to how it would appear on a résumé that would get me . . . what? Someplace my parents had always expected me to wind up, even if it would surprise the rest of the world to bump into a black girl there.

If Trey had been a bit off-kilter in that conversation in the Lightkeeper's Cottage about the crabs, it was beginning to seem just another piece of something innocent and unthreatening, a fella who tried to understand his world. If I was finding something sinister in that, surely I should be looking inside myself.

After the last sliver of moon disappeared, we turned back to the east, our arms touching as we joked about how sturdy the lighthouse might be and whether it could take all this weight on one side—at the top, no less. The horizon continued to brighten with our laughter, and the sky reddened, and the water purpled until the first lovely smack of sunlight shocked our eyes.

Doug sang out then, "Morning has broken," his voice joining the lap of the bay and the fading crickets, the rising clamor of morning birds. Beau's voice joined Doug's after a moment, followed by Frank's and

Trey's. And then we joined in, too, even Betts moving her lips to the words. It's hard to describe how lovely it was. I'd forgotten that: how really lovely it was.

We went back to Chawterley and fixed breakfast, all eight of us crammed into the kitchen, as on top of each other as we'd been in the skiffs. We made griddle cakes and sausage we ate in the Sun Room, and after breakfast I found a sketch pad and charcoal pencil in the Painter's Studio. I took them back into the Sun Room and sketched with Ginger observing over my shoulder. I remember the sensual odor of salt air and sausage and scotch clinging to her long hair, which was loose for once, not confined in a barrette but hanging long and untamed all the way to her fanny.

"I wish I had all your long, long hair, Ginge," I said.

She reached down and fingered the edge of my sketch pad. "I wish I could draw, but Beau took all the artist genes."

Beau, stretched out on the floor, raised his head to protest, but it was true: Ginger's drawing would never be any better than my hopes for fanny-brushing hair.

Mia came and sat next to me on the couch, admiring my sketch with Ginger: the pier, the twin boats, the bay, and the endless horizon.

"I wish we could stay like this forever," she said.

We all looked at her for a fond moment before Betts said, "'I wish that I had duck feet. And I can tell you why . . .'"

We laughed, looking down at our feet as Betts hopped up and duck-walked around, and Frank obliged her with a comic quack. We were at that point you get to when you've been up all night, when you aren't exactly drunk anymore but you aren't exactly sober, when life seems full of endless hope. Betts kept duck-walking, tapping on heads now, saying, "Duck. Duck. Duck." But Mia was the one who shouted, "Goose!" She leaned over and tapped Beau's head and then hopped up and sprinted out the back door and down the stone path, Beau a puppy dog at her heels.

He trapped her at the end of the pier, playing like he was going to push her into the water to join his sleeping bag lost on the murky bottom all those years ago. Betts's freckled face was so full of disappointment and frustration and longing as she watched them that I moved closer to her, thinking *poor Betts,* pitying this friend I knew even then was truly extraordinary. Pitying her in a way I don't expect I ever would have pitied a fella. Why did we do that to ourselves? Why did we buy into the notion that the fella we married was as important, or more, than the people we were our own selves?

I fell asleep in the Sun Room not much later, my head and Ginger's feet against one armrest of the sofa, my feet and her head at the other end. I woke sometime in the early afternoon to find us covered with a light blanket. Betts was asleep on the other sofa, lightly covered, too, and the fellas were stretched out on the carpet, fast asleep.

I picked up my sketch pad and charcoal and slipped out, heading for the Painter's Studio, thinking I'd poke around there while everyone else slept. I heard soft voices as I approached, though: Beau standing at an easel while Mia curled up on the window seat.

"Right there, just like that," Beau was saying. "The light catches the gold in your hair and makes your eyes laugh."

Mia giggled lightly, her head tipping back and her hair falling away from her face so I could see her blushing from her cowlick to her tiny ears to her narrow chin. "Makes my eyes *laugh*?"

As I edged backward from the doorway, I wondered if I'd ever seen her look so happy with Andy. And yet Andy was such a great fella. Andy was so good to her. We all wanted an Andy back then.

I went back later that day to sneak a look at Beau's sketch. It was charming, effortless, the way I wanted to draw but could never quite manage to. He'd caught the light in Mia's hair and in her eyes, even limited by the gray of the charcoal. He'd caught the sweep of cowlick at her forehead and whatever it was in her expression that made her both joyous and vulnerable. I remember thinking for the first time that maybe Mia *was* the prettiest Ms. Bradwell, at least in that moment. I remember wishing I were in love with someone who loved me back, and thinking it really was time to let go of Carl, time for me to let go of the bitterness I'd clung to for a whole long year by then.

Mia

~

LAW QUADRANGLE NOTES, Summer 2009: Mary Ellen ("Mia") Porter (JD '82) won the Holga Inspire Award at this year's Krappy Kamera Competition, for her photograph "Women of Kabul." Her photographic work is shown at the Left Coast Gallery in San Francisco, owned by Andrew ("Dartmouth") Cooper IV (JD '82).

BEAU'S LIPS ON mine that Monday in the Chawterley Painter's Studio, with the sun through the windowpane warm on my shoulders, and the lingering smell of oil-based paint. I had seen that kiss coming and I had wanted it to come, I had invited it from the moment we sat in the skiff together, from even before that, in the Captain's Library. I'd like to say there was more to it than that. I'd like to think my attraction to him arose out of the soft, thoughtful way he explained the difficulties of establishing economic stability in third world countries and the near-impossibility of instilling hope in people who've never seen anything but downsides to having dreams. I'd like to say I was charmed by his tales of adventure with Ginger: climbing around the moss-covered foundation of the original Chawterley kitchen; sailing all the way around the island for the first time without a parent aboard, and then from the island to the mainland just because they could; setting out with Max McKee in search of pirate treasures buried, legend had it, deep in Mad Man Barley's Grove—a few acres of hackberries and persimmon and locust trees on the other side of the no-name road, where they would in later years meet the island kids to smoke dope. But the truth is, the attraction I felt for Beau was immediate and physical. The fact is that if he'd kissed me in the Captain's Library even before we'd been introduced, I'd have done what I did the next afternoon in the Painter's Studio: slid the diamond of my engagement ring palmward, closed my fist around it, and kissed him back.

One shortish kiss, followed by another, longer one, his beard tickling my cheek, my chin, the vulnerable spot at the join of my jaw and ear and neck. He ran a finger from my cowlick down my nose and over my lips, to the tip of my chin, ever so gently, as if to make sure I was real. Then down my neck, to the indent at my collarbone where the clasp of Ginger's black pearls I'd worn to the Crease Ball my first date with Andy had sat.

"Want to hunt for pirate treasure with me?" he asked, his eyes as bright as they must have been on those childhood adventures with Ginger.

I glanced out the door—no one else awake yet.

He kissed me again, and I kissed him back again.

"We go halfsies on anything we find?" I said.

He set the charcoal pencil back on the easel and I stood, stretching tall. "Agreed," he said, "even though I'm the one who knows the island."

"Such amazing expertise, and yet you've failed to find any treasure to date."

He smiled, Ginger's wide grin surrounded by his soft beard. "You haven't seen my collection of arrowheads."

We slipped out the side door from the studio and down a narrow path into the woods. He didn't take my hand until we were out of sight of the house, and when he did, he took my right hand in his left, maybe because he was a southpaw like his sister, or because he was a gentleman, or because he was as aware as I was of the ring on my left hand, the promise I'd made that everything about this moment broke.

Andy deserves better than this, I thought as I linked my fingers in Beau's. Andy deserves better than me.

WE'D ALL GOTTEN pretty comfortable with each other by the Wednesday evening when the eight of us went to dinner at the Pointway Inn. We piled into the jeep the Conrads kept at Chawterley, and we headed down the island, across the no-name road, and into the little crabbing town. Frank drove and the rest of us squeezed in wherever we fit, sitting on laps and in the back where grocery bags might ride. My head bumped up against the ceiling, but my back nestled against Beau's chest, my legs on his legs, so I wasn't about to move.

We drank cocktails on a charming glassed-in porch overlooking the bay, watching the sun sink and redden over the water. I tried to remain engaged in the conversation despite the distraction of Beau's thigh warm against mine, his fingers surreptitiously brushing along my jeans.

"How long does it take from the moment the sun's blazing bottom touches the horizon until its last cut of light disappears?" Laney asked.

"It depends," Trey said.

"It *depends*?" Betts raspberried her lips, very sophisticated. "Doesn't the earth always turn at the same rate? Isn't that what determines how fast the sun disappears?"

"The time it takes the sun to set depends on the latitude you're watching from, the season, and even the atmosphere," Trey said, meeting Betts's incredulity with facts: "The fastest sunsets occur around the times of the equinoxes, on March twenty-first and September twenty-third, and the slowest near the solstices, June twenty-first and December twenty-first. There's a mathematical formula for the approximate time it takes the sun to set on those dates, the variable being latitude. It rises faster at the equator, and more slowly as you approach the poles."

I thought of the long days that summer Mom dragged us to Alaska. Mom's friend that year was Miss Georgia, and she was pretty enough to be the Miss America contestant her name suggested rather than the schoolteacher she was. We stayed in a cabin on the coast, where even in August I was never quite warm enough. Bobby was in his *Harriet the Spy* phase; he had a spy costume he put together from an old hunting vest of Dad's, with binoculars and sunglasses to hide behind, a notebook, and a toy camera, a Holga. I was uncomfortable enough with the idea of him turning his spying eye on Mom that I walked into the little town with him every morning to spy on absolute strangers instead, although I couldn't have told you why. But I did the spying on Mom myself the last night we were there. I stayed up with the midnight sun, watching the straight set of Mom's lips as she and her friend sat on the front porch steps, arguing. I couldn't quite hear their voices from the bushes I hid behind, and I was afraid to move closer, afraid I'd be seen, so I just watched Miss Georgia's angry face, Mom's more impassive one, hoping the sun would set and Miss Georgia would leave and Mom would go inside to sleep.

Sometimes the sun never does set.

"The world land speed record for sunset is two minutes and eight seconds," Trey said as the cocktail waitress brought a fresh round of drinks.

"Here—we're at about thirty-eight degrees latitude—the range will be from about two minutes and forty-five seconds to about three and a quarter minutes."

"That's all?" Betts asked.

"Don't blink."

Laney asked—in what Betts would call her best I'm-working-with-this-guy-next-fall-so-why-not-flatter-him voice—why the atmosphere made a difference.

"It doesn't much," Trey conceded. "Refraction by the atmosphere lifts things a little near the horizon, so they look higher in the sky than they are, but that works at both the top and bottom."

"Both instants are delayed by the same amount so their difference remains the same," I said.

The sole of Beau's foot pressed gently over the laces of mine.

"Exactly," Trey said.

"Unless conditions in the atmosphere change as the sun is setting."

"Exactly," Trey said again.

"Here it goes," Doug said, and we all looked to see the sun kiss the horizon. We watched quietly as the bottom arc flattened, and then Doug began to sing softly: "Is this the little girl I carried?"

Beau's hand settled quietly on my upper thigh as he joined Frank and Trey and Doug for the chorus of "Sunrise, Sunset," the four of them singing in such melancholy tones that the song seemed to bubble up through me as I listened, as I sat mutely watching the sun sink under the darkening bruise of sky.

We ate early-season crabs in the inn's cozy dining room, and drank a delicious French chardonnay, and we talked, and we laughed, and we flirted. It felt right, as though we Ms. Bradwells were completed by this guy gang, as though they were just what we should have been looking for had we known we needed to look. Laney was a little quiet, and she didn't eat much, but maybe she wasn't much for crab, or maybe it was weird for her to be the only black person in the room, although I didn't think that was it. Laney's family had been the only black family in her neighborhood in Denver when she was a kid.

"Dessert is a required course tonight," Trey insisted. "Mrs. Kitching's Smith Island Cake." Eight thin layers of yellow cake interspersed with chocolate icing, brought over by boat from Ewell on Smith Island, which we ate with a slender bottle of dessert wine. And then it was dark, dark,

dark. "Time to see this syzygy," Trey said, and no one objected, no one pointed out that Venus and Mercury wouldn't rise until almost dawn, that if we started now we would be there all night. We wanted to be there all night.

BACK AT THE lighthouse, Doug ducked into the Lightkeeper's Cottage to grab a bottle of scotch while the rest of us headed up the winding stairs. I don't know what I'd expected Trey's telescope to look like— something small and precise, scientific, I suppose—but the one in the middle of the watch room was a fat red tube that even today's supersized me would easily have fit inside. It looked like it should be too heavy to move, but Trey took the bottom end and Frank the top, and they carried it easily up the winding stairs to the lantern deck.

"It's just an empty light bucket," Trey said to Laney. "It doesn't have a lot of bells and whistles, but you're going to love the view, Miss Weils."

Ms. Weils. But Ginger didn't correct him.

"First up: the Roman war god's very own Mars," Trey said.

He used binoculars to scan the sky, then pointed the telescope and looked through an eyepiece near the top of the scope. After a moment, he said, "There she is."

Ginger moved toward the telescope, but Trey said, "How about you first, Mia?"

I hesitated, but Ginger didn't move, so I put my eye to the viewfinder. A reddish bowling ball of a planet loomed big enough that you could see a deep tear in the swirly-patterned fabric of its surface.

"Valles Marineris," Trey said.

"Mariner's Valleys," Laney said.

Trey looked her up and down carefully, like she was a racehorse he might like to bet on. "You know Mars?"

"Just Latin," Ginger answered for Laney, a little dismissively, I thought.

"Greek, too?" Trey asked.

When Laney allowed that she didn't know Greek, he told us the canyon we were looking at was also called Agathadaemon, "the sanctuary of the good spirit." It was ten times as long and three and a half times as deep as the Grand Canyon, he said, on a planet with a radius half that of Earth.

"An eighth the size," I said.

The looks I got . . .

"The volume of a sphere?" I said. "Four-thirds pi times the radius cubed?"

"Mia, the fucking Savant," Ginger said.

We spent the whole night taking turns looking through the telescope and talking about what we saw. Jupiter and Saturn were in fairly straight alignment with Mars so that when Trey showed us where to look—"near that really bright star, which is Spica"—we could identify three starlike dots in a line of not-stars without the telescope. Laney, the first to step up to the telescope to see Saturn, said in an astonished voice, "Saturn looks just exactly like you expect it to—which is so unexpected!" Its rings looked like the ones on the plastic solar system model Bobby had when we were kids, oddly unreal.

In no time at all, it was nearly dawn and we'd seen Uranus and Neptune and Pluto—still a planet in those days—leaving only Venus and Mercury.

"Prepare yourself for the end of the world!" Betts warned, and as always, she was the first to laugh.

It was so easy to laugh back then at doomsday predictions: the earth pulling off its axis, out of its orbit, away from the only warmth we knew. We couldn't imagine our lives could be changed so dramatically in a single moment. When Laney asked Trey, seriously, if scientists expected anything unusual, Ginger offered to make her doomsday placards, help her grow a beard, and feature her in a *New Yorker* cartoon.

"But seriously," Laney repeated.

"Seriously," Trey said, "they expect all the planets to be aligned on the same side of the sun, an event that won't repeat for almost two hundred years. Isn't that unusual enough?"

We all took turns stepping up to the telescope as Venus rose. Then Mercury rose, too, and the world didn't end as near as we could tell. The eight of us—oddly energized despite the glow of light at the horizon—peered eastward as if we might see this final planet without need of the telescope. Trey scanned the horizon with the binoculars, and fiddled with the telescope again, and peered for a long moment before saying quietly, reverently, "There she is."

"Laney," he said as he stepped away from the eyepiece, and she didn't have to be asked twice to take his place.

"Just at the horizon?" she said uncertainly.

Trey motioned Beau to step forward next, but he said no, we ought to let the girls go first, and I felt the warmth of his hand on my back, moving me forward.

I pressed my eye to the glass, but I could see nothing but horizon and lightening sky. Maybe the light still had been dim enough for Trey to see the planet, but it had changed now. Maybe the atmosphere was changing so fast that by the time even Laney put her eye to the viewfinder it had disappeared into the wash of dawn. I don't know. I remember feeling oddly embarrassed, though, as if I'd lost Mercury in something I'd done wrong and my failure would deprive the others of the last chance in our lifetime to glimpse a syzygy.

Trey looked through the eyepiece himself again and adjusted the scope, then peered and adjusted again. "Too much sunlight," he said. "It's gone."

Leaving me remembering again that last night at that cabin in Alaska, with Miss Georgia: I'd stumbled forward, probably nodding off to sleep as I'd spied on Mom and her friend, and the noise had attracted their attention. "Oh hell, Ellen," Miss Georgia had said, and she stood and walked to her car. *"Georgia,"* my mom called softly, but she only stood watching from the porch as Miss Georgia closed the car door and drove away. I remember thinking if I'd known it would be that easy I'd have let Bobby loose with his hunting vest and binoculars and camera the day we'd arrived. But then I'd looked to my mother, seen her expression as she watched the car disappear down the road. I understood even then, I think, that she was in love with Miss Georgia, and that she'd never see her again.

Betts

LANEY HAS DISAPPEARED up the steps to the lantern room and the deck outside it. I hate to leave her there by herself. But I hate to leave Ginger alone here in the watch room. Maybe what happened to Laney is worse than losing your mother or maybe it isn't. It's an ugly scar. No doubt about that. A healed-over-in-a-long-thick-psychological-gash scar. But Laney's scar is hardened and white now. Ginger's is new and raw.

"Ginge?" I say gently.

She looks lost as she turns to me. It's such a not-Ginger thing to do, to appear vulnerable, that I link my arm in hers. A not-me thing to do.

As we stare through the glass to the gray-churning bay, I imagine Ginger having a bonfire out on the waterfront. Sending her mom's books heavenward to Faith in a rising plume of flame and smoke and ash.

"She was an amazing person, your mom was," I say.

Ginger unlinks our arms. Her wide lips press together. "That's a total crock of shit," she says. She's going for light and funny. It was one of Faith's favorite phrases, "a total crock." But "shit" is Ginger's own addition. Her voice betrays the hurt she's trying to hide. It makes me think of that miniature book with the peacock cover she stole.

"Ginge," I say gently. I want to do the your-mother-loved-you-really-she-did thing. But Ginger would see my needing to say it as doubt. Doubt and, worse, pity. Ginger can stand anything but pity.

"It would have been worse if we'd gone to Mother about it," she insists. "I know you don't think so, but it would have been."

I should tell her the truth: that I did go to her mother. But I don't know how to begin that conversation.

"Laney wouldn't have been able to bear the public humiliation," she insists, taking my silence as disagreement. "You know that. You fucking knew it at the time."

You fucking knew it, or thought you did. That's the sudden anger I almost spit out. You fucking knew it and wouldn't listen to anyone else. And here we are now. Here I am now. About to be the one bearing the public humiliation. Having to withdraw my name from consideration for the Court under a cloud that will hang over me the rest of my life. Doomed to have the mention of my name in the press forever followed by "whose nomination for the Supreme Court was withdrawn when questions arose about a death on Cook Island in 1982." And I will never be appointed to any bench, much less the Supreme Court.

You fucking never listen, I almost say. You never listen, and look where it's gotten you. Passed over for partner. Let out to pasture. Doing nothing at all with your life.

The bitterness in Ginger's voice stops me, though. Not just because she might be right about Laney. Not just because she might be right about what I thought. But because of the certainty revealed in her tone: she believes her mother went to her grave thinking Trey was the golden boy. The child Ginger herself could never be. And I never told her differently. I let this misunderstanding separate them when I might have brought Ginger closer to her mom. And now it's too late.

Mia

LAW QUADRANGLE NOTES, Winter 2002: Mary Ellen ("Mia") Porter (JD '82) is delighted to report that her goddaughter Isabelle Johnson took second place in the high school division of the national chess championships held in Memphis this winter. Ms. Johnson's mother, Elsbieta ("Betts") Zhukovski (JD '82) can claim no role in her daughter's accomplishment, as, despite her Eastern European heritage and years of Ms. Porter's tutoring, she can't grasp the concept that "the horsey-guy" can jump over even a king.

I REMEMBER WAKING in the Chawterley Sun Room to Faith's voice booming, "Well, good afternoon, everyone!" and the sight of the crab-eating, gut-running, sunrise-watching gang—or most of us—startling awake on the rattan couches and the floor. She stood looking from the back foyer into the Sun Room with a man I recognized from photos as Ginger's father. He had the same fair skin and broad hands, and the same hint of almost-arrogance in the angle of his not insubstantial nose. In Ginger, the hint was in her eyes more than her nose, though, and was just a cover for the many shortcomings she meant to hide from the world.

The fact of her parents' arrival registered in those almost-arrogant, sleep-faded eyes of Ginger's as Trey and Frank came in, each holding one handle of a cooler. While we'd slept—maybe dreaming of seeing the syzygy we'd missed or maybe not—her brother and cousin had taken the boat across the bay to fetch her parents. Ginger was the one her parents hadn't seen in months, the one you'd think they'd be most anxious to see, but they'd asked Frank and Trey rather than her to come for them.

She snapped up to a sitting position, then stood and smoothed her rumpled clothes. "Daddy! Happy birthday!" She hurried to her father and gave him a big hug.

If her mother felt excluded from the greeting, she didn't show it, she only raised her eyebrows slightly at a woman who stepped into the foyer behind her, as if to say *See, I told you they'd be slugs.* "There are things to be brought in from the boat, gang, if you all don't mind waking now that it's"—Faith eyed her watch—"two in the afternoon?"

"Aunt Margaret!" Ginger exclaimed. "Brody. I didn't know you two were coming today."

While I was trying to interpret her tone—surprise, clearly, but was she pleased or not?—she turned to Laney and Betts and me. "This is Mother's friend from *her* law school days, Margaret Traurig. Aunt Margaret, this is Betts. I told you about her, remember?"

Betts stood and shook her hand, and Ginger introduced Laney and me. Following Betts's lead, I shook Margaret's hand, conscious of my unbrushed teeth, my unwashed face.

Ginger moved to the side of the woman's husband, saying, "This is Brody, who can drop a duck from about three million yards away with his eyes closed."

Brody wrapped an arm around her shoulders and mussed her hair as if she were a little girl.

"You're the shooter here, sweetheart," he insisted. Then to us, "First time I shared a blind with this little girl, she took down a duck from an incoming flock over one pond and turned and shot one just leaving another hole while I was still pumping my gun."

"Anyone can do that from the Triangle," Ginger said.

"Well, only you and Trey here ever have, far as I know," Brody said.

Trey, wide awake and windblown from the trip across the bay, said, "The duck stops here," provoking chuckles from Mr. Conrad and Brody, and groans from Ginger and Frank.

"You're coming out with us Saturday morning?" Brody asked Ginger. Then to Beau, as if an afterthought, "You too, son?"

Beau glanced at me, and I raised my eyebrows, noticing Betts watching us, trying to appear not to be—the expression on her freckled face saying *Pick, for God's sake, Mia. Beau or Andy. I'll take your leftovers, and wear them well.*

I felt guilty, I did, I felt selfish. I could see Betts liked Beau, and I had Andy. But I didn't want to pick.

Trey touched Laney's arm lightly. "You're all welcome to tag along. It's an amazing way to experience dawn."

Laney frowned in my direction: how far did she have to go to make nice with a partner in her firm? I shook my head ever so slightly; Laney would lose her breakfast the moment anything was shot in front of her, and that would be a story Frank, and probably Trey, too, would get a kick out of telling to anyone who'd listen.

"Not so many pairs of waders to fit them, I'm afraid," Frank said. "And Ginger never *has* been much for sharing her hunting gear."

"It was *my gun*," Ginger said, her tone truly light this time; this was a conversation that had played out before, all in good fun. "I share fine, but I can't hunt without my gun."

Laney pulled at the shirt I was wearing. "Ginger's shirt." Then at the shirt she was wearing herself. "Ginger's shirt. We vouch. She shares."

"We vouch," I agreed.

"My *gun,* Frankie," Ginger repeated, "which I clean while you dump yours in the closet and forget about it until the next time we hunt. So I'm supposed to give you mine because we're out shooting and yours is so gunked up it barely fires?"

She sounded so reasonable that I wondered what little fact she was leaving out. Ginger tends to sound most reasonable when she is least entitled to lay claim to the word.

Trey leaned close to her and whispered theatrically, "You *had* shot your limit an hour earlier, Ginger. You shot your limit in about eight seconds that day."

Ah. There it was: her gun that she no longer needed but still didn't want to share.

Ginger rubbed her ear, grinning that way she did whenever she stepped up to the grade wall and saw an A beside her number. She never blinked when she didn't get an A, but we could always tell by the absence of her wide, unabashed grin.

"And that's a bad thing?" she said. "That's a reason for me to hand my gun over so Frankie can fail to take care of it like he fails to take care of his own gun? I didn't see you handing yours over that morning, Trey."

"Of course, *I* hadn't shot my limit yet. I still needed my gun."

Again, the grin: she'd just gotten Trey to admit she was a better shot than he was, which was so much sweeter than having to say it herself.

"After you shot your limit, though," she said.

Trey said, "Frank was still up on me for the season."

Frank said, "But I wasn't up on you, Ginge. You were still way ahead of me. Besides, you were . . . what? Maybe fifteen?"

Trey extracted his Marlboros from his pocket and lit one. "Thirteen."

When Frankie balked, Trey insisted, "She was only thirteen, and she still outbagged you, boy."

"Enough!" Faith interrupted with more exasperation than I would have imagined, although that might have had as much to do with too much work left behind in D.C. and too much party preparation ahead of her at Chawterley as it did with her children needing more attention than she could give. "Enough." She found a cigarette, and Trey lit it for her, the menthol of hers mingling with the grittier smell of his. "It's your father's birthday weekend. We have a hundred people coming. Let's all make nice in the sandbox for just these four days, shall we? Now, out to the boat, everyone."

That was Thursday about 2:00 in the afternoon, as Faith didn't let us forget all the rest of that day, or on into the evening. Despite our explanation that we'd stayed up all night to watch the syzygy, despite the hunting guns and suitcases and many bottles of birthday champagne we schlepped from boat to house without complaint, her disapproval hung thick in the Chawterley air. I felt the keen shot of her disappointment not so much through any coldness to us, but through her warmth toward Frank and Trey, who'd taken the boat across to fetch them while the rest of us slept. I think that was when I began to understand a little better Ginger's relationship with her mom.

Betts

~∿~

GINGER GLANCES UP at a sound from above us, Laney out on the lantern deck. "Shit, she went up by herself?" she says. Without waiting for an answer, she charges the last flight of lighthouse stairs. Two at a time. Despite her bare feet. I feel a little bubble in my heart as I watch her go. Which is maybe affection. Or maybe jealousy. Or maybe both. All the Ms. Bradwells are close. But there are no closer friends in this world than Laney and Ginge. We are a foursome composed of two pairs. If I have a best friend it's Mia. How can I think she would have written that blog?

Anyone at Mr. Conrad's party might have written it. *Someone turns up dead like that, anyone at that party might have doubts.* Mia is right about that. Anyone on the island, even. But she was so quick with that answer.

Not that I really imagine Mia is jealous enough of me to say those particular unsaid things in an anonymous blog. But why didn't she tell me she'd lost her job? Or if she didn't want to bother me during the hearings, then Ginger or Laney. Ginger, because Laney has enough to worry about with her campaign.

Upstairs, the door creaks. Ginger going to Laney.

A speck appears on the horizon. It remains after I blink. A fishing boat. A yacht out for a morning cruise. I push back the irrational hope that it's Izzy and Anne; if anyone is headed to this island this morning it's the press. I push back the thought of Trey found dead in this room. The memory of Zack in his hospital bed.

Zack, when he knew he was dying, asked me to play two songs on my zhaleika at his funeral service. He had always loved to hear me play. He said Laney could accompany me on the piano for the first song just like we had in the law school talent show; she and I always played together when we visited. But Zack wanted me to play the second song by myself. He never said why. He just asked me to promise I would play it alone.

"You aren't going to die," I'd said.

"I know," he said. "But promise me, just in case."

When the moment for me to play at the funeral came I sat in the pew holding on to Izzy. Unable to move. Laney was at the piano and the silence in the church was interminable. Mia asked in a low whisper if I wanted her to tell Laney to play alone. But Matka was already standing. She took Isabelle from my arms and placed her in Mia's hands. Mia, who I know will take care of Izzy if ever she needs taking care of and I'm not there. Mia was the only one other than Matka to whom I could have entrusted my daughter in that moment.

She put my instrument in my hands and she extracted her own zhaleika from the bag she'd carried mine in. She took my hand and walked with me to the seat set up by the piano where I was to play. "Our music will rise up to Zack," she whispered as she guided me. "He will know you and Isabelle will be okay, and he can be at peace."

The three of us played Lynyrd Skynyrd's "None of Us Are Free," Zack's personal anthem. He'd gone to Yale Law School meaning to change the world. Izzy started cooing as we finished the song, the way she always did whenever Zack tickled her. As if his spirit was with us in the church.

I looked to Matka, sure I couldn't possibly play the second song alone. She blew the first notes of "Let It Be," and I raised my zhaleika to my mouth and joined her. Only as I was blowing the last note did I realize that I was playing alone. That I had been doing so for most of the song.

The whole church was almost sacredly silent after I lowered my zhaleika. Even Izzy no longer making a sound. Stifled sniffles from around the room. The quiet drip as my own tears splashed onto my instrument.

Izzy exploded into such an enraged wail then that she captured how everyone in that church felt about Zack's dying so young. Oddly, the whole church erupted in laughter. To this day I can't explain why. But even I had laughed.

I measure that funeral now against the way Ginger and her brothers buried Faith: after Frank and his family returned from their uninterrupted European vacation. In a ceremony that excluded even their closest friends. I can't now imagine how I ever thought I'd trade Matka in for Faith. Or even for Ginger's whole extended family.

I thought I wanted Izzy to have a big family like that. But if I did, why have I never reached out to anyone else after Zack? I didn't even have the excuse Matka did. The possibility my husband might still be alive somewhere.

Perhaps we're better off having only each other. Like Matka and me. Perhaps an abundance of family inevitably leaves one taking them for granted the same way we take for granted so many things we have more than enough of. More than we need.

THE DOT ON the horizon is taking shape. A large power boat. The kind I'd look for if I were a reporter trying to cross the Chesapeake to Cook Island. We've reached no conclusions about what we should do or what we should make public. What we should admit and what we should continue to deny. But the fact that we aren't ready for the cameras and reporters isn't going to slow their descent on us.

How powerful are their lenses? Can they see us here if they know where to look? Would withdrawing my name from consideration for the Court take us out of this spotlight? Or would it just fuel the flames?

The unsubstantiated whiff of scandal already in the air will sink my appointment. I'm suspect to start with. An immigrant woman who, as smart as I might be, has no judicial experience. I suppose it shouldn't matter: Is having my particular mind deciding the law more important than remaining a professor and having it shape thousands of young minds to do so in the future? It's hard to say which would have the bigger impact. And yet I want this appointment to the bench. I think I would be a good justice. Perhaps it's bragging to think so, but I'm good at considering all sides of a thing. I'm fair. I think I can imagine lives different from my own. I think I have a good sense of what isn't right. And what is.

This you must remember, Elsbieta.

Having an immigrant on the Court will make a difference, too, the way the justices serving with Thurgood Marshall said he made a difference just by being there. Not the daughter of an immigrant like Justice Sotomayor. Someone who was actually brought to this country from another world. A physical representation of what closing our borders costs us. A symbol of what denying immigrant children a public school education might mean.

Having more women on the Court is important, too: women who understand what it means to be denied equal wages because of gender. Who know how difficult it is to do one's best in a work environment where our breasts are more closely examined than our work. (Okay, maybe not *my* particular breasts.) And Faith taught me well what rights women used be denied, and where we are now, and what we still need to insist upon. She taught me how to compromise, too. And how and when not to. But there is more to it than that. The truth is I want this for myself. I want to reach this goal I set even before I was a Ms. Bradwell. When only Matka believed I could reach goals like this. I want it for Isabelle. So her future will hold more possibility. I want it for Matka. For all the sacrifices she made for me. For her certainty that choosing to do the right thing was always the better path.

I *could* have told her I was pregnant in law school. She wouldn't have been ashamed of me. She would have felt only love. She was a mother. The worst that could happen to her no longer had anything to do with what might happen to *her* and everything to do with what might happen to *me*, her daughter. There was nothing she wouldn't endure for me. Just as there is nothing I wouldn't endure for Izzy. Nothing Ginger wouldn't endure for Annie. Or Laney for Gem. Or Mia for any of the girls. It's a mother's lot. I suppose it must have been Faith's lot, too.

So what do we do now? Can we possibly ask Laney to tell the world about her rape? How could that do anything but undermine Gemmy's sense of safety? How can a daughter feel safe if the mother who is supposed to keep her from harm can't even protect herself? Is that the lesson she would be teaching? That the world is as dangerous a place for our daughters as it was for us? What could possibly be gained by telling that truth?

And yet how can I ask for a place on the Court without laying the truth of what happened at Cook Island out in the open? *This you must remember, Elsbieta: to be leader you must lead, even when it will harm you. To be leader, you must always do what is right.*

Laney

〜〜〜

LAW QUADRANGLE NOTES, Summer 1987: Helen ("Laney") Weils (JD '82) married William Robeson on July 3 in Atlanta, Georgia. The bride will keep her name and, after considerable negotiation, the groom will, too.

AFTER TWO WILD nights of gut-running and stargazing and falling asleep after dawn, we went to bed with the chickens the night Faith and Mr. Conrad arrived at Chawterley. We set the alarm for 5:15 a.m., an hour before the sun would show itself, not to please Faith but to have one more opportunity to see Mercury rise. We didn't precisely leap from bed when it went off, but we did dress and make our way to the lighthouse by the light of a not quite full moon. *Non est ad astra mollis e terris via.* There is no easy way from the earth to the stars.

This time, I insisted on having the last turn at the telescope, and we all did see Mercury there at the horizon, or we all said we did. It was as close as we were going to get to seeing all the planets on the same night.

We spent the rest of Friday helping unload the boats each time Trey and Ginger or Frank and Beau returned with guests, carrying luggage and pouring iced tea and lemonade and, later in the afternoon, cocktails. We ought to have been beat by the time dinner was served Friday evening, a buffet catered by the Pointway Inn so guests could eat whenever they arrived. But we were so young then, and the house so chock-full of the older Conrads' friends that we jumped at Mr. Conrad's suggestion that we "kids" go for a swim. We put on our bikinis and Frank dug sweatshirts from the dresser in the Captain's Office—his bedroom he'd turned over to guests for the weekend—not wanting us to freeze our fannies off *again,* he said.

We weren't in the icy water a quick minute before Ginger shed her suit. We'd been sipping cocktails all evening, and Ginger always did get wild when she drank. Beau mentioned that Mia and Betts and I might be uncomfortable skinny-dipping with a bunch of fellas we'd hardly been introduced to, but Ginger insisted we "were cool," and Trey was already adding his suit to Ginger's on the pier, telling Beau not to be a "sissy-assed prude." Even Mia was untying her top in the moonlight.

The sun was long set and the moon not yet risen, at least there was that. I tried to shrug off my discomfort as we splashed each other, as we raced to the buoy and back, working up a little warmth, our own laughter mixing with that spilling from the house. Breathless from the race, we tilted our heads back to see the stars, and we talked about people all over the world seeing the same sky, and what might be up there, and whether there was life anywhere else in the universe. I was starting to shiver in a serious way when I had the sense someone was missing. Had Mia and Beau swum off somewhere? But then Beau directed us all to observe the moon rising big and bright at the horizon, the light soft on the gentle waves.

"Does the moon rise as quickly as the sun sets?" Mia asked. *Two minutes and eight seconds. Don't blink.*

When no one answered, I knew Trey was the one missing.

I climbed Fool's Hill in a hurry searching for my suit again. I tried to stay low in the water, but I couldn't sort through the pile on the pier without my breasts peeking up into the moonlight. Only Mia's face was turned toward me, though, so I pulled myself partway out of the water, pressed myself against the waterlogged wood, and dug. I had half a mind to put on whichever bottom I came to first, if only mine might've fit anyone else. But I had to stand twice in the same place to cast a good shadow back in those days.

Everyone was getting out then, Ginger saying, "Shit, it's cold." That's when I saw Trey still in the water, floating alone on the far side of the pier.

IN THE WARMTH of the fire at the Lightkeeper's Cottage, we all had a good laugh over my bikini bottoms being inside out under my borrowed sweatshirt. By the time I'd rectified that particular situation in the light-keeper's primitive bathroom, the others were sitting around a Risk game map of the world with a newly opened bottle of scotch and glasses all around.

"You sit here, Lane," Ginger said, patting the floor between her and Doug. "You're purple."

"A world domination color," Frank joked, and he handed me a glass of scotch I didn't much want.

"You have to change more quickly if you want a say in what color you are," Ginger said.

Trey lit a cigarette, grabbed a cheap tin ashtray from a table, and said, "Purple. The pope's color."

"Laney the Good Girl," Mia said.

"She's not Roman Catholic any more than you are," Betts said with an edge in her voice that was all about how close Mia sat to Beau.

"I'm sorry to say, you also pick last, Lane," Ginger said. "I rolled the die for you, fair and square."

Everyone else had set colored blocks of wood on the board: armies, Doug explained when it was clear I had no idea how to play this game. At his suggestion, I set my first block on Brazil, and settled in.

I was playing well enough with Doug's help—never you mind all Ginger's protests that he was guiding me to attack everyone but him—when Trey picked up the bottle and started refilling glasses. I alone needed no refill.

"Sadly, gentlemen, our scotch does not meet with Miss Weils's standards," he said.

I protested and took a polite sip.

"Like this, Lane." Ginger drained her refilled glass and held it out to Trey again.

"Cheers," Beau said, and lifted his glass and did the same, perhaps with a sideways glance at Mia. Which was probably why Betts, without hesitating, drained her glass. And Mia never will be outdone by Betts. I was left the last Ms. Bradwell standing, too self-conscious not to drain my glass.

Ginger cleared Trey out of Australia on the next turn, gaining additional armies by possessing that whole continent.

"You unfriendly slut," Trey said, joking, yes, and Ginger laughed and held her glass out for more scotch, but still the word left me uneasy. Trey dutifully refilled her glass, then went around the group, playing host. When he got to my still full glass, he tapped the edge of the bottle against its side. I hoped I didn't look as stupid as I felt. Why was I like that, feeling as dumb as dirty dishwater just because I didn't like to get drunk? I wasn't much used to folks noticing, was the thing.

I lifted my glass and I said, *"Meus calix inebriat me!"* and took a substantial slug of scotch.

Ginger had a no-Latin finger cross up faster than any half-drunk Risk player ought to have managed, and Betts and Mia followed suit.

"An inside joke," I told the fellas.

"Clearly our cups are making us *all* drunk," Trey said. "Not just you."

And somehow that comment left me feeling all right. Maybe it was the fact that he'd understood the Latin, or that he was still sober enough to translate, or that he wasn't embarrassed that he could. If Ginger hadn't been between us, I might have leaned a head on his shoulder affectionately, as she sometimes did. I might have done it before it occurred to me I shouldn't, that it might not be appropriate to be that comfortable with someone I would work with, someone who'd told everyone at the office who would listen how brilliant he thought I was. Who'd taken the liberty of kissing me, yes, but only that once.

Beau was the first to lose all his armies, followed quickly by Mia; if they were throwing the game so they could go off alone together, they had the good sense to lose their countries to Ginger. As Mia tossed her last army back into its little box, Beau asked her if she'd like to take another peek at the sky. Mia hopped up and brushed off the seat of her bikini, and off they headed to the lighthouse. Betts, across the board from me, rolled her eyes.

Ginger established a second line of attack on the Risk board, in North America, but that was later, after Trey had been eliminated and I'd been reduced to a few insupportable armies. Doug eliminated me altogether by attacking my South American holdings through Africa. "To establish a bulkhead against Ginger's North American flank," he explained with no hint of real regret. "The battle for world domination is serious stuff."

Trey stubbed a half-smoked cigarette out in the now-full tin ashtray and said this gang could be playing for some time yet, and would I like to join Mia and Beau?

THE LIGHTHOUSE LANTERN had been flashing when we went into the cottage, but it was off by the time Trey and I emerged. Who knew what Mia and Beau were doing up there? I challenged Trey to a race to the top, calling out, "First one to the watch room," already sprinting off ahead of him, intent on making enough noise that Mia would hear us coming. I thought I could stall at the watch room on the excuse of catching my breath to buy Mia just a little more time to, say, put her panties back on.

I made the most unprofessional ruckus racing up the stairs, whooping and calling out taunts to Trey. By the time I got to the watch room I truly did need to catch my breath. Trey would have won our little race if I'd given him a chance to get by me on the narrow stairs.

As we stood collecting ourselves, Trey reached a hand to the back of my neck and pulled me to him, and kissed me. I closed my lips to the stale cigarette and scotch taste of his mouth, and after a moment he took the hint, stepping back and turning away from me.

"Beau!" he called out as he sprinted up the last flight of stairs from the watch room to the lantern room. "You better be handling that telescope as lovingly as you handle your own little friend."

I did hesitate then. I know I did. I felt a jolt of unease. But he'd seemed embarrassed when I didn't kiss him back, and maybe he meant Mia rather than the part of Beau's anatomy I was imagining he meant. He'd been drinking, and so had I, and he'd just followed my bikini-covered fanny up more than a hundred stairs. Not everything was as clear as it should have been. Nothing seemed clear except that Mia would be up on the lantern deck, and when we Ms. Bradwells stuck together, we were always just fine.

Trey was already at the telescope when I emerged from the lantern room. I don't expect I realized he was alone until I was beside him, until he reached out and took my arm and said, "Look, you have to see this." And so I put my eye to the telescope.

He put his arms around me again, began kissing my neck. I stiffened. I said no. I'm sure I must have said no.

"Yes," he said gently.

And when I resisted, he said, "You like that game? I can play that game." And before I knew what was happening, it was happening. I was up against the railing, looking out over the wave-crashing darkness, with my arm twisted behind my back. Pressed so hard against the rail that I was sure I was going to plummet all that way to the hard earth. He was stripping my bikini bottom down to my knees with his other hand. He was pressing his body against mine, the heat and scotch of his breath on my ear. I started to scream into the crash of waves below, but he slapped a hand over my mouth.

"Careful," he said. "I like that, I do, and probably no one can hear you, but we don't really want a crowd.

"You know how the crabs do it?" he said, his breath hot and stale in my ear as he stripped my suit the rest of the way down with his foot. "The she-crab pisses a scent that sends the jimmy all into a lather. Do you do that, Laney? Do you piss like that?"

I tried to bite his hand and he drew back, but in a way that left me feeling I would surely fall over the rail. And then he was stuffing my bikini bottom into my mouth, laughing, pressing me up against that high, high rail again.

"A month from now, bobbing corks will scatter across all the water you can see from here, each attached to a caged jimmy crab who wants to fuck all the ladies he can," he said, his voice in my ear again as he stripped off his own suit. "The silly sooks swim right into his cage, wanting him to fuck them. They crowd into the cages until there are fifty or a hundred or more ladies all wanting the one jimmy to fuck them. Do you think they get hot then, all those slutty ladies panting after the same man?" His fingers squeezing my breast so hard. "He fucks as many as he can before the crabber pulls the pot up. And then you know what happens?" He shoved himself into me, then, my insides ripping so that I screamed in pain, choking on the cloth. "The slutty ladies go to the boiling pot while the jimmy goes back into the water, to a whole new slew of lady crabs climbing into his cage."

Laney

~~~~

THE DOOR FROM the lantern room scrapes open behind me, and the sound of Ginger's rushed breath mixes with the lap of the bay below and the smell of wet cement, the awful aftertaste of remembering Trey.

"He called me a slut," I say, wanting suddenly to hand it all over to her, to have her lift it from me. But I don't turn to her, I can't face her.

She doesn't move on the lantern deck behind me. She just stands dumbly, not even approaching the rail. She didn't believe me then and she doesn't believe me now. She'll never alter her notion of what happened that night. How could she if she'd been sleeping with Trey for years by then? It's why I've never told the awful details even to her, my closest friend. Because she can't bear to hear them. She can't bear to face what it means about who she is, what she thinks it means about who she is.

What kind of woman loves a man who rapes?

I keep staring out at the bay that had been dark that night, until the door from the lantern room opens again, Betts joining us.

"A nigger slut, that's what he called me," I say, throwing the bitter words at Ginger. *A whole new bunch of lady crabs present their backsides to him, little nigger sluts like you wanting to skip the kissing and romance and go straight to the fuck.*

Betts and Ginger close ranks, one on either side of me, and I want Ginger to just go away, and I don't. The three of us stare out at the sea, at the faraway spit of mainland and the little dot on the water at the horizon. Betts's hand covers mine.

When Ginger gently fingers my hair, I'm back in the bunkroom, with

Ginger climbing into bed with me that next night, wrapping herself around me, protecting me. Would things have been different if I'd told them this then?

I expect there was only so much I could say, though, not just because Ginger didn't want to hear it, but because I couldn't bear to believe it myself.

"I didn't worry about getting pregnant," I say. "It wasn't that way."

Betts's hand tightens over mine, and Ginger leans her head on my shoulder. They don't look at me. I expect they know this is hard to admit even without having to face them, without them being able to see the shame in my eyes.

Why does it shame me, this thing I had no control over? But there it is, even after all these years. Maybe I ought to be thankful that he took me in a way that wouldn't leave me pregnant, but it only makes the shame worse, even with the Ms. Bradwells, even now that I'm trying to get past it, now that I'm running for office and thinking I've decided my past be damned, it wasn't my fault.

I don't know if I would ever have told even William if it wasn't for a midnight call from Mia a few months ago, not very long after Faith passed. My telephone ringing off the hook in the middle of the night, an East Coast number I'm sure it was because I thought it was Faith's number, I had that moment of thinking *Faith? I hope she's okay* as I picked up the receiver, before remembering Faith wasn't okay at all, Faith was dead. It was Mia saying she was thinking of getting married again, ringing me in the middle of the night like she needed my approval or my permission or maybe just my advice before she could accept a fella's ring.

"Well, do you love him, Mi?" I asked. Not terribly original, but I wasn't half awake.

"He sings beautifully, Lane," she answered.

The sun could have risen and set again in the time I tried to make sense of that one, before I decided she must mean it as a euphemism. For as much sex as Mia has, her reluctance to talk about it is a thing to behold.

"Mi," I said. "A good voice is certainly an important thing to look for in a husband. A good voice does go a long way."

She said, "Remember Doug Pemberley from Cook Island?"

Just a name, not even Trey's name, but I sat in my bed in the darkness, William asleep beside me, the shame catching me by surprise.

I think I stammered something like, "Well, I do suppose if he sings *that* well . . ."

She seemed as at loss for words as I was, which is very un-Mia.

"The ring is gorgeous," she said finally, in a way that made me wonder if this ring was such an ugly thing that it made her doubt her choice of this fella, whoever he was. Made me think this was more difficult somehow than I imagined it was for her. Made me set aside my own feelings and try to attend to hers.

"But do you *love* him, Mi?" I insisted.

Her answer to that question was even odder than the thing about the singing: "I want to, Lane. Maybe I even do. Maybe I do love him. But I don't think I should. I don't think any of us would be happy, do you?"

I didn't know what to say to that. *Any of us?* And when I didn't say anything she thanked me for always being there to listen and she told me she loved me and said goodbye and hung up before I could say another thing. I rang her right back on the number she'd called from, but there was no answer, just an endless ringing at the end of the line. And when I rang her cell, I got the message on the first ring, her phone turned off. William was awake by then, asking who it was, if the children were all right, and so I let go of thinking about Mia to assure my husband our children were fine.

I couldn't reach Mia that next morning, but that never did worry me much; so often she's in remote places where cellphones simply don't work. I did call Betts, though. I told her about the call, and she said maybe Mia was seeing someone new, but then when wasn't she? And when I finally heard from Mia again she clearly wasn't meaning to marry anybody anytime soon. She's not wearing a ring now, anyway, and when I mentioned that I guessed she'd decided not to marry the fella with the ugly ring, she looked confused for a moment, and then said she'd decided I was right, that she didn't love him. Which I hadn't said at all. But if Mia wants to lay the responsibility of her remaining single on my shoulders, it's all right by me. Lord knows she's done enough kindnesses for me over the years that I'm glad of the chance to pay a small kindness back.

GINGER WIPES HER eyes, I can feel her hand moving to her face on my shoulder, but I just keep staring out at the not-endless sea, at the sunlight sharp in my eyes.

"I'm sorry I ever doubted you," she says.

An anger I thought I let go of that night talking to William rises up in me, the long familiar tightening in my throat and my spine and my fists. What kind of fool is she, thinking she can just apologize thirty years after the fact and have everything be fine? She was the only person in this whole world I could have talked to, and she pushed me away without even trying to hide her disgust.

When we parted after graduation, I walked away from that friendship just as surely as I walked away from everything else. I called Maynard and told him I'd like to work in the mayor's office after all. I called Tyler & McCoy and told them I'd been offered a political appointment, and they deferred me for a year, and the year came and went and I stayed in Atlanta. I chose an apartment that was more expensive than I could afford but had a security desk and cameras monitoring all the public spaces. I didn't realize until I moved in that what I'd like about the security desk was that the security guard who'd been there when I signed the lease was a confident, heavyset older woman named Mildred, who would have been no defense against anyone with a weapon but who seemed likely to interrogate any fella coming in with me so aggressively that he wouldn't stay. She wasn't there when I moved in; her role that morning was played by a younger fella I never did find comforting. But Mildred turned out to be the evening shift, and was for a long time the closest thing I had to an Atlanta friend.

I didn't date that first year. I didn't go out at night. I didn't even want a roommate. Roommates were only good for betraying you when you most needed them. I bought a used exercise bicycle, and I came home at night and locked myself in my secure apartment, and I bicycled off to nowhere, and watched television and read and slept not all that well. I was depressed, I see that now, but maybe only because I know the statistics: rape victims suffer from depression ten times more often than others do. I was depressed but I had this notion that I was just fine, that I was moving on with my life.

So many times, I thought about telling Mama. I would start conversations in my mind: Mama, can I tell you about something that happened to me? But telling my parents only would have caused them pain; they'd have felt they should have protected me even though no one could have protected me. That's what I told myself. I started conversations with Faith, too. I thought I might tell Faith. But she, as much as my parents, would have taken the guilt on herself: it was her home, her nephew.

And there was the shame of it, too. I see that now. The shame that if I was raped it was my fault. The shame simply of being able to be taken, of not being strong enough or in control enough, or pure enough. *Cogi qui potest nescit mori.* She who can be forced does not know how to die.

I never told my parents that I slept with Carl either, or anything else I did sexually when I was young. All of it would have made them think less of me, I was so sure of that. It never occurred to me that they ever might have felt the same things. What is it about parents that makes you think they never do live life?

Years later, when I first met William, I didn't want what had happened to be part of the way he thought of me, I just wanted to leave it behind. I knew what happened wasn't my fault. I knew that. But knowing a thing is not the same as believing it. And maybe I didn't even want to believe it.

My silence left me lonely, and angry at Ginger but also, in the little eddies where the anger ebbed, understanding better why Ginger was so messed up when it came to men. How do you get over being seduced when you're just a child? When you think what is happening is love and then, when you begin to realize at some level, probably not even consciously, that it isn't love, you try so hard to make it become love? And how can you possibly make love out of something that is at best a young man's sickness? Poor Ginge.

You feel at fault. You know you were meaning for this man to like you. You know the way you've always gotten men to like you is by being attractive to them. That's what men like: pretty gals who flirt with them. And I was flirting with Trey that night. I was. There it is. Maybe I was flirting with him that day at the firm, before he kissed me in the elevator. Maybe I don't know how to talk to a man and not flirt a little bit. It's not even sexual, exactly. It's more that Southern hostess thing, the compulsion to make sure everyone is having a good time. Mama always flirted with Daddy's friends, and Daddy with Mama's, and I don't imagine either of them ever went home with anyone else.

You feel at fault because in retrospect everything you did looks like something different than just trying to be a nice girl. It looks like the opposite of trying to be a nice girl.

Or maybe it isn't that at all. Maybe you *want* it to be your fault. The thing about it being your fault is that it means you have some control over it, that you have some ability to keep it from happening again. Maybe you'd rather be a slut who can control your world than a victim who can't.

Ginger called me a few days after I moved to Atlanta, just after I'd started my bar review course. "Hey, I was just calling to see how you're settling in," she said. "Is your apartment nice? Have you met anyone yet?" And then, without giving me a chance to answer, she said, "I miss you, Lane. I wish we'd all gone to the same city. I miss everyone, but especially you."

And I remembered then the feel of her arms wrapped around me in bed the night Trey Humphrey died, her quiet weeping, and I saw that I'd forgiven her already. I saw that she was sorry even if she'd never said the words, that she'd seen the truth that night on Cook Island but just couldn't admit it, even to herself. That she probably never would.

GINGER

LAW QUADRANGLE NOTES, Summer 1990: Virginia ("Ginger") Cook Conrad (JD '82) has moved with her family to Shaker Heights, Ohio, where she is enjoying retirement almost as much as is her nine iron, which was retired into the pond on the third hole of the Canterbury Country Club, in full view of the clubhouse. Visitors to the city should contact her for sailboat tours of the lakefront. Golfers should contact her husband, Ted.

I'M NOT SURE I can say to this day exactly what happened after I won that late-night Risk game, and in celebration had another shot of scotch, or maybe two. But I do remember Mia saying we should call the police. "Evidence of rape needs to be collected as soon as possible," she insisted. She had no idea what the hell she was talking about, though, how awful it is to go to the police as a rape victim. It's like being violated all over again, that's what Mother always said. "The largely male police force collecting evidence doesn't often have the good sense to treat a rape victim's body better than any other crime scene they secure."

Not long before Mother died, she forwarded to pretty much everyone she knew a link to a *New York Times* column that described how rape victims have to undress over paper so every speck of anything on you can be collected: a strand of your husband's hair from his morning goodbye kiss, the little bit of ash from the cigarette you snuck after he left, a crumb from the cookie your daughter ate in your lap at the park, which you finished when she'd had enough. They examine every pore of your body with sterile swabs and ultraviolet light, and they photograph the details. God forbid you should have had sex, or masturbated, or taken a fucking bubble bath. Then the rape kit more often than not sits untested for months or even years while the rapist runs free. All those poor women (or girls; half of rape victims are minors) going through all that humiliation for nothing.

When Mother forwarded that column, I wondered if she had an inkling of what had happened that spring break. But the prosecution of domestic violence and sexual assault cases had been high on her agenda for years by then. She'd been involved in the passage of the Violence Against Women Act and in the unsuccessful defense of its civil provisions in the *Morrison* case. She'd pushed for the Debbie Smith Act in 2004, then fumed when the $500 million it provided to process rape kits was funneled elsewhere. She'd made sure everyone she knew heard that New York City's efforts to process rape kits resulted in a doubling of arrests for reported rapes. She'd spent countless hours on a case in Pennsylvania where ten women testified that the accused had drugged and raped them. *Ten women.* And that wasn't enough for a jury to convict that dickhead. He actually kept a "Yearly Calendar of Women" and lied about who he was, but the jury chose to believe he was a playboy rather than a rapist because his victims had each had a drink with him. The jury chose to believe all those women lied under oath, that they all wanted what they got.

The idea that women want to be taken by force is deeply imbedded in our culture: Zeus, Apollo, and Poseidon all raped with shocking frequency and enthusiasm, their victims emerging unharmed and with the blessing of a godly child. Revered authors like Updike write "as a raped woman might struggle, to intensify the deed" and "You know what a rape usually is? It's a woman who changed her mind afterward." *He knows, or thinks he knows, what you secretly wanted.* Not that men are the only ones to beat that drum. Perhaps the worst offender is Ayn Rand, whose character Dominique in *The Fountainhead* thinks, after having a week to contemplate the fact of her rape, "I've been raped . . . Through the fierce sense of humiliation, the words gave her the same kind of pleasure she had felt in his arms." How do you fight that deeply imbedded idea that at some level any woman can be charged with "wanting it"?

And yet I can imagine Mother analyzing Laney's story, deciding whether to try to take it to a jury. "You were skinny-dipping with him just hours before the alleged rape? You'd drunk how many glasses of scotch? Drank it straight up, not even with a little ice?" She would walk through the details, then: Laney's first sexual experience with Carl, who'd been sleeping with another girl at the time and Laney knew that, but she was head over heels for him. In a bout of anger and hurt in the aftermath of their breakup, she'd gone down on a business student at Michigan, a guy she'd just met at a party that night. A white guy, like Trey, which shouldn't matter, but would. And Laney's words as we'd played Risk in the Lightkeeper's Cottage, *"Meus calix inebriat me,"* and her raising her glass to our no-Latin finger crosses, laughing when Trey said he thought our cups were making us *all* drunk, not just her. A flirtatious laugh? I couldn't swear under oath that it wasn't.

Trey had returned Laney's look, too. Even I, who didn't want to see Trey wanting anyone but me, saw that Trey wanted Laney. I remember thinking I shouldn't make anything of it, that she was like the island girls he flirted with when he was up, but when he was down he always came back to me.

Were we wrong not to tell anyone? The "broad distaste for rape cases as murky, ambiguous and difficult to prosecute, particularly when they involve (as they so often do) alcohol or acquaintance rape," as that *New York Times* column Mother sent around had put it, leaves juries reluctant to convict even today. Instead, they find victims who have been, say, so "promiscuous" as to have a glass of scotch with a rapist around a Risk board in a room full of friends to have consented even if those victims have said no. And even when a rapist is found guilty, the victim is left stained. There are always people who question what she wanted, or asked for, or deserved.

"There isn't anything we can do tonight," I'd insisted that Friday night. "The island has no police force. We'd have to cross the bay, and none of us is in any shape to take out a boat even if it weren't dark as hell out there."

That was when Betts suggested dragging Mother into it.

"You want to tell my *mother*?" I turned to Laney and I said (God help me, I did, I said), "Let's say for a minute that this awful thing you're accusing him of really did happen through no fault of yours. You tell Mother, you become the headline in every paper. Every paper, Lane. It has all the makings of great tabloid coverage: a wealthy, successful, and dare I say handsome alleged rapist no one in this world is going to believe needs to force himself on any girl. A white-on-black rape, which always titillates. A well-known feminist lawyer defending the accused, if it comes to that, because you can't imagine Mother won't defend Trey.

Trey is the son Mother always wanted, the one she took under her wing when none of her real children were quite good enough."

I think I actually believed I was trying to protect Laney from herself. I was so sure that Trey wasn't like she was suggesting. That he didn't go after girls. That if he didn't always turn them away when they offered themselves to him, well, neither did Frankie or Doug, and maybe even Beau.

"Can you even begin to imagine how much press coverage this would get?" I demanded. "Mother—who made headlines trying to stop President Reagan from denying funding for abortions for rape and incest victims—taking the other side for a rich white nephew accused of raping a drunk, skinny-dipping young black law student? It would be the end of your career *and* hers, Laney. You must know that. It would sink you before you started. Shit, do you think *anyone* at Tyler & McCoy would believe their young superstar partner is a predator?"

It would sink her *anywhere* if she spoke up and wasn't believed, and why would she be? It would sink the rest of us, too; we'd be dragged through the mud with her.

Betts grabbed my arm and pulled me into the hall, then, blasting me the way only Betts ever has. "Ginger, can you not *see* the bruise on the back of her neck? Can you not *see* that she can barely move her arm?" All in a hushed but forceful tone, because we were standing in a hall in a house overflowing with guests.

"Maybe she likes it kinky," I whispered. "What do you know about what Laney likes?"

I still remember Betts's unblinking gaze, crystal cold where Mother's eyes were a grittier green, but still they had the same look of disappointment in them, of disgust.

"Christ, Ginge—"

"Be *quiet,* Betts. Do you want everyone in this whole fucking house to hear you rant? You think *that's* going to help Laney?"

It was Mia who raised the possibility that Laney might end up pregnant, or with a sexually transmitted disease. (Not AIDS, we didn't know about AIDS yet.) This was after Laney was asleep, when Mia and Betts and I were back in the room, speaking in hushed tones. This was when I came to Trey's defense, when I told them Trey and I had made love almost every night since he'd arrived at Chawterley.

I could see the doubt creep into Mia's brown eyes as she began to grill me: exactly how long had we been lovers? I wasn't sure what she was beginning to doubt: what I was telling her, or whether Trey had so much as touched Laney, whether this wasn't all some bizarre domination fantasy Laney had concocted because even still, after a year, she couldn't get over Carl.

"Jesus, Ginge, that's statutory rape," Mia said.

Which was when I called her a complete fucking fool. If Trey and I loved each other, how would that be rape?

"Maybe we just need to get Laney out of here," Betts said. "Maybe we just need to pack up and head back to Ann Arbor first thing in the morning, before anyone else is up."

"Everyone will be up long before dawn to go hunting," I said. "And it sure won't help keep this quiet if we disappear on the morning of the party we came here to attend."

So in the end we left it that I would go duck hunting and they would stay with Laney, and whatever she wanted to do when I got back, we would do.

I didn't sleep at all the few hours left in that night. I lay in the bottom bunk while Laney slept in the bunk above me. I listened to the breaths of my friends, and watched the shadows of the branches outside the window shifting with the slowly moving moon. I got up before dawn, brushed my teeth, washed my face, took another two aspirin, drank two glasses of water, put on my hunting gear, and got my gun.

"You and me in the Triangle Blind," I said to Trey.

He shot well that morning, and I shot poorly, and he was giving me grief about it when I lowered my gun and made myself look straight at him.

"Did you fuck Laney?" I asked.

His eyes looked the gray-black of the moon through the telescope, the gray-black of craters cut into dust.

"Did you fuck her, Trey?" I insisted. "She says you did."

"Shit, Ginge," he said. "What the hell are you talking about?"

And maybe I believed him that morning and maybe I didn't. I don't even know anymore, if I ever did. So often, I've come to understand, I choose to believe what I want to believe, instead of what I see.

Mia

~

LAW QUADRANGLE NOTES, Winter 2010: Mary Ellen ("Mia") Porter (JD '82) won an International Women's Media Foundation Courage in Reporting Award for her article "Acid Girls," about the gritty determination with which Afghan girls who were splashed with acid on their way to school returned to their classes. Even her Law School roommate, Professor Elsbieta ("Betts") Zhukovski (JD '82), can find nothing funny in this.

TO BE HONEST, Betts and I were glad Ginger went hunting that Saturday morning, we were relieved to be rid of her for a bit. *"She was thirteen?"* we whispered to each other after she left, while Laney slept. What twenty-year-old man seducing a thirteen-year-old was well intentioned? What decent person thought that wasn't sick? Young children were so often vulnerable, so eager to please, and you could see that in Ginger, in the way she adored her big brothers, breaking her arm in a boat and not blinking at the pain because she wanted to keep up with them, she wanted to belong.

At the same time, we couldn't much believe it. *I Know Why the Caged Bird Sings* had been published a dozen years earlier, but none of us had read it. We didn't know that Virginia Woolf had been molested by a half brother when she was just six, or that Billie Holiday was raped by a neighbor when she was ten. No one wanted us to know those things happened, any more than we want Izzy or Annie or Gem to know now, although young girls do know so much more these days.

We didn't talk much about sex together even among ourselves back in law school, despite that business about Ginger hating to wake up next to a man she didn't know. The rest of us felt too naïve and inexperienced to call her bluff, to poke at the hurt we must have begun to see underlying Ginger's relationships with men long before that spring break. And that left us reluctant to talk about sex at all. Maybe that was why Ginger said it. Maybe it was her way of putting the topic of sex safely out of bounds. But maybe that's just me longing to change history, to have whispered to Laney or Betts that Friday night over the Risk game board that I was going off to make love with Beau, rather than saying I was going to the lighthouse to look at the sky.

How different would our futures have been if I'd simply told the Ms. Bradwells the truth? That I wanted to sleep with Beau even though I was engaged to Andy. That I wasn't sure I wanted to marry Andy. That when Beau and I left the cottage that night, I knew we wouldn't spend much time at the lighthouse. That long before he suggested we go to the boat, I knew I would sleep with him. I didn't need to be seduced.

I was careful to make sure we got back to the cottage before the Risk game would likely be over. I remember thinking, when I noticed Laney and Trey were gone, that that was a bad idea, that she ought not to have been flirting with a partner in the firm where she was going to work, much less go off alone with him.

And then finding her in the bunkroom. Trying to get her to talk. Laney answering in single words, or less. Laney, who would do nothing but sit hunched over her books in her bedroom the rest of that term, who would abandon her plans to go to D.C. and take instead a low-paying city job in Atlanta, because she couldn't sit in an office at Tyler & McCoy without being glad Trey Humphrey was dead.

That was such an awful thing, to be glad a man was dead, but we'd all felt it. Or at least I had. Not thirty hours later he turns up with his guts shot out, and I was glad.

But even with Trey dead, it could still happen again. There are men like Trey everywhere.

Back in Ann Arbor, I'd tried to talk to Betts about what had happened, and maybe I could have if we'd still been sharing that little room in N Section, when we used to lie awake in the darkness and talk. But we each had our own room on Division Street, and when I'd worked up my nerve to tell her, when I'd said, finally, "Can I ask you something? It's about Ginger's brother Beau," she'd given me such an unforgiving look, and she'd asked if I didn't think I'd hurt enough people already that spring: "Don't you think enough people have been hurt already this spring?" she asked. She'd said she had to get to class then, even though her class—Jackson's International Law seminar—didn't start for almost an hour. And she got up and left me sitting alone on the porch, sure finally that she must have seen me slip from the boat with Beau the night Trey died, sure she must be as disgusted as I was with the person I'd become.

The irony is that the night she must have seen me—Saturday, after the party—I didn't sleep with Beau. The night I did—the night Laney was raped—Betts and I had whispered together, still as close as we ever have been. "Is Ginger making this up?" Betts had asked while Ginger was in the bathroom. But it explained why Ginger and Trey had been gone such a long time that first night the guys arrived, getting the second skiff. It explained why she was as reluctant for us to befriend her cousin as she was to introduce us to that jerk she dated that first summer, and then the jerk's younger brother, and even Ted. It made some little sense of her forever choosing total dicks over nicer guys. So often matters of sexuality are more complicated than we ever imagine. I've come to see that with my mom, with facing the choices I now see she made over the years to give Bobby and me a normal life, giving up her own happiness in favor of ours. She never did divorce Dad, but she held on to her summer wanderings until she began to let go of everything, until the only past left in her mind was that of her childhood, before breasts or periods or sex, when everything was simple and she was happy, never imagining she would have sexual desires of any kind.

How does a thirteen-year-old make sense of anything a man does to her? How does any man begin to understand how vulnerable a young girl feels when her body is beginning to change in ways that confuse and horrify her, that cause boys and men she's known her whole life to treat her differently, to become suddenly uncomfortable? How can any man understand how desperately we want just to fit into a world that we're never quite sure we'll fit into, how unsure even girls like Ginger who have mothers like Faith are about what women are supposed to be and do?

There is, I've come to realize, nothing I wouldn't do to help Betts get on the Court. A woman like Betts? How many of them can there be? There aren't many people—male or female—as smart and thoughtful and, yes, empathetic as she is. Empathetic. That word was kicked around like a dirty old sock when Justice Sotomayor was being confirmed, as if an intelligent person who lacked empathy might be something other than a sociopath.

And yet this whole disaster is my fault. Betts's appointment is at risk because of me.

Betts was wonderful with Laney that Saturday morning at Chawterley, when Laney woke to the horror of what had happened. She said in the most gentle way you could imagine that we supported whatever Laney wanted to do, or not do. She left no doubt that we believed her, that even Ginger believed her. That was probably why Ginger was ranting, Betts said: because she loved Laney, and she wanted to protect her, and she didn't know how.

Betts offered to go to Faith herself if Laney wanted her to, or to take Laney to the police. "We just want to help however you want us to, Laney," she said softly, and yet underneath her words was a steeliness that left me with the startled sense that what she really wanted to do was shoot the bastard and have it over with.

Maybe that's hindsight, though. Maybe after Trey turned up dead I inserted something into my memory that wasn't real in trying to make sense of what had happened, Trey turning up dead just when we all wanted him dead.

Laney didn't want to go home to her parents: her mother would know something was wrong and Laney couldn't bear to tell her what happened. Laney's father, who never was much for white guys who were attracted to his daughter, could not be trusted to know. Not that she said much of this. She nodded yes or no to our questions and suggestions. And when it became clear, through the nods, that she wanted to stay in the room until Sunday morning, and then she wanted to go back to Ann Arbor and pretend none of this had happened, Betts said she would let the rest of the house know that Laney was not feeling well, she would get her out of the party that night, and we'd leave the next morning, as early as we could.

After Laney fell asleep again—or pretended to—Betts directed me to stay with her, and she disappeared. To ask for an aspirin, I supposed. To lay the groundwork for the claim that Laney felt unwell. It sure was taking her long enough, though. It was well over an hour before she returned, sallow-faced and silent.

"What?" I asked. "Betts, where have you been all this time?"

"I . . . I talked to Faith," she said. "She won't expect Laney at the party."

. . .

THAT NIGHT, GINGER and Betts and I put on our dresses and went to the party, made small talk, avoided Trey and, with him, Frank and Doug and Beau. Even Ginger seemed to be avoiding Trey. When Beau finally caught up with me, he knew something was wrong. I see in retrospect what he must have imagined: that I was confused, or full of guilt or remorse for having slept with him.

"I have to see you again," he said. "When can I see you?"

I wanted to see him again, too, but I was engaged to Andy, we were getting married after graduation. And I loved Andy. I did. I couldn't possibly walk away from my relationship with him for someone I'd just met, for nothing but one ill-considered night of great sex and perhaps nothing else. I couldn't exactly take off for a weekend in Chicago before finals. Beau couldn't come visit me in the San Francisco apartment Andy and I had already rented. If my sleeping with Beau was anything, it was wedding jitters. Cold feet.

Still, I whispered for him to meet me on his mother's boat, where we had made love after we left the lighthouse the night before.

After everyone else was asleep the night of the party—Saturday night—I climbed from the top bunk and went out to meet Beau. I can't imagine I meant to sleep with him in the aftermath of Laney's rape, but I wanted to be with him, to have him hold me. I never imagined having him hold me would break the dam of mixed-up emotions, would leave me sobbing, "It's my fault, it's all my fault, if I'd been at the lighthouse like I told her I would, if I'd just not *told* her I was going there . . ."

"What are you talking about?" he'd asked me over and over again.

"Laney and *Trey*," I managed, and maybe I said the word "rape" and maybe I didn't, maybe he understood me and maybe he couldn't make out a word I said, I don't know. All I know is he wrapped me in his arms and kissed the top of my head and held me for a long time, until I'd cried myself out and the night was almost over and if I didn't get back to the bunkroom I would be missed.

When I slipped back into the room, Betts was standing by the window. I nearly had a heart attack seeing her there, looking out the window as if she'd been watching Beau and me.

I quietly climbed into the top bunk, pulled the covers over me. Betts turned just as I'd closed my eyes, pretending sleep. I listened as she stood there for the longest moment. I was sure she'd seen me or heard me come in, that she knew I'd been with Beau. She stood there for an eternity before the soft inhale and exhale of her breath moved toward me. Then the bed sank as she settled into the bunk underneath me, and she pulled her covers up. Her breath never slowed, though. She lay there as I did, with the room lightening around us and no better idea than I had what to do, how to help Laney, how to make this right.

Mr. Conrad—looking uncharacteristically disheveled—came into the kitchen not much later that morning, as I was putting together snacks so we wouldn't have to stop on the way back to Ann Arbor for anything other than gas. He looked to be in serious need of a couple of aspirin.

"Are the other girls up yet?" he asked.

I concentrated on the sandwiches I was making, afraid that if he focused on my face he would be able to tell everything: that his nephew had raped my friend; that I'd slept with his son. "We're just about ready to take off," I said.

"To take off? Oh, Christ, you meant to leave early." He poured himself a cup of coffee, measuring his words. "I'm afraid you girls will have to delay your departure for just a bit," he said finally. "We've had some terrible news."

Dr. Pilgrim, one of the guests and an old friend of the family, had already examined the body; he had no doubt that it was an accident, from the close range of the shot, the gun-cleaning equipment found beside Trey, the fact that he'd been hunting that day, and the almost-empty glass of scotch beside the cleaning equipment. But all the guests needed to stay until the police, who were on their way from the mainland, could determine which of us they might need to question.

We had a long drive home, everyone knew that, Mr. Conrad said, but the police boat ought to arrive at the pier any moment, and he would make sure that if they needed to talk to anyone, they would talk to us first.

"Will you send Ginger down?" he asked, and then, after a long pause as he tried to rein in his emotions, "I don't know how I'm going to break this to her. Trey has been like a brother to her her whole life."

Betts

THE LANTERN DECK, COOK ISLAND LIGHTHOUSE
SATURDAY, OCTOBER 9

GINGER AND I remain standing on the lantern deck with Laney for some time. Our silent friendship a balm for the memory of "nigger slut" and "It wasn't that way," I hope. There aren't words to say to bring comfort. There is only touch. So we stand touching her. Looking out at the water that was purple at dawn. That is now an unwelcoming green.

"Shit, it's the press," Ginger says. She points. "That boat. It's heading straight for Chawterley."

Laney lets go of my hand. Raises it to shade her eyes. "It might be the girls," she says. But she doesn't believe that, really. And Ginger doesn't recognize the boat.

"We should head back to the house, anyway," Ginger says. "It's probably neither, but Mia will be wondering what happened to us."

"Maybe not," I say. "She's with Max."

Ginger frowns. Which ticks me off. After all these years you'd think Ginger would be able to let go of the need to have every man within sight want her. It's pathetic, really. She's not happy in Cleveland either. I've visited her enough over the years to see that. She's fifty-two years old and she still doesn't know what she wants. Even Mia, who never knew what she wanted when we were young, has settled into a life that suits her.

"I think there's pretty definitely something starting there," I say.

"Then you'd best wave goodbye to Mia," she snaps. "Max's boat is heading out. And, shit, isn't that another one coming in? Another two?"

She's right. A boat is just heading out from down island. Near Max's house. Two others loom at the horizon. I slip back inside the lantern room. Away from the cameras. We're almost certainly too far away to be caught on film. But who knows?

I try to imagine what I'm going to say to the press as Ginger leads us down the winding steps. I'm the one who is going to have to say whatever is said. I'm the one they'll look to for explanations. I'm the one being considered for the Court. And I'm the one—the only one—who knows the facts. The only one who has kept silent. I only meant to protect Laney. Not to bury a crime I wasn't even sure was a crime. But that won't be the way it's seen.

So what do I do here? Do I stick to the story we've been telling all these years? The story we've been declining to tell, pretending there isn't any story. Do I stick to a story I know isn't quite true?

I remember what Faith said that Saturday in the Captain's Library: *The press can make a nice girl into a slut without even trying.* I'd thought she was talking about Laney. But she was talking about Ginger, too. She was talking about us all. How much it must have angered her that it was still true thirty years later.

MIA IS JUST heading out the Chawterley door to find us when we return from the lighthouse. That silly plastic camera in her hands. We duck back inside. Scatter to close drapes. Lock windows and doors. We peek through the blinds in the Sun Room to see four boats drawing closer.

"So what's the plan?" I ask.

"If we've learned anything from politicians lately," Ginger says, "it's that if you keep repeating even the most ridiculous statements over and over, people eventually believe they're true."

It is what is better in this country, Elsbieta: the rules apply to all the peoples.

So much of life is guided by chance. Outside our control. There are so many things we can't stop or can't see that we should change. Laney's rape. Zack's death. Mia's marriage to Andy. Ginger's relationship with Trey. We're all scarred by every one of those things because they happened to us or they happened to someone we love. I suppose it's those scars that make us refuse to step back and allow things we *don't* want to happen to take their course just because the law requires it. Which is an untenable position for a judge to hold, of course. I do see that.

Is that what we were doing that spring break? Putting ourselves above the law? We didn't see it that way. We thought we were putting our reputations before our rights in a way that had nothing to do with anyone else. Making choices that hurt no one. That saved us from hurt. The facts had changed, though. Trey had turned up dead. A different set of facts we never stopped to consider.

The first boat arrives. A wiry guy jumps onto the pier and secures a large powerboat across from the *Row v. Wade* as a string of eight or ten more boats streams toward us. A heavyset guy hands a TV camera up. A perfectly coiffed blonde emerges from the cabin.

" 'We got the bubble-headed-bleach-blonde / who comes on at five.'" I sing off-tune. Even Matka would tell you that.

"That's no bubblehead." Mia raises her wreck of a camera and eyes me through the viewfinder. She doesn't take the shot. "That's Fran Halpern."

Fran looks a bit sick to her stomach. I take some small pleasure in that.

Another boat is not far behind them. Someone shouting from the bow. One of the crew in the first boat yells back, "We're unloading as fast as we can!" But the last of the crew is dawdling. Checking around to make sure all the gear has been unloaded. Which it has. They have everything to gain and nothing to lose by stalling. Their camera is already rolling on Ms. Halpern. As long as their boat is tied up to the pier there isn't room for another to dock.

"Imagine how well exclusive footage of a still house front plays on television," I say.

Ginger points out that it's actually the back of the house.

"Saturday is a slow news day," Mia says. "You'd be surprised what they'll run."

I hesitate as we head toward the servants' stairs. I have half a mind to stick my head out the door and tell these bastards they're trespassing on private property. But they would take my photograph before I got a word out. And who knows how they'd twist anything I might say. What *would* I say, anyway? That if they didn't leave I'd call the police? There are no police on Cook Island. A blessing in 1982 coming back to bite us.

Was it a blessing? Would we have done things differently if we hadn't had the night to think over what to do before we could go to the police? Would our lives have been better in the long run, or worse?

The doorbell rings. Rings again. And again. We don't even think about answering.

"The nerve," I say.

We all laugh as we hurry upstairs.

We duck into the first bedroom. The Captain's Bedchamber, which was Faith's room. The double bed with a massive mahogany German-grandfather-clock-look-alike headboard must be where she died. Where Max found her. I'm not sure about this, though. Ginger never shared the details with us.

A white terry-cloth robe hangs on a hook on the closet door. A crystal decanter of what is probably bourbon sits beside an empty ashtray on the nightstand. An open pack of Virginia Slims. A bitten pencil. A pleading clip. This was Faith's life until it wasn't anymore. She died with her activist boots firmly on her feet.

I think it was a disappointment to Faith that I never took up the banner of gender issues directly myself. I used the excuse of Catharine MacKinnon being more expert than I ever could be. I focused on immigration issues instead. I think Faith understood but was disappointed nonetheless.

One closet door and the bottom drawer of a mahogany dresser are slightly ajar. Was it only yesterday that Ginger came in here looking for clothes? She stares at the crystal decanter and the pleading clip as if her mother might emerge, white-robed, from the shower to ask if we've written our congressman about the Equal Rights Amendment this month. It's Saturday. The day she always called to remind us. *Carter and Ford both support the amendment.* I can almost hear her voice. *More than eighty percent of Americans, after they've actually read the ERA, support it.* It fell three states short of ratification that June, though. Seventy-five percent of women state legislators in the four key states voted to ratify, but only forty-six percent of the men did. I'd been in D.C. clerking for Judge Ginsburg when the time for ratification expired. Laney and I mourned it together by phone instead of at the apartment we'd planned to share.

I wonder, sometimes, if Faith was happier in her last years than she had ever been. Living alone here. Accomplishing what she meant to accomplish. With no distractions. No children to raise. No husband who needed a weekend-long birthday party thrown in his honor.

Is that selfish, living like that, or is it selfless? Is it foolish, or is it wise?

"There'll be as good a view from Emma's Peek as there is from here," Mia suggests.

"Or the Captain's Office," Laney says.

Ginger walks to the window. Peers out. Laney joins her as I remember that story Beau told about Ginger hauling a skiff from the mud with a broken arm.

The first boat has cleared the pier now. A second boat has taken its place. A second gang of journalists is unloading.

"WJLA?" Laney says.

Mia answers, "The D.C. affiliate for ABC."

I step behind Laney. Finger a ringlet of dark hair. She turns to meet my look. Raises a hand to her neck and rubs it. Aging skin to aging skin. Though there is still so much youth in her face.

"If I had ever imagined this would get so much attention," I say, "I would have said no when they offered me the Court."

Something in her dark eyes leaves me thinking she doesn't believe me. Leaves me wondering if I believe myself. I did imagine someone might ask about Trey's death; I armed myself with an answer. Did I never imagine this would blow up into such a public mess? That Laney, too, would be dragged into it? Or did I want the nomination too badly to admit to the sight of it in my path?

Laney takes my hand. Her fingers interweave darkly with mine. "I knew it might happen when I decided to run for office," she says. Taking onto herself the burden I should bear.

Betts

⧯⧯

THE CAPTAIN'S BEDCHAMBER, CHAWTERLEY HOUSE
SATURDAY, OCTOBER 9

"I THOUGHT THE Ben thing might come out in the confirmation hearings," I say. I hesitate. There is a brief I-could-make-something-up-and-present-it-as-truth moment. An I-can-protect-myself-as-I've-been-doing-all-these-years chance. But I let it pass. I take a peek through the curtains: Yes, this is really happening. I sit in a chair beside Faith's empty fireplace. I slip off my shoes and pull my feet up into half lotus. And I tell them about my affair with Ben.

They settle into the sitting area with me as I talk. Ginger and Laney on the couch facing the fireplace. Mia in the chair on the other side of it. Mia and Laney skin off their shoes as I have and pull their feet up under them. Ginger wears no shoes.

"Jesus, Betts," Ginger says. "Even I never slept with a married man."

Mia's spine straightens. Her one foot is still up on the seat but the other moves flat to the floor. "How would you *know*, Ginger?" she says. "You're the one who always hated waking up next to men whose names you didn't know. So you ask marital status but not names?"

I quash the urge to shush her. To suggest Faith can hear us. That her spirit is here. Anger presses into Ginger's wide lips. But then her overbite disappears into an apologetic almost-smile.

"You're right, you're right," she says. "That I know of."

Mia confesses to having slept with a married man once. It surprises me how grateful I am for this disclosure. It crosses my mind that it might not even be true. Mia might be confessing to a sin she never committed just so I won't feel alone.

"What a sorry bunch of hussies we turn out to be," I say.

"You never told us," Laney says to me.

I shrug. I don't want to admit my distrust of them any more clearly.

"Ambition makes lonely bedfellows," Ginger says. A simple statement that makes me ache with loneliness even as I set the loneliness aside. As I hand it over to Laney and Mia and Ginge.

"Justice William O. Douglas plowed through four wives while he was on the bench, each one younger and blonder than the gal before," Laney says. "Are you thinking he never started seeing one before he left the other?"

"That's no doubt why he found a right to privacy in the bill of rights," I say. I'm the first to laugh but they laugh with me. Gallows humor. What is there to do but laugh?

"Clarence Thomas," Mia says. "Long Dong Silver and pubic hairs in Coke. Why would Anita Hill volunteer to have her name dragged through that mud if that wasn't true?"

"But women are held to higher standards," Ginger says. "In all that ImClone insider trading mess, who was the only one who ended up serving time? Martha fucking Stewart. Who took the fall for employing an illegal immigrant nanny? Zoe Baird and Kimba Wood because of course we can't have an attorney general who breaks the law, never mind that our very male secretary of the treasury had $34,000 of unpaid taxes on an illegal nanny before he was confirmed. Do you think there's a double standard?"

I smile despite the situation. We'll have to arrange an exorcism here. The ghost of Faith Cook Conrad has clearly taken up residence in her daughter's wide mouth.

"A double standard we perhaps impose on ourselves," I say. "Giving up the Supreme Court to care for a husband who doesn't even know who we are anymore. Only to have him die and leave us with nothing to do but watch as the justice who replaced us undoes half the good we've done."

"Betts," Mia says gently. Not Sandra Day O'Connor's name, but mine. In the gentleness of her voice I see that it isn't the demands of working another life around my ambitions that I've avoided all these years. It's the demands of another dying. Not just the grief of losing someone I love, but the care it takes to see them through the process of dying. I might love again if I were guaranteed I would be the first of us to die, or even if I just knew my new lover would die the way Matka did: in her sleep one Sunday night. After we'd spent the weekend together in Chicago. She'd moved there years earlier for a job as a medical researcher, work she loved. "We had such a nice weekend, didn't we, Betsy?" Those were her last words.

Laney, sitting closest to me, reaches a hand across the gap between the couch and my chair. Rests it on mine. "Did y'all know Justice Hugo Black was a member of the Ku Klux Klan?" she asks, seeing I need to move on to something else. "Everyone in Alabama knew it," she says. "It's how he got elected to the Senate, with the Klan's support. Then *he's* the one to insist separate can never be equal."

"Making up for past wrongs?" I suggest.

She removes her hand from mine. Fingers her neck again. Her expression is somewhere between angry and sad. I can't imagine what I've said.

"So you're suggesting that's what I need to do here, Betts?" she demands. "Make up for my past wrongs?"

"Of course not! I was talking about Justice Black, Lane!"

"Not reporting it wasn't wrong, Laney," Mia says gently. "No one is obligated to report an assault on themselves. It was a reasonable decision, to choose not to subject yourself to . . . to all that."

"Except then Trey ended up dead," Laney says.

Outside: the sounds of boat horns and people calling to each other. Journalists, cameras, and equipment continue to come ashore. The pier, jutting out over the water, is public property. Theoretically we could stop them from coming above the high tide line. But as my students would say, good luck with that.

I wonder if the press will go away if we hole up here long enough. What do they have to wait for? They don't have a stick of evidence suggesting Trey's death was anything but an accident. They just have the suggestion of one blogger who won't even step up to identify him or herself. They don't even have Laney's rape.

"I'm thinking maybe it's time I just say what happened," Laney says. "I'm thinking part of what I was looking for in this campaign was to put this behind me once and for all, to go ahead and live my life. So maybe this is it, maybe this is what I've got to do now."

But it's not just you. A selfish thought. If she confesses the rape now the press will have a field day speculating about which of us might have killed Trey. Which of us might have known about it. Might have helped cover up a murder.

"But it's not just you, Laney," Ginger says, reading my mind. "And it would be terrible timing for you and Betts both." With a judgmental glance at Mia she continues, "Great timing for the anonymous blogger who surfaced this, though."

Connections and timing. You girls are going to have both. How many times did I hear Faith say that? Every time I came to D.C. she introduced me to everyone she could: To Ruth Bader Ginsburg. To Justice Stevens, for whom I also clerked. To Hillary when it looked like she'd be the nominee. To the president when he came through Michigan on the campaign and again after he was elected, when he was making his list of potential Court nominees.

The way Ginger looks at Mia. Oh hell, she's going to accuse Mia about this blogger thing with the press outside waiting to hear us when the shouting starts.

"Ginger," I say. Trying to reel the thread back onto the bobbin.

Ginger shoots me an overbitey-and-annoyed look. "I'm just saying that whoever this blogger is has just set herself up for some nice advertising revenues, which is what I might do if I were a recently unemployed journalist. Wouldn't you, Mi?"

Mia fixes her paper-bag brown eyes on Ginger. She doesn't blink even once. "I don't know, Ginge," she says evenly. "If I were that blogger, I'd figure there was some good juicy stuff to be had in the story of the daughter of a prominent feminist lawyer who is so concerned about the disclosure of her own sordid sexual history that she does everything she can to convince a dear friend who has been sexually assaulted to let it go."

"No one but the four of us knows about this," Ginger shoots back. "And Betts and Laney have everything to lose here. So that leaves either you or me, Mia. Me and my 'sordid sexual history,' right? You can imagine how excited I am to announce to the whole world what a fucking slut I was."

Laney and I share a glance. Mia has never let go of feeling we ought to have gone to the police. Feeling she was right and we were wrong and we ought to have listened to her. But Ginger had been insistent that going to the police or even just to her mother would have made things worse. Laney hadn't wanted to talk to anyone either. And I'd come back from talking to Faith with my mind changed.

But there has never been any point in getting between Ginger and Mia when their tempers fly.

Mia doesn't say anything, though. She smiles a little sadly. Lifts her goofy toy camera. Focuses on Ginger's wide feet wedged between her legs and the worn fabric of her mother's chair. A single cheap plastic *snap* interrupts the silence.

She stands and goes to the window. Peeks through the curtain. "Fox," she says. "CBS and, damn, is that Judy Woodruff? We've moved from scandal to legitimate story if the *NewsHour* is here." She turns and looks at the three of us sitting around Faith's cold fireplace. "You suppose that's the good news, or the bad?"

Mia

~

WE'VE BEEN SITTING in the Captain's Bedchamber for hours—all of us taking surreptitious peeks out the window while I've been taking surreptitious peeks inside myself—when Betts spots yet another boat headed for the Chawterley pier. "There aren't enough journalists squashing the flowers already?" she asks. As Laney rises to have a look, too, I stuff down the urge to defend the press, to defend myself.

"Not many flowers on that side of the house," I say.

"You think there aren't reporters and photographers on every side of this house?" Ginger says. "But the flowers are all dying, anyway." She, too, goes to the window, leaving me alone to wonder how many times Faith sat here by the fireplace, with no one to share the night.

"It's Max!" Ginger says. "That's Max's boat. And, shit, that's Annie helping him dock. Annie and Iz."

I join them at the window just in time to see the horde of journalists swarm the pier as the boat approaches, already clicking photos and shouting questions. They have no idea who they're photographing, but they don't want to miss the shot, just in case. In this digital age, they waste nothing but the time it will take to delete what they don't use.

Betts moves toward the door, but Ginger grabs her sleeve before she gets very far.

"Max will get Izzy in, Betts," she says. "Believe me, Max will get Izzy and Annie both into the house unharmed. If we go out there, especially if *you* go out there, it's just worse for them. Trust me this once: let Max get them in the house."

"It's locked," Betts says. "All the doors are locked."

"I'll get the door," I say, heading out into the hall before anyone can object.

"Max is such a nice guy," I hear Laney say as I'm leaving. "Why do you suppose his wife left him?" Her words register in my pathetic little brain only as my feet hit the marble of the back foyer: Max and his wife have split? But there is no time for that now.

I peek through the backdoor sidelights, my hand on the doorknob as Max barrels through the press, one arm around each girl. Tiny Isabelle is practically buried in the crook of his arm, where the photographers can't get much of a shot of her, but Annie, at six feet, is all there for everyone to see. I silently will her to reach up and release the clip holding her hair back, to let the veil of blond loose to cover her face. And I see in Annie how Ginger, too, must have been as a girl: taller by a margin than all the middle-school boys, gawky tall until she got used to her height, everyone-turning-to-look tall, and beanpole thin. It's the last pin clicking into place, why Ginger never has seen herself as beautiful: she was a gawky virgin, and then Trey seduced her without falling in love with her, and she became a gawky slut. How many years does it take to get over the burden of the teenage girls we were?

I throw the lock and open the door. "You are not even thinking about using tape of a minor, or stepping on this porch," I announce loudly to the cameras still pointed at the arriving threesome. "You're all from reputable news sources, Fran," I say, picking Fran off from the pack to personalize this. "You have standards of conduct." Which maybe they would all remember without my help, but there is no percentage in testing that.

My words have the intended effect: everyone turns to me, their cameras rolling, their shutters snapping, but no one steps beyond the path as Max and the girls break free of them and hurry inside.

Annie has just had a birthday, I remember as I close the door and throw the lock again. She's eighteen now, not a minor. An honest mistake on my part, though, and it will take them some time to figure it out.

Annie isn't the story here, anyway, and now they have a clip of me.

I'm glad I put on makeup in the little moment before I headed to Max's house this morning—a vain thought, I admit it, but my squishy fairness looks bad enough in photos *with* makeup.

I kiss first Annie, then Iz, telling them they look beautiful, which they do. Gawky, almost grown-up beautiful in Annie's case, and dark hair and pale skin intelligent beautiful in Izzy's. "Hollywood agents are going to be knocking on your doors based on just that little bit of film," I say, trying to keep this light.

Max hikes up the sagging butt of his jeans, bracing himself for the plunge back outside. The thought of his boxers showing in the TV footage makes me oddly fonder of him. I tell the girls their moms are up in the Captain's Bedchamber, and suggest Max come say hello. He demurs: he's already intruded on us once today.

"You brought us the *newspaper*," I say. "That isn't intruding, that's doing a favor. And now you've brought us the girls, which is exactly what we need. At least come upstairs and let everyone thank you for that."

GINGER, AFTER HUGGING both the girls, asks Max how he knew to get them. I can't decide if she's oblivious to her daughter's trauma at being run over by the press, or if she is handling it by letting her get over it quietly in a way her own mother never would have allowed her to do.

"I called him." Annie takes in the empty ashtray, the pleading clip, the robe that perhaps Faith wore when she drank her morning coffee. "I used to call him a lot when Grammie was alive, just to make sure she was okay."

I don't know which surprises me more, hearing Faith called "Grammie" or the idea of a teenage girl who worries about her grandmother, who calls a neighbor to check up on her. Maybe Faith found the relationship she'd always wanted to have with her daughter in her granddaughter instead.

The girls are famished; they've been traveling without stopping to eat. I offer to fix something for dinner, and Max again starts making excuses to leave.

"You'll be hounded by the press, Maxie," Ginger says. "You're bound to say something stupid. Just about anyone with a microphone thrust in his face manages to sound stupid. Besides, Mia can't cook worth shit."

"I can cook," I say, but Laney and Betts agree: I can't cook worth shit.

Max says he'll stay if I'll sous-chef for him and, honestly, I'm happy for the excuse to get away from the other Ms. Bradwells. I'm still stinging from Ginger's words, even if I do deserve them: *So that leaves either you or me, Mia. Me and my 'sordid sexual history,' right? I'm going to be publicizing that, for sure.* I can't imagine how Max isn't stinging from the charge that he'll be stupid in front of a microphone—which I say once we're settled in the kitchen.

"Ginger never will get past thinking of me as an island boy," he says. "You end up with a warped perspective when a place like Chawterley is your summerhouse. But she has such a big heart, even if she isn't always quite as socially graceful as she might be. She's like her mother that way. It's easy to forgive them both, because they have so much bigger hearts than they recognize."

Ginger startles us by appearing at the bottom of the servants' stairs. If she's heard us, she pretends not to have. "We've decided to dine in the Tea Parlor," she says, and she heads across the kitchen and out through the Ladies' Salon. The others follow her into one of the few rooms downstairs that has no window to the outside.

"Set a place for Faith's Ghost," Betts whispers as she brings up the rear.

Max puts me to dicing onions, then takes the knife back. "Maybe you can just be the soundtrack to my cooking?" he suggests.

"I can sing better than Betts, but that isn't saying much."

"Better than you dice?" He grins his nerdy-glasses grin. "Think talk radio."

And then we're talking easily, like we've known each other forever. At some point in the conversation, I remember my Holga, and I frame him in the viewfinder. He has a whole mess of things cooking together in the pan, and he's boiled a pot of pasta he's now dumping into a colander. I click the shutter, catching the steam and the falling pasta and Max's age-stained hands, remembering for some reason the rearview mirror of my mother's car. Am I looking backward still, or am I looking ahead?

He dumps the drained pasta into the pan of things he's been cooking, then cracks a few eggs in and stirs it all around. I want to tell him that I wasn't the blogger but that it was my fault, that I told someone I wasn't so sure that Trey shot himself. It would compound my sin to tell Max this, though, sharing my doubts with yet another non–Ms. Bradwell. So I lower the camera and hold the wide, flat serving bowl while he dumps the pasta mixture in.

"Ginger tells me . . . ," I start, and I almost say "that your wife left you." But I remember how I reclaimed my name, quit my job, left San Francisco, and headed as far away from Andy as I could get, far away from everyone who might see how I'd failed him. ". . . that you're divorced," I say. "That must have been hard, with kids and all."

He looks at me like he has no clue where this is going, and I sure don't either, but I kiss him anyway. Not a long kiss, just a tentative one. He tastes like the pasta smells, all olive-oil buttery and herby.

He looks at me through his goofy glasses, and he says, "Pasta's getting cold."

I nod, thinking, *Well, it serves you right, blowing off what any idiot ought to have seen were his advances.*

"They think I'm the blogger," I say.

"Who does?"

"Ginger."

It feels like she has been beating me up over whether I'm the anonymous blogger for about a hundred years now. It was just a suspicion when she first suggested it . . . this morning? yesterday? She said it with a rise in her voice at the end, the only way you can ever tell when Ginger doubts herself, because Lord knows she never admits to doubting anything. But she's convinced herself she's right now, that this is my fault. And of course it is my fault.

"Ah, Ginger," Max says. "Ginger is wrong about so many people. Always has been, even when she was a kid. It's her Achilles' heel."

"I thought it was only men she was always wrong about," I say.

He shoots me what Betts would call a raised-brows-behind-the-lenses-surely-you-can't-be-serious look before taking the pasta bowl in one hand and a stack of smaller bowls, napkins, and forks in the other. He nods toward the jelly glasses and wine bottle on the counter. I pick them up and follow him through the Ladies' Salon.

The reporters outside have settled in to keeping a looser kind of vigil. They might see us hurrying across the hall and into the Tea Parlor, or they might be too busy sharing shots from flasks like the ones we drank from that night we went gut-running. They're huddling closer together against the wind that rattles the windowpanes, that any minute now will hoot down the chimney in the Captain's Library, sending the low moan of the Captain's Ghost through the house.

I hope they have no blankets or flashlights or food. It's a long walk to town from here, and I didn't see them unloading a car or even a bicycle from those boats they came over on, boats which are long gone. I hope the Pointway Inn is already full, although of course it won't be in October. Still, I can hope. I can hope they have no choice but to sleep uneasily on the pier, in danger of rolling into the bay and joining Beau's lost sleeping bag. I can hope the wind whips Fran Halpern's perfect coif into a rat's nest that even her wonderful hair and makeup crew can't tame. I can hope the skies will open up and a downpour will wash their damned cameras into the Chesapeake, that the sunrise will find them floating like crab-pot markers strung across the bay: MSNBC, FOX, CBS, APTN.

DINNER IS SURPRISINGLY relaxing. We linger in the skirted chairs circling the round wooden tea table, forgetting about the cameras outside, or at least pretending to. One of the delights of having Baby Bradwells around is that the focus turns inevitably to them. They're walking, talking yellow-triangle caution signs: yield to the concerns of this young person; it will do you a world of good.

Annie is planning to study archaeology at Princeton, and the girls on her hall seem nice. Her classes aren't too tough and everyone brings their laptops to class, not just her. "It's like I'm just regular," she says. "Normal." It makes my heart break for all those years she was the little girl weighed down with a backpack containing a computer nearly as heavy as she was, before students brought laptops to college classes, much less to the fourth grade. It makes me wonder about Ginger, too: how much did her schooling suffer because her handwriting was so difficult to read? Would she have made law review if she'd grown up in a world where everyone learned to keyboard, or even just without a feminist mother who forbade her learning to type?

Isabelle tells us she's interviewing for jobs for after she graduates. The high-paying law firms all want her, but the low-paying public interest jobs she wants are ironically harder to come by. She does have a paid position at a legal clinic in New Haven for the school year, which helps cover her expenses. And she's seeing a guy.

"You are?" Betts's gaze behind her lenses is both hopeful and apprehensive.

Izzy's dark eyes—her father's eyes in her mother's freckled face—don't blink. "He's from Tennessee originally," she says. "He's a business school guy."

Betts crosses her yoga-toned arms. "The business school," she repeats, and although she tries to hide it, you can hear the vision of rich, Southern, country-club bigot she is imaging in the words.

"He's specializes in micro-investment. He's putting together a program in Appalachia, like people have been doing in Africa with some success. That's where he's from, originally, a little town in Appalachia."

Betts uncrosses her arms, lifts her fork, and twirls a length of pasta and julienned vegetables, then sets it back down.

"He sounds wonderful, Iz," I say. "What's his name?"

Is it possible she's just gotten even smaller? I wish I could withdraw the question. It's just a name, and she doesn't have to take it on herself. It's too much to risk, anyway, giving up your name.

"His name is Zack," she says. "Zack Bloom."

Betts's breath deepens as if she's entering a meditative state. To her credit, she doesn't flinch at the fact that her daughter is dating a man who shares the name of the father she never knew.

"He's a student?" she asks, and in the question I see that she's right: he isn't.

Izzy folds her hands together as if meaning to say grace. "A professor, Mom. He's thirty-nine. Divorced. Two kids, a twelve-year-old son named Pete and a ten-year-old daughter, Rebecca." Laying all the unacceptable cards out on the polished and polite tea-table top in a way I doubt any of us Ms. Bradwells ever could have done. Is this a generational thing?

Betts nods, knowing she needs to respond but unwilling to approve. Maybe she's thinking of her married man from that summer at Caruthers. Maybe she's hoping, like I am, that this romance started only after this Professor Zack split with Mrs. Bloom, so Izzy will never have to fault herself the way I did when Doug left Sharon. Or maybe Betts is thinking about Izzy's father, maybe she's awash in a moment of missing him. Maybe what I take for disapproval is only Betts's unwillingness to let her daughter see her pain.

"Rebecca. That's a great name," Max says, as if that has anything to do with anything.

Betts wraps a hand around her jelly glass of chardonnay. At least Max didn't say Zack was a great name, too.

Izzy gets up from the tea table and slips away, into the Music Room. She doesn't turn on the lights there, and the drapes are drawn. A minute later, over the soft tinkle of piano keys, Izzy begins to sing.

She sings beautifully. It's one of the miracles of mixing genes that Betts and Zack, neither of whom could carry a tune, produced a child with such a lovely voice. The tune is familiar, yet not, and the words are foreign, guttural. It takes me a minute to realize it's a song Betts used to play on her zhaleika, a Polish folk song.

"You taught her this one," I say to Betts. The only Polish she ever learned was the words of songs.

Betts is listening to her daughter play. Maybe she's heard me, or maybe she hasn't. She takes a sip of her wine. She hasn't eaten a bite of her dinner. She hasn't had a single dessert this weekend despite my resolve back in the Hart Building hearing room. Her eyes are moist.

"Betts?" I say into the silence after the song ends.

"Matka taught it to her just before she died," Betts says. "They did it as a surprise for me. To make me happy."

"It's beautiful," Laney says softly. "Happy beautiful, not sad."

In the Music Room, Izzy starts playing another piece.

Betts pushes her still-full plate away, sits back in her flowered chair, stares up at the four-candle chandelier. "Matka taught it to Izzy," she says, "so I would have someone to play music with after she was gone."

Mia

~

THERE IS NO moon outside, no stars, and the wind continues to blow, but the rain I'm hoping for still hasn't come when Laney, Ginger, Betts, Max, and I settle into the sitting area in the Captain's Office. The girls are already sharing the twin beds in Hamlet's Retreat, and the rest of us are comfortably settled on the settee and chairs, our backs to the twin beds, the armoire, the Captain's rolltop desk and the secret doorway into Emma's Peek. We've turned out the lights and opened the curtains, tired of being so closed in. Below us, the journalists huddle together in small groups, sharing cigarettes and flasks and old war stories that have long ago grown past mythical and on to stale.

"She wants a family. That's what this is about," Betts says. "Instant family. Add Izzy and stir."

We kick that around for a while. Max and I seem to be the only ones who can imagine Izzy might actually love this guy, that not all first love comes in a virgin package. Betts can't get over the idea that this Zack—a name she never says—is a father replacement like she's decided the Caruthers partner she had her affair with was, although she doesn't say that either, not with Max here.

"It took me years to shrug off the embarrassment of having no father," she says. "Of having a mother who spoke a language no one could understand even when she was speaking English. The crappy little apartment over the dry cleaners I never wanted you guys to see. The fact that I was nowhere if I lost my scholarships. I was back in the crappy little apartment over the dry cleaners with Matka."

A ghostlike sound answers, startling me although it's not unexpected.

"It's just the Captain's Ghost," Ginger assures us.

We listen as the sound repeats: the wind whistling across the chimney top, this time in a higher register, Faith's Ghost joining the Captain on his late-night haunt.

"I wonder if we all feel a little like we don't belong, even in our own families," Ginger says. "I got along well enough with Daddy and my brothers, but I was never quite one of them because I was a girl."

"Even though you could shoot better than any of them," Max says.

"Even though," Ginger agrees. "And Mother—sometimes I think I've lived my whole life trying to impress her."

"We all wanted to impress your mom, Ginge," I say.

When I'd realized Doug was married, my thought hadn't been that I should break it off, it had been that I didn't want Faith to know I was seeing him.

Laney tells us about always hurrying from work the summer she spent in D.C. so she wouldn't arrive late for dinner with Faith. "Faith meant to see great things from us and she made not a single sorry bone about it," she says. "She was so sure we *could* better the world if we set our minds to the task."

"I'm pretty sure she expected the world to help us out a little more here," Betts says. "I don't think her crystal ball contemplated that forty years after the second wave women would still comprise only . . . what, *seventeen* of the country's one hundred senators? Thank God for California and Maine. Twenty percent of the federal bench. And maybe two CEOs of the Fortune 500 companies."

"It killed her that Hillary didn't get the nomination," Max says. He adjusts his glasses as what he's said dawns on him. "Not literally," he says, and he grins goofily.

Even Ginger laughs.

"But your mama was like that, too, Betts," Laney says. "She believed in us, too."

"It was different, though," Betts says. "Matka believed. But Faith led."

"The way your father led?" Laney asks Betts.

We all know the story of Betts's father helping lead a resistance against the Soviet government in Poland, and disappearing; Mrs. Z escaping to the States with Baby Betts.

"I expect I should be pleased my mama and daddy weren't civil rights activists," Laney says, "watching the way you and Ginger think you never can accomplish half of what your parents did."

"I still imagine I'll find him," Betts says. "I can't say, honestly, that it isn't that little bit of hope that persuaded me to keep my name. This idea that someday I'd be . . ." She shrugs.

"Nominated for the Supreme Court," Ginger says, flashing her wide grin.

Betts smiles back at Ginger, the little fatty deposit disappearing into the fold of her smile line, her eyes flashing in a way that makes me think she doesn't mind being caught out in this unlikely, middle-aged dream of finding her father.

"My dad will hear my name on the evening news while he's cooking a sausage for dinner," she says. "Maybe while he's cooking for a whole other family. I wouldn't even mind that. I think I'd like to know I had siblings somewhere. He'll hear 'Elsbieta Zhukovski.' He'll focus on the television screen. He'll see my face. He'll say to my brother or sister or both, 'That's my daughter. Sweet Lord, that's my daughter. She looks just like her *matka*.' And then somehow we'll be reconnected. Izzy will have a grandfather. I'll have a dad. We'll be a family. Instead of just the two of us."

Outside, a journalist swears. They, too, are getting tired and cranky. At least we're comfortable and warm.

"Two is family," I say quietly, though I'm embarrassed to say it with Max here. A family of two is what my brother, Bobby, and I are going to be soon, with my dad failing physically, my mom disappearing into Alzheimer's. A family of two who don't even see each other much. I'm not unlike Izzy, I realize, or not unlike how Betts thinks Izzy is: part of my attraction to Doug was the fact that he had kids. I know so many women who don't like children, but I'm not one of them.

"Two is family," Max agrees, and something in his voice makes me imagine he must understand what I'm feeling, the longing I feel every time I see the Baby Bradwells. I've thought about adopting a child, raising her on my own like Mrs. Z raised Betts. But I'm not Mrs. Z. I'm not settled. I can't imagine myself with a lawn, much less a fence and a swing set. How could I give up the life I have for a life I might forever long to flee, the way my mother had?

"Don't doubt yourself, Ms. Professor Drug-Lord-Bradwell," Ginger says to Betts. "Wanting to find your father isn't why you've led the life you've led, any more than Laney's mother's dreams are the reason Laney is running for office. Don't talk yourself into thinking what you're doing isn't real. Would your mother be proud of you now? You know she would. Just like Laney's mother would be proud of her. And your daddy would be proud of you, too. Just like you busted your damned chest open when Izzy was accepted at Yale, this little girl of yours who was making her own way in the world. It's important to you because of who *you* are. Because you're kind and thoughtful. Because you're generous with your talents. Because you care."

I look from Ginger to the window, realizing Max is right about Ginger's heart being bigger than she knows.

The red tips of two cigarettes move toward the end of the pier, the way Ginger's and Trey's had that first night when they left to steal Max's skiff, the path Beau and I took toward his mother's boat that Friday night.

"And what about you, then, Ginger?" Laney asks. "If we've made our choices for ourselves, then haven't you, too?"

"Who the hell have I chosen to become?" Ginger says. "A 'wet brown bag of a woman / who used to be the best looking gal in Georgia.'"

"Georgia?" Knocked off center by my mother's lover's name.

"A poet," a soft voice says from the direction of the arched doorway.

How long has Annie stood there? How much has she overheard?

"It's from a poem, Aunt Mia," she says. Then to Ginger, "You're a poet, Mom. You are."

As Ginger looks away to the rolltop desk and the little door behind it, connecting this room to Emma's Peek, it strikes me that Annie calls Ginger "Mom," where Ginger always called Faith "Mother." It strikes me that Izzy calls Betts "Mom," too, where Betts always called Mrs. Z "Matka," which means "Mother," not "Mom." It strikes me how different Faith and Mrs. Z were, and yet how similar. How different Ginger's and Betts's relationships with their mothers were, and how similar, too. Were Laney and I luckier, to have mothers who wanted for us but didn't expect? Wanted us to have whatever we wanted, to be happy. Even my mom's idea that I should go to law school was rooted in her believing she would have been happier if she had, and so maybe I would be.

"If literature and art can't change the world, then we're all lost, aren't we?" Annie says.

She smiles sleepily, looking so like a twelve-year-old that it leaves me reconsidering her words, thinking how untrite they are when they come from someone so young and lacking in cynicism, thinking that she's right, that the arts *can* expose the truth sometimes in ways that make people notice, that move people beyond what a headline and a few columns of newspaper print ever can.

"I can't sleep," she says. "I just keep thinking about that guy shooting himself in the lighthouse. I mean, I've heard about Trey Humphrey's Ghost from the island kids, but I never thought he was a real guy. Have you seen the blog they're talking about?"

They, meaning pretty much everyone.

"We haven't, honey," Ginger says. "We came straight here."

I don't contradict her.

Annie sits beside me and hugs me as if she sees the guilt on my face and wants to wash it away. She smells of soap and salt air and just the faintest trace of sweat, and she leaves me thinking this is why I sometimes imagine I want children, for the hugs.

"Grammie has an Internet connection," she says. "She couldn't get cable or DSL out here, but she has dial-up."

The sounds of the journalists and the sea again fill the silence.

"Not anymore," Betts says gently.

"Well, the blog doesn't really say anything," Annie says. "I get how you could think after you read it that maybe Uncle Frank or Uncle Beau or Mom killed this guy, but it doesn't even mention you." She twists her long neck toward Betts. "Like you would ever hurt *anyone,* Aunt Betts, much less kill someone."

Ginger says, "I, on the other hand . . ."

"Oh!" Annie laughs. "I didn't mean *that,* Mom."

"It was an accident," Ginger says. "He was cleaning his gun."

"After he'd been drinking," Annie says.

"After he'd been drinking," Ginger agrees.

Annie yawns, then turns to Max. "Will you make something good for breakfast, Max? I haven't eaten anything half as good as that pasta since I left for school."

"Cinnamon apple crêpes or eggs Benedict?" Max asks. "Eggs Benedict without the meat, I'm afraid."

"Eggs Benedict," Ginger answers just as her daughter says, "Cinnamon apple crêpes."

"Eggs Benedict is your favorite," Ginger says to Annie.

"How about both?" Max says. "Tomorrow is Sunday. What kind of Sunday brunch doesn't offer a choice of what to eat?"

The clock in the front foyer begins to chime, twelve calm gongs.

Annie kisses first me and then her mother, then heads back to bed, leaving us no further along on deciding a course of action than we had been before. We should talk, but we decide instead to play Scrabble, and Max fetches the game from the Sun Room for us before saying he thinks he'll catch some shut-eye himself. That's the way he says it, "catch some shut-eye." The cliché seems to go with his goofy glasses and baggy jeans, if not with the fancy pasta and eggs Benedict and crêpes.

"Don't concern yourselves too much about those reporters: they won't be staying overlong," he says as he hands Ginger the Scrabble box. "Isn't a soul on this whole island who'll rent them a room. Rose down to the café will burn their toast and tell them she's out of breakfast meat, and when old Mr. Dodie comes in for his usual two eggs over easy and six pieces of bacon, she'll fry it up and insist that's all she's got. 'I cain't be givin' Mr. Dodie's bacon to a bunch of mainlanders,' she'll tell them, 'much less a slimy bunch of lie-spewing reporters.'" Max laughs, then. He has a lovely laugh. "Rose, she doesn't ever mince her words," he says. "Well, g'night."

He leaves, and we huddle around the Scrabble board in the Captain's Office, and we draw tiles. Laney, who draws an *X* and so gets to play first, looks at her tiles and then up at us. "The truth," she says, and as I'm trying to make sense of this—is she asking how to spell the word?—she says, "It's time I tell the truth. I need to tell the truth."

"What is the truth, exactly?" Betts asks. "Do we even know anymore?"

"Did we ever?" I ask.

Ginger says, "'Tell all the Truth but tell it slant—'"

"Stop it, Ginger!" Laney insists. "For the Good Lord's sake, stop with the poetry. Stop shoving all the bad things you feel into someone else's words and disowning them. Or don't. I don't care. But quit disposing of my hurt along with yours. What happened to me happened to *me* and I'm sorry it dug up your own mess but what I say about it is *my* decision, not yours. I'll say what I need to say in my own words."

I'm not sure which surprises me more: Laney lashing out at Ginger, or the fact that our friendship has survived so many years of this boiling under the surface, all this second-guessing about the choices we never did really agree upon.

"You're not a failure just because a group of fellas who have never invited a woman lawyer to join their silly little club didn't invite you, Ginge," Laney continues. "Though why you were so hell-bent on helping rich old misers add money to their already overfull pockets, I don't know. That's not you any more than that Ginny character that playwright fella wrote was you."

Her words are followed by a sharp silence. The journalists are looking up toward our window; if we can hear their outbursts, they can hear ours. Although they're closer to the lapping water, which should help wash over the sounds of us.

I try to shush us, but Ginger won't be shushed.

"You what? Went to see that asshole's play?" she demands.

We did, although Laney doesn't admit this. Laney and I went on a whim one time we both happened to be in London while it was playing, but we've never told Ginger that.

"Lordy, sometimes I think you *still* wonder if the whole world doesn't see you that way," Laney says. "As the unloved and unlovable Ginny that idiot wrote into his play."

In Ginger's pale eyes: devastation on top of devastation. First she fails at her career and then her best friends betray her in the worst way she can imagine, we pay money to that asshole to see the shit he'd written about her. And now we're grinding the grit of it into her. Her face is thick with the awful thought: *But that is me, Laney. That Ginny character, she* is *me.*

"That fella delivered the worst of you, exaggerated and untempered by your strengths, Ginge," Laney says more gently. "He delivered the surface of you without tilling up the good earth underneath."

Her intelligence; that jerk left out how smart Ginger is. And her generosity, too, her preference for the comfort of others over her own.

"That fella is the selfish one, Ginger, not you. You aren't as selfish as that character he wrote. You aren't that spoiled and you aren't that pathetic. You only think you are. You need to stop looking for a sad little pair of twos long enough to see you're holding a flush."

Ginger stares at her for a moment, then flips the Scrabble board. The tiles scatter in angry clicks all over the room. "Fuck you, Laney," she says. "Fuck you. I'm not half as selfish as you are. And if you think I'm pathetic, take a look in the mirror at yourself."

Laney and Betts and I watch as her bare heels stomp across the center hallway and disappear into the family wing. She's long gone before

Laney says angrily, "I didn't *say* she was pathetic. I said she *wasn't* pathetic."

Not *that* pathetic. Not *that* selfish. Not *that* spoiled.

We set about gathering up the game pieces together, my knees aching against the wood floor long before I find a final *N* under the Captain's desk, up against the secret passageway into Emma's Peek. Ginger still hasn't returned. Laney secures the lid on the box with a firmness that suggests she has no intention of going after her.

Betts, staring at Laney's long, dark fingers on the taped-up game box top, says, "I'll . . . head to bed, I guess."

I slip out a minute later, on the excuse of looking for something to read, and wait in the hallway for Betts.

"I knocked, but she won't answer," she says when she emerges from the family wing. Yes, Ginger's door is locked.

Perhaps she just needs some time alone, to cool off, we decide.

"She's cooling off with my contact lens solution," Betts says.

I tell her she can borrow mine.

"You don't think she'll hurt herself, do you?" Betts says.

The two of us stand in the hallway, whispering. We decide, finally, that she won't, that Ginger's weapon of choice for hurting herself is men, and the only man here—Max—appears to have no sharp edges on which she might cut herself.

It isn't until Laney and I are in bed with the lights out that I ask, "What about your political campaign, Lane? What if you just wait until after the election?"

Her words float up in the darkness, quiet and unsure: "If the good voters of the Georgia Forty-second want to hold against me something that was no fault of my own, they don't deserve my representation anyway."

I lie awake wondering if she really believes what happened was no fault of her own. She should, but I wonder if she does. Her sentence sounds as rehearsed as Betts's did when she said she didn't have anything to add to the public record on Trey's death. And her words ring equally untrue.

Mia

___

∼

THE GRANDFATHER CLOCK is striking three in the morning when I slip out from under the sheets in the bedroom Laney and I share; she's not snoring her light snore, so maybe she's only pretending sleep. I head down the dark stairway into the dark kitchen, and pour wine from the bottle we didn't finish at dinner into the first glass my fingers find, a coffee cup. In the Painter's Studio, the blinds are open to a huddle of journalists in the electric light of film equipment outside, but that isn't what stops me in the doorway. The shadow of a man sits at the window inside, where I posed when Beau sketched me, when the light made my eyes laugh, or that's what he'd claimed. For a moment, I'm sure it's Ginger's brother there again even though it can't be, of course: Beau is in Chicago with Laura, his wife of twenty-some years.

"They're not sleeping, but they look like they want to." It's Max's whisper, of course. "It's too dark for them to see inside." He pats the window seat. "Come enjoy the show. They're sharing now, at least there's that."

He means the light: the journalists are dealing cards under a single filming light, taking turns providing the light so no one runs out of juice to film us in the unlikely event we should emerge to make a statement in the middle of the night. I watch Fran Halpern for a moment. She manages to stay professional even around a journalists' film-light campfire in the middle of the night. She's one of my favorite television journalists, actually. A stand-up person who stays after the truth when others settle for the cheap headline and move on. If it were only Fran out there, I might open the door and invite her in.

"So often as a kid I hoped to be asked to a sleepover at the big house," Max says. "Used to watch Ginger and Trey steal my skiff, and I'd let them. Didn't want to be a snitch, just wanted to be invited to the parties here. Even after I was down to New York for architecture school, old enough to know better, still I sat watching out the window while they took my skiff."

I smile at the funny syntax: down *to* New York. This island has a language all its own.

"Who knew it would be the last time?" He says, and he stares out at the journalists, who are laughing. "So now here I am—in Governor Waller's Room, no less—and I can't sleep a wink."

"The week Trey Humphrey died?" I say, the journalist in me.

"Can't tell you how many islanders breathed a sigh of relief when that asshole shot himself." He blinks back at me through his geeky glasses. "I didn't mean that the way it sounded." A small note of alarm, quickly reined in. "We weren't glad he was dead, just glad it was by his own hand. Enough folks around here didn't care too much for Trey Humphrey."

He's talking about himself or I haven't been a journalist for twenty-some years. That "asshole"? Maybe he knows what they said about his sister, Tessie McKee.

I sit next to him, wanting to kiss him as surely as I wanted to kiss Beau the first time I sat in this room. Am I drawn to him because he hates Trey Humphrey as much as I do? How sick a reason would that be to fall for a guy? But no, I already made the first move earlier, kissing Max in the kitchen. And I've never been one to make the first move, really. It's one of the many ways I cling to the good girl I once was, the girl I left behind long ago.

Where was the turning point, the moment I crossed the line? Was it when I slept with Beau when I was engaged to Andy? When I lied to Andy afterward? When I told Andy the truth—or some version of the truth—after our marriage was through? Was it that first one-night stand in the chaos of my divorce? The first time I woke in the bed of a man whose name I didn't know? The moment I told Doug Pemberley more than I should have in an effort to shake off my past mistakes?

The night after I called Laney from the Cook Island pay phone, Doug and I sat on our balcony at the Pointway Inn, overlooking the sand he'd proposed in and sipping champagne even though the engagement ring still sat in its little velvet box. Not our first bottle that night, and still we'd just poured the last of it, drinking champagne in abundance as if I might still say yes, I'd marry Doug.

He'd married Sharon six months after Trey died, he was telling me. "When Trey was no longer around to tell me I was making a mistake." He smiled a little, his crooked smile in his charmingly crooked face. "Sometimes I still can't believe he's gone."

"Frankie was my best man. Frankie stood where Trey should have," he said. "I think I won't have a best man this time. I think I'll stand by myself, knowing Trey is beside me."

He set his hand on mine, caressing my ringless finger. "Not that I'm taking anything for granted. Not that I'm trying to pressure you."

He touched my forehead, my cowlick. "Trey would have approved of my marrying you. Even he was taken with the four Ms. Bradwells."

"Taken," I said, thinking Trey was a taker, and flashing rage and disgust and grief at all he'd taken from us. Thinking even if I could marry Doug—even if Laney could bear that—I couldn't bear the thought of Trey standing beside my happily-ever-after-to-be.

"Trey made me uncomfortable," I said. "I thought he wasn't . . . that maybe he wasn't who he seemed to be."

"He wasn't," Doug agreed. "He acted the hardass, but he was a nice guy, really. It was just that everyone always expected so much of him. And there was his dad killing himself over some woman, some black woman. I don't think he ever got over that."

I looked away, to the light sweeping across the water, the new lighthouse.

"That was weird, wasn't it," he said. "His attraction to your black friend? Do you think they slept together?"

"No." The one word all I could manage.

"I think they did," Doug said almost gleefully. "Not that he ever said that. Trey was nothing if not a gentleman."

"No!" I said. "I'm sure Laney never—"

"Hey, hey. I didn't mean to . . . I *liked* her. Helen. Laney. I didn't mean to disparage her. I just thought Trey was . . ." He laughed. "Well, I thought maybe you and Beau, too, but that was ridiculous, you were *engaged* to some guy back at school, right?"

The bubbles in my champagne surfaced and popped, and surfaced again.

"That was ridiculous," he repeated.

When I didn't respond, he drained his glass and stood and opened another bottle, poured a fresh glass, drank half of it, and topped it off again. His narrow face looked at me as if I'd slept with my cousin like Ginger had. He went to the balcony rail, looked out at the water, the light circling again and again.

"You didn't sleep with Trey, too?"

"Me?" I said, unsure whether he meant "too" as in he knew Trey had sex with Ginger or Laney that spring break, or "too" as in he understood from my silence that I'd slept with Beau. "No! Of course not!" Pushing back the memory of Trey's hand on mine in the skiff as we sped through the guts. "I'd never have slept with that asshole." Knowing the moment I said the word that I couldn't call his dead childhood hero-friend an asshole, but not knowing what to say to take it back. Not wanting to take it back.

Whatever I meant to happen, the words we said to each other only got more hurtful, the way they do when you rip apart someone somebody loves, when you are both angry and one of you has no idea where the anger is coming from and the other can't explain without making the hurt worse. When one person wants a relationship to last forever and the other doesn't know how to love like that. When one person has been expecting every moment for days that the other will say yes, she wants to spend the rest of her life with him, while she's been counting the minutes left in their week together, wanting to escape to a place where the men she might sleep with are journalists like her who don't expect anything more.

When that argument was over, so was our relationship. At least I understood it was. Doug spent the night in the sailboat we'd come over in, and I lay awake in our bed at the inn until the light came up and I could pack and catch the early morning ferry back to the mainland. Somewhere in the process, one truly lovely engagement ring found its way to the bottom of the Chesapeake, joining Beau's old sleeping bag.

I see now that I'd wanted him to be angry, because what else could I do? I'd called Laney. I'd told her I wanted to marry Doug Pemberley. I'd said his name, "Remember Doug Pemberley from Cook Island," so she would know exactly who I was engaged to. I'd said it was a bad idea, knowing if there was any chance she could stand to see Trey Humphrey's best friend every time she saw me, she would disagree with me, she would say she thought I should marry Doug. Because Laney does love me.

Laney does want me to be happy. She would have given me that if she could.

She hadn't answered, though. She'd let her silence be her answer. And I couldn't bear to cash in a thirty-year friendship for a marriage that probably wouldn't last anyway.

Or maybe that's not the way it was at all. Maybe I never wanted to marry Doug Pemberley. Maybe Laney was just my excuse for hurting him. Maybe I'd been looking for a wedge to free me from him when I went out to that public phone.

I hadn't wanted to hurt him, but he was hurt. After he got over the anger, he was hurt. He called me and apologized, and told me about pitching the ring in the bay. He didn't say anything about Beau or Trey or Laney.

"Let's try this again," he suggested. "Can't we try this again?"

I hadn't said yes, but I hadn't exactly said no either. I'd been on the other side of the world by then, with the excuse of never quite knowing where I'd be next. But there was no getting around that I would be in D.C. for Betts's confirmation.

"Just have dinner with me, Mia?" he'd asked the last time we'd spoken, just a few days ago, when I was in Madagascar to hear the Indri love song.

"I can't," I said.

"I said I was sorry, Mia. What more do you want from me? I said I was sorry."

"I know, Doug."

"I didn't have anything to do with Trey's death, Mia. Is that what this is about? This sudden change in how you feel? Did something I said make you think that?"

Outside my hotel room window, the thrum of insects. Inside, a tidy, impersonal room. Generic art. No books.

"No, of course not."

"The police only questioned me because I was the last one to see him."

"I know, Doug. I know that."

"I was such a mess after that. I thought it was my fault. I was his best friend. I knew he had moods. I should have stopped him. I should have seen it coming."

"Doug, you can't . . . He didn't . . . You don't believe he killed himself. You don't."

"I sure don't believe he took his gun up to the top of that fucking lighthouse to clean it."

"No," I said. "No. I don't either, Doug."

"But you don't think I—"

"No, of course not."

"Then why—"

"I *can't,* Doug. I can't marry you."

"I get that," he said gently. "I understand that. I'm, you know, old-fashioned. I think every woman wants to be married. But I know you're not every woman."

"I can't, Doug."

"I don't *care* who you slept with back then, Mia. Trey. Beau. Fucking both of them! I don't care."

"I can't."

"But you *love* me. You do love me, Mia."

In the silence, I remembered the call of the Indri I'd heard in the forest, that love song till death do them part. But I didn't call out. I let the silence cut the tie for me.

"MAX?" I SAY now, and some part of me knows this is just another mistake in a long line of them, but I do it anyway: I kiss him. With the window ajar and the view of the press huddled out in the darkness together, enjoying the same kind of noncommittal friendship I've spent so many nights sharing, I kiss him. I don't know why it surprises me when he kisses me back this time, but it does. Maybe because I know he doesn't approach this the way I do. He's not a one-night-stand kind of guy. He's a guy who would still be with his wife if she hadn't left him. He won't be someplace else tomorrow. He can be hurt as easily as Doug was.

With the kiss comes the memory of the night Beau kissed me here: the same ocean smell and faint overhang of turpentine, though staler now. So much has gone stale.

And I think of Andy then, of how everyone thought it must be easier for me that he was gay, that his leaving wasn't a rejection of me. But it wasn't any easier. It left me feeling I'd driven him away not just from me but from all women. It left me feeling he'd seen how I'd betrayed his trust, and thrown out all women with me. I know it isn't true. Andy was gay the day I met him; he just didn't know it yet. I do know that. What I know and what I feel are so often two different things, though. What I feel doesn't always make sense.

Betts

~~~

IF THE IDYLLIC-weekend-with-Iz-and-Annie idea wasn't shattered before we went to bed last night, it is by the time we finish Sunday brunch. There were no English muffins for eggs Benedict. The sad remains of Max's cinnamon apple crêpes lie scattered before us. The chef himself declined to join us for breakfast on the excuse of not wanting to intrude on our time with the girls. But the truth is the bickering started before we sat down. Bickering and worse. Laney and Ginger are each acting like the other simply is not here.

Iz sits across from me, still in the oversized-man's-shirt-and-boxer-shorts pajamas that no doubt have their origin in this divorced man I'm supposed to embrace. A man nearly as close in age to me as to her.

"Does he want more children?" I ask. "He already has—"

"We've barely been dating a month, Mom," she protests.

"But it's one thing to love a man and another thing entirely to love a whole family, Iz. To be denied children of your own when—"

"We're not planning our futures together yet, Mom! So why don't you just chill?"

The closed-in Tea Parlor is beginning to feel claustrophobic. Amazing what an effect lack of sunshine will have on you.

"Maybe I don't want children," Izzy says. "Aunt Mia doesn't have children, and she's the happiest one of you."

Mia's startled brown eyes fix on this daughter of mine who adores her. *Maybe Izzy doesn't want children?*

"Oh good lord, Isabelle, you can't want to be like Mia," I say. "She can't even hold a relationship together. She doesn't know *how* to love!"

The untruth of my words rushes over me as Mia picks up her fork and pushes the cold, gelatinous remains of a crêpe around.

Annie rises to Mia's defense, saying, "That never stopped anyone in my family." Probably referring to her Uncle Frank, who is on his third wife, his third set of kids, and his third law firm. But her dagger hits Ginger's heart. You can see it in the way her pale eyes and her wide mouth soften. Laney and Mia and I all suspect Ginger's marriage isn't as Midwestern-idyllic as Ginger likes to project. But this is the first crack in the façade any of us has actually seen.

I need to say something funny here. Something that apologizes to Mia and lets Ginger know her daughter isn't talking about her. But I don't feel funny. I don't feel apologetic or forgiving.

I want Ginger to explain how she could possibly ever have thought it was okay to have sex with her cousin.

I want Mia to stop forever thinking she knows better than everyone else. I want to throw Faith's words in her face: *It's not fair, but it's the way it is.* Get over it, Mia. Let go of it. Move on.

Iz is the one who moves on, though. She excuses herself to shower and dress. I want to stop her, but there is no reasoning with Isabelle when she's upset.

Annie announces she needs to dress, too. She's always been Izzy's loyal puppy. She hurries across the hall after my daughter.

Laney watches the empty hallway long after the girls disappear into the Ladies' Salon and up the servants' stairs. I'm pretty sure it's her daughter Gem she's thinking of rather than my Iz or Ginger's Anne. Her brown slacks and turquoise three-quarter-sleeve blouse are fresh and pressed but her eyes are weary.

"I didn't kill Trey," she whispers.

Only then does she focus on the pink-walled room and the round table. The four of us sitting in the flowered chairs. She's lain awake all night rethinking her decision to go public about her rape, thank God. It's the way Laney has always been. Mia makes a decision and never looks back. Ginger is the same although perhaps she *ought* to rethink her decisions. I'm a worrier like Laney, but it rarely keeps me awake all night. Not since those early months after Zack died. Laney though? She goes over and over her choices even when there is no longer anything to do about them. Maybe she was like this before the rape. Or maybe she wasn't. I don't remember anymore.

Have we seen her bright smile at all this weekend?

"If I go public with . . . with what Trey did, the whole world will think I killed Trey and y'all helped me cover it up. I didn't, but they'll be mighty sure I did anyway. Who else would have done it?"

"Any of us might have, Lane," Mia insists.

"But none of us did," I whisper. We're all whispering. We can't get away from the fact of the reporters outside. Their attention was raised by my outburst about Mia. Cranky journalists who've had no decent sleep. Who need to justify their discomfort with news.

"We were all together in that little bunkroom the night he died," I say without conviction.

In the long silence that follows I stare out through the archway, into the Ballroom Salon and the door to Faith's Library beyond on the far wall. This is one of the questions I worried someone would ask me back then. It was one of the questions I held my breath for as the Judiciary Committee grilled me. The question I've never put to Mia because I haven't wanted to know for sure. One of the uncertainties I hang my hat on when I'm assuring myself I don't really *know* what happened to Trey Humphrey. That I have nothing to add to the public record.

"I wasn't, not all night," Ginger says.

I turn to her, confused. This is the confession I expected but not the source. Ginger was in the bunk with Laney. It was Mia who was out. Mia who tried to slip in without being seen.

"I went out for a walk, just for a short walk," Ginger says. "Trying to sort things out."

"I wasn't either," Mia says. "I was out for . . . for a while."

"But you weren't alone, Mia," I say. Launching into a choice selection of the little speech I'd prepared for the Senate Judiciary Committee before Mia talked me into the single "nothing to add to the public record" line: Mia wasn't alone.

Ginger's hand goes to her lips. "You and Dougie?" she says. "I *knew* you were with him that week. You can't say I didn't warn you not to listen to him sing."

Mia looks to the Music Room and the Painter's Studio, the journalists on the pier outside. "With Beau," she whispers, maybe because of the journalists or maybe because that's all the air she can get behind the confession.

"No way." Ginger looks for support. Finds none. "No way," she repeats. She crosses her arms at her chest. Trying to communicate a conviction she doesn't feel. "Shit, Mia," she says. "You're seducing my brother while you're engaged to Andy?"

I'm pretty sure what Laney told me she saw in the Painter's Studio was Beau seducing Mia. But I don't say this. No one says this.

"You're fucking *fucking* my brother while my cousin is drowning in his own blood?"

Mia doesn't protest. As if this attack isn't about her at all.

The anger in Ginger's voice improbably bubbles over into something else. Sadness or fear or some other emotion that has her touching her hair for comfort that way she does. Trying so hard not to cry.

"He was dead when I got there," she sobs. "Or maybe he was alive, a little alive, I don't know." She sinks back into her chair. Focuses on the emptiness in front of her as if the ghost of Trey Humphrey were floating in the stale-breakfast air under the chandelier. "But he'd already shot himself, the blood was all over the place." She closes her eyes against the horror she's buried under layers of pretend happiness for thirty years. "The blood was all over the place."

Mia

~

TREY WAS DEAD when Ginger got there? As we sit in stunned silence, the journalists outside laugh, just another day at work. It seems so bizarre that it stops me. How many times have I been laughing just outside, passing the time waiting for news to drop into my lap?

Laney is the first of us to recover. She moves to the chair beside Ginger and takes her hand, saying, "Hey, Ginge," comforting Ginger the same way we've so often seen Ginger comfort Laney. "Hey," she says again. "Hey." I half expect her to offer up a line of Latin in apology for the blast she gave Ginger last night. If Ginger tucks her emotions into lines of other people's poetry to cast them off, Laney tucks hers into Latin words no one can understand.

Max emerges from the Ladies' Salon and crosses the hall. Before I can figure out how to turn him back, he blunders into the Tea Parlor, saying, "Rain's going to start within the hour." He stops when he sees Ginger, who is working hard to recover her composure. He shoots me a look, as if I might have some clue how to help him out here. He's interrupted something, he sees that. But he's in it now.

"I'm making a run across for groceries," he says as nonchalantly as he can muster. "Any special requests?"

"Across?" Ginger's voice so artificially light it sounds ridiculous. "To the mainland?"

Max runs a hand over his thinning hair. "Don't worry, Ginge," he says, grinning in a way that is almost convincing. "I've been practicing my 'No comment' all morning. I think I've got it down." And he's in the hallway and headed out the back door before we can put in the special requests we haven't thought of yet.

Ginger bolts from the windowless Tea Parlor through the Ballroom Salon and into Faith's Library, Betts and Laney following her. I bring up the rear, thinking Ginger really *is* smarter than I am; I'd have gone straight for the closer Music Room windows, where we would more likely be seen peering out.

We peek through the tinted glass of the low-e windows, through the tree branches beyond the glass. Outside, Max faces a large bouquet of microphones offered by the swarm of reporters. If we'd planned this, we could easily be slipping out of Chawterley while they're distracted, but Iz and Annie are upstairs showering, and where would we go, anyway?

Ginger cracks open a window just in time to hear Max say, "The only comment I have for you folks is that the sky up there looks mighty ugly." They all look up, and he pushes through them and throws the lines, hops onto his boat. Not the skiff, but the larger boat he brought the girls over in. A minute later, he's headed out.

"He's not going to the mainland," Ginger says as we watch the boat grow smaller. "He's headed to town. That makes more sense."

The loud motor of a boat approaching not much later makes me glad of the fact we'll have food. With a quick peer through the drapes, though, we see that the boat is not Max's but rather the ugly wreck that takes the day's catch across to the mainland, a.k.a. "the ferry."

"What the hell is Arthur doing here?" Ginger asks.

It's started spitting; the microphones thrust toward the poor guy trying to secure the boat are held by slightly damp journalists. With the press distracted, Ginger again opens a window slightly so we can hear what's going on.

The guy looks at the journalists like they are poisonous.

Max emerges from the ferry cabin, hiking up his baggy jeans. The press turn as one, offering him their bouquet as he hops to the pier. His expression is almost smug.

"Oh, shit, he's going to talk," Ginger says.

Cameramen are wiping the drizzle from their lenses and focusing. Max seems to be waiting for them to be ready. His glasses are misting over, too, but he doesn't clear them.

"Does he know anything?" Betts asks Ginger. She turns to me. "You didn't—"

"Of course not!"

"Good afternoon," Max calls out. The sound guys all flinch, and adjust. "Occurred to me some of you folks might like to catch a ride with me before your equipment gets soaked. I figure I have just enough time to cross the bay and get back with some champagne a friend of mine needs. Anyone wants a ride, you're welcome."

The journalists laugh but eye the clouds uneasily and wipe their lenses again.

I say, "They won't leave the island, it's too hard to get back here. If it starts raining, they'll figure they can find a hotel in town."

"Only the one little inn," Ginger says.

Outside, Max says, "Tide's coming up, too. It's already crested the break and headed up the walkway at the inn." He eyes the pier. " 'Course this ground is a little higher. Probably won't come much above the third step here, I don't think."

The cameramen frown at their equipment.

"The inn is closed for the weekend," Max continues. "Even if you don't mind the long walk in the pouring rain, there aren't rooms. Restaurant's closed, too. They're having a little party for the innkeepers' anniversary. Everyone in town will be there, 'less they have to cancel on account of the weather. The owner of Brophy's and the barmaid, too."

He offers this little bit with such conviction that I'm pretty sure the whole thing is untrue, although the champagne is a nice touch. A flurry of questions from the press follows. They, too, are skeptical.

"Suit yourself," Max says. "Not sure there's room enough for everyone, but first come first served. Arthur and I have got to get going, or we'll be late for the party. He's promised he'll return to the mainland to fetch you tomorrow morning if you like, though. Island hospitality."

Arthur nods, a man of few words.

"Hate for anyone to catch pneumonia out here in the rain all night," Max says.

The rain starts coming harder then.

"Like he's planned the downpour," I say gleefully.

"Anyone who grew up on the island can read the weather without the need of news channel satellite data," Ginger says. "Every choice people make here is governed by the weather."

"The bit about the tide on the Pointway Inn walkway is a little over the top," Betts says.

"That, actually," Ginger says, "is one of the few things he said that's probably true."

Arthur heads below and fires up the engine. Max takes the line, preparing to leave. We watch as reporters start loading on like Max is Noah sent by God to collect them. The only holdout is Fran Halpern, whose carefully casual coif is protected by an attractive hat, her makeup still perfect. I make a mental note to get a hat like that.

Her camera crew motions her to join them on the boat. We can't hear what they're saying over the rain now, but Max clearly says something to her before he squats down to the near cleat and takes the line in his hand. Her body language is all protest, but he stands and says something more, then extends his hand. She looks from him to her crew, her lips forming angry words: not the f-word, but that's the idea.

Ignoring his hand and that of her cameraman offered from the boat, she steps from the pier unassisted. Max tosses the line aboard, releases the other line, and hops aboard himself.

As the boat clears the pier and heads out into the bay, Ginger says softly, "'As if a shipwrecked Pagan, safe in port, / His guardian sea-god to commemorate' . . ."

She backs away from the window and heads toward the shelves with the miniature books.

"It's one of the sonnets," she says.

"From the peacock volume, Ginge?" I ask.

Ginger pulls the tiny book from a shelf and opens it, reads the whole sonnet aloud. Laney doesn't turn from the window, but she is listening intently, as if Ginger has written the poem herself. Betts, too, remains with her back to the room, watching the rain wash away the last glimpse of the ferry, as if those journalists are taking her last hope of being appointed to the Supreme Court away with them.

"What does it mean?" Betts asks when Ginger finishes reading, asking about the poem or the fact that we're alone here at Chawterley again, or both.

Ginger sets the book on her mother's desk, next to a volume titled *Transformations.* "I'm not really sure," she says. "Maybe that's why Mother left the volume to Aunt Margaret, because I had it all those years and still I don't understand half the poems."

Her hand as she picks up the larger volume looks old, suddenly, despite her expensive creams. We're all growing old and worn like so many of the books surrounding us—old and worn and misunderstood.

"Mother left this one to Aunt Margaret, too," Ginger says. "Her favorite book of poetry, and I'm the poet, but she leaves it to a fucking friend."

She flips open the book. The pages split at a point where something has been inserted, a foggy old photograph. She stares at it for a long moment before moving it aside to reveal a small cream-colored envelope underneath.

Laney turns from the window to us as Ginger stares at the writing on the envelope.

"What is it, Ginge?" I ask.

Betts

~~~

FAITH'S LIBRARY, CHAWTERLEY HOUSE
SUNDAY, OCTOBER 10

"You *saw* him, Ginge?" Laney whispers. She hasn't said a word since the Max-entering-press-exiting-poem-reading began. A fact I realize only as she speaks. Her dark cheeks and dark eyes are sunken. Her tone leaves no doubt that she's had the image of Trey dead in the chair in mind ever since Ginger said she saw him. That her initial rush to comfort Ginger has given way to something else.

"Lordy, why didn't you tell us?" she asks.

Ginger sets the envelope back in the poetry book and closes it. Stands staring at her mother's desktop. Not the desktop from the Captain's Library where Faith sat talking with me that Saturday morning after the rape. But similar. A large expanse of wood inlaid with leather. It's bare but for the tiny peacock book where that earlier desktop was covered with papers. Whoever cleared her kitchen has tidied her life here, too.

"Ginge, we all know you didn't . . ." Laney says. "None of us . . . How could any of us have done something like that and not told the rest of us?"

I finger a drawer pull on the desk as if I might slide it open to find a chewed pencil. Chewed reading glasses, too. "If I'd killed Trey, I wouldn't have told you," I say. "It would make you guys accessories after the fact. It would be asking you to go to jail for me."

Was that what I'd made Faith by seeking her help? Or what she'd chosen to become?

Laney's frown leaves me searching for the words of that poem Ginger mentioned. Something about silence and restraint.

"You think you were that calculating when you were twenty-five, Betts?" Laney says. "And isn't that what y'all did for me, anyway? Make yourselves accessories after the fact by agreeing to keep quiet for my sake?"

"We made that decision together," Mia says. "And we weren't protecting you from the legal consequences of anything you did, Lane."

"She didn't tell us about being pregnant," Ginger says. "Betts didn't." She thinks I'm plenty calculating. That's what she's saying. Or she means to offend us all in one easy weekend. Or both.

Mia picks up the framed "Curse of the Naked Women." To get Ginger's attention. To piss her off. If this foursome cracks in two, Mia is on my side.

"The only person protected by us remaining quiet was Trey Humphrey," she says.

Which isn't exactly true. Or I'm not exactly sure it is.

"Trey, who was already dead," Ginger says.

"We didn't know that," I say. "Not when we made that decision." And he *wasn't* dead when we decided to bury the rape. That decision was made in the sometime-after-midnight hours of Friday. Trey didn't die until late Saturday night. Or in the dark early hours of Sunday.

"We thought we were protecting each other," Mia says. "Not just your reputation, Laney. All of our reputations. That's why we kept quiet about what happened. Not to protect Trey. Not even just to protect you. To protect *ourselves*."

"From something none of us did!" Ginger insists. "We aren't guilty of anything."

Mia studies the poetry book in Ginger's hand as if there might be some answer in the title. *Transformations*. "Any one of us might have slipped out and killed Trey and slipped back in while the rest of us slept," she says. "It only takes a minute to shoot someone."

"You don't believe that, Mi," Ginger says.

"That's not the point, what we believe," I say. "The point is that's the way it plays in the press. There's a . . . a rape, right?" Even when the word was there on the Scrabble board none of us said it aloud. Not in Laney's presence. "And then just coincidentally the guy turns up dead the very next night. The facts start coming out. Maybe Laney was in the room all night. But you two were—"

"But I wasn't," Laney says quietly. "I put the book back."

"The book?" Mia runs her fingers through her hair at her cowlick.

"The peacock book," Laney says. She nods at the miniature book on Faith's desktop. "I slipped it into the Captain's Library during the party."

"Oh, shit," Ginger says.

"But the doctor said it was all an accident," Laney says. "Trey was drunk and he was cleaning his gun."

"The doctor who was the best man at my parents' damn wedding," Ginger says. "Who was Daddy's best friend from before they started lower school. Everyone already thinks Trey committed suicide. Everyone already assumes Dr. Pilgrim lied. It's no great leap to conclude he lied to hide a murder rather than a suicide."

"Well, maybe a little bit of a leap?" I suggest.

"But you're off the hook, Betts," Laney says. "You and Mia both. Why would y'all have shot Trey Humphrey?" She fingers a small turquoise button at the fitted waist of her blouse. "If I admit what happened, that clears your name, clears your way to the Court."

"But what about Gemmy, Lane?" Ginger asks quietly. "How does a mom tell a daughter she's been ... been raped?" She gulps the word. Giving voice to the same thing I've been struggling with.

"None of us can keep ourselves safe all the time, Ginge," I say.

Laney leans against the window as if to steady herself. "I could have, though," she says. "That's the thing. I *chose* to go drinking with Trey Humphrey. I *chose* to go skinny-dipping. I *chose* to go to the lighthouse."

I touch her hair. The curls she's finally set free. "You thought Mia was there," I say. "It's where Beau and Mia *said* they were going. Really, no one can fault you, Lane."

"But they will," Ginger says. "They will fault Laney. And now what does she do? Let Gemmy learn about it from the headlines? Tell her over a damned long-distance phone?"

Laney

LAW QUADRANGLE NOTES, Spring 1992: Ms. Helen Weils (JD '82) and her husband, Will Robeson, are happy to announce the birth of their third child, Ginger Elsbieta Mary Robeson, a.k.a. Ms. Gem Robeson-Bradwell.

RAPE, FROM THE Latin *rapere,* meaning to seize, a term used in Roman law for crimes of theft. Theft of a fella's property, women being the property of men under Roman law. If it had been anyone but William with me when I hung up the phone from talking with Mia that night she called to ask about marrying again, I might have begun the conversation about what happened on Cook Island with that Latin, if I'd begun it at all. I might have held the rape away from me, wrapped it up in a single word in a dead language that I could explain.

In retrospect, I see so many ways I might have reached out for help in the aftermath of Cook Island. There was rape counseling available in Ann Arbor. There was a twenty-four-hour peer counseling hotline, 76-GUIDE, I could have called; I could have been a nameless gal helped by a faceless voice over an anonymous telephone line. But I wasn't behaving in a particularly rational way in the aftermath of Cook Island. How could I act sensibly in a world that no longer made sense? And what would I have told the voice that answered the telephone anyway? That I'd gone skinny-dipping with Trey Humphrey. That I'd gotten drunk with him. That when he asked me to leave everyone else in that cottage behind and go to the lighthouse with him, I had gone.

It got no easier to talk after I moved to Atlanta, either, after I started working in the mayor's office. Once I was part of Maynard's team, my behavior reflected on him, whether it should have or not. A story about a sex scandal involving a young female aid to the mayor and a dead Washington lawyer was no longer just about me. And there was that, too, of course: Trey was dead. I couldn't talk to anyone without raising questions about that.

Whenever I start in on the Latin, though, William gives me a look that says I can't hide from him. Maybe he gave me that look even before I'd finished assuring him the kids were fine that night, that the caller had been Mia. Or maybe I finally asked myself *why* I couldn't I tell this man who loved me about something I ought not to be ashamed of, something that wasn't my fault. I'd never have forgiven myself if he learned about what happened to me the way, a few weeks later, I would learn that Betts was nominated for the Court: by reading it in the news.

"William," I said, "can I tell you about something that happened to me a long time ago? A long time before I even met you. I don't know why I never told you before."

He didn't answer exactly, but William has a way of letting you know he's with you without saying a word. And he listened, and he held me, and when I was finished he just kept on holding me. He didn't say anything, but he didn't need to. It was as if he always did know.

"I think I need to tell the children about it," I said finally. "But how do I tell Gemmy?"

William took my hand then. Wrapped both my bony hands in his beautiful ones.

"How do I tell Gemmy this happened to her own mama?" I asked him. "How do I say that in a way that doesn't leave her forever worrying about herself?"

THE MORNING GEMMY was born, late morning after a sleepless night in labor, I looked at her long skinny feet and her long skinny fingers, her perfect little nails, and I wondered if there ever was a more beautiful girl in the world. "Beautiful" was the word I used, but I didn't mean it in a physical sense, I meant it as a reflection of the way she makes me feel every time I look at her.

Okay, not every time. Not at 7:45 in the morning her senior year in high school, when first bell was just minutes away and her not yet dressed. Maybe not during those annual September ordeals when I dragged her around to every store in Atlanta in search of new school shoes only to have her decide, invariably, on the first pair she'd tried on at the first store we'd left hours before. But *most* every time.

I had two sons before I had Gemmy, and then the surprise of Little

Joe after her. I don't love her more or less than them, or even differently. But it's special, having a daughter, even when she's thirteen and doesn't much want a mama.

It was William's idea to name her after the Ms. Bradwells: Virginia Elsbieta Mary, that was his thought. But she was born such a willowy little thing, and those names all seemed so stocky. We considered Libby or Beth, but that didn't seem right, either. It was the whole of us we wanted to capture the spirit of, anyway. That's what I told Mia when she called from wherever in the world she was after Ginger called her with my news.

"Gem," Mia said. "Ginger Elsbieta Mary. Or you could do Elizabeth if Elsbieta is too much."

I said I never really thought of Betts as an Elizabeth, and William said, "Gemmy." And she has been ever thus.

There is so much in a name, I told myself as the days grew into weeks after I'd told William about being raped and still I hadn't told the children. I began to rationalize that I didn't need to tell them, I wasn't going to get the nomination, never you mind the polls moving in my direction. And even if I did, how would anyone find out about what had happened? No one knew except the Ms. Bradwells and now William, and none of us would ever tell.

Then I did get the Democratic nomination. I remember watching the primary results come in on the Internet, the spread widening until finally the last of my opponents called to concede. I remember Gemmy hugging me like she didn't often do in her teenage years. My daughter calling me "Senator Mama" and looking so proud, like she might want to be more me than Mia after all. Gemmy asking if she could call her friend Tara to tell her, forgetting it was the middle of the night. I resolved then that I would tell her about what happened to me on Cook Island, that I wasn't ashamed and I didn't want her to think she should ever be. I was about to go up against a Republican opponent who wouldn't hesitate to smear me the way someone in my own party would, and I wouldn't leave any of my children emotionally unarmed for this.

But in the bright light of the next morning, I was less sure. Knowing her mother was raped would change my daughter's sense of security in the world in a way I just couldn't bear. And she never would be raped. She was smarter than I was. More cautious. And I would never allow it. As if it were something I could control.

Then Betts was nominated for the Court.

Ginger called me the minute she heard; she couldn't understand why Betts hadn't told us before it was made public, why Betts didn't trust us with her secret. But I didn't think it had anything to do with not trusting us with secrets, and I still don't, even now that I know about her affair with that partner fella in New York. I thought it had to do with her fearing I would ask her not to accept the nomination. But I wouldn't have. I'd have told her she ought to. I'd have told her the Court needed her.

The way they dig into a Supreme Court nominee's past, though, surely someone would question her being there that night Trey Humphrey was said to have shot himself. I couldn't help wondering what they might ask her and what she might say, whether she would be under oath if the questions came and if it would matter if she wasn't. The planets were gathering the way they had that week on Cook Island, lining up against me with Mercury about to rise.

And so I told the boys first. Willie J and Manny were home from college for the summer, so I told them together with Little Joe. I told them in a different way than I would tell Gemmy, but it gave me a little practice at the children reacting. I said this happened to me, and I wanted them to know in case it came out in the press. I said I wasn't at fault, that bad things happen to good people, that I wasn't ashamed. I told them if it did come out, that was what I would say: I'm not ashamed. And being boys, their reaction was less complicated; boys do get raped, but they never imagine they will. My sons' reactions focused on me, on what it meant about me, and it was enough for them to know that it was a long time ago, before I'd even met their daddy, and that the fella was dead. I expect they heard it as much as anything as a caution to be gentle with girls, to make sure they weren't pushing anyone. The boys didn't ask too many questions, and at the first pause Manny wondered if Little Joe was getting enough practice at the hoop in the off season, and the three of them took a ball to the high school nets. They might have talked among themselves there, but I expect they did not.

That left me alone to talk with Gemmy, in the quiet of the house that had been the only home she'd ever known. I found her in her bedroom, leaning back against her pink pillows, the matching comforter on the floor in the company of yesterday's underwear and socks. I believe I smiled when I saw them. I believe I thought how very young an eighteen-year-old girl is. I believe I wondered how I could ever let her go away to college in September, and how my own mama had let me—her only child—go.

But what I said was, "Gemmy." And then I repeated her name, "Gem," remembering that a gem was a good thing, beautiful and strong. I sat at the end of her bed, on the sheet where the comforter wasn't, and I set my hand on her long, skinny, bare foot, and said, "Gemmy, can I tell you about something that happened to me a long time ago?"

THE COOL OF the window glass against my shoulders soothes me, as do Betts's gentle fingers on my hair. Poor Ginger, I think. She's standing there at her dead mama's desk watching Mia wipe dust from Faith's framed copy of her African women piece, one of the few things Faith kept in this room other than her books. How many times over the years have I listened to Ginger carry on about her mama framing that thing? Nearly as many times as the two of us talked about getting our daughters to tell us things we surely never told our mamas when we were their age.

I think of the way Izzy gave Betts what-for this morning when Betts was poking around about this new fella of hers. Annie and Gem never sass Ginger or me the way Izzy has sassed Betts her whole life. I believe we've privately welcomed that as evidence that we're the better mamas. But it strikes me now that Izzy does tell Betts everything, and I wonder if there aren't things my daughter doesn't tell me.

"Gemmy already knows about what happened, Ginge," I say quietly. "I don't have to tell her over the telephone. I told her this summer." I hesitate, but then I do ask, "Does Annie know?"

In the silence that follows we all know the answer. Ginger has never told another soul about her and Trey. Our reaction back then had shown her what she surely knew on some level but likely couldn't face and maybe still can't: that her relationship with Trey would be considered sick. *His* sickness, but she didn't see that, she saw it as her own.

Ginger sinks down into one of the guest chairs, fingering the back of her head where all that long hair I used to so envy no longer is. "If you say anything, Lane, they'll find out everything there is to find out about me, too. That I slept with him. That I found him and maybe he was dead or maybe I left him to die instead of going for help. That maybe I killed him."

"But the Lord's truth is he shot *himself*," I insist. "It was an accident."

"And whether there are other truths that did or didn't happen around that truth isn't the point," Betts agrees. "I think we need to back up here. No one is asking if Trey Humphrey did anything to anyone Friday night."

"No one has the rape," Mia says.

"And how will they get it if none of us talks?" Betts says. "Talking about it just muddies the truth."

"Which is that Trey fucking shot himself," Ginger says.

"But how can we be sure they don't have it?" I ask. "How can we be sure this blogger fella doesn't have everything that happened that night?"

Mia rubs her temple at her cowlick. She looks like she needs air, like the extra weight she's picked up is stressing her poor heart.

Ginger crosses her arms, hugging the *Transformations* to her chest. I silently will her not to say what I know she thinks, that Mia is the blogger. If Mia is the blogger, let her say so herself.

What Mia says, though, is, "I didn't tell him anything about what Trey did. Honestly. I might have told Beau the night after it happened, I don't know, I was so upset I'm not sure what I said. But I never told Doug a thing about the rape."

Mia

~

"I WANTED TO marry Doug," I say to Laney, trying to make her understand I never meant to hurt her. "I thought I *would* marry him. I know you didn't want me to but I thought . . . I thought maybe with time. And I wanted to start it right, not like with Andy, not with secrets. I thought . . . I don't know. I thought I wanted to marry him, but maybe I didn't even really want that. Maybe I was just going to make the same mistake I made with Andy, marrying someone I liked well enough because I wanted to be married. Because I wanted to be part of a family and if I didn't marry him, who would I ever marry? I wasn't trying to tell him anything about Trey, I was trying to explain about Beau. Because they were friends. I wanted him to know about Beau."

Laney doesn't move from the rain-streaked window. She just stares at me, as does Betts, standing beside her, and Ginger, in the chair by Faith's desk. It's so quiet you can hear the blowing of pressurized air, Faith's careful measures to protect these books she also drenched in tobacco smoke. The things we are willing to give up, and the things we can't.

Was that what I was doing, trying to tell Doug about Beau? Or was I trying to break it off with him in a way that allowed me to hold on to the idea that I did love him, that I wasn't so selfish as to destroy a twenty-five-year marriage for a thing that had never even been love?

"Doug Pemberley wrote the blog, everything about it is his style," I say. It has my almost-fiancé's fingerprints all over it: the overuse of the word "probable," the lack of commas, the short, clipped sentences that so remind me of Betts.

"He knows everyone in D.C. from his years as a lobbyist."

Ginger pulls the damned book she's holding even more tightly to her chest, as if to shield her heart. "He wanted to be a writer when we were kids," she says, the doubt in her voice falling away with each successive word. "He tried to be a writer, but he couldn't make enough money."

I try to imagine again how Doug could have done this to us. He's hurt, sure. I hurt him. I left him months ago, but he didn't really understand it was over until I refused to have dinner with him in D.C. this week. If I were him, I'd want to hurt me back, too. Like I'd wanted to hurt Andy. Which is, I suppose, why I fled after our breakup, to put some distance between us. Why I suppose my mom left my dad every summer: trying to avoid hurting him. But that doesn't justify Doug's dragging this out now. If he wanted to stir up a scandal to kill my chances of finding another job, fine. But coldly ignoring the collateral damage to Betts, which he must have anticipated—that's inexcusable.

Except that Doug isn't like that. It's not just his singing voice that's sweet. I think that's why I couldn't believe the post was his when I first saw it in the airport, even though I'd been following the blog for a few weeks by then, even though I was pretty sure it was Doug's. It wasn't until I read the post at Max's, until I reread it carefully, that I was sure. And even then, not sure enough to tell Ginger and Laney and Betts.

So maybe it's something more forgivable than bitterness? Maybe he thinks no one should be considered for the Supreme Court without all the facts? You couldn't exactly fault him for that. You might even find him honorable—a good guy, really, who maybe has never gotten over finding his best friend dead in a pool of blood when they were both young men. You might think it's high time he be allowed to understand the truth about what happened to his friend. You might even think he would have been a great husband, if only you could have figured out a way to save your own dear friend the hurt your marrying him might have caused her. You might hurt as much as he does, even knowing you made the right choice. You might think you've become your mother, or even something less. All those summer friends, but she gave them up for Bobby and me. Could I do that? I'm not the giving-up type. I'm better with borrowed children, Baby Bradwells I can love when it's convenient, who don't have to rely on my love.

"I don't know why he wrote it," I say. "I've tried to understand why he wrote it, and to be honest I think maybe he just thought it was the right thing to do, that if there are questions about Trey's death they ought to be answered."

Betts frowns. "Then why didn't he name me?"

I focus on the rain on the window, the tree branches and stone steps and pier distorted through the wet glass. "Because he doesn't really believe you're involved?" I suggest. "But he isn't sure? He's not sure enough about anything to name names, but he's been carrying the guilt of Trey's suicide his whole life, and he wants to set it down."

I recognize the truth of this as I say it. Doug just meant to set his own hurt down, finally. If he'd meant to hurt me, he would have welcomed tossing my name toward scandal in pursuit of the truth. He would have justified naming me on the excuse of my knowing something I haven't admitted, to give the questioners a place to start. But the only name he gave them was Trey's name and the mention of the Conrad summer home. A home more than a few friends from Washington had visited over the years. Faith Cook Conrad's house. Faith, whose protégée, Elsbieta Zhukovski, was now the nominee for the Supreme Court—people would know that because Faith introduced us Ms. Bradwells to everyone she could. Connections and timing, that's what she thought it took for women to succeed, and she shared every connection she could with us.

Elsbieta Zhukovski, who'd been a law school friend of Faith's wild daughter, someone would have remembered—after which any of the party guests might recall that the daughter had had her law school roommates with her that weekend, hadn't she? Half the guests and probably a few people who hadn't even attended would have remembered meeting Betts at Mr. Conrad's birthday party then, because who doesn't want to have known a Supreme Court justice since she was a girl? And any single one of them wondering aloud whether Betts had known the dead nephew would have fired up the rumor mill. The public loves a scandal. We always have.

"Doug doesn't *know* anything," I insist. "All he knows is that I had doubts about Trey's death."

"But how can you be sure?" Betts asks quietly.

"I just said I—"

The thought registers then: we aren't the only ones who knew what happened. Trey knew what happened, too. Trey knew what he had done for a whole day before he blew his guts out. Or before someone else did it for him. All this time we've been thinking we could control this, but who knows what Trey himself might have told someone? Not rape, probably. But he might have talked about Laney without calling it rape.

"That's why you made me rehearse that line over and over," Betts says. "You *knew* this was going to surface—"

"I didn't, Betts. I swear I didn't have any idea. I was as shocked by the WOWD blog as you were. When I saw it in the airport—"

"You saw it in the *airport*? *Before* the hearing?"

"You were already at the microphone, Betts. By the time I got off the plane, the afternoon session had already begun."

"And you had no idea it was coming? You just happened to check one single blog at the airport and it happened to be this one?"

"It wasn't like that, Betts. I swear it wasn't like that. I've been reading his blog for weeks. I . . . He's a nice guy, Betts, and he just wanted to have dinner while I was in town, he was just trying to understand what he did wrong and he didn't do anything wrong, *I* was a schmuck, I just— How could I—"

Laney won't even look at me now. She stares at the gray-black television screen over the fireplace.

"There just was no way to make that relationship work," I say.

"You made me practice that line a million times, Mi," Betts insists. " 'I have nothing to add to the public record on that.' Like you knew it was coming."

"But Mia has always been like that, Betts," Ginger says. She sets the book in her lap and settles her manicured hands over the title, *Transformations*. "She always knows without knowing she knows. Mia, the Savant."

"Mia, the *asked*," I say. "You asked me, Betts. That first phone call, when I was in Madagascar, you asked me. 'What do I say if someone asks about Cook Island?' I thought maybe *you* knew it was coming. I thought maybe you somehow knew something none of the rest of us did."

Betts

"I THINK WE should go for a walk," Laney says. Just like that. As if I'm not about to bludgeon Mia. As if we're only discussing whether the storm has passed enough to go outside.

"It would be a nice thing to do with the girls," she says.

Ginger looks as astonished as I feel. But she sets the book with the photo and envelope beside the miniature peacock book. She says Annie would like that. In her response I see what she sees: Laney has hit a wall. She can't talk about this anymore. She can't listen anymore.

Ginger prods Mia to call the girls. They'll come for her, she says. "They all think you hung the fucking moon."

A minute later, the girls tumble down the center stairs like three-year-olds just offered a ride on a merry-go-round.

"Umbrellas in the mudroom," Ginger says.

But she hesitates when we get to the mudroom. Her bare feet sit wide and long across a join of tile. "You guys go," she says. "I think I'll stay here and start going through Mother's things."

Annie bends her long, thin neck to study the mudroom floor. Ginger must see how much her daughter wants her to come. Still, she doesn't move to put on shoes.

"Do you still keep those boot things you wear duck hunting, Ginge?" I ask. "Seems like a perfect day for them."

Ginger stares at me the way she did the night in the hot tub when she claimed to hate waking up next to a guy she doesn't know. I hold her gaze as steadily as I did then. This time it's for her rather than for me. *It's okay,* I try to say with my eyes. *I've been sleeping in Zack's old shirts for almost thirty years now, and I couldn't wear my mother's shoes either.* I want to tell her that she has no idea how very much her mother loved her. That Faith loved her as much as she herself loves Annie. I want to tell her that Annie needs her just as much as she needed her own mother. That all this indifference is just an act, a way of defending herself from the fear of being rejected by rejecting her mother first.

Give her a few years and she'll come back to you, I want to say. But I can't say it. I can't say any of it. Not with our daughters here and probably not even if they weren't. So I just keep meeting her gaze.

She opens a closet door and pulls out a pair of waders. "Anyone who wants them is welcome to them," she says.

We all decline.

"I'm sure I couldn't walk any distance in boots like that," Mia says with a note of challenge shaded in her plain brown eyes: *Go ahead, Ginge. Show everyone you can outdo me.*

Maybe Ginger sees Mia is trying to play her or maybe she doesn't. Probably she doesn't, because she pulls the heavy boots on and leads the way out the door.

GINGER

❧❧❧

WHAT VOYAGE THIS, little girl? The damned "Briar Rose" line echoes through my mind as my old hunting boots (which have always been as comfortable as a second skin) rub at my bare heels. We're walking along the bay, my own little girl forgoing Mia's proffered umbrella to share mine. It's hard to say why this makes me want to cry, but it does, as surely as seeing that photo of Trey and me stuck in the pages of that damned poem has.

I look younger in that photo than Annie does now. Still with braces on my teeth. Trey and I standing together after a morning of duck hunting, me wearing these very same boots. Had we fucked in the Triangle Blind the morning it was taken? *Fucked.* It's such a brutal word, and yet there it is. I thought what Trey and I did back then was making love, those quick takings in a skiff late at night, or in the Triangle Blind while everyone else was focused on shooting the damned ducks, or up in the fucking lighthouse that sits abandoned ahead of us, its darkness inviting ships to crash onto Misty Vista Rock.

We haven't intentionally headed toward the island's end, but we seem irresistibly drawn toward the lighthouse. There is no direction I can go on this island without facing something, though. The other direction leads to the Triangle Blind.

Trey liked the Triangle Blind best, the nearness of my father and my brothers. Quick, frantic sex that he came to already hard. Sometimes I could see his anticipation even as he was putting on his boots in the mudroom, as he was first loading his gun. How very long I hung on to the idea that that first time at Fog's Ghost Cove was the beginning of love.

Mother must have known all along. Why else would she leave our photo stuck into "Briar Rose," a poem about incest, as if she might actually have approved? Her thirteen-year-old daughter and the golden boy. Golden man.

I take Annie's arm, handing her the umbrella, ceding that little bit of control to her. If any man had so much as touched her when she was thirteen, I'd have had him in jail for eternity.

She's eighteen now. No longer a minor. No more actionable than I was when I took off with Scratch. If she decided to run off to South Africa with a sleazy playwright, what could I do? Seethe, like Betts is doing now over Izzy and her divorced business school professor, to be sure. But is that it?

Izzy is walking with Mia, ignoring her mother, leaving Betts to share an umbrella with Laney, with no idea that the two of them have convinced themselves that their futures are behind them, that there will be no Drug-Lord Bradwell Supreme Court justice, no Cicero-Bradwell state senator to represent the Georgia Forty-second or anyplace else. Which is the problem I should be solving, but it's impossible to focus on any problem other than my daughter's with her walking beside me. Sweet eighteen and never been kissed, which I would choose for her over what I chose for myself. I would choose it for myself if I could choose again, over not-so-sweet thirteen and already fucked. Still, I worry that Annie is lonely. Still I think the solution to loneliness is a boy.

I was lonely when I first met the Ms. Bradwells, despite all the boys, or maybe because of them. Laney was lonely, and Mia and Betts, too, I think. We all had friends, family, relationships, but we none of us ever quite fit in anywhere until we met each other. Sometimes I think I want that kind of friendship for Annie even more than I want her to find romance: a friend who will stand by her the way we stood by Laney. The way, I see now, Mia and Laney and Betts all stood by me. It isn't that our friendship has saved me from loneliness or anything else, really. But our friendship makes it all easier to bear. Our friendship leaves us with someone to call when we need to. Friends we know love us even when it seems no one else does. Friends who are sometimes lonely, too.

It must be menopause, all this wanting to cry I've got going on here. Bring the bloody bloodless change on and be done with it.

What voyage this, little girl?

Mother must have known, that must be what she is telling me, leaving a photo of Trey and me wedged into "Briar Rose" with a note for Margaret. *For Margaret, should the time come.* Whatever the hell that means. Should Mother be the first of them to die, I guess. But Aunt Margaret is dead, too. The time has come and gone.

It's impossible that Mother would have approved of me having sex with Trey when I was thirteen, though. Even with the golden boy. Which means what? That she knew and disapproved, but did nothing to stop me? Could she not get past the idea of the publicity it would stir if the word got out that the thirteen-year-old daughter of a prominent feminist lawyer was promiscuous, and with an older cousin, no less? Mother loved publicity when it promoted one of her causes, and hated it when it intruded into her personal life. I remember the calls from Beau when I was living in South Africa with Scratch: "Mother would haul you back here by your long hair if she could. But you're not a minor anymore so there's nothing she can do, and it would only fuel the press."

Fuel the press. Those words had stung so, although I'd pretended they didn't. I'd pretended I was too busy living the life of the darling muse of the soon-to-be-famous playwright to care what Mother thought. Pattie Boyd to Scratch's Eric Clapton, a relationship that ended badly, too.

Shit, I would shoot Annie if she ran off with someone like Scratch. I would get on a plane and fly to South Africa and shoot them both.

Annie adjusts the angle of the umbrella as the rain blows sideways, soaking us despite her efforts. Iz turns to Annie and sings the first few silly doo-doo-doo-doo notes of "Singin' in the Rain."

"Don't you dare," Mia warns Izzy good-humoredly. "If you're gonna dance here, you just leave the umbrella with me."

She and Laney and Betts are already laughing as Izzy grins just the way Betts used to do in law school, and sometimes still does. I wonder if humor is hereditary or learned. Betts, the Funny One; me, the Rebel; Laney, the Good Girl; and Mia, the Savant. That's what I'm thinking as Izzy pirouettes away from Mia, taking the umbrella with her, swirling it around her as if she's Gene Kelly, the start of a routine our three girls have done in pairs or all together so many times over the years, and yet still I never tire of it.

And then the rain is pouring down on me, and Annie is spinning away into the unlit grayness with her umbrella lowered, too. *Our* umbrella lowered. Our umbrella that is doing me not one bit of good. Only my bare feet in the heavy boots are dry.

Mia and I scurry to join Laney and Betts, our faces leaning close as we try to squeeze in under the single umbrella. All four of our asses hang out in the rain, getting soaked. We watch the two girls dancing and singing, stomping in puddles and kicking up muddy water, intentionally splashing us.

We breathed in rain, I think. A line I would like to have written.

I guess Laney is right about how I hide my feelings away in other people's poems. I'm afraid to put them in my own poems, for fear they might be seen.

"They need a lamppost," Betts says. "What kind of establishment do you run here, Ginger, that you don't even provide a lamppost?"

The girls have closed the umbrellas now and are strumming them like guitars. They open them again, and flip them; and I remember the first time they actually caught the umbrellas, so surprised to succeed that they'd dissolved into laughter and never finished the routine. Now, they move right into what Betts calls the big-swirling-with-umbrellas part, and then the part where Gene Kelly goes up and down on the curb. There's no curb here, but the granite rocks that edge the path serve well enough.

"Do you think they even imagine harm can ever come to them?" Laney asks.

Mia crosses her arms like the cop who comes in at the end of the scene in the movie, a role the girls persuaded her to play years ago.

"Do we want them to?" she asks.

"Doo doo doo doo doo doo doo," Laney begins singing, the winddown. I join her, "Doo doo doo doo." Fortunately for all of us, Betts doesn't sing.

GINGER

~~~~~~~~~

THE SEXTON VOLUME with the photo and the note were already in Nana's Room when I climbed into my childhood bed; I had slipped away from dinner on the excuse of going to the bathroom and hidden them here. I want to open the note, and I don't want to; I want to tear the photo into pieces, and I don't want that either. I guess mostly I don't want anyone else to connect this photo and this poem, although I can't even say why. The Ms. Bradwells know I slept with Trey, and I can't imagine Izzy or Annie would make anything of the photo wedged into these particular pages. Perhaps I'm mortified by the idea of the Ms. Bradwells knowing that Mother knew about Trey and me. It makes no sense: why should I care? But I could feel it in the way I slipped into the library to fetch the book on the pretext of finding Band-Aids for the heel blisters I hadn't, quite frankly, even felt until Betts pointed them out.

I'm like a child waking from a nightmare, afraid to climb from the bed for fear that the monster will come out to get me. Holding the blanket to my chin and imagining if I lie still enough I won't be seen. I want to climb from this bed and pull on my boots again, walk out into the dark by myself, damn the blisters. *A possessed witch, / haunting the black air, braver at night.* I'm not brave, though. I dread what haunts the black air everywhere on this island.

All night I am laying / poems away in a long box. But my box is empty, it has none of Sexton's "starving windows." No *skinless / trees . . . / in shapes of agony.* No *and what of the dead? They lie without shoes / in their stone boats.*

My poems are no sadder than the years' worth of words I wasted chasing partnership at Caruthers, though, Laney is right about that. Wanting to be a permanent female cog in a tired old male wheel that would never change anything except perhaps which few hands held a lot of dollars. How foolish was I, really, to think anything about that would bring me immortality? Mother had tried to tell me, but I wouldn't listen. All I could hear were the echoes of her anthem for my teenage years, her voice all those mornings shouting, "It's nearly noon, Ginger! Get up and make something of yourself, for God's sake."

It's nowhere near noon; it's an hour or two before daybreak, but I heed Mother's long-stale advice, and I get out of bed, thinking of the two books Mother left to Aunt Margaret, and the blisters on my heels, and the dreadful journal pages filled with my poems. I take the book I brought to read on the train from New York, John Felstiner's *Can Poetry Save the Earth?*, to the chair by the fireplace, and I open it and read what he has to say about the biblical litany of Jane Kenyon's "Let Evening Come." I consider skipping to the next chapter; I'm not much for God or the Bible. But since he calls the poem "as fine as it gets in our time" I read to see what he means:

> Let the light of late afternoon
> shine through chinks in the barn, moving
> up the bales as the sun moves down.
>
> Let the crickets take up chafing
> as a woman takes up her needles
> and her yarn. Let evening come.
>
> Let dew collect on the hoe abandoned
> in long grass. Let the stars appear
> and the moon disclose her silver horn.
>
> Let the fox go back to his sandy den.
> Let the wind die down. Let the shed
> go black inside. Let evening come.
>
> To the bottle in the ditch, to the scoop
> in the oats, to the air in the lung
> let evening come.

Let it come, as it will, and don't
be afraid. God does not leave us
comfortless, so let evening come.

I am weeping as I read the last line: for the loss of Mother, for all the things we never said to each other, everything we never shared. For the pain she must have felt at being unable to protect me. Could I have borne it if Annie did what I did and refused to listen to me? I weep for Laney, for everything she endured without my support. For what I went through myself without any idea how to make sense of it. For what Betts is going through now, and Laney, too, and even Mia, who must feel this is her fault. It's all so awful, and yet it's brought me to this place where Mother died; it has brought me here not alone, as I've dreaded coming, but in the company of my dearest friends. It's brought us all together when we need each others' comfort as much as we ever have.

RAINDROPS TICK AGAINST the windows as I slip into the Captain's Office, with the book and the photo and the note. Before I can even whisper Laney's name, a bedside light clicks on, and Mia says, "Ginger! God, you scared me to death."

As I blink against the brightness, Laney, too, sits up in bed.

Mia reaches for her eyeglasses on the nightstand. "I thought you were . . . I don't know. Hamlet's ghost or something."

My mother's ghost. Faith Cook Conrad's Ghost.

I'm wearing the underwear and blouse I wore to the Judiciary Committee hearing, the same thing I've slept in each night since we've been here.

"Ginge," Mia says. "You okay?"

"I thought you were with Max," I say, I don't even know why. "I thought you were, you know, slipping out to screw him like you did with Beau."

"Ginge," Laney says, soothing and scolding all at once.

Some part of me knows I should take the words back. I hate myself for saying them. I don't have any idea why I'm saying them. They aren't even true. Max is sleeping in his own bed in his own house tonight, and even I haven't imagined Mia would slip out of Chawterley and make her way through the unfamiliar darkness of Cook Island to Max's house even if he's left the light on like he did for Mother.

"What's wrong, Ginger?" Mia says. "What's wrong?"

In the soft tone of her voice, I hear how perfectly ridiculous it is for me to hold Mia's sleeping with my brother against her after all this time. Still, I don't take the words back. I push my glasses into place and look to the rain outside.

The empty swivel chair at the Captain's rolltop desk inexplicably moves, as if the Captain's Ghost is pushing back from his after-death work. My heart is whacking against my fucking chest before I hear Betts's voice from under the center drawer say, "Other than the fact that half the world thinks one of us shot Trey Humphrey?"

"Lordy, Betts! You scared me half to death!" Laney says as Betts emerges like some fantastic sea creature arising from the waves.

"I couldn't sleep when we went to bed," Betts explains, "so I opened the connecting door." She shrugs her square diver's shoulders. "I could hear Laney's little snore, which is oddly comforting."

"I don't snore," Laney protests.

Mia rolls her eyes.

"Well, glad I could help you sleep," Laney says.

"Oh, you didn't," Betts says. "But I did feel less alone as I lay awake."

They all turn to me standing there in just my underwear and blouse.

"Trey Humphrey's Ghost," Mia says. "I didn't think you were Hamlet's ghost, Ginge. I thought you were Trey Humphrey's Ghost."

Laney scoots over and thumps her hand on the bed. "It's cold in here," she says, an invitation to climb in next to her, under the covers of the twin that I still think of as Frankie's bed although he and his succession of wives sleep in Emma's Peek these days. Laney hands the extra pillow to me, and I snuggle under the covers next to her, feeling the weight of the Sexton volume pressing the soft cotton sheet against the skin of my bare thighs. The last time I climbed into bed with Laney was after finding Trey in the watch room, dead or almost dead.

Betts sits on the end of Mia's bed, her legs falling as if by memory into that yoga pose she does with both soles facing upward, like she's about to start chanting a mantra. She untucks the bedspread from around one of the end posts and pulls it up over her legs.

"That's one of the books your mom didn't leave you," she says. The way she says it doesn't make me feel bad, though. It leaves me thinking maybe Mrs. Z left her favorite zhaleika to a friend.

"The Sexton poems," Laney says. "Like the poems you write."

"I wish," I say. I smooth my hand over the front cover of the book, as if smoothing the wrinkles from the sheet underneath. And then I'm spilling it all, about the photograph and the note for Aunt Margaret stuck into a poem about incest. "I don't even know why I care that Mother knew about Trey and me," I say. "But I hate the idea of her thinking of it. I hate the idea of her agonizing with Aunt Margaret about whether the press will get hold of the scandal of her promiscuous thirteen-year-old."

"Ginge." Betts runs a hand along the smooth wood of the bedpost, shaking her head as if she disapproves of me as much as Mother ever did.

"*You* should have been her daughter, Betts," I say. "She would have liked that: perfect little virgin Betts who will go on to be appointed to the fucking Supreme Court." I feel the tears begin to stream down my cheeks, but I will not acknowledge them.

"Ginge," Laney says, and she puts her arm around my shoulders.

Let the wind die down. Let the shed / go black inside.

Mia gets up and looks for a tissue but can't find one. Betts says she has some in her briefcase, which is just in the closet. She climbs under the desk on her hands and knees so that her skinny little yoga-toned butt sticks out under the drawer, then reemerges with her swanky black leather briefcase. She climbs back onto the bed and sits cross-legged again, zips open the briefcase, and looks inside.

What she pulls out is not a tissue but rather the strand of black pearls she wore at the hearing. Mother's pearls. She sets them aside and pulls out a small plastic packet of tissues, which she tosses to me.

"I'm sorry," I say. "I'm so sorry. I don't mean any of that. I don't know why I say things like that."

I take a tissue from the package and blow my nose.

"So you're absconding with my mother's pearls?" I say, trying to sound lighter than I feel.

Betts holds them out across the gap between the beds. "Guess I won't be needing them anymore."

The gold clasp is cool against my palm, but it warms as I close my fingers over it, remembering the smell of Mother's perfume on evenings when she and Daddy were going out, the luster of the blue/green/purple-gray pearls around the matte skin of her graceful neck. Remembering Daddy's expression as he turned to see Mother descend the stairs, the tendons of his neck (as thick and ungraceful as mine) straining just before he stepped to the bottom of the stairs to take her in his arms. He always kissed her, then, and told her she looked stunning. Not just beautiful, but stunning. I never could understand why he loved her. They were so different, and I was like him.

I lean back against the headboard. "What kind of mother lets her thirteen-year-old-daughter sleep with her twenty-year-old cousin?" I pull another tissue from the pack. "What kind of mother doesn't at least try to put a stop to that?"

"She couldn't have known, Ginge," Laney says quietly.

"She left our photo in a . . . in a fucking poem about incest."

What voyage this, little girl?

Betts worries her bare big toe, sliding her fingers over a callus. "She didn't know before I told her," she says quietly, "and then Trey was dead."

A rush of wind crushes tiny raindrops against the windows in a gust, the panes rattling with the force of nothing more than condensed mist.

"I told her the day after Laney . . . I couldn't believe we should just do nothing about it all, you know?" Betts explains.

"You told Mother about Laney?"

"The day of your father's birthday party, while you were out hunting. I went to her office and I told her."

"About Laney," I whisper.

She pulls her top leg more tightly toward her hip, reminding me of Justice Bradwell, the contortionist gargoyle in the Law Quad, where we used to meet. "About everything," she says. "I know I shouldn't have, it wasn't my place to do it, but I thought she would help, I thought she would know what to do." She looks up at me. "And then she didn't. She just told me not to say anything to anyone. Even to you."

"You told my mother," I repeat, trying to absorb this. "She didn't know, and you told her?"

The morning of the day Trey shot himself.

"I . . . I just assumed she knew," Betts stutters. "But she didn't. I'm sorry, Ginge."

"She didn't know," I repeat dumbly, trying to make sense of it, thinking Mother *didn't* know then, Mother *didn't* allow it to go on. Maybe she should have known but she didn't, she just didn't know.

And then she did?

"Her reaction . . ." Betts looks from my face to the pearls, the book, the letter. "It was more than just . . . you know. Concern that I knew. She didn't know."

"Quandoque bonus dormitat Homerus," Laney says.

Betts stands and moves to Laney's bed, then, sits next to me and picks up the book. She sets aside the photograph and examines the sealed note: *For Margaret, should the time come.*

"She wouldn't have let it go on if she'd known," she says. She turns the envelope over to the sealed triangle, Mother's signature sprawling across the joined edges. "Your mother? She wouldn't have let it go on, Ginge. You must see that."

I wipe my eyes with the tissue again, and I say I do see, even though I don't see, I don't understand anything except that I need to stop Betts from saying anything more until I've sorted this out. "I do see," I say again, to prevent a silence she might need to fill, trying to imagine Betts telling Mother, and Mother hearing. How do you tell a mother she's failed to protect her daughter for years? How can a mother bear to hear that?

I climb from Laney's bed, trying to imagine Mother telling Daddy. Would she have? Or even telling Margaret. There is the sealed envelope and there is the photo and there is the poem "Briar Rose." But that can't be Mother speaking from the grave, to tell Margaret about a relationship her daughter had thirty years ago. That doesn't make sense either.

I walk to the window, look out into the rain. The drapes are open; Mia or Laney must have opened them this afternoon. To hell with the press if they come back.

When I turn back to the room, Betts is still studying me, watching my hands, which, I come to realize, are worrying the pearls Mother gave me, that we all have worn. She stands and comes to me, rests her hands on my shoulders, her face close to mine, her hair gray where it was such a pretty red, her face lined and marked but still freckled, her eyes through the bifocals still the same intelligent blue gold green.

"Your mother loved you, Ginge," she says. "Surely you must know that by now."

I look down at the manicured nails of hands that look more and more like my father's, fingering these pearls that have been mine for nearly as long as I can remember. Mother's favorite pearls, which she gave to me years ago, when she still wore them. Betts is trying to tell me something without saying it. I don't know if I am trying to hear her or trying not to, but all I can think of is the way Mother and Daddy came in from a walk around the island the night Mother gave me the pearls. She came in to the Sun Room to find Frankie and Beau and me all huddled around the Risk board. Trey was there, too, I remember, because I was sitting on the couch and he was sitting next to me but not touching me, and I wanted him to touch me like he sometimes touched the island girls when we were all hanging out together, and since he wouldn't I was being merciless, about to wipe him out. I was acting all gleeful about it, but I wasn't feeling gleeful. And then Mother and Daddy came in, laughing. I remember thinking they were laughing at me, although I couldn't say why. Maybe because I felt Trey laughing at me, and my brothers, too. And then Mother was standing behind me, setting her pearls around my neck, lifting my hair to fix the clasp and then gently turning the necklace so that the clasp would sit at the base of my throat, like it did on her. She didn't even say anything. She just latched them there and kissed the top of my head and said good night, and when I turned to see her, she and Daddy were headed up the stairs, holding hands.

How odd I'd felt with those pearls around my neck. Confused. Like I was playing dress up. Like Mother was dressing me up, making me her. The weight of the dark pearls where I rarely wore more than a thin silver chain. *Next to my own skin, her pearls. My mistress / bids me wear them, warm them.* But they came to my skin already warm.

None of the boys said anything, but they ganged up on me then; I'd been about to wipe Trey off the board before Mother and Daddy came in, and Frankie and Beau were all for it, and then they weren't and I lost, and the funny thing was I didn't really care.

After they wiped me out, Trey said he didn't want to play anymore, he thought we should all go gut-running, Frankie and Beau against him and me. I remember not wanting to go out in the skiff with Trey, and going anyway. I must have been fourteen, because I'd already been out to Fog's Ghost Cove with him, and not just that summer. I remember thinking I didn't want to have sex with him anymore, and not knowing how to say no, and going with him even though I didn't want to, knowing that we would lose Frankie and Beau somewhere in the darkness of Tizzie's Ditch or Rock Creek or Midden Gut. And then we would have sex out in the skiff, quick sex on the little wooden centerboard, or more often with me lying down on the smelly hull and Trey over me. But maybe that memory isn't even real. Maybe I didn't hesitate that night any more than I had any other night. Maybe that's just gauze I've overlaid in the intervening years, wanting to be someone other than the girl I was.

I don't know how long I waited for Mother to ask for the pearls back, dreaded her asking for them back and dreaded her not doing so. That whole summer, I think. And it was only after I came downstairs in a new dress I'd picked out especially for our annual end-of-summer party that she mentioned them again. I was at the top of the front stairs and she was greeting someone at the door. Daddy's partner, Mr. Johns, I remember, because he whistled up at me like he thought I looked hot, then looked as surprised as I felt. I'd giggled, and he'd laughed, and Mother had said, "Why don't you wear your black pearls tonight, sweetheart? They'll look beautiful with that dress." And I did wear them, and I suppose they did look beautiful, but I never could get used to wearing them, I never could come to think of them as anything other than Mother's pearls.

Mother, whom Betts had told. Who'd learned about Trey and me the day before I watched Trey bleed to death.

I reach up and hold the pearls at Betts's throat. I don't even know why. These pearls I so love to loan, but never wear. They seem to belong on Betts as surely as they ever belonged on Mother, even though Betts looks nothing like Mother, even though the pearls are a different thing against her skin than they are in my memory of my mom.

"They've never looked better than they did around your neck in the hearing," I say.

"They bring out the gray-blue of your eyes," Mother had said when I'd reappeared at that end-of-the-summer party. No, what she'd said was, "They *pick up* the gray-blue of your eyes." Not them bestowing beauty on me but me bringing my beauty to them.

I loop the pearls around Betts's too thin neck, under the edge of her driftwood hair. I fasten the clasp at her throat just as Mother did when she gave them to me, except that I am facing Betts, she can see my face.

"They'll look stunning with your black robes," I say.

Betts smiles wryly. "My orange prison garb, you mean."

I touch the clasp that nestles into the dip between her collar bones, the pearls on either side. "Mother would be so pleased to know her pearls adorn the neck of a Supreme Court justice," I say. "I want her to have that."

Betts, fingering the pearls herself now, starts to protest.

"I want her to have that," I repeat, "and you want her to have it, too."

"I can't accept your mother's pearls," Betts says.

A circle of unmatched black pearls, each one bringing something different to the connected whole.

"You'll no doubt feel them spontaneously strangling you if you even think about overturning *Roe v. Wade*," I say.

"I can't accept your mother's pearls, Ginge," Betts insists.

"They're not Mother's pearls," I say. "They're my pearls, that Mother gave me. And now I'm giving them to you."

Betts

"I NEVER THOUGHT I would be like Matka. I thought I would be like your mother, Ginge," I say. Because I have to say something. Some thank you for her gift of these pearls. And I'm not ready to say what I know I need to say here. Which has nothing and everything to do with the gift.

"And here I am," I say. "Exactly like Matka. And Izzy is turning out the same way."

I dip my chin but of course I can't see my own neck. Then catch a glimpse of myself in the window glass. A dim outline against the darkness outside.

"'A woman is her mother. / That's the main thing,'" Ginger says.

She denies the credit Laney wants to give her for the line; it's from Anne Sexton's "Housewife."

I wonder if it's true. Is Ginger her mother? Would she do the things Faith has done?

"'A woman is her mother. / That's the main thing,'" Laney repeats as if saying penance for blasting Ginger about her poetry last night.

"I never thought I'd be my mom either," Mia says. "All the friends she met on those summer trips? I thought I'd marry Andy and never have another lover. I thought I'd be loyal and chaste. Then I blew it even before the wedding, and now the only difference between Mom and me is that I prefer men."

"And you're not married," Laney says.

"Rub it in, Lane," Mia says.

"That's not what I mean," Laney says. "I mean you're not betraying a single soul."

"And you live a life that makes you happy," Ginger says. She settles again on Laney's bed.

I feel awkward standing here by myself. Still wanting to make Ginger take the pearls back. But it seems that moment has passed.

Outside the rain has slowed. It spits against the glass. The last little cough of the dying storm.

"You're doing something you love to do, Mia," Ginger says as I settle back on the end of Mia's bed. "Don't underrate that."

"Except I'm unemployed now," Mia says.

"Me, too," Laney says. "Or as good as unemployed. I have no job, and the odds of my gaining the one I've set my sights for are looking slim to none, with the smart money betting on none. You at least might write a book about this whole fiasco to make a dollar or two. And seriously, I didn't mean to swipe at you for not having a man. I just meant you're not living through your daughter, like your mama did."

"I don't have a daughter to live through," Mia says.

"But you're living a life you *chose*, Mi. Living choices your mama didn't have, or didn't think she did. Even if you did have a Gemmy or an Izzy or an Anne, you wouldn't be living your life through her. None of the rest of us is."

"Well, I might be just a little," I say. "I practically strung Izzy's Phi Beta Kappa key from a chain and wore it around my neck."

"There wasn't a soul at the club in Cleveland who didn't get a chance to congratulate me on Annie getting into Princeton," Ginger says.

"That's not living vicariously," Laney says. "That's delight at your children's success. Or at worst, maybe a little competitive parenting, gloating over the notion that since your baby is looking more successful than your friends', y'all must be the better mamas."

Mia says, "On that basis, I'm the best mom here since I claim all the Baby Bradwells as mine."

Ginger pulls Laney's sheet over her bare legs. "It's not too late to have a child if you want to, Mi," she says gently. "You could adopt. These days you could probably even still have a baby. Some woman in India gave birth to twins when she was *seventy*."

Mia laughs. "I'm not even *thinking* of running around after a two-year-old when I'm seventy." Her eyes lack their usual confidence, though.

I wonder if she isn't.

She says, "If I wanted to raise a child, wouldn't I have figured out a way to make that happen by now? But I feel like that makes me a bad person, not to want to parent."

I set a hand on her foot under the covers. It's as bare as Ginger's have been all weekend.

Ginger says, "A bad *woman*? How many of the men you work with don't have children and don't want them, and no one thinks to frown on them."

"The happy bachelor," I say. "The old maid."

"You'll just have to let me keep borrowing your kids," Mia says. She says "borrow" but she means love.

Laney says, "I sometimes think I'm becoming my *daddy*. Like I'm running for office because I was starting to look at my daddy in the mirror every morning, taking the safe path, living my life to keep my children out of danger."

"We can't keep our children out of danger," Ginger says. "We can't even keep them out of the press."

"I suppose Max will be along with the morning papers any minute now," I say.

"I suppose Max will be along with the press themselves," Mia says. "It's stopped raining."

We all look to the dark windows.

Ginger says, "I would have killed Trey if I were my mother."

She says it casually. As if she doesn't mean it. As if she's saying she'll kill her son if she has to remind him to take out the garbage again. She looks to the window as she says it. Ginger never likes anyone to see her pain.

So there it is, finally. The thing I've wondered since the morning Trey Humphrey turned up dead in the lighthouse. Would Faith have killed her nephew? I dismissed it at the time as my own hysterical imaginings. But I wasn't yet a mother then.

I think of Matka for a moment. I never told her it was me, not Ginger, who couldn't afford an abortion. I thought it was because I didn't want her to feel my shame. But now I wonder. Maybe I didn't tell her because I knew she would have done what I asked. That she'd have gone against her every principle for my sake.

I wonder sometimes if she can see all my life from heaven, where she must be now. But would that be heaven? To know all there is to know about the people you loved most in life? Or would that be hell?

"I think it's time for a swim," Ginger says, still looking to the darkness outside the window. "If we go now, we can get in a quick dip before the sun rises and the press arrive."

"So would I have, Ginge," I say quietly.

When Ginger turns to me I plunge ahead before I lose my nerve. "I would have killed Trey if it had been Isabelle. I wouldn't have been able to bear seeing him walk free. But I couldn't have borne for Isabelle to have endured what it would take to put him away."

"God, you're not serious," Mia whispers.

The long silence is brutal. No wind. No rain. No hint of early morning life. Not even the sound of a heater kicking in or a daughter stirring elsewhere in the house. Only our own breathing as we sit here on the two beds much as we sat on the lower mattresses in the bunkroom all those years ago. I don't think Ginger even breathes.

The silence is broken finally by a fresh gust of wind blowing across the chimney top. The plaintive howl of the Captain's Ghost. Or Faith's Ghost. Or perhaps Trey's.

"I think it's time for a swim," Ginger says again.

Laney's bony, spotted hands stroke the edge of the sheet. "We don't have swimsuits."

The sad blinking of Mia's plain brown eyes suggests she's working her way toward the same conclusion I did years ago. That it's impossible. And that it's probably true.

It has always seemed such a coincidence that Trey turned up dead that morning. I think Mia has always sensed that. Mia, the Savant. But her choice before tonight has always been to think it was one of us who killed him. And how could she believe it was one of us?

I was the only one who knew that Faith knew about the rape. Who knew that Faith had just learned about Trey's seducing Ginger when she was a girl. I was the only one with facts that might have led the way to whatever the truth was about what happened all those years ago, when justice might have been served.

I've thought about it so many times since. I've thought that I should say something. But to whom? And what? I didn't know anything at all, really. I had only fantastical suspicions that flew in the face of all the evidence doctors and policemen assured me was something else. And what kind of justice would it have been to punish a mother for protecting a child against the failures of a legal system anyway? Against the failures of a whole society.

"When have we ever swum in suits?" Ginger says. "Not even at that first hot tub party did we keep our suits on."

It isn't true. Or that isn't my memory anyway. I kept my suit on at that hot tub party and so did Mia. The first time we all bared ourselves in so many ways was here on Cook Island. But I don't say that. I don't do anything but remember how close we'd been that first night, swimming together in the star-thick night.

We've seen one another regularly over the years since then. Vacations. Reunions. Weekends. But we've never again shed our clothes together. We let Trey Humphrey steal that reckless abandon from our friendship. That complete trust in each other that we were just gaining. That trust that is so impossible to find in friends, but there it was in our grasp. We've all of us let what one man did make us ashamed of who we are. Because he hurt one of us. Because none of us stopped it. We hadn't recognized what was happening. We hadn't known anything needed to be stopped until it was too late. But that hasn't saved us from feeling that failure. From feeling our friendship wasn't enough.

Ginger stands and takes Laney's hand. "Come on, Lane," she says. "The water is good and cold out there. Let's swim."

PART III

What would happen if one woman told the truth about her life?
The world would split open.

—from "Käthe Kollwitz," by Muriel Rukeyser

Betts

～

IT'S CHILLY AS we stand on the pier. The sky is still dark and cloudy. The water black and hard, unyielding. There is a hint of light at the horizon. Or maybe there isn't. Maybe that's just me hoping there is.

"The girls will be horrified if they see us skinny-dipping," I say.

"It might be good for them to be horrified by something their mothers do," Mia says.

I bristle. Why does Mia need to contradict me? Even on something she knows nothing about: motherhood.

She says, "I think maybe it allows you a little freedom yourself, if you can get over the shock." Speaking not as a mother but as a daughter. It's not a way I see myself anymore. But maybe I should. Maybe I'd be a better mother if I did.

"Annie and Iz are students," Ginger says. "Virtual teenagers. And it isn't even dawn. There is not a chance in the world they'll wake up and see us."

She dumps the towels she's had the good sense to grab onto the raw wood of the pier.

"'I fold my towel with what grace I can / Not young and not renewable, but . . .' *woman*?"

She pulls off her blouse and stands in her underwear. Probably her own that she wore to the hearing Friday. If Faith's shoes and pajamas are too intimate to wear surely her underwear is.

"What do I do about the note to Aunt Margaret?" she asks. Speaking, I guess, of being horrified by the things one's mother has done.

"She died just before Mother did," she says.

The rest of us begin shedding our pajamas as Ginger drops her under-wear and dives off the dock. She disappears into the darkness. Emerges with a quiet splash. "Shit, it's cold!"

"What do you think the note says, Ginge?" I ask.

Her voice floats up from the dark water below us. "I don't know. My first thought was that she wanted Margaret to know about . . . about Trey and me, I guess. But if she didn't tell her before, why now? It's just that the note was there, with the picture and the poem. But maybe that's ran-dom."

And maybe Trey really did just happen to shoot himself the night we all wanted him dead.

Ginger splashes water toward us. Cold drops sting the tops of my feet.

"I'm thinking I should open it," she says.

I consider this for a long moment. Then jump in after her. Come up sputtering. " 'Supreme Court Nominee Body Found Frozen and Naked in Waters Off Cook Island,' " I say. Not, suddenly, giving a damn about the press. I imagine it might even be funny if a crowd of reporters showed up in a boat just now. I imagine that instead of climbing from the water and rushing into the house the way we did when Trey and the guy gang arrived that spring break, we might wave and say hello. Finish our swim and our conversation. I imagine for a moment that our bodies are just our bodies. The caretakers for our brains.

Someone plunges into the water to the right. A shadow head emerges in the darkness between Ginger and me.

"You can't open the letter, Ginge," Mia says.

Laney jumps in feet first. Close enough that I wonder if she's trying to sink me. I can see the whites of her eyes, maybe because mine have ad-justed to the darkness. Or maybe because it's a little lighter. The sun isn't coming up quite yet. But there is a grayness in the sky where the moon is trying to break through.

"Ginger can do anything she wants with the note," I say to Mia. "The woman it's addressed to is dead. The note is technically in Faith's estate. And you're the residual heir, right Ginge?" Ginger inherits everything not specifically given to anyone else in her mother's will. "The two books were left to Margaret. If she had survived Faith then her heirs would be entitled to the books. Maybe there would be a case that they're entitled to what's inside the books, too. But likely not. Anyway, she didn't survive

Faith. So the books stay in the estate and go to Ginger as the residual heir."

The water laps in my direction as Mia says, "Ginger isn't asking for a legal opinion, Professor Drug-Lord-Bradwell. Faith signed her name across a sealed envelope, Faith who was a lawyer and a damned good one, for God's sake. Why would she have done that on a note to a friend?"

"You two don't need to one-up each other anymore," Laney says quietly. "You don't need to be smarter than each other. You're already smarter than everyone else."

My face warms at the charge even in the cold water. I want to protest. But the thought that comes to me in my defense has nothing to do with smartness. *I'm not the one who slept with Beau when I was engaged to Andy.* It's even more mortifying than still needing to be smarter after all these years: still needing to be more attractive.

I remember Mia's face that night in the Lightkeeper's Cottage when she and Beau threw the Risk game to Ginger so they could be alone. I've been imagining Mia as the least scarred by all this. She wasn't the one who was raped. She wasn't the one who was seduced when she was a girl. She isn't even the one whose life dream is now at risk. But she's the one whose budding love was polluted by everything that happened. I see that now. And in seeing it I can't imagine how I failed to see it before. Mia and Beau might have ridden off into the nerdy-smart sunset together. Mia's life could have been a different thing, too, if not for Trey.

"I think Mother wanted to make sure Margaret could show she didn't know what was in the note until after Mother died," Ginger quietly agrees with Mia. "To protect her friend."

I nod. They probably can't see me nodding. "That makes sense," I say.

Laney floats on her back in the water. Her face and her breasts break the surface. But the rest of her is submerged. Mia paddles over to the wooden post anchoring the pier. She puts a hand up on the wood slats above her so she no longer has to tread water. The skin of her arm is pale in the moonlight just breaking through the clouds now. Pale as it was thirty years ago when we went skinny-dipping with the guys.

How stupid I'd been back then. I hadn't given a thought to how bad it would look for Laney and me should Trey or Frank mention our skinny-dipping to anyone at Tyler & McCoy. The firm she was going to work for and the firm I meant to join after my clerkship. I'd been all tied up in my jealousy of Mia. Trying to find a way to turn Beau's attention from her to me.

"If Margaret didn't know what was in the envelope," I say, thinking it through, "then how would she know when 'the time' had come? We're saying Faith left the note to . . . to protect anyone else who might be accused of"—I hesitate, but then I say—"of killing Trey, right? But how does Margaret know that's what it's for?"

If Ginger is half as cold as I am she doesn't show it as she dips back in the water to clear her hair from her face. It doesn't float out across the water like fine seaweed as it did when we were young. I was so surprised the first time I'd seen her after she cut it. She's pretty by any measure. But it was all that hair that turned men's heads. She'd only shrugged, though, and said she'd needed a change. It was Laney who told me, and years later, too, that Ginger had donated it to make a wig for a child who was as bald as Zack had been when he died. It's the side of herself I think Ginger least understands. The place her poetry comes from. It's what keeps us loving her. Will always keep us loving her despite the total pain in the ass she sometimes is.

"Margaret knows the same way we would know," Ginger says. "Because she was Mother's best friend. It isn't exactly that she knows at the time so much as that, when she receives the envelope, she realizes what maybe she's always known about her friend but hasn't been quite able to piece together."

"Or maybe hasn't wanted to," Mia says.

"But Aunt Margaret is dead now, too," Ginger says. "If she was an accessory after the fact, it's too late to hang her for that now. So I can just burn it?"

I imagine the headline: ADVOCATE FOR WOMEN'S RIGHTS INVOLVED IN BIZARRE SEX-RELATED MURDER. I think of the irony of this. After years of resisting Faith, Ginger now wants to protect her mother's reputation. But it's not that simple. In protecting her mother's reputation she protects her own.

"If the note says anything about this, Ginge," Mia says, "it could save Betts's chance of the Court."

"If the note says anything that will destroy Faith's reputation," I say, "it will cast a pall on so much of the work she's done. Not that it should. Not that this has anything to do with that. But it will."

"She'll be tried in the press," Laney says, "and everything she did'll be dragged out and reconsidered, found flawed."

"It will set us back," I say.

"By 'us' you mean women in general?" Mia says. "Not us in particular? But *you* in particular, Betts, *Laney* in particular—that's progress, too."

"Progress that maybe happens if the explanation for Trey's death doesn't involve you loading up a rifle with bullets, Betts," Laney says. "Mia is right. We need to clear your name."

"Loading a *shotgun* with bullets," Mia says. "A twelve-gauge. The kind Hemingway used to kill himself."

"Shells," Ginger says. "You don't load a shotgun with bullets. You load it with shells."

"It doesn't save my appointment," I say. "An explanation that involves me knowing facts I withheld?"

"Suspicions," Laney insists.

"The *fact* that Faith might have had a motive for killing Trey," I say.

"A motive for the *accidental* death of Trey Humphrey?" Ginger says. "No one thought it was anything but an accident."

"No one but me," I say.

"Shit, I'm freezing," Laney says.

"Laney said 'shit'?" Ginger says.

"Laney said 'shit,'" Mia confirms.

"Shit, it must be time to get out, then," Ginger says.

We climb from the water. Wrap ourselves in the towels. Stand there for a moment trying to get warm.

"Are you really that smart, Betts?" Mia asks. Her face in the moonlight looks almost young.

I look up to see the moon through a thin gauze of cloud now. Its light sifting through.

"Did you really sort this all out so quickly back then?" Mia insists. "Trey shows up dead and you deduce in the space of the few chaotic hours we had between when he was found and when we left that it wasn't an accident? That a woman you'd spent the last three years aspiring to be like did something you could never in a million years have imagined her doing?"

The question stops me. I want to say that of course I knew. But did I? How could I have put that all together so quickly when I still couldn't believe that Trey raped Laney. When I was still thinking Ginger's story about Trey and her might just be Ginger trying to hold everyone's attention, not wanting to share even such an awful spotlight?

"The thing is, y'all, we just need to tell whatever truth we know *now*," Laney says. She speaks so softly that we all step toward her. Our heads bend together like football players waiting for the quarterback to call the play. "I need to do that," she says. "I need to say 'This is what happened to me.' I need it for myself and I need it for Gemmy. I need to reclaim my . . . my certainty about who I am." She pulls her towel more tightly. "If it costs me the election, then it costs me the election. I don't want to feel shamed anymore."

I look to the horizon. Definitely lightening now. I think of Matka. Wonder how it would feel not to be ashamed anymore.

"I don't think the question is what we say about Faith or even about Trey," Laney says. "I think the question is what we say about our own selves."

Again I think of my mom. It's the way she lived her life. She went from being a doctor in her country to cleaning toilets to put me through school. Living in that crappy little apartment. But she never doubted her choices. She is the kind of woman I should aspire to be. She even more than Faith. All that stuff I was saying to the Judiciary Committee about how great Matka was. The Widow Zhukovski stories Mia urged me to tell. I thought I was just saying all that because it sounded good. But it turns out to be true.

"The only thing is, I don't want to be the one to have to say it," Laney says. "I just want to have it be done. It's not even that I'm a coward, although I expect I am. It's just that I'm afraid I'll do it poorly. It's important that it be said well, and I don't know that I can."

I shiver in the cold silence. We all do.

"I can do it, Lane," Ginger whispers. "I'd like to do it."

Let me do this for you, this one small thing.

"Call it an homage to my mother," she says.

Laney balks. She didn't mean to foist this off on anyone else. She was just talking about how she *feels*.

"It will keep you and Betts out of the limelight," Ginger says, "and it doesn't really matter to my life. I'm not anyone."

I want to object. But the objection that comes to mind is that she is the daughter of Faith Cook Conrad. Which would only make her feel worse. She is the daughter of Faith Cook Conrad with no accomplishment to claim as her own.

"The weird thing is that if Mother had been raped, she would have endured all the humiliation in the world to change things," Ginger says, "but she wouldn't put us through shit."

She's more surprised than any of us at the truth of this.

"We wouldn't put Izzy or Annie or Gem through anything either," I say.

"Which is why we have to speak up now," Ginger says. "If change is needed and it doesn't start with us, then where the hell does it start?"

"If it doesn't *continue* with us," I say.

"If it doesn't continue with us," Ginger agrees.

A shock of sunlight bruises the horizon then, leaking mauve through the thinning clouds.

"*Carpe diem,*" I say. "Seize the day."

"Hey, *I'm* Ms. Cicero-Bradwell," Laney says with a raised finger cross to me. She smiles in a way that (I know when I see it) I haven't seen since we left the Hart Building. "And *pluck* the day is the more precise translation, actually."

Mia

GINGER AND I stand and watch for a moment as Laney and Betts pad up the pier. It strikes me that I feel comfortable in my nakedness despite the fact that I'm no taller and certainly no thinner than I've ever been. I'm cold as hell, but comfortable.

"You think either of them stands a chance no matter what I tell the press?" Ginger asks.

I look to the horizon, to the first edge of sun smearing an intense red across a friendly horizon of clouds, like lamplight between sill and shade. That this day has finally come seems no more real than the sunrise looks.

"An homage to your mom?" I ask. "The way your mom would have done it?"

Ginger looks at me then. She smiles ever so slightly, her wide lips pressed together with the barest upturn at the edges. She lifts her arm and touches the back of her neck. I wonder if she's conscious of the gesture, if she is surprised her fair trade, eco-conscious, fruit of the gods hair clip isn't there any more than her long hair is. I wonder where the child she gave her hair to is today. Or children, I suppose; all that taffy apple hair would have made wigs enough for a few children.

"I don't suppose Mother ever told you she kept that African women article all these years, did she?" she says.

I shake my head. "I'd probably still be a lousy, unhappy, somewhat more well-to-do lawyer if not for your mom."

"I should have told you," she says.

As I'm considering this, imagining how much confidence it would have given me to know Faith framed that article, she asks, "Are you happy, Mi?"

I say, "Instead I'm a lousy, unhappy, *penniless and unemployed* journalist. Thanks, Faith!"

Ginger watches the sunrise for a moment. How long does it take to rise at this latitude, this time of the year, in this atmosphere?

"Seriously," she says. "Being a journalist, I mean."

I look out at the sea, thinking of the many places I've listened to water lap against shore, how different the backdrops to it are and yet there is some consistency to the water itself, something that doesn't ever really change.

"I like to write," I say. "I feel like I . . ."

Contribute, I guess is the word, but I don't say it.

"Are you happy being a poet?" I ask.

"'There is no happiness like mine. / I have been eating poetry.'"

"Seriously," I say.

Her hand again goes to the back of her neck, where her hair is plastered flat. "I'm . . . less sad when I write." She pauses, considering what she has just said, perhaps recognizing only now that she is sad, that she has carried around a deep sadness for as long as I have known her.

"I figure I have to tell the whole truth," she says.

She might be talking about the poetry she writes—telling all the truth, but telling it slant, like Dickinson suggests—but I don't think she is.

"Everything?" I say.

"About me and Trey, too. But I have to explain it to Annie first."

We both look to Laney and Betts making their way up the stone path toward the warmth inside the house.

"How do I explain it to Annie, Mi?" she says.

We stand watching as a boat heads out from Max's pier, the ferry taking him across to collect the journalists again, as he'd promised; Max is a man of his word. I don't have an answer for her. I don't think she expects one.

"I'd like to stand beside you when you speak to the press, Ginge," I say.

"I can do that part. No point in more than one of us exposing ourselves." She smiles slightly, adjusting the hand that holds her towel. "No pun intended."

"I'd like to," I say. "I have my own penance to pay." I wasn't the blogger, but I may as well have been. "I thought I loved him. Doug Pemberley. I thought he loved me." I reached out and lifted her wet hair from her neck. "I wasn't the one who was raped, but somehow it's always felt like I was violated back then, too."

"We all were, weren't we?" Ginger says. "Yes, we all were."

She's right, of course. We were all different people when we got back into Mrs. Z's dented-bumper Ford at the yacht club than we had been when we'd arrived.

"I'd like to stand beside you, Ginge," I repeat. "Everything is easier with a friend."

Ginger doesn't agree, but she doesn't object again either. She says, "I warned you not to let Doug Pemberley sing to you, you know." Then, "I'm thinking right here. What do you think?"

"On this pier?" I look down at the wood under my feet, at Laney and Betts now standing in the Chawterley doorway, looking back at us.

"Where it began," Ginger says.

I want to object, to say the fact that we skinny-dipped with her brothers and Doug and Trey didn't set the whole thing off, no matter what people might think when they hear the details. But I see in the way she studies the wood planks herself—not the water glittering with sunlight now, but the worn wood planks—that her beginning starts long before mine does.

"There will be TV, you know," I say.

The corners of her wide mouth turn upward again, just barely. "I guess I hope so, right?"

She looks up the path at Laney and Betts and, beyond them, to Faith's Library and its impenetrable glass.

"There's got to be a book to write about this little adventure we're having, don't you think, Mi?" she says. "Wouldn't you like to write a book someday? And there's a very nice library here to write it in."

"It would be a very nice library from which to write a book of poems, Ginge," I say.

At the horizon, the full circle of the sun sits fat on the edge of the world now. It won't be long before a boat shows up, before the press are upon us again and this all begins.

"I have other things to do," Ginger says. "I have Mother's affairs to sort out. I have to put her work in good hands."

I say, "I've always liked your hands, Ginge."

"I hate my hands," she says.

"Good, strong hands," I say. "So maybe this is the start of a new career for you?"

A little more upturn. "Maybe it is," she says, and although I was joking, she repeats the words with a knot of surprise in her voice: "Maybe it is."

The realization of what she's saying hits her then. Can she fill her mother's shoes? Could any of us?

"You need a partner?" I ask.

Her pale gray-blue eyes look almost as pleased as they do when she looks at her daughter. "I think I do, in fact," she says. "Someone with press contacts would be ideal."

"I don't suppose I can lose ten pounds off my hips before this plays out," I say. "I'm sorry to say that the camera really does add ten pounds."

Ginger tips her head to the side a little and studies me. "You have beautiful hips, Mia," she says finally.

"Well, we can hope for camera blur," I say.

She laughs out loud, a wonderful sound that draws Laney and Betts back outside. She sounds like her mother in that moment. I half expect her to pull out a menthol cigarette and light it up and say, *Humor is a much more effective way to get press coverage for something you care about than is rage.*

"You guys coming?" Betts calls.

"I think we can hope for camera blur," Ginger says as we head up the pier together. "In fact, I'd bet on that if I were you, if I were a betting kind of gal. But that's not the kind of help I need today, Mi."

Betts

⤜⤐⤐⤐⤐

WE WAKE ANNIE and Iz not long after we've dried off and dressed. We make pancakes with Faith's flour and we sit in the Sun Room with the drapes open. We tell them the story of what happened that spring break.

We say we made some choices that look pretty bad in retrospect. Drinking and skinny-dipping. Details we've never shared. We say the consequences of telling anyone had seemed worse than the consequences of not telling. Maybe we were right and maybe we were wrong, we say. But now it's time to admit the truth.

"I'm as much to blame as anyone," Ginger says. "I . . . I had a relationship with Trey when I was a young girl."

Her daughter's eyes the practical green Faith's were.

"A sexual relationship that started when I thought I was old enough to understand, but I wasn't," Ginger says. "I'm going to have to speak about that, too, Annie. So I wanted you to know first."

"Laney feels she needs to tell the truth now," I explain. "It's important for her to say this happened to her. To make the world see that it isn't the victim's fault."

When we finish explaining, the girls are silent for a long time.

"It will cost you the Court, Mom," Izzy finally says.

I say nothing. She is probably right.

"Have you told . . . who do you tell this to?" my ever-practical daughter asks. In her expression I see the same little girl who insisted on making her own peanut butter sandwiches to take to school. God, how she loved peanut butter.

"The president?" she asks. We all laugh. It seems so improbable. But there it is.

"I'll go into town when we're done with breakfast," I say. "But we wanted to tell you girls first."

"You're going to, like, call the president of the United States from a pay phone on some street corner?" Izzy says.

"Outside the market," Annie says.

"Sometimes we have to make do with the resources we have," I say.

"You could call from Max's phone," Annie suggests. But Max is out on the ferry collecting the press.

"This will cost you the *Court*, Mom," Isabelle repeats. "It will be a scandal. A woman who was wild like that now up for the Court?"

"A woman," Ginger says. "Would you feel differently if we were talking about a man?"

Izzy looks like her father in that moment. She wants to say no, but can't. She *would* feel differently. Even her generation holds to the imbedded double standard. Boys sow oats, with all the implications of something positive and sustaining growing from their youthful indiscretions, while girls are loose. Or sluts. Or asking for it.

Asking for what? I wonder as Ginger and I make our way to town in the little skiff not much later; I have no idea how to steer a boat much less how to find my way through the island guts.

Asking for what? I think as Ginger ties the skiff up at the public pier.

A fishing boat unloads an odiferous pile of crabs beside us, the season not quite over.

We walk across the road to an old-fashioned phone booth with an accordion door. Ginger smiles at me through the dirty glass as I close it. She continues to watch me as I dial the number. As I wait on hold. As I say my piece. And listen. And insist that, yes, this is something that simply has to be said. It ought to bother me to be watched in this moment. But Ginger's presence leaves me comforted.

I tender the withdrawal of my name for the Court. It's taken from me and bantered about a room increasingly full of advisers. I cover the receiver with a hand and push the phone booth door open. The guys on the dock across the road are having a big time. I don't suppose they would quiet down if I told them I had the president on the phone. I suppose they'd be quite sure I was pulling their sturdy legs. Or perhaps the blue-tinged crab legs they are still offloading from their boats.

"Imagine Matka looking down from the mother-heaven," I whisper to Ginger. "Saying, 'Look at my Betsy. She's stirred up a whole lot of excitement, hasn't she?'"

"Mother is sitting beside her," Ginger says, "saying, 'I always knew that daughter of yours would go far, Mrs. Z. I figured if she could make it halfway across the country in that wreck of a car you loaned them, she could get anywhere she ever wanted to go.'"

"*You* drove the last leg, Ginge," I say. "You're the one who got us here. And got us home, too."

Ginger grins her double-wide grin. "Your mother up in the mother-heaven is saying, 'Betsy, honey, that's the president of the United States on the telephone. Stop talking to your friend and pay attention, for heaven's sake.'"

The room full of advisers is beginning to talk about the language. What exactly should be said about why exactly I don't want to be a Supreme Court justice after all, thank you very much. The secretary of state pipes up, then. This isn't her bailiwick of course. But she happened to be meeting with the president when I called and no one has asked her to leave.

"Gentlemen," she says, "I don't want to be a naysayer here or intrude where I don't belong." This draws a chuckle from the whole room. "But isn't anyone concerned about how this is going to look? We've staked a claim on this whole gender agenda thing, we've been telling the world how important women's issues are to us, and here we are with a chance to show we mean it and instead we're slipping out the back door?"

There's a long silence at the other end. Then the conversation comes right around the bend, turning to the details of exactly how this all should be presented to the press. I mention Ginger and everyone leaps on that idea. A non-official breaking the news. If it doesn't go over well we can rewrite the script and deny anything Ginger has said, the idea seems to be.

"I think you better hear this, Ginge," I say.

She crowds into the narrow booth with me to listen on the same receiver. Our heads press together. People go in and out of the grocery store. Onto the dock just yards away, fishermen unload the last of the season's crabs.

Betts

~~~

A SKING FOR WHAT? I wonder again as the six of us, the Ms. Bradwells and Izzy and Anne, stand looking out the windows in Faith's Library. The returning ferry is on the horizon. We take a silent, collective gulp.

Asking to be accepted. Asking to be loved.

Ginger squares her shoulders. "Okay, then," she says. "Game on."

Mia says, "We're sure about this, right?"

We all turn to Laney. She nods slowly. "I am."

"We're sure," Ginger says. She looks at me. "If you are, Betts."

"I'm not going to be the one to call the president again if we're changing our minds," I say.

The rest of us stand by the window as Ginger heads down the path. "Don't worry, Lane," she calls back to us, "the press won't even be facing the house, they'll be focused on me." She crosses the rough wood of the pier. Walking the plank. And disappears below deck of the *Row v. Wade*.

Izzy asks if we should close the drapes. Annie moves to do so but Laney says no. "I think we ought to leave them open," she says. "I think Ginger deserves that, at least."

We watch the ferry creep toward the pier. The journalists are all out on deck. Cameras point toward the house. I take a step back. But the tree branches and the tinted low-e glass would make it hard to see in under any circumstances. And it's bright out and dim inside. They can't see us watching them. We can hold on to the illusion we're being brave while remaining invisible.

"We should turn on the television," Laney says. "I want to hear what Ginger says."

Down on the pier Arthur jumps from the ferry to secure it.

"They won't run it live," I say.

Annie finds the remote in a lower cabinet of her grandmother's library. Clicks the television on to a commercial. CBS. "Grammie liked Katie Couric," she says. "Katie and the *NewsHour.*"

"I'd have thought she would have preferred Diane Sawyer," Mia says.

Annie shrugs. "Grammie didn't like to be predictable."

The reporters climb from the boat. They look fresher and considerably drier. Hungry for news. It's Monday. I have to be back in the capital tomorrow. Within twenty-four hours they'll get their shot at me and they know that. They're willing to get wet today if need be. Although the sky has cleared now. It's a bright, sunny, unseasonably warm October morning. One last glimpse back at summer before winter sets in.

We all stand watching as Ginger steps from the *Row v. Wade* onto the pier.

"What is Aunt Ginger wearing?" Izzy asks.

"A towel?" Laney says.

"Maybe she's trying to look like she just happened to be out for a swim?" I suggest uncertainly. "Was that the plan?"

Mia smiles slightly. Laney frowns.

Annie flips through the morning talk shows until she finds CNN. The newscaster is saying they are about to go live to Cook Island in the Chesapeake Bay. They've just received word that some announcement is about to be made by Elsbieta Zhukovski, the nominee for the Supreme Court.

"Not me," I say. "I'm the coward here."

The newscaster is laying out the details. My confirmation for the Supreme Court appointment had been expected to be swift until questions arose at Friday's hearing "about a death in Professor Zhukovski's past that may or may not have been accidental." Emphasis on "may not." They won't come out and say it but they're hoping I killed him. Wouldn't their ratings soar on that news.

"Professor Zhukovski has reportedly been holed up with friends all weekend at a remote summer home on Cook Island . . ." the newsman is saying.

"'Professor,'" I say. "At least they're giving me that."

". . . with, among others, Helen Robeson-Weils, who is in a tight race for the Georgia state senate."

"My campaign manager is throwing things at the TV now," Laney says, "having conniptions."

"What exactly *are* conniptions?" I ask.

Mia, ignoring me, says, "Name recognition, Laney. Most voters will remember your name but not why they know it."

Laney rolls her eyes.

"Most voters," Mia repeats without conviction.

And then there is Ginger on the television screen. The microphones are being thrust at her so aggressively that she takes a step back.

"She's definitely wearing a towel," Izzy says.

The camera focuses tightly on Ginger's face. She is clearly about to speak when a startled murmur arises from the journalist crowd. A gasp, really.

We turn back to the windows as Ginger's steady voice comes over the television: "I have a note from my mother, Faith Cook Conrad, which I believe may have some bearing on the death of Trey Humphrey on this island thirty years ago."

She is standing naked on the pier.

"Shit!" Laney and I say together. She takes my hand in hers. Mia's in her other hand.

"What in the good Lord's name is she doing?" Laney says. "What is she saying? Why is she talking about Faith?"

I squeeze her hand as Isabelle takes my arm. Her shoulder presses re-assuringly against mine.

"If she doesn't talk about Faith," Izzy says, "you lose your election, Aunt Laney. And Mom doesn't get confirmed."

"Or probably even if she does," I say.

Izzy shrugs. "Some chance is better than none, Mom."

"We're both long shots anyway," Laney says quietly.

"But you always have been, Aunt Laney," Izzy says. "You and Mom both, and look how far you've come."

My daughter's words overwhelm me for a moment. She sounds as proud of me as I am of her.

"But what the hell is she doing with no clothes on?" I say.

"You didn't clear this particular wardrobe choice with the president, I'm guessing," my daughter says.

Annie smiles: her mother's wide mouth under her grandmother's pa-trician nose. "That's the way Grammie would have done it," she says. "'If you want to draw attention to an issue, you have to be willing to draw attention to yourself.'"

"What better way to draw attention to the issue of how female sexuality is bungled by our society than by stripping down naked?" Mia says.

Annie is laughing now, actually laughing. Her mother is standing naked in front of the world and she is completely unfazed. There is a hint of her grandmother behind her quiet façade after all. "Grammie would be so proud of Mom now," she says. And she is right.

I remember Matka talking about watching me play the zhaleika onstage by myself that first time. Wanting to go with me and knowing it was time for me to play alone. *One person plays alone, it is one thing, but two plays together is so much more.* I suppose I always knew she was proud of me. I suppose this is something Ginger wanted that I always took for granted: a mother who was proud of me. Who I knew was proud of me. *Even though you miss half the notes, I am so very proud. I am always be proud.*

Laney steps closer to the television. "So the good news is all those folks are only focusing on Ginger's face."

Annie points the remote and clicks through a few stations. And there is Ginger standing on the pier. Her breasts and her crotch are blurred, but there is no doubt that she is standing in the altogether. Standing confidently despite the sag of her breasts. The cellulite on her slender legs, which aren't blurred.

Ginger begins to describe in detail what happened. The rape. Her own insistence that we not reveal it for fear of what it would do to Laney's professional reputation to bring rape charges against an important young partner in her law firm. The improbability of those charges being believed. The history of Ginger's own relationship with Trey.

"Aunt Laney?" I hear Izzy say.

Laney has skinned her shoes off and shed her slacks and underwear all at once. She is already heading from Faith's Library into the Ballroom Salon. Toward the back foyer. She pulls her top over her head as she hurries without quite seeming to hurry. No trace of the gawky girl she once was. *Festina lente,* I remember her saying. Hurry slowly. A phrase Laney often used to describe the way Ginger slipped into class without interrupting whenever she was late. As she so often was.

Laney moves smoothly. With incredible grace. She makes fifty-something look awfully good.

"Laney, you can't," Mia calls out.

Laney glances back at us and shrugs. *"Veritas omnia vincit,"* she calls to me. "Truth defeats all things." She keeps walking, her long, dark body moving toward the door and the press and the certainty, finally, that the things that happened to her only happened *to* her. Not *because* of her. Not because she deserved anything but the best from this world. Her mother would be so proud of her, I think as I skin off my shoes. And so would Faith.

This you must remember, Elsbieta: To be a leader, you must always do what is right.

On the television Ginger is talking about me having gone to Faith for advice on what we should do even though Ginger herself had directed me not to. "Betts never does follow directions she doesn't agree with," she says. "And she always has had the good judgment to solicit opinions from people she respects. Both of which are just some of the reasons why she's so well suited for the Supreme Court, an institution that expects each justice to consider the wisdom of the justices sitting alongside him or her as well as those whose shoes they try to fill. Some of the current justices who put themselves above *stare decisis* might learn quite a lot from Betts."

Ginger. Ms. Decisis-Bradwell.

"Oh—" Ginger's lips are clearly forming "shit" but it's bleeped out. She is looking beyond the cameras. Toward the house. She's just spotted Laney at the back door.

But Mia is already there. Her arm is on Laney's arm. She has already pulled Laney back inside.

The reporters and the cameras turn just in time to catch the door clicking shut again as Mia hurries Laney away from the leaded-glass windows. Too bad for them. A naked political candidate would have been news ratings paradise.

"You can't either, Betts," Mia calls to me.

I've unzipped my slacks but I'm still more or less respectable. I'm still in Faith's library.

"It's too much to expect the voting public to accept a Supreme Court justice who has appeared naked in public, Betts," Mia says as she bursts back into Faith's Library, a strand of hair at her cowlick flipping in the blow of the pressurized air. "You simply can't."

"Fortunately, it's not an elected position," I say as I drop my slacks. "So it doesn't matter quite as much what the folks watching on the TV will or will not accept."

"But it *does* still matter," Mia insists, and Iz and Annie chime in to support her.

"Really, Aunt Betts," Annie insists. "Mom is doing this to eliminate the questions. Mom is doing this so you end up on the Court."

"Your mom is doing this because it's the right thing to do," I say to Annie. "This is what matters. This is what's important. That we say what happened, finally. That we say we are not ashamed." I slip off my underwear. This feels even more awkward than I would have imagined in front of my daughter.

"How will it look that I lacked the guts Ginger has?" I ask as I pull my shirt over my head and unhook my bra. "No one wants a coward on the Supreme Court. Besides, I think that 'Curse of the Naked Women' thing Mia wrote about draws strength in numbers.

"In manus tuas, Domine," I say. Putting myself in the hands of a god who is my own mother and Ginger's. The god who must have been watching over those Nigerian women who'd bared themselves to gain a healthier world for their children.

It's Mia's hand that is tight on my arm, though. Not God's. And she is not letting go.

"You can't, Betts," she says. "You can't and Laney can't and I can't."

"I *can,*" I insist. "If Massachusetts can elect a male senator who posed naked for a centerfold—"

"Men are studs, women are sluts," Annie interrupts.

"*You* can't, Mia?" I demand. Thinking this is about Mia being a coward. Mia not wanting her ample thighs out there for the world to see. "Why can't *you?*"

"I can't," she insists.

I see in her paper-bag-brown eyes then that I am wrong about her. That she knew Ginger was going to do this. That she has already offered to join Ginger.

"But she's all alone out there," Laney says.

"She's all alone out there," I repeat.

"She's not," Mia says. "She's no more alone than you were sitting at that table in front of the Judiciary Committee, Betts."

I see then that Mia is right. That Ginger knows Mia and Laney and I have her back now. Just as I knew they had mine. That she knows her mother has always had her back, too, just as Matka has had mine. That her mother loves her and always has.

I turn and watch Ginger on the television. I think of her that night in the hot tub, her breasts pale where Laney's were dark. She looks comfortable with her body in a way that she didn't back then. That she never has before.

"Besides," Mia says, "Ginger has a better body than any of us."

"I wouldn't go *that* far," Laney says.

"Me either," I say.

Mia gives us a you-must-be-joking look.

"You're right, you're right," I say. "I can admit it now. Ginger has a better body than I do."

We turn back to watch her through the window again. Listen to her clear voice on the television.

"And more courage, too," I say.

Because that's what Mia is saying. Mia is saying that if I step out that door I will only be riding on Ginger's courage. I will only diminish what Ginger has done in stepping out there herself.

"'A woman is her mother. / That's the main thing,'" Laney says. She's remembering that line of poetry Ginger said in the Captain's Office after she gave me her mother's pearls.

"Except more so; she declined my offer to find her a gorilla mask." Mia smiles that wry smile that somehow makes us all feel good about ourselves. "She wouldn't even let me borrow *your* black pearls for her, Betts."

I stand looking out from the safety of Chawterley. Watching as Ginger continues on with her one small thing she is doing for Laney and for herself and for us all. She is speaking as well as any of us ever has. Even that first day in law school Ginger was good on her feet.

"I hope we have a better getaway plan than we had Friday," I say.

"I hope so, too," Mia says.

Mia

～

THE PRESS CONFERENCE, we'll call it for lack of a better name, ends when Ginger tells all those eager journalists that she means to open the envelope Faith left only after she returns to the mainland. Then she climbs aboard the *Row v. Wade*. She's awfully certain she knows what she's promising, what the note will say. When the journalists move to follow her she says, "You won't even be thinking about stepping onto this boat, which is private property." She fires up the engine. "But I'm guessing the ferry will take you across the bay if you're quick about getting on," she calls out.

The stampede onto the ferry would make wonderful footage, but not a single one of those turkeys stays to film it. Sadly, my Holga is upstairs in the Captain's Office, and the boats are already heading out.

The ferry follows the *Row v. Wade,* the press snapping photos again, the TV cameras filming from the unsteady boat. A naked woman stretching up to hoist the sail on a boat called the *Row v. Wade*—that will make good press.

Ginger never does hoist that sail, though. Not far out into the bay, she cranks one of the two big white wheels, as if she means to turn right into Boat Scrape Gut. While Max and the ferry continue alone toward the mainland, she keeps turning, heading back to the pier and to Chawterley, her house that was her mother's house.

IT'S GINGER'S IDEA, when she returns, to have lunch with the girls before we sail back across and return to D.C. The press can wait. After all

these years, what difference can an hour possibly make? And having decided we can wait an hour, it isn't any great stretch to conclude that we
can wait until morning, we can have a whole afternoon and evening with
Isabelle and Anne.

"I guess we're going to let it be interesting at the Capitol in the morning?" I ask over lunch in the sunroom, with the drapes wide open to the
day.

"I guess we are," Betts agrees. "What better forum than the place
where all those laws we don't trust to be enforced are made?"

What follows is a long negotiation about who, exactly, will stand on
the Capitol steps. Betts and Ginger are sure Isabelle and Annie will need
to get back to school for classes, but their daughters don't quite see it that
way.

"I want to stand with you, Mom," Isabelle says to Betts.

"I want to stand with you, Mom," Annie tells her mom.

We talk for a good hour about the press and the cameras, the publicity. Laney tries to broker a compromise between Ginger's and Betts's rising unwillingness to include their daughters and Iz's and Annie's refusal
to be prohibited.

"How about we let Izzy and Anne come with us to Washington," she
proposes, "but they wait inside while you open the envelope on the Capitol steps, Ginge, and then Betts addresses the press. That adviser fella
could arrange to stow them somewhere, couldn't he?"

"Aunt Mia says we both look great on film," Annie replies. Not *I disagree,* but the more effective *Have you considered this?*

Ginger looks like she's about to throttle me.

"When they had to make their way through all the reporters here Saturday," I admit.

"You'll have microphones thrust in your face, Annie," Ginger insists.
"You'll say something idiotic. Everyone does."

Annie is so young, just eighteen. And she has always been so eager to
follow after Isabelle, even when she's not ready.

"You two don't need to be out there," Ginger says, tamping back her
exasperation. "You don't need to expose yourselves."

For a minute, I think Izzy is going to agree to Laney's compromise.
Before she can, though, Annie fixes a gaze the caper green of her grandmother's on Ginger and says, "Neither of us said anything idiotic to the

press Saturday, Mom. And we had plenty of microphones. Besides, you yourself said, 'If change is needed and it doesn't start with us, then where the hell does it start?'"

"If change doesn't *continue* with us," Izzy says.

To Ginger's credit, she manages to fall back from an argument she sees she's lost. "You don't say one word to the press, Annie," she says. "Not one word." Then to Laney, "Next time you and Gemmy disagree on something, I get to mediate."

Betts says to Isabelle, "You don't say a word even to the janitors. Are we clear on that?"

Izzy grins back at her mother and says, "'I have nothing to add to the public record on that.'"

IT'S LATE AFTERNOON when Laney and Betts and Ginger and I retire to Faith's Library, where Ginger pulls open the middle drawer to her mother's desk and pulls out blank paper and a chewed pencil.

"You write, Mi," she says. She hands me the pencil, and we settle in on the floor by the fireplace to lay out together the things we want to say.

Mia

~

BY THE TIME we stand with Betts on the Capitol steps, the heavy bronze Columbus doors looming behind us and Isabelle and Anne at our sides, we've begun to come to terms with the idea that Faith shot Trey, that she figured, as we all had, that there was not another way to protect Laney and Ginger, that the cost to them would be too high. When Ginger opens the envelope and reads the note, though—in front of a crowd of witnesses and with cameras rolling—it's simpler and far less dramatic than any of us expect: a single line from Trey Humphrey, saying he was sorry, that he didn't deserve the love of the Conrad family, that he would never cause them pain again. With it is a short note from Faith, explaining that Trey was bipolar—manic-depressive, it was called at the time—and that she'd concealed the note, wanting to spare her sister, Grace, the pain of feeling she'd failed her son as surely as she felt she'd failed Trey's father when he'd killed himself.

Ginger stares into the roar of questions and then down at her mother's handwriting again, her pale eyes filled with relief at not having to blacken her mother's name. That first response is quickly washed away by something stronger, though, an emotion I initially read as grief: just as she's embracing the idea that Faith would have done anything for her, that version of her mother slips through her fingers, reverting back to the one who loved her nephew more than anyone else. But then I'm less certain. There is something in her expression that reminds me of the way she looks at Annie, that looks almost like pride.

One of the journalists yells, "But you yourself thought Faith Cook

Conrad shot Trey Humphrey," and I can see my ex-editor jumping at that headline: DAUGHTER BELIEVED PROMINENT FEMINIST LAWYER FAITH COOK CONRAD MURDERED NEPHEW. It isn't PROMINENT FEMINIST LAWYER FAITH COOK CONRAD MURDERED NEPHEW, but it's not bad.

I shout over the fray, "That is not what anyone has ever said here!" And when I have their attention: "You have the footage. I'm quite sure it will show what Ms. Conrad said yesterday was that she had a note she believed 'may have some bearing on the death of Trey Humphrey.' Ms. Conrad has never suggested her mother was guilty of *any* wrongdoing."

The press turn their disappointed attention to Betts, still in search of a headline.

"Mrs. Zhukovski," one calls out, "what do you think this might do to your prospects of being confirmed?" Leaving behind the question of what might have driven Trey Humphrey to kill himself.

"*Ms.* Zhukovski," Ginger insists.

"Pardon?"

"*Ms.* Zhukovski," Ginger repeats. "Not 'Mrs.' The idea that a woman should be identified by her marital status is demeaning."

"And it's Professor Zhukovski, actually," Laney says. Then under her breath, "Y'all know that, you mealy-mouthed toads. You're just trying to yank her chain."

"Professor Drug-Lord-Bradwell," I whisper, pushing back the thoughts crowding in: the image of Trey with his eye to the telescope, searching the sky; that photo of Ginger as a young girl with her dad and brothers, all holding guns; Faith's careful signature over the seal of the envelope; the sound of her rough voice urging me to write about the curse of the naked women. "Imagine what a difference it would make in this world if more of us were willing to take risks like that," she'd said. "I wish I had the courage those women do. I wish I was willing to risk like that." Words that left me wondering when in her life Faith had ever lacked courage.

What might have driven Trey to kill himself? Remorse for what he did to Laney? He *might* have regretted it afterward. He *might* have carried his gun and the things to clean it up all those steps to the watch room, meaning to kill himself.

The alternative: That Faith collected Trey's gun and the cleaning gear and took them up to the watch room herself? That she loaded the gun and then brought Trey up there, where no one would hear them, insisting they needed to talk? That she made him write . . . what? "I'm sorry. I don't deserve the love of the Conrad family. I will never cause you pain again."

An apology that might look like a suicide note if the writer were to be found shot dead.

Would a mother do that? And live with it the whole rest of her life? Never telling a soul? Or perhaps telling only the one friend she knew would understand. A smart friend, who knew the law. Who could help support the conclusion that Trey Humphrey killed himself if his death was questioned after Faith died, or claim not to have known of the sham suicide note if evidence that Trey's gunshot wound had not been self-inflicted ever came to light. A friend who could save Faith's reputation if it needed saving, or give it up for the sake of Ginger or Laney or Betts or me, or anyone else who might ever be suspected of having shot Trey.

As we watch the crowd pepper Betts with questions, I wonder if Ginger, too, is questioning the "truth" of this note from Trey, or if she's content to settle back into the belief that Trey Humphrey, in a fit of remorse and depression, climbed 136 stairs to shoot himself just when we wanted him dead. I suppose if I were her, I would choose that easier reality. Something in the soft set of her overbite leaves me thinking she has. But maybe that's my imagining Ginger is more like me than she is. For all my journalistic searching for the truth, I still think of all those women my mother met over all those summers as her "friends." Ginger is the Rebel, though, with all the courage that nickname implies. And if there was ever any thought that she lacked courage, she put that to bed out on the pier yesterday.

"Thanks for saving me there, Mi," she whispers.

"Anytime," I reply, realizing that whatever Ginger or I believe happened, Trey Humphrey's death occurred thirty years ago, under circumstances so murky that the truth will never be known.

"Consider it the first official act of the firm of Porter and Conrad, Ginge," I whisper. "And by the way, you'll need to turn the phone and Internet back on."

"Conrad and Porter," she says, her little bit of overbite disappearing into her wide smile.

Betts is still answering questions, saying now, "As Michelle Obama has said, real change occurs one determined woman at a time. Almost thirty years ago now, my dear friend Laney Robeson-Weils was raped. At the time, we remained silent. She did. I did. Our friends did. Even the prominent feminist lawyer Faith Cook Conrad did. We decided it would be too personally devastating to stand up for our friend.

"Perhaps it was a decision that made sense. Perhaps it wasn't. The fact remains even today that it is a very hard thing for a woman who has been raped to stand up for herself. Particularly a woman raped by someone she knows. No young woman ought to have to make the decision to risk her own reputation in order to bring a criminal to justice. No woman— young or old—ought to. Like it or not, a change in the way our society thinks about violent crimes against women has to start with women like my friend Laney who are willing to stand up and say 'this happened to me and it wasn't my fault.'"

The cameras adjust to catch Laney, shots that perhaps will be seen differently than they might have a few days ago, now that her story is known. Her rape will be a part of her biography for a long time to come. But she's standing tall, starting finally to make some good of the bad things that happened to her. I think of Gemmy watching from Palo Alto, and I wonder if we were right to talk her out of taking the red-eye to be here with her mom.

"Senator Cicero-Bradwell," I whisper.

"And Justice Drug-Lord-Bradwell!" Ginger says.

"*Chief* Justice Drug-Lord-Bradwell by . . . what was the date in your gum-wrapper note?" I say. "2016?"

"2018," Ginger says. "She may need every minute of that."

"*Progressio advenit sensim,*" Laney whispers.

Progress does come slowly, I think as Ginger and I raise discreet finger crosses at Laney.

And I can almost hear, then, over the clamor of the gathered reporters, the quiet *tick* of a gum wrapper note landing on my Constitutional Law casebook spread open under the green lights of the Michigan Law School Reading Room. So many planets need to align on one side of your sun to reach any dream. But Betts is right. Faith was right. The change starts with the reaching itself, whether the goal is attained or even attainable be damned. If enough of us reach, the syzygy will occur someday. And if we don't reach, every planet in the universe aligning will do no good.

"I think I might write a book," I whisper, listening as Betts continues to answer questions, working in the prepared bits I wrote for her last night. As I say it, I see that this is my way of reaching and always has been: through words.

The way Ginger and Laney look at me, I'm not sure if they realize I've finally, after all these years, come to embrace my own dream, or if they think I've lost my mind.

"I think I'll write a novel titled *The All-True Tales of the Ms. Bradwells of Cook Island* so everyone will assume it's true," I say, "and I'll write myself as the pretty one *and* the smart one!"

I don't think either of them hears that last part because Ginger is saying (perhaps a bit more loudly than she should), "That's us! The law firm of Bradwell and Bradwell!"

Neither she nor Laney is laughing at my dream.

"Bradwell and Bradwell—and of course we'll be sure to bring 'the natural and proper timidity and delicacy which belongs to the female sex' to our efforts," I agree.

"Bradwell and Bradwell and Baby Bradwell," Izzy says. "I graduate this spring, you know. And I'm still looking for just the right job."

"Bradwell and Daughters," I say, taking the hand of this goddaughter of mine.

Betts is coming to a close, saying, "Women need to step forward. To run for office like my friend Laney is. To seek out and accept judiciary appointments. To participate in shaping the law and determining what, exactly, a Constitution that didn't contemplate our participation in the world beyond the home means for us. We need to grab for the reins at corporations and trade unions and universities, where we can foster environments in which women are treated with respect. Because that's what it all comes down to: Insisting on the respect we deserve. Saying we are powerful, too."

She opens the heavy bronze door behind us, the panels of Columbus discovering a new world. She doesn't pass through, though. She pauses as if she is going to say one more thing, but she doesn't do that either. She only touches a finger to the black pearls she wears, and she stands there holding the door open for Laney and Ginger and me, and for our daughters, too.

ACKNOWLEDGMENTS

SO MANY PEOPLE were so graciously helpful on this novel, starting with my husband (and tireless reader), Mac; my sons, Chris and Nick; and my parents, Don and Anna Waite. Also my brothers, Pat, Mike, Mark, and David, my wonderful sister-in-law Ginny and niece Stephanie, and Cord and Yvonne and Grant and Molly. An extra-special thanks to booktrailer master, Ashley Clayton. Every writer should be blessed with such love and support.

Evan Caminker and Margaret Leary made me feel at home again when I came to poke around at the University of Michigan Law School on the possibility I might find a novel hiding there; thank you for the wealth of information, the tour, the yearbook, and your delightful company then and since. Brian Pascal's lovely gargoyle photos allowed me to see detail from afar. And the spirit of friendship among the Ms. Bradwells draws heavily from my many Michigan Law friends—too numerous to name, but you know who you are. A very special thanks, though, to the women who shared a home with me—Jenn Belt DuChene, Darby Bayliss, and Sheri Young; to Stacy Fox for her hot tub gathering; to Paul Salvodelli for the note-tossing thing; and to Chuck Jarrett, Steve Barth, and André Jackson for allowing me to name characters who are not them after them.

My fascination with miniature books also began at Michigan, thanks to Margie McKinley and Paul Courant. When Margie proposed a reception in the Special Collections Library at Hatcher, I had no idea how moving an experience it would be to wander among such beautiful books, much less to have the benefit of Peggy Daub's and Kathleen Dow's expertise as we did. Bookseller Joe McKernan was kind enough to provide me details of the miniature *Sonnets from the Portuguese* I put into Faith's collection.

My copy of Tom Horton's lovely *An Island Out of Time* has nearly as much ink on the pages—underlining and margin notes—as the first draft of *The Four Ms. Bradwells* did; his graceful depiction of life on a Chesapeake Bay island might have made my own trip to one unnecessary, but left me all the more eager to go. I am indebted to him also for taking me boating to and from a lovely photo exhibit one rainy, spooky-dark night, and to Susan Evans, for her hospitality during my very memorable visit to Smith Island.

One of the great pleasures of writing this book was the excuse to spend afternoons reading poetry and call that "work." I'm grateful to Phyllis Koestenbaum for pointing me in the direction of Anne Sexton when I had no idea which way to head, and to John Felstiner for his extraordinary reading of Jane Kenyon's "Let Evening Come" from his book *Can Poetry Save the Earth?* Two wonderful texts on poetry I turned to were Mary Oliver's *A Poetry Handbook* and *The Making of a Poem* by Mark Strand and Eavan Boland. A complete list of poems referenced in the novel is included on my website; I hope readers will be inspired by the lines included in this novel to read and buy more poetry.

Other works I turned to in the writing of this novel include Catharine MacKinnon's *Women's Lives, Men's Laws*, Susan Brownmiller's *Against Our Will*, Sarah Evans's *Tidal Wave*, Susan Faludi's *Backlash*, and Ellen Sussman's moving essay "How Would My Rape Shape My Kids' Lives?" It's thanks to the wonderful talents of Ilsa Brink that my Web presence looks so beautiful. And to John Downey that the Latin Laney speaks is not gibberish. Adrienne Defendi introduced me to the Holga camera and gave me one to try myself; would that I could make photos as beautiful as hers. Camilla Olson allowed me to dress Ginger in a suit of her design. Brenda Rickman Vantrease . . . well, if I start here on how much Brenda does for me as a friend and fellow novelist, this book might never end. And Terry Gamble included me in a few wonderful days spent writing with friends at her lovely Sonoma home, where I managed to get a little water on this oar while waiting to see if *The Wednesday Sisters* would float.

A very special thank-you to Target stores, and to the booksellers, librarians, bloggers, and readers who helped that novel float along so nicely, allowing this one to find water, too. Two bookstores in particular, Kepler's and Books Inc., have been truly amazing in their support. And with reluctance that I can't thank every reader whose enthusiasm helped *The Wednesday Sisters* succeed, I'd like to specifically thank Nancy Salmon at Kepler's and Margie Scott Tucker at Books Inc.

I am blessed to have found a literary home at Ballantine Books, and am grateful to Libby McGuire and Kim Hovey for making it such a comfortable one. Anika Streitfeld's help in shaping this book in the proposal stages was indispensable. Caitlin Alexander brought moral support, friendship, and more enthusiasm than I could have asked for as I was writing, as well as the kind of editorial insight, guidance, and *stamina* that is a writer's dream. Thanks to Victoria Allen and Georgia Feldman for the gorgeous cover and Victoria Wong for the lovely interior design, and to everyone else at Ballantine, especially Katie Rudkin, Jen Ramage (not Damage!), and Beth Pearson.

And last but not least: Marly Rusoff, who walks on agent water, and Michael Radelescu, who makes sure she doesn't sink.

The Four
Ms. Bradwells

Meg Waite Clayton

A Reader's Guide

A Conversation with Meg Waite Clayton

Meg Waite Clayton sat down with Amy Sue Nathan of Women's Fiction Writers to talk about ensemble novels, being organized, and writing what no one expects. This interview originally appeared at womensfictionwriters .wordpress.com, and an edited version is reprinted by permission.

To preface this interview, an ensemble novel is one where there is more than one main character. Where, if you will, a group of characters shares center stage. Think of a play or a musical where the last curtain call is two actors onstage together, holding hands, taking a bow simultaneously, and then each stepping aside to honor the other because they were equally important to the story and to the audience. Yep, just like that, but in a book. —ASN

Amy Sue Nathan: Your novels fall under the women's fiction umbrella. What do you think of the label "women's fiction"?

Meg Waite Clayton: It troubles me because there is no companion "men's fiction" label. It's this whole idea that if it's about women, it must be meant only for women, whereas if it's about men then everybody can read it. But fortunately for those of us who write novels about women, the great bulk of novel readers are women.

ASN: What do you like most about writing a novel with an ensemble of characters?

MWC: My first novel, *The Language of Light,* was not an ensemble novel in the way you think of it, although it does cover four characters in depth. *The Language of Light* is very centered around one of the characters, as opposed to being evenly balanced among several characters.

One of the things I found is that I craved that balance. That's why I took an ensemble approach with *The Wednesday Sisters*. It allowed me, as an author, to explore more possibilities. If I hang a bunch of problems on one character, that character tends to get weighed down—not a problem if I have a few different characters with something in common they're exploring in addition to their personal concerns. It gives me a lot of freedom to explore things I'm interested in. I really like that.

ASN: So when you set out to write *The Wednesday Sisters,* you knew it would be an ensemble novel?

MWC: I did. Before I had anything else, I had the title *The Wednesday Sisters,* and having the title suggested that the book would be centered on more than one person. Since I have only brothers, and I understand that sister relationships can be very complicated, I knew from the start it was going to be about friends—and I knew I wanted the story to be balanced among the friends.

ASN: Do you take the same approach with your newest book, *The Four Ms. Bradwells?*

MWC: Yes, *The Four Ms. Bradwells* is the same approach. There are four friends who first meet in law school who come together in the present when one of them is a nominee for the Supreme Court. It's very much an exploration of the decisions they made as young women together and the separate paths each of them has taken. So it's definitely an ensemble novel.

ASN: I find ensemble novels very appealing. You write them—do you also read them?

MWC: I do. I've seen it in Ann Hood's books. J. Courtney Sullivan's *Commencement* is written that way. Certainly Karen Joy Fowler's *Jane Austen Book Club* is an ensemble novel as well.

ASN: What do you think is the most appealing about ensemble novels?

MWC: From a reader's standpoint, it gives me a number of people to connect with. So the possibility of finding someone in the novel to identify with and to stay close to as I'm reading is expanded. It allows me to consider characters less like me, but in the context of at least one character with whom I can strongly identify. As a reader, I like to strongly identify with one of the characters. I find it more engaging read that way.

ASN: How do you keep these ensembles organized so that you can write about each character separately and also as a group?

MWC: The answer to that is: every way I can! One of the things I find very helpful for writing an ensemble novel is a character scrapbook. It is, quite literally, like your high school scrapbook or a scrapbook from your childhood. It's a collection of all sorts of bits that help me define each character. It often starts with pictures I've torn from magazines. I start with the physical, but it's not one picture of a person, it tends to be one person's eyes and another person's nose and another's physique and another's wardrobe choices, all put together on the page. I set aside pages for each character, and for settings, too. For *The Four Ms. Bradwells,* because one of the characters is a poet, there are poems that I identify with each of the characters (and which my poet character identifies with them as well). There are also things nobody needs to know—like what their offices look like or what their cars look like or what their childhood boyfriends look like—but it helps me to flesh out the characters in a way that makes them feel real to me. They need to feel real to me for me to make them feel real for the reader. I also add snatches of dialogue. And I continue adding to the pages of the scrapbook as I go along.

I also use outlines and flow charts. One of the things I find useful about a flow chart set up by chapter and character is that you can see if, perhaps, you haven't touched on any particular character's story in four or five chapters. It's a very helpful visual aid. Also, in my office, I surround myself with inspiring, thought-provoking pictures.

ASN: Do you see benefits to these visual aids beyond helping you stay organized?

MWC: When you need choices and you need details, I think—or hope—it comes more easily because you have a real sense of the character. You can describe something about her the way you would something about your best friend. Your characters, in a way, become your best friends, at least for the time you're writing about them.

ASN: You are so organized, it's a little overwhelming for someone like me, who's not. [Meg was very gracious when I admitted to not being nearly as organized as she is. She believes it is very important to be organized. I'm working on it.]

MWC: I don't even think of it as being organized, but rather as just being in the game. The more ways I have into a manuscript each day, the easier it is to get into the manuscript. And this has evolved over time. For my first novel I outlined and my husband did a flow chart for me because there were pacing issues and it helped me with that. That's where I got the idea to use flow charts. But I didn't do a character scrapbook for that one, although I did do character sketches. *The Wednesday Sisters* was the first novel where I used a scrapbook.

ASN: You were a lawyer before you became a novelist. What prompted you to write fiction?

MWC: The better question is, what prompted me to go to law school? I always wanted to write fiction. I was a huge reader growing up, and it was my dream to become a novelist, but nobody I ever knew in my life growing up was any kind of artist. Becoming a novelist would have been like being able to leap tall literary buildings in a single bound—something I didn't think I was capable of doing. I went to law school because I didn't know what else to do, and I practiced law because I thought I would be good at it and it would give me a nice paycheck and it was something to do. But it was really a conversation I had with my husband where I confessed that if I could do anything in my life, my dream would be to write novels. And he said, "How will you know if you don't give it a try?" His vote of confidence and support has meant a tremendous amount to me. And it's very much what *The Wednesday Sisters* is about—how much we all need that kind of support in our lives.

ASN: Many readers are writing their first novel or trying to get their first novel published. What's a lesson you learned from your first novel?

MWC: One of the things I learned writing my first book, *The Language of Light,* is that it makes sense to go forward in the draft and not reread what I've written as much as possible until I get to the end of the first draft. With my first novel I spent months revising the first one hundred fifty pages, and then in the end I deleted about one hundred of those. So there was all this finely honed prose that ended up on the cutting-room floor. It wasn't until I got to the end of the novel—and this is still true to a large extent—that I knew what it was really about and what the truly important things in it were. Once I had a sense of that, it was much easier to revise with an eye toward bringing out the things that were important and discarding the things that were not.

ASN: Do you make notes for yourself as you write about things you want to change when you go back to page one?

MWC: I put notes to myself in square brackets in the manuscript to remind myself of things I want to change. Then I can do a search for a square bracket in order to make those changes. I learned when I was practicing law that if I don't have a list of things to do, I forget to do them.

ASN: Can you share with us what you're working on now?

MWC: I signed a contract with Random House last fall for a new novel to be published in 2013. It's also an ensemble novel—a follow-up to the *The Wednesday Sisters.* It follows three of the daughters of the characters from that book. I'm having a lot of fun with it. It's interesting to explore how some of the issues that *The Wednesday Sisters* faced in their lives are echoed in their daughters' lives. It allows me further exploration of the Wednesday Sisters themselves without telling a story that focuses on the improbable scenario of them having another transformative moment at the same time, as they had in *The Wednesday Sisters.* But it is really nice to revisit those old friends, and it is fun taking their children into adulthood.

ASN: Did you ever consider writing an actual sequel to *The Wednesday Sisters*?

MWC: I have had so many requests from readers for a sequel, but it was not something I'd ever contemplated. The epilogue to *The Wednesday Sisters* brings the reader into the present, so it doesn't leave a lot of room for flexibility for other stories in the interim. I think I did that in some ways to shut off the possibility of a sequel. I think that most characters do not have multiple stories that will keep the reader interested in the same way the first story does. But I like the idea of having a whole new cast of characters to explore in the comfort of their familiar mothers.

ASN: What's your best advice for aspiring women's fiction authors?

MWC: The best piece of writing advice I've ever gotten—and it's not just for writers of women's fiction at all—comes from the author Tim O'Brien, with whom I was fortunate to study. To paraphrase, he said, "Use extraordinary actions by your characters to illuminate ordinary emotions." When he said that, a scene from his novel *July, July* leapt into my head. It gave me permission to go beyond the things we would expect people to do, and to explore the possibility of things people might do even though those things are a little more out there. Doing that allows readers to have a catharsis they wouldn't otherwise have. It was a liberating piece of advice for me.

Questions and Topics for Discussion

1. *The Four Ms. Bradwells* have distinct Bradwell nicknames based on things that they revealed during their first law school class. Do you think these nicknames suit them? In what ways do you think each stays true to her nickname? In what ways do the women flout them?

2. What did you learn from the *Law Quadrangle Notes* chapter epigraphs? What insights did they give you into the evolution of the Ms. Bradwells' friendships that wasn't conveyed in the narrative?

3. Ginger goes to visit Annie on her eighteenth birthday, just as Faith came to visit on her twenty-first. How do the two different visits reflect the different mother-daughter relationships? What do you think Ginger absorbed about mothering from Faith? Is she a better mother, or worse?

4. How do you think race factored into the Ms. Bradwells' decision not to go public with the rape? Do you think it would have turned out differently if Betts or Mia had been raped instead of Laney?

5. At one point, Mia muses on the four Bradwell mothers: "It strikes me how different Faith and Mrs. Z were, and yet how similar. How different Ginger's and Betts's relationships with their mothers were, and how similar, too. Were Laney and I luckier, to have mothers who wanted for us but didn't expect?" (page 232) What do you think she means by this? How would you compare Matka and Faith? How have their similarities and differences shaped their daughters?

6. Isabelle, in a fight with her mother, says that Mia is the happiest of the Ms. Bradwells. Do you think that's true? Why do you think Mia never remarried?

7. Mothers are very important to the story, but fathers mostly lurk behind the scenes. Why do you think this is? How do you think each of the Ms. Bradwells was influenced by her male role models or lack thereof? In what ways do you see this reflected in the next generation of Bradwells?

8. Why does Betts keep her conversation with Faith to herself for so many years? Do you agree with her that talking about it could have helped Ginger and Faith's relationship? Do you think Betts suspected Faith of killing Trey? Did you?

9. Would *The Four Ms. Bradwells* have been a different reading experience without Ginger's poetry, Laney's Latin, Betts's quirky turns of phrase, and Mia's photojournalist's eye for defining details?

10. Why is it significant that Faith left the letter to Margaret wedged into the pages of Anne Sexton's "Briar Rose"?

11. Reread the epigraphs to Parts II and III, as well as Ginger's thoughts on pages 200–202 about the *New York Times* article. Were you surprised by the statistics? How, if at all, did this novel change your perceptions about violence against women? Do you agree with Muriel Rukeyser's answer to the question "What would happen if one woman told the truth about her life?" (page 287)

12. When Ginger arrives on Cook Island, she quotes from Elizabeth Bishop: "Should we have stayed at home and thought of here? / Where should we be today?" (page 71) How do you think she would have answered that question at the end of the book?

13. The book ends with Betts opening both a literal and figurative door for the Ms. Bradwells and their daughters. What do you

imagine the future holds for Annie and Izzy and Gemmy and the rest of their generation? What sacrifices have their mothers and grandmothers made in their names, and what sacrifices will they make for their own daughters? What aspects of these relationships resonated with you most personally? Would you share this novel with your daughter? Your mother? Your best friend?

The Wednesday Daughters

~

So I will share this room with you
And you can have this heart to break.

—Billy Joel, "And So It Goes"

1

Autumn is far away the best time at the Lakes.

—Beatrix Potter in a September 1903 letter to her then publisher
and eventual fiancé, Normal Warne

IT NEVER STRUCK me until I was grown up myself how often one of the Wednesday Sisters would tell me what to do. We Wednesday Children are all pretty good at defying our parents, but less practiced at the art of defying our parents' friends. I see in retrospect how they used that, Aunt Frankie, for example, poking her head out her door to send me home from the park when I'd been ignoring Mom's calls. It's why Anna Page and Julie came to the English Lakes with me last fall, some thirty years later. It's perhaps how I ended up crossing the narrow ribbon of Lake Windermere myself, the daylight softening from blue to salmon to steel with each hushed push of the wood oars, our little boat sliding as silently forward as time itself.

"You'll want to be hearing the quiet of the evening coming up," the man rowing us—Robbie, he'd said his name was—had suggested as he'd directed us past a motorized launch to a rowboat. Such a funny phrase, "hearing the quiet." Like so many of the expressions Mom had brought home from that side of the world: "queue" and "toff" and "fancy," "single-track" instead of "one lane" to describe the long, winding trip around the lake by car. But I *could* hear the quiet of the evening coming up, even with the squabble of geese down the shoreline, the occasional gunshot clap of a car passing over a trestle echoing across the lake.

Behind us, the stone walls on the dwindling hillside sharpened into a dark maze, the bracken marooning and the green fields deepening, the green gold orange woods as well. The black-faced sheep we'd seen out the train window faded to nothing as lights blinked on in the shops trailing downhill from the town of Windermere to hug up together at Bowness, the boats in the harbor bare-masted as full sails were exchanged for fire-side seats in restaurants and pubs and homes. A few hundred yards ahead, two swans dug at the lake grasses, and the thick woods on the shore beyond them took shape as individual trees. A stone chimney poked above the treetops upslope, collecting more stone around it: an-other chimney, a square tower, various slants of roof that were all of a same.

"*That's* your mama's cottage?" Anna Page asked.

Robbie glanced over his shoulder without breaking the rhythm of the oars, reminding me somehow of the boys who used to show up at our door when Anna Page babysat my brother and me. "That one's the big house, idn' it?" he said, ending with a question. The same way he'd said, "They'll be my boats now, won't they?" when explaining he'd bought the boats that had belonged to the grizzled old character Mom had de-scribed. I could almost hear her admonishing me that the ghost of the old man who'd always ferried her across this lake ought to be taking us now.

"There's a small cottage to the right, there through the scrub?" Rob-bie continued, his voice Irish rather than English; perhaps that was the hint of not-quite-belonging I sensed in him. He raised the oars and stilled them with one hand, touching Anna Page's red-jacketed elbow with the other, then pointing to a less majestic stone chimney tucked be-hind the trees at the lake's edge. A glimpse of cornflower blue took shape through the tangle of branches: a door overhung with vines on a cottage I'd seen only in photographs. A simple rectangle of gray stone. Low walls around a patio. A last straggle of geraniums in a window box.

I trailed a hand over the boat's edge, the echo wake of my fingers fold-ing into that of the drifting boat as I imagined Mom writing at a wrought-iron table on the patio, her feet up on a second chair. When it was colder, she would have moved inside, written at a desk beside a wood fire, or at a table piled with books and papers, pens and paper clips and Post-it notes, empty teacups scattered as if to catch drops from a leaking ceiling in a life that held little rain, except maybe the disapproval of my dad's mom, my Ama, who spent a lifetime trying to make a proper Indian wife of her Caucasian daughter-in-law.

"It's an evening, sure it is." Robbie ran a hand through his short blond hair, leaving it spiky and rather chaotic. He wasn't bad-looking, in a ruggedly sun-worn way. He was older than I'd first thought, too. Perhaps the forty I was or even more.

The four of us sat in the drifting boat, watching and listening, the grayness settling over even the swans, the air fresh with the smell of woods and the promise of frost.

A light appeared high on the hill, a dot-dash of Morse code but with the dash overlong. When it disappeared again, Julie asked if we'd all seen it, and what it was.

It had gotten dark so quickly.

"That'd be the Crier of Claife, folks here say," Robbie said softly. "'That old Crier of Claife on Furness Fell, / as long as ivy evergreens shall twine, / May sally forth from his ravine, / And rouse the boatmen with his human yell.'"

"A ghost," Julie said, blinking back surprise at the fact of this boatman spouting poetry—relevant poetry, of course, to amuse the folks he took on tours of the lake, poetry he probably knew only because the old man he'd bought the boats from used it before him, but still.

A ghost who played the piano, I thought, whom Mom might have brought from home and left behind. Aunt Frankie used to joke about a ghost that belonged to my mother, one who'd haunted an old mansion in the park across the street from us in Palo Alto before I was born. The ghost seemed to be some secret Frankie and Mom kept even from the other Wednesday Sisters.

Robbie's gaze lingered on the chimneys high on the hill, or perhaps at the place where the light had been, his fingers wrapped around the rough wood of the oars surprisingly well kempt. "We ought to be carrying on to the cottage before it gets any darker," he said.

Anna Page started to speak as she ran her hand through her hair— wavy-dark and wild even in the still of the approaching evening. Julie pressed her foot gently over Anna Page's and raised an eyebrow, but Anna Page, undeterred, said to Robbie, "Don't you think my friend Julie here has gorgeous eyebrows?" She leaned close to him and whispered in his ear, a sprinkle of grays showing at her part line. There was nothing to keep her from flirting with Robbie, she had no marriage to end first. She could have as many doors as she wanted. She could paint them any color she liked. And Julie could too. Her divorce papers were filed now. I was the only one of us who'd left a husband at home.

Robbie looked from Anna Page to Julie—to her eyebrows (which are in fact pretty gorgeous: straight across and not insubstantial, not over-thinned or over-arched or over-anythinged, really) and her long, straight arms and nose and neck, long straight fingers abundant with rings that ought to be too much but aren't. Julie has no hips whatsoever, no hint of wave in her highlighted hair. The only interruption in her straight-line elegance is the occasional ear peeking through her hair, always sporting silver earrings, which, like her rings, she designs herself. Simple and elegant, no-nonsense jewelry for the no-nonsense librarian she is.

I said, "The guy who owns the big house, that's the pier he lets Mom use, I guess." Imagining my mom—tiny-faced and tiny boned like me, but pale where my skin is dark—pulling on the oars of her own boat, although of course hers would have a motor. "She keeps a bicycle and a small boat here, so she doesn't need a car."

Used to let. Kept a bicycle. Didn't need. Mom didn't need anything else in this world anymore except for me to pack up what was left of her life in England the way I'd already packed up her clothes and jewelry and toiletries at home, her manuscript drafts of the children's books she never did share with anyone but my brother and me. "Your books," she called them.

Robbie set his weight into the oars, moving us toward the cottage again, measuring his words as if he might know something about my mother's life here that I didn't know, after all.

"They say he killed someone," he said.

Anna Page's laughter cracked the evening. "Lordy, did my ma pay you to say that?" In a near perfect mimic of her mother's Southern accent (although Anna Page is even less Southern than I am Indian), she quoted a Gatsby line our moms all whipped out at the slightest provocation, "'You look at him sometimes when he thinks nobody's looking at him. I'll bet he killed a man!'"

I heard my own mother's voice wrapped around the words, my mother's laughter.

"The Crier," Robbie insisted. "The ghost. They say he killed someone. Not a bloke, but a lady. His British wife."

"His British wife," Anna Page repeated, teasing him with the tone of her voice, charming him in that way that always worked so well with men, that lifted my own spirits, too.

"He had two, didn'e?" Robbie said to her. "One wife in India and a proper British wife as well." He laughed uncomfortably, glancing my way as if his words might offend me when they wouldn't offend Julie or Anna Page. He thought I was Indian; people who aren't Indian always do.

"Not that I know anything about it," he said, dipping one oar and raising another to ease us toward a narrow pier. "But that's what folks here say." He hopped out to secure us to a mossy post, the swan pair watching suspiciously from a jetty of flat rocks on the other side of a dilapidated boathouse. "They say old man Wyndham, who killed his British wife, is the Crier of Claife—that he's the ghost who calls across to the ferrymen at Nab. But none will go to him. The only one who ever did, the poor bloke wouldn't speak of what he'd seen, and then he died the next day."

An awful animal sound broke the silence then: the bay of a wolf or a coyote, deep and primitive. The light appeared on the hill again, a long dash that gave me a chill, that left me thinking about the ashes that were all that was left of my mother. Ashes that weren't even ashes, really: they were dry bone fragments left after the rest of Mom was vaporized, crushed by machine into a fine sand and tucked neatly into her favorite puzzle box.

Robbie said, "'Course, another story has a monk taking a Bible and a bell across the lake on Christmas Day, plying the ghost 'with candle, book, and bell' and confining him to the quarry and woods 'until men should walk dryshod across the lake.'"

"Couldn't just exorcise him away altogether, I guess," Anna Page said.

Robbie met her amused gaze and kept it. "That'd be no fun, now, would it? How's a body to claim he's been followed in the woods at dusk by a hooded figure if the ghost has been exorcised?" Offered with a grin that left you doubting anything Robbie ever might say.

THE GENTLE LAP of lake and the *cheep-cheep* and *tit-tit-tit* of evening birds added to the quiet as I removed the key from the latch and pushed open the cornflower-blue door. Inside, the pitched ceiling gave the illusion of space, but the only furniture in the single room was a double bed and nightstand, a love seat, and a china cabinet filled with books. A barn-style door to the right, we would find, led down a narrow stairway to a small kitchen, and another across the room opened to a hand sink with no mirror in a bathroom so narrow you had to leave the door open to wash your face. A deep, claw-footed slipper tub sat improbably not in the bathroom but on a rectangle of limestone set in the wide-planked floor between the fireplace and the end of the bed.

Julie said, "Oh, this is going to be cozy!"

I stood rubbing the raised ERA of the cast-iron key to my mother's empty cottage, taking in her empty bed, her empty tub where she could bathe alone, the one little part of her life not even my father shared.

Julie clicked the lamp switch beside the bed. Nothing happened. "Your mom still in London, Anna Page?" she said with an ironic smile. "All alone in that swanky four-bedroom flat where she begged us to stay?"

"Lord, Ma thinks we're still sixteen and can't survive in England without a chaperone," Anna Page answered, dismissing the suggestion. I love Anna Page, really I do, but she thinks everything her mother does is solely to vex her rather than, say, to visit one of her authors who's a favorite for the Pulitzer Prize.

Julie's ring-laden fingers followed the cord to the plug, and a small click sounded as the light popped on, illuminating a spider motionless on a trail of web. "How funny—it was plugged in," she said, "but there's an on-off switch on the damned outlet." She squashed the spider with a swift pinch of finger and thumb before I could begin to say *Go away, you bold, bad spider! Leaving ends of cobwebs all over my nice clean house.*

I fingered the cold porcelain edge of the slipper tub, remembering the way Mom quoted those lines from *The Tale of Mrs. Tittlemouse* as she corralled spiders and put them out, the same way the Wednesday Sisters quoted that Gatsby line, I suppose. Remembering how I'd forever barged in on Mom's bubble baths as a child, the smell of vanilla candles mixing with the smell of vanilla bubble bath as Mom laid a wet washcloth over her breasts.

Julie peered at a photo on the nightstand—my brother and me when we were toddlers—while Anna Page spotted a radiator and went to turn it on.

"I imagined little plates of crumbs resting on the pages of open books, like your mama's dining room at home," Anna Page said. "How do you write a biography without piles and piles of books?"

Julie picked up a second, unframed photo and studied it for a moment. "My mom says Aunt Ally was searching for her family here, that the Beatrix Potter biography was just an excuse to come." Her voice as certain as her mother's, but her words less direct; Aunt Linda would have said something more like, "Ally is just looking for the family that abandoned her."

Aunt Ally, they call my mom, just as I call Julie's mom Aunt Linda and Anna Page's mom Aunt Kath, although we're no blood relation, we're just daughters of best friends who started calling themselves the Wednesday Sisters long before I was born. Daughters who've ended up best friends ourselves the way children who grow up together sometimes do, whether they have much in common or not. It's a lot to have in common, though, I suppose: a shared childhood. People who knew you before you knew yourself.

Julie handed me the unframed photo: my mom's father and mother as a young couple—such an odd pair, he with poor teeth and not much better hair, she as Britishly fair-skinned and doe-eyed as my mother, beautiful even with mousy-thin hair where Mom's was thick and dark or, later, the gray of the ashes in the puzzle box. I never met those grandparents; like this cottage, I know them only through photos. They disowned Mom when she married Dad, because he wasn't white.

"I don't think this thing is working," Anna Page said. "The radiator."

Julie went to have a look, as if there might be some other way to turn the single knob and she'd do it better than Anna Page could.

Anna Page shifted her attention to a cast-iron contraption in the fireplace: bars and cabinets that left no room for any self-respecting log. "What in the world is going on with this fireplace?" she asked.

Two quick raps on the door startled us then, and a man burst in without waiting for an answer, saying, "Allison! You didn't call! You'll freeze without— Oh!" He was all broad chest and broad jaw, older than any of us but younger than our mothers. His mahogany eyes registered just a hint of ire behind silver wire-rims.

He said something under his breath that might or might not have been a cuss as he turned the hard black door handle, still in his grasp, and back-stepped over the threshold. He nearly knocked his head against the doorframe not because he was tall but because the door was low. Behind him, a huge dog—black and white, with a lionlike head and long hair— sat unmoving on the stone path, giving me a start.

"I beg your pardon," he said in that imperious tone older men deliver so well, not begging anything. "But do you *belong* here?"

"Do *you?*" Julie demanded. She looked disapprovingly at the little bit of mud his hiking boots left on my mother's cottage floor.

"Oh!" he repeated again as I swallowed back the urge to defend this slightly frightening stranger from the frankness of my closest friend. It was the dog, I decided; he hadn't seemed quite so frightening until I'd seen the dog.

"The gate is marked 'Private'; you're quite off the public bridleway," he said. "I was just having a look-in on Allison, who keeps the cottage." He let go of the handle without closing the door, and crossed his arms. "I don't mean to be rude, but perhaps you could tell me who you are?"

Before Julie could verbally whack him, I said, "I'm Hope Tantry."

He looked perplexed for a moment, before a light of recognition registered. "Oh! You are, aren't you!" he said. "You're Allison's daughter. You're Asha." He stepped forward again and offered his hand as, behind him, the dog settled back just a little. "And one of you is— No, neither of you is Santosh, are you?" He smiled: charmingly imperfect teeth, healthy but not battered into picket fence submission, in a face that had more color than average here. The lines at his eyes deepened, and a dimple appeared on his right cheek. "Sorry!" He said the word brightly, as if it were the most delightful thing in the world to own up to a mistake. "You're Asha's friends here with her on holiday at her mum's cottage, of course you are."

On holiday. We didn't deny it. Tucked into Anna Page's bag was a booklet for easy walks in Grasmere and Ambleside and, unbeknownst to Julie, two of Alfred Wainwright's volumes of more ambitious hikes. Julie, who isn't much for bugs or dirt, brought a collection of Wordsworth poems for this land of Dove Cottage and "A host, of golden daffodils," and she'd arranged "cookery lessons" at a place called Lucy's that offered "Proper Puds and Sweet Solutions," "Afternoon Tea and Temptations," and "Cakes Fit for a Queen"—British comfort food. But it was the contents of the personal secret box that brought us to the English Lakes. My mother's ashes, to be scattered here.

The neighbor glanced around the cottage, doing the same arithmetic we'd been doing on bodies and beds. "I meant to see if your mum wouldn't like help setting a fire in the grate, and perhaps a tipple after her journey, but I don't suppose she'll be joining you, then, will she?"

Anna Page slipped her clean, gentle fingers—surgeon's fingers—through mine.

"Mrs. Tantry died a few weeks ago," she said.

He reached behind himself and wrapped a hand around the edge of the still-open door. "Allison? But Allison isn't—"

The dog seemed to surge forward without coming any closer, his tail lowered and still.

"I . . . Forgive me, I . . ." He turned abruptly as if to leave, then turned back.

"Are you okay?" Anna Page asked. "Do you need help?"

He looked to me, blinking as if I were just coming into focus. "You'll have the desk, of course. And the pictures, yes, you must have the pictures," he said, and he stepped out the door then, latching it behind him, leaving us alone again in the glow of the single bulb.

MEG WAITE CLAYTON is the author of the nation-
ally bestselling novel *The Wednesday Sisters*. Her first
novel, *The Language of Light*, was a finalist for the
Bellwether Prize. She is a graduate of the University of
Michigan Law School and was a Tennessee Williams
Scholar at the Sewanee Writers' Conference. She lives
in Palo Alto, California, with her husband and their
two sons.

Chat.
Comment.
Connect.

Visit our online book club community at
www.randomhousereaderscircle.com

Chat
Meet fellow book lovers and discuss what you're reading.

Comment
Post reviews of books, ask—and answer—thought-provoking
questions, or give and receive book club ideas.

Connect
Find an author on tour, visit our author blog, or invite one of
our 150 available authors to chat with your group on the phone.

Explore
Also visit our site for discussion questions, excerpts, author
interviews, videos, free books, news on the latest releases,
and more.

Books are better with buddies.
www.RandomHouseReadersCircle.com

RANDOM HOUSE
READER'S CIRCLE
®

THE RANDOM HOUSE PUBLISHING GROUP